THE SWEETEST DREAM

THE SWEETEST DREAM

Love, Lies, & Assassination

A Novel of the Thirties

Lillian Pollak

iUniverse, Inc.
New York Bloomington Shanghai

The Sweetest Dream
Love, Lies, & Assassination

iUniverse books may be ordered through booksellers or by contacting:

iUniverse
1663 Liberty Drive
Bloomington, IN 47403
www.iuniverse.com
1-800-Authors (1-800-288-4677)

Because of the dynamic nature of the Internet, any Web addresses or links contained in this book may have changed since publication and may no longer be valid.

This is a work of fiction. All of the characters, names, incidents, organizations, and dialogue in this novel are either the products of the author's imagination or are used fictitiously.

Front cover design by avi@javendesign.com
Cover photo, from left to right, Natalya Sedova, Leon Trotsky, the author, "Bunny", Van Heijenoort

ISBN: 978-0-595-49069-1 (pbk)
ISBN: 978-0-595-60956-7 (ebk)

Printed in the United States of America

To Richard and Nomi, who guided me through the labyrinths of cyberspace, and to my loyal and loving family and friends, who waited patiently, knowing that someday, eventually, I'd finish this book. With all my love, Lillian.

Dear Patient Reader,

In the following pages you will find romance, intrigue and sadness. The two young girls you meet in the first chapter are, like you, no matter what your age, seeking life's meaning and self-realization. They are fictional characters but, having been drawn from my own life experience, how fictional can they really be? Aside from Ketzel's and Miriam's families and lovers, all the characters are real or made up from several people I have known.

In Notes in the back I've included more details about people and organizations that prevailed during the "Great Depression" period. I was a young woman in the '30's, active in radical politics when I met and knew Trotsky. I've supplemented my memories with extensive research in order to depict accurately what took place during those years.

Today at 93, I'm still active and engaged in the struggle for peace and a better world. While I don't know when you will read this book, I'd like to think that if you have any questions, I will still be around to answer them. In any case, *Avanti!*

Lillian Pollak
Spring 2008
New York City

Prologue

1917
REVOLUTION

In the midst of World War I, a small revolutionary party seizes power in Russia and declares an end to fighting. The people cry, "Peace, land and bread!" Two men rise to power: Lenin (unswerving, pink-cheeked, good-natured) and Trotsky (handsome, sharp, fiery) guide the country. For seven years they are at the helm, the acknowledged leaders of the Union of Soviet Socialist Republics. Then, in 1924, Lenin suffers a series of strokes.

As Lenin lies dying, snow blankets Moscow's low buildings and high steeples. The sky is gray, leaden; the cold is intense. Crowds of bundled figures wait, men with patched coats, women wrapped in thick shawls. Grim faces, tears icicles on frozen faces. Krupskaya, Lenin's wife, speaks, her voice deep, sorrowful: "Vladimir Illich has died. Our very own has died."

Four men carry the bier. Trotsky is not one of them. A murmur goes through the crowd: "Where is he? Why isn't he here?" Next to Lenin he is the most popular man in Russia. The people roar, dismayed, disappointed. They do not know that Stalin—chief pall-bearer, patient Bolshevik—has pulled a trick and lied to Trotsky about the date so he will miss the funeral.

This is the beginning.

"To choose the victim carefully, prepare the blow, satisfy an implacable vengeance, then go to bed. There is nothing sweeter in the world."

—Josef Stalin, 1923

CHAPTER 1

New York City, 1925

The morning sun, rising above low rooftops, throws long shafts of dazzling light, promising another day of summer heat. Sunday morning, nine o'clock, and 117th Street is still quiet except for the clang of a trolley car on Lenox Avenue and the hourly chime from a nearby church. Faint odors of sweat and cooked cabbage drift through sultry air. Lining the block are graceful two-and three-story brownstones with wide curving balustrades which were once private dwellings of prosperous families but now are mostly furnished rooms for porters, cooks and bookkeepers.

One of the brownstones is still home to the Ortega family. Jaime Ortega, Ketzel's father, Fanny's husband, stands at the foot of his stoop, waiting for the rest to come down with picnic baskets and blankets. The portable phonograph has already been stashed away in the new automobile in front of the house. He calls up to the open window, keeping his voice soft: "Ketzel, shall I go see if your friend is ready?"

As soon as the words leave his mouth he knows he's made a mistake. Ketzel yells down, her voice resounding in the empty street: "Sure—tell her to get a move on. *Ahorrita!*"

Jaime, frowning, walks across the street to the brownstone where Miriam and her mother live. Hesitant, he stands in the aerieway; he knows how hard Clara works all week, and she may be sleeping. He presses the bell lightly.

"I'm sorry. I didn't mean to be late," Miriam says when she appears a moment later, the iron gate creaking shut behind her. She's carrying a blanket, a bag of fruit and a box of Uneeda Biscuits, her black gym bloomers peeking out from under her skirt.

She laughs, a little shyly. "I didn't know what to wear for a picnic. I never went on one before. Is this middy-blouse okay?" Her small face is flushed, her eyes shining, her thick, dark curls slightly damp.

Jaime smiles at her. "Don't worry. We wouldn't leave without you. Ketzel wouldn't allow it—and neither would I."

Earlier that week Miriam told her mother about the Sunday picnic: "I'm going with Ketzel and her family. Elena and Arthur, too. It's a going-away party." Arthur and his widowed mother live upstairs in two rooms and are planning to leave for the U.S.S.R. in a few days.

Clara shrugged. Miriam knows her mother has too much on her mind to be concerned about other people's woes; she only knows she has to get another tenant as soon as possible. And she misses Bertha, Miriam's older sister, who's away in Chicago, misses her every day. Her dark look reminded Miriam of the day a week before when she'd told her mother about the Ortegas' car. It was Sunday morning then, too. Her mother was loading sheets from all the tenants into big tub in the kitchen in their basement apartment; she works every day except Shabbos.

"You should see Jaime's new car. It's a Model T Ford, brand new." Miriam can't help talking about it. "Ketzel calls it Lucille because she knows a song that goes like this: 'Come away with me, Lucille, in my shiny Oldsmobile.' The back seat is open but when it rains, you can pull over the top. And it has an electric starter …" Clara said nothing, her face clouded as she scrubbed the sheets. She doesn't seem to be listening and Miriam stops.

Now Lucille waits across the street, shining black, adorned with two great headlights, looking like the queen of automobiles. As Miriam approaches, Ketzel is scrambling in and out of the rumble seat and while they wait for Fanny, they have a contest to see who climbs in and out faster.

Fanny comes down looking very demure in an outfit she's sewed herself, a pink organdy blouse, a white skirt and jacket. A wide picture hat frames her blonde hair and Miriam keeps looking at her, she's so beautiful.

"Are we ready?" Jaime asks. He's wearing a leather jacket but takes it off and hands it to Fanny. "Put on your black cap with the visor," Ketzel tells him. "It makes you look like an airplane pilot. Isn't my father handsome?" she asks Miriam, who nods in agreement. Ketzel is very lucky, in a lot of ways.

They drive up 125th Street to Riverside Drive, then along the Hudson River, its deep, swift water glinting in the morning sun. Homes of the wealthy with lavish entrances and uniformed doormen line the waterfront. The Drive ends at Dyckman Street and as Jaime makes a turn onto Broadway, he says, "Look, girls, we're in the country already." In the yards of the wooden houses they can see chickens and an occasional goat tied to a fence.

"Okay, Daddy, we're not on a sight-seeing tour. Let's get there already!" Ketzel complains. The drive is long for Miriam also: she was too excited to eat breakfast and now she's hungry.

"We're meeting the others at our favorite spot," Fanny says, and Ketzel groans. Their favorite spot is away from activities; a wide green lawn with tall trees, a swift, icy-cold wading brook and where it's cool, even on the warmest day. "Quiet as a cemetery here," Ketzel grumbles as they settle in the shade.

"Okay, Ketzel, that's enough," Jaime tells her. "Your mother has to get some rest today. There's plenty for you to do here." He's busy putting up a hammock for Fanny.

The others arrive soon after, and once they've had a drink and some pretzels Ketzel, Miriam and Arthur take off. They run across a rustic bridge, hike down one of the paths, then scramble down to a stream. There they strip off their stockings and wade, splashing and disturbing the little fish in the cold water, waking up a garter snake sleeping under a shady rock. Later they head back to the grown-ups and persuade Jaime and some of the others to play running bases with them.

At last they gather for the picnic. A feast! Everyone's brought their favorite foods: corned beef, salami, rye bread with seeds, pickles, olives; for dessert, ruggelah, raisins, nuts and halvah; and to wash it down, lemony tea from a huge thermos.

Leaning against a tree, Elena murmurs, "I feel sad we're going back to Russia. Yesterday was wonderful. A big meeting, a crowd—maybe 40,000 people from my union, Cloakmakers, from all the unions. We vote, we will make work stoppage but officials say they will throw out left-wing locals. I tell you, so exciting."

Fanny sighs. "I would like to go but Jaime said no. I didn't have such a good day yesterday."

Miriam looks over at Ketzel, lying on the grass, busy looking for a lucky four-leaf clover. Ketzel has told her that her mother is sick, that she's overheard the doctor say that Fanny has TB. "I don't know what TB is," Ketzel said, "but Jaime worries a lot."

They were walking home from school; after Ketzel said that, she began to run, fast, leaving Miriam behind. Miriam was annoyed; she would have liked to tell Ketzel that she knew about TB. But Ketzel always did that—when she didn't want to talk about something, she'd run away.

The setting sun's rays shimmer through the trees. A fresh breeze springs up and everyone except Fanny stretches out on cool grass, looking for Orion and the Big Dipper, admiring the clear dark blue sky and the bright crescent moon. When the girls lie on their backs, their stomachs are so full they bulge up. Says Ketzel, "We're pregnant ladies."

Fanny and Elena start to sing union songs, "Hold the fort for we are coming, union men be strong" and "I dreamed I saw Joe Hill." Then, sitting beside Fanny's hammock, Jaime sings a Spanish song to Fanny about green eyes, "Aquellos ojos verdes." His voice sweet and rich like chocolate or brown sugar, and all chime in when Jaime begins "La Golondrina" and then goes to "Cielito Lindo" and "Ramona."

While they are singing, Ketzel gets up, raises her arms and begins to pirouette on her toes, as she does in her ballet class. After a few minutes she yells, "C'mon, everybody, let's do the Charleston!" and starts to swing her legs.

"Go ahead, Miriam, you too," Jaime urges. So Miriam gets up to dance with Ketzel and then Arthur joins in, too. All three of them dance on the thick grass, kicking, crossing their arms over their knees while the grown-ups laugh and clap their hands and sing:

> Pack up all my cares and woe
> Here I go, singing low
> Bye-bye blackbird.
> Where somebody waits for me
> Sugar's sweet and so is she
> Blackbird, bye-bye

Later, as they are packing up, Fanny starts to sing one of the old Jewish songs she likes, "Ofen den pripishuk brent a fierlih, In der shteib is heis," and Elena sings a Russian revolutionary song, "Varshavianka." It sounds so serious and mournful that Miriam asks her what the words mean. "It says that whirlwinds of danger are raging around us," Elena answers.

"Is it dangerous now in Russia?" Miriam wants to know, folding up a blanket. She's read about the new government in *The Mirror* and *The Graphic*, about how terrible everything is over there, they had an awful famine and people were hungry. "Aren't you afraid to go back?"

Elena smiles, a little sadly, and starts to answer but Ketzel breaks in, crying, "Oh, Miriam, you're such a 'fraidy-cat. You get so serious. C'mon, let's sing

American songs." She begins, "Daisy, Daisy, give me your answer true, I'm half crazy all for the love of you."

Miriam doesn't sing with her. She wants to ask Elena about Russia. Ketzel sometimes annoys her, cutting off any conversation she isn't interested in, calls her a 'fraidy cat.

But she likes Ketzel a lot. She's glad they met on the street two years ago and found out they went to the same school. So what if Ketzel calls her 'fraidy cat'? And she'd been as frightened as Miriam that day.

They'd been playing potsy in front of Miriam's house when it started to get dark. "The eclipse—the eclipse," Ketzel yelled, and they ran to get the little pieces of broken glass they had smoked over a candle, the way their teachers had told them to. Peering through the smoked glass, the two girls watched the sun disappear behind the moon and when it got totally dark—pitch dark in the middle of the day—they'd screamed and clutched each other, playing at being frightened but frightened for real.

After a few minutes, when the sun slowly emerged and the sky became bright again.. Ketzel said, "You really were scared, weren't you?" Before Miriam could protest, Ketzel said, "It's my turn—I go," she said.

When she jumped, she'd leap into the air, her sailor dress billowing as she turned. Ketzel was tall for her age, quick, darting like a silver fish through water. She fascinated Miriam, who moved more slowly, in a thoughtful way,. "Wait," Miriam said. "Let's do something else. Did you bring the jump rope?"

"Okay, I'll go first," Ketzel answered and ran to the top of the stoop to get it. She began to skip slowly at first, then faster, singing, "Charlie Chaplin went to France, To teach the ladies how to dance. Lady, lady, show your pants, Lady, lady, please skidoo." She loved that song; it was such fun to flip up your skirt. The rest of that day they forgot about being scared.

Ketzel's family owned the brownstone house across the street. A few days later, when it was raining, Ketzel invited Miriam in to play. She showed Miriam her father's study, where he did his writing on a hand-carved desk from Mexico, where he came from. For the rest of the house Jaime had brought congitas, serapes made from churro sheep, straw-inlay frames, tin hanging lamps, gilded mirrors and for the kitchen, blue and yellow pots. To Miriam the house was a magical place, full of light and laughter. She always wanted to play there, even when it wasn't cold or rainy.

They would go upstairs to Ketzel's room to play house, Ketzel always the Mommy, Miriam the Daddy and their baby was a Betsy-Wetsy doll who miraculously drank from a bottle and could make wee-wee. On the shelves in her room were dolls, hundreds of them, it seemed to Miriam—a Russian girl with golden pigtails, a China Poblana from Mexico in a wide red skirt, a Pancho Villa on a horse. They both especially loved the Pilgrim doll with her white apron and cap, because they had read the romantic story of Priscilla and Captain John Smith in their fourth grade class. They'd act the same scene over and over again, with Ketzel as Priscilla, who would whisper softly, "Why don't you speak for yourself, John?" Miriam always had to be John.

"Ketzel, that's a funny name," Miriam says one day. They're sitting on the floor, making up a love story about Natasha, the Russian doll, and Pancho Villa, who kidnaps her. "You know what a *ketzel* is, don't you?"

"Of course I know. It means kitten in Yiddish. My mother always calls me *ketzelah*. That means little kitten. Do you think I look like a kitten?"

"Your eyes are like a cat's, like my cat, Kootah." Miriam leans over to look into Ketzel's eyes. "Green and wide. But Kootah is gray and your hair is gold and red. It's nice, the way you wear it with ribbons at the end." Ketzel had a habit of tossing her head and making her red-gold pigtails fly around.

Ketzel loved to talk about her father. He studied at the Sorbonne in Paris, she tells Miriam, and he writes for newspapers in Mexico and for magazines like *Colliers* and *The Saturday Evening Post* in New York. He and Fanny would go to Greenwich Village to the John Reed Club and sometimes up to Harlem, where he'd read some of his poetry and they'd often invite guests for dinner. Once, as Miriam is going up the stoop, a round-faced Negro man comes up right behind her and they went in together. "That's Countee Cullen," Ketzel tells her when they're up in her room. "Daddy says he's a wonderful poet."

"He has a kind face," Miriam says.

"My daddy does, too," Ketzel says. "His hair is so shiny and he has squinty dark eyes. That's his Indian blood. He's good too, cause he doesn't act snobby, the way some of those other writers do."

"He's very nice," Miriam agreed. "I think he's handsome, too. He likes to talk and explain things, even to kids."

Miriam wishes she had something interesting to say about her own family, but all she can think of is that her father died when she was three years old. "I remember he had a big mustache and he was nice. He played games with us; he'd make believe he was going to hit my sister and me. We'd be on the bed, under a sheet, and he'd take his belt off his pants and smack it down where we weren't, of course. As if he didn't know! We'd laugh so hard!"

"What happened to him?" Ketzel asks.

"There was a big 'flu epidemic. I ws only three years old, so I don't remember that. My mother says he came home with a fever, got into bed … he had a 105 temperature. He died three days later. She said in those days people used to sing a song, 'I had a little bird and her name was Enza, I opened the window and in flew Enza'. So now, well, we're poor …"

Before Miriam could go on, Ketzel throws her arms around her. "You'll come to Mexico with me someday," she says. "We'll have lots of fun. My parents will pay for you. They have lots of money."

Jaime grew up on a a large hacienda in Mexico; his parents are dead and his sister, who still lives there, is running it now. That's why Ketzel's family can afford to live in a whole brownstone, why Jaime is able to buy a new Model T. Fanny still insists on working, though, as much as she can, when she's well enough. She's a pattern maker and tries to be active in her union and the Communist Party. Sometimes, if Miriam is there at night, she sees Fanny coming home late, wearily climbing the stairs. The nights she comes home early Jaime is waiting for her, with dinner ready and the phonograph playing Vienna waltzes or the "Barcarolle" from *The Tales of Hoffman*—"Doesn't it remind you of waves dancing?" Ketzel asks Miriam. The table is always set with fresh flowers and a white tablecloth, as if it's a special holiday, even if it's a school day.

"In my house," Miriam tells Ketzel, "my mother puts newspapers on the table unless it's Friday night. Then we have a tablecloth like you. Kootah sits there until we chase him off."

When Miriam tells her mother she's going to Ketzel's for supper, which is quite often, Clara will ask irritably, "Again? You haven't got a home anymore?" Miriam knows her mother can't help nagging her. But she doesn't want to tell Clara about the delicious dinners at her friend's house, or how much she loves the creamy ice-cold milk that is always on the table. Sometimes, for supper, she and Ketzel will run down to the candy store on the corner with an empty pitcher and bring it back full of frothy cherry soda. But most of all she loves going to the Ortegas because it's so lively and cheerful there, Jaime and Ketzel always talking and joking and Fanny smiling at all of them.

They often take Miriam with them when they go to the movies. Jaime always pays, even though Miriam fishes ten cents out of her pocket and offers it to him while they stand waiting at the box office. They usually go to the Regun nearby, old, damp and very dark except up in front, near the screen, where a small light glows for the piano player. When he stops every once in a while for a rest, the big room is quiet except for the rasping clickety-clack of the movie projector. The pianist always plays the same music, like "The Poet and Peasant

Overture," except when someone on the screen is dying; then he plays "Drigo's Serenade."

On warm summer nights they go up to the roof garden, one flight above the theater. A sign outside the movie says the rooftop theater is "air-cooled," but it's just an ordinary tar roof with rows of seats, a screen and a pianola. The girls like going there; they think it's romantic, and when the movie is boring or dumb they look up at the stars and whisper to each other. If it starts to rain, everyone dashes downstairs to the regular theater. Jaime always buys them ice cream and Charlotte Russes, little round spongecakes in a cardboard tube, topped with swirls of whipped cream and a bright red cherry. The girls try to eat them very, very slowly, but somehow, no matter how small the bites they take are, the sweets disappear in two minutes. Why don't good things last longer? Miriam wonders.

The girls love comedies best of all. Their all-time favorite film is *The Gold Rush* with Charlie Chaplin, especially the scene where Charlie's little wooden house in the snow slides down to the brink of a precipice and stops there—right at the edge! Then, when he runs to the other end of the room, the house tips back to safety. The girls scream so hard every time it looks like the shack is going to fall, Jaime has to lean over and whisper, "Girls, try to be a little more quiet!" Miriam tries to laugh more softly, but Ketzel says, "Oh, Daddy," and goes on screaming. But most of Jaime's attention goes to his wife. He circles his arm around her shoulder and every once in a while presses his lips to her cheek. When he does this, Ketzel nudges Miriam and grins.

One winter night Miriam and Ketzel are lying on a woolen rug in Ketzel's living room in front of the fire, doing their homework. "It was so romantic how my father and mother met," Ketzel says. "At a lecture at Cooper Union."

"That's where Abraham Lincoln gave a speech." Miriam shuts her arithmetic notebook, rolls over on her back, closes her eyes, knows she is going to hear a long story. "Miss Finnerty told us about that when we were studying the Civil War."

"While they were sitting, waiting for the program to begin my father kept staring at her. She was the most beautiful girl he ever saw."

"My mother was pretty, too," Miriam says softly. "If she didn't have to work so hard she'd still be."

"Let me finish my story," Ketzel says. "My mother didn't know what to do. She felt uncomfortable so she kept pretending she was reading the program. My father began to hum a song and you'll never guess what he did next." Ketzel giggles. "He told her, 'That song must have been written for you. It's called

"Green eyes, beautiful green eyes.' My mother blushed and when she got up she dropped her purse. He picked it up and began talking about the lecture. It took her a little longer than him to fall in love, but not too long."

Fanny, who'd come from Russia, just a few years before, had been going to classes at night for English. One night she tells the girls after dinner while they're washing dishes that after she and Jaime met, she never went back to school. "I didn't need to. I learned English talking to my husband. We would read *The Masses* together. If you are lucky, you will find a man like Jaime," she tells the girls.

Fanny and Jaime became socialists when they married, but five years later they split away and became members of a new organization, the Communist Party of the U.S.A. They went to lots of meetings downtown, including the fancy home of Mable Dodge on Fifth Avenue, where Big Bill Haywood and John Reed used to go. Now their house on ll7th Street is a hub for activity also. Many of their guests are Party members, Ketzel tells Miriam, who thinks it's so exciting, these great writers, leaders and poets coming to this house!

One day after school they're in the kitchen making My-T-Fine chocolate pudding, taking turns stirring the mixture on the stove. Upstairs a meeting is going on, with Jaime and a dozen or so other men and women. "These two Italian guys, Sacco and Vanzetti, are in a lot of trouble," Ketzel explains to Miriam. "Right now they're in jail but they're going to put them in an electric chair and electrocute them. But people are trying hard to save them. Jaime said there's a lot of committees working on it."

"But why are they going to be electrocuted?" Miriam asks, horrified.

"The government says it's because they killed a man, but it's really because they're anarchists. Jaime says it's a frame-up."

"What's an anarchist?" Miriam asks.

"They're people who think that you should do whatever you think is right, even if it's against the law. They don't believe in laws or having a government. Anarchists are wrong," Ketzel says, shaking her head, "but they don't deserve to be killed."

"No one should ever be killed," Miriam says. "Bad people should be put in jail, never killed." As she spoke, a frightening vision crept into her mind.

"You better stir a little faster," Ketzel says. "It smells like it's burning on the bottom. In Russia, communists make laws for all the people," she goes on. "Good laws people like. They don't kill people, even the bad ones."

"My mother says communists are terrible." Miriam says, as Ketzel sets out four cups on the table. "She says they drink too much. She's glad she's in

America. She told me when she was a little girl in Poland, Cossacks used to ride into her village. They'd burn houses and kill." Miriam talks fast so Ketzel won't interrupt her. "My grandmother stuck my mother under a puffy featherbed once when the Cossacks came. When they rode away, she crawled out. She was crying so hard she couldn't stand up; she kept falling over, her legs were so wobbly."

"Your mother doesn't know anything about Russia now," Ketzel says, her cheeks red.

Miriam says nothing further, just stirs the pudding. She thinks of the paper she saw, one of Clara's roomers had left a copy of *The Graphic* in the bedroom. On the front page was a picture of a man in a chair, his hands strapped down on the arms, his head in a helmet, blindfolded, his body stiff with fear. The headline read, "When Will They Pull the Switch?" The story reported that Sacco and Vanzetti were to be executed in the electric chair.

As she drifts off to sleep that night, she dreams she is the kitchen, alone with Kootah. All at once police break down the door, pushing her away, grabbing the cat. They want to shove him into a black box but he screeches and scratches them so hard they say, "Let's just electrocute him." They tie a wire around his neck and connect it to the light and string him up. He begins to howl, his body twitching, dancing, electricity sizzling through him. Miriam screams, "Stop, stop!" but the people in the room just stand and watch. She keeps crying and yelling until she wakes up. When she tries to go back to sleep, the same nightmare comes again.

She remembers the dream the next evening, just after she and Clara finish eating—noodle soup her mother made with rinse meat, parsnips and carrots. Through the window she can see the rain pattering into the backyard, a cold wind lashing the old ailanthus tree, but it's warm and peaceful in the basement room. Kootah, curled up in his corner on an old woolen scarf, is fast asleep, making sounds like a small meat grinder.

"That was good soup, Mama," Miriam says.

"We could have tea," Clara says. "I bought sponge cake today."

"I'll make the tea," Miriam says, hopping up and looking for the matchbox so she can light the stove. She wants to talk about her dream, but then she decides it might be better not to. Her mother isn't interested in Sacco and Vanzetti, in politics, in dreams; they're not important to her. And her mother is in a good mood tonight, because Bertha will be coming home when school finishes this year. Better not say anything to spoil it.

Her older sister has been living with a well-to-do couple, childless, distant relatives, who took her to live with them in Chicago four years ago. But Clara missed her terribly and now she wants her home. With a sigh she'll tell anyone, a stranger on the bus, "My Bertha, she's the smart one, beautiful, my everything."

Miriam is used to this. It doesn't upset her very much. Her sister is smart, was very grown-up even when she was a little kid. At times Bertha was mean to Miriam; she'd even throw a book at her when she got angry. For the most part, though, she'd act as though Miriam wasn't there. All her life Miriam has thought how nice it would be to have a sister who liked her. Now she has Ketzel.

Ketzel isn't always nice, though. The next day, when they're walking home from school, Miriam tries to tell Ketzel about her dream. As soon as she describes the electricity jolting through poor Kootah, Ketzel puts her hands over her ears and yells, "Cut it out! I don't want to hear any more! They're not going to kill Sacco and Vanzetti! People will stop them. They're protesting, all over the world. My father said so. The communists will stop them."

"But it was such a scary dream," Miriam starts to say.

"I don't want to hear about it!" Ketzel whirls away, dashing up the icy steps of her stoop, almost stumbling at the top. Today she's not inviting Miriam in. Miriam bites her lip hard to keep from crying. She scrambles over the hard, dirty gray mounds of snow piled high in front of her building. "Why did I say anything?" she thinks. The next day, though, Ketzel is friendly again.

The snows melt and spring finally arrives. Sun warms the damp earth and the light wind is sharp and vinegary. The forsythia bushes in front of Ketzel's house blossom with lacy, light-green and yellow sprays. Miriam, watching Kootah sniff the air and then leap over the back fence to visit his pals, still doesn't understand how people can do terrible things like kill men in electric chairs, but she knows enough to keep these thoughts to herself.

Now that it's nice outside, Ketzel and Miriam spend the afternoons after school playing movie games with Arthur, the littleboy who lives upstairs in Miriam's building. They love Douglas Fairbanks and Mary Pickford, have seen almost all of their pictures—*The Thief of Baghdad, Robin Hood, The Mark of Zorro.* Arthur, two years younger and a head shorter than both girls, with rust-colored hair and full lips, must always be the hero, dashing about, flourishing a cape, a tin sword or a black mask. Ketzel is the damsel, wearing Fanny's silky blue dressing gown, fluttering her eyes behind a Japanese fan, while Arthur fights a fierce duel against twenty or more villains, all of them played by Miriam. When Arthur's vanquished them all, he says to his fair lady, "Now you must bind up all my wounds and kiss me." Ketzel is willing to put her arms around him but she only allows him to kiss the fan she holds it in front of her face. Too bad Arthur is only ten years old, Miriam thinks. If he were older and taller, maybe Ketzel would let him kiss her cheek.

They play for hours, stopping only when Ketzel has to leave for her ballet lessons. She goes twice a week. At first she wasn't interested, but after seeing Anna Pavlova in *The Dying Swan* she is full of enthusiasm. "Miriam, it's unbelievable! She really looked like a swan, all in white—her tutu, the cap on her head, her slippers—she ripples her arms and her own neck is as long as a swan's!"

Jaime takes the two girls to see some performances of Les Ballets Russes. Ketzel is enthralled, but Miriam can't conceal that she's bored. "I think it's kind of phony and artificial," she says afterwards, alone with Ketzel. "All that plié and paté."

"It's plié and elevée," Ketzel says, laughing. "Paté is goose liver—which you've probably never had." Ketzel acts a little snobby, sometimes, Miriam thinks.

"Let's go to 125th Street," Ketzel says one afternoon. "I need some ribbon for my tutu sash".

The girls like to walk up the wide, busy street, stopping to look into the windows of Woolworth's, Kresge's and Blumstein's department store and admiring the French soaps and pretty bottles of perfume at Hegeman's. As they pass Hotel Theresa, a huge, white-glazed building on Seventh Avenue, Ketzel says, "Jaime told me colored people aren't allowed to stay there."

"I don't understand," Miriam says. "They let negroes go into white stores to buy stuff." She is careful to say "colored people" and "negroes," the way they do at Ketzel's house, not 'schwartze' like her mother does.

"Yeah, that's funny," Ketzel agrees. "I wonder why. I'll ask my dad."

When they arrive at the 5 & 10 off Lenox Avenue, Miriam goes to get a blank book for school, Ketzel her ribbon. A little later they meet at the candy counter, where Miriam counts out her pennies and buys some yellow "chicken corn." She notices that Ketzel is empty-handed. "It's getting late," she says. "Go get your ribbon."

But Ketzel hurries to the exit, calling, "Let's go" over her shoulder.

"Didn't they have the ribbon?" Miriam asks as they walk down the street. She's having trouble keeping up with Ketzel. "Why are you going so fast?"

Ketzel doesn't answer. When they cross Lenox Avenue she pulls out her hanky and out falls a large roll of pink satin ribbon.

"You took it," Miriam gasps. "You stole it."

"I really didn't mean to," Ketzel grins, picking it up. "It just happened. I just looked at it and then, all of a sudden, it was in my pocket."

"Like fun! You don't steal things. We could be arrested! You—"

"Pooh," said Ketzel. "You're just a fuddy-duddy. *Ish kabbible!* I should worry, I should care, I should marry a millionaire." She runs away down the street, her dark blue woolen cape billowing behind her, waving the ribbon. "See you tomorrow!"

At times like this, Miriam wonders about being Ketzel's friend. She's so different but she loves Ketzel, Jaime and Fanny and their house full of music and people. In the two years since she's known Ketzel she's learned to ignore things that make her uncomfortable so that she can enjoy everything else.

The picnic for Elena and Arthur has been one of those enchanting days that only happen when Miriam is with Ketzel and her family. It's been such a happy day that no one wants to stop singing and leave the green, tranquil grotto. But it's late, the sky is darkening, and reluctantly everyone carries the blankets and baskets and pillows to the cars, kissing each other and murmuring good-byes.

"Why so serious, Miriam? Didn't you have a good time?" Jaime asks, looking for a place to stash the large thermos.

"Oh, Jaime, I wished it would never end," she says, so fervently that he turns around to look at her. She's embarrassed—what a dumb answer, she thinks. But when he smiles at her she's glad she said it.

Arthur wants to ride home with Ketzel and Miriam, so they squeeze him into the rumble seat between them. He falls asleep as soon as they take off and it's almost eleven when the overflowing automobiles chug into their street. The exhausted children sway, yawning under the street lamp, while the grown-ups busily remove bags and bottles. All of a sudden Arthur, standing and swaying, starts to cry, deep tearing sobs.

"Madre de Dios, what's going on?" Jaime demands.

"I don't want to go away. I don't want to leave America," Arthur implores. "Mama, please, don't let's go away. Let's stay here," he cries, tears pouring from his eyes. His mother and the others are embarrassed. Alana tries to hold him but he pushes her aside.

"We are going on a big boat—your uncle Nick will be with us. Don't be afraid." Tenderly, Alana tries to reassure him but the little boy keeps sobbing until Ketzel runs to him. She wraps her thin arms around him and says softly,

"We'll come and see you, Arthur. You'll come back soon, too. You'll see, Arthur. It'll be all right." She hugs him until the sobs end. At last he lets his mother lead him into the house.

Clara has come outside at the sound of the crying and stands there, her arms akimbo. When Miriam runs across to her, she says, "Come, you said good-night. It's late." As they go down the steps to the aerie way entrance, Miriam hears her mother murmur, "Ich hub rachmounis fa den kint"—I have pity for that child.

Trotsky—Exile

Prinkipo, Turkey, 1928

Within a few years after Lenin's death, Stalin seizes the power he has long plotted to acquire. In1928 agents of the secret police, the GPU, arrive to arrest Trotsky. "I will not let you in," Trotsky shouts. The agents smash the door open and one of the agents, a Red Army officer who served under Trotsky, cries out, anguished, "Shoot me, shoot me." But Trotsky consoles him and says, "You must follow your orders."

Through the quiet streets of Moscow the car rushes away the leader of the October Revolution, the founder of the Red Army, and his wife, Natalya, and sons Lyova and Sergei. Twice before, Trotsky remembers, he was exiled from Russia and returned. The last time, he came back and took power, became a great leader.

He will never see his homeland again, but he does not know this.

Trotsky is sent first to Kazakhstan. His son, Lyova with him, takes care of everything. "He is secretary, bodyguard and organizer of hunting trips with his fathe, r" writes Natalya. "It gave him great pleasure." Then, in 1929, he is permanently exiled from the Soviet Union and deported to Prinkipo, an island near Istanbul. Lyova remains with him but Sergei is in Russia, his future uncertain, and Trotsky's daughter, in Moscow, dies of consumption. "My daughter, Nina, my ardent supporter, was only 26 years old, continuing her oppositionist work until quick consumption carried her off," writes Trotsky in his Diary. Grieving, he refuses to believe Stalin will prevail. He is full of energy, ready to fight. But for now, Prinkipo is his new home.

The household runs like clockwork. Trotsky writes every day at set hours. He dictates in Russian, briskly walking up and down; sits at his desk when he speaks to his three secretaries in German, English and French. Punctuality is a must; if a meal is not ready on time, he leaves the room, refusing to wait.

Security is a constant concern. Counterrevolutionary White emigres as well as GPU agents are a constant threat. On a few occasions someone posing as a devoted follower turns out to be in reality a member of the GPU; during one period, a man who later was revealed to be a Latvian agent lived with the family for as long as five months.

In 1931 Trotsky's other daughter, Zina, arrives with her little son, Seva. A month later Lyova leaves for Western Europe. Soon Zina follows, leaving Seva with his grandparents. Lyova is working with the European opposition to Stalin; his sister, a troubled woman, will seek psychiatric help in Berlin.

In the USSR, the noose is tightening. Yakov Blumkin, a GPU agent, visits his old friend Trotsky in Turkey and, when he returns to Moscow is charged with plotting against the state. Before the firing squad cuts him down, Blumkin shouts, "Long Live Trotsky!" "His execution will raise a storm of protest," says Trotsky. But he is mistaken; there is no public reaction. More executions of oppositionists follow.

CHAPTER 2

New York City, June 1931

Ketzel likes her classroom in the high school in Washington Heights. "It's on the third floor, up on a hill, and it's like being on a giant ship," she tells her mother. "I can see the water from my seat. The Dutch used to called the place where the two rivers, the Hudson and the East rivers met, "Spuyten Duyvil" 'cause it was so dangerous that if a person was able to get across, it was in spite of the devil."

Today she sits in a corner so she's not noticed and can daydream. There is so much going on in her life and she feels as if she's being carried by events she has little control over. It's a warm day, the end of a crazy week; her head rests on one arm; the afternoon sun streams in, warming her shoulders. She falls into an easy doze, only to be awakened by Mrs. Carlucci, calling on her to name the parts of a flower. Stanley, sitting on her left, snickers, but Ketzel, after giving him a scathing look, reels off the answer quickly and settles again, resuming her revery.

So ridiculous, she thinks, having to take Biology 1 in her senior year in high school, but rules are rules, stupid and arbitrary. Jaime had made the decision to return to New York and to have Ketzel finish her high-school education in a public school. The only consolation, once she stopped grumbling, was that George Washington High was new and beautiful, in neo-classical style with an elegant entrance and graceful columns, something like Jefferson's Monticello.

She's still tired from last night, her arms aching, a bruise on her knee from banging it against a heavy old bureau she and some comrades had lugged up the stairs. They were carrying rickety chairs, smelly mattresses and chipped cooking pots back into the apartment of a family that had been evicted that day. Right after that she'd had to rush to her dance rehearsal, but she couldn't stand seeing a family, kicked out of their home, standing on the street, the father, helpless, his face grim, the kids yelling, clutching broken toys, the mother, frantic.... Besides, she knew how important her doing these things were to Fanny.

A sharp ring announcing the end of the final period startles her. Stretching her long legs out into the aisle, she pulls herself up. Stanley lingers a little and she's amused. He loves to look at silk stockings. That dopey little boy has a yen for me, she thinks. He starts to say, "I really wasn't ..." but Ketzel interrupts him. "Forget it," she says. "Have a nice summer" and then adds "kid." But realizing that isn't nice, she gives him a friendly little push, smiles and says, "I mean it."

As she walks down the hall, thinking she won't miss the stuffy smells of leather briefcases and dusty chalk for a few months, all at once she hears a yell and someone from behind is calling "Ketzel, hey, wait!" And then right in front of her is a short, pretty girl with unruly brown curls, breathless, grinning ... someone she knows! A friend she hasn't seen for years.

"Miriam!" Ketzel shrieks "It's you! I can't believe it!" They fall into each other's arms, hugging, kissing, talking, hugging again.

"Why didn't you ever write me?" Miriam asks.

"I wanted to." Ketzel hesitates. "But I lost your address—and then you didn't write again! We went to Mexico and then Switzerland ... I sort of stopped writing to everyone. It's hard when you're traveling around so much."

"All those places! You're lucky. How are Fanny and Jaime?"

"He's fine. Wow, will he be glad—he always liked you. Hey, we've gotta talk. Where to?"

They race down the hill to Goldstein's candy store. The chubby, wispy-haired owner behind the gray marble counter fills the tall glasses with so much ice cream the milky foam runs down the sides. He was just about to close up for Shabbosh but for these two nice kids he'll wait a few minutes more. Sitting on high stools, sipping through long straws, they smile with delight at each other. "It's so great to see you again, Miriam. I didn't have a clue where you were."

Miriam busies herself for a moment, wiping up a little pool of ice cream on the marble. She doesn't want to sound as if the years had been dull, sometimes awful. Shortly after that summer picnic, after Arthur and his mother had left for the Soviet Union, Ketzel and her family had moved, away and she'd been very lonely without them. Then, two years later, she and Clara moved uptown.

Her mother, feeling rich with the few thousand dollars she'd saved up from scrubbing furnished rooms, bought an apartment building on 156th Street. It was in 1927, the same year they electrocuted Sacco and Vanzetti, and Miriam can still remember how she cried that night. Things were okay for awhile, the twenty tenants paid rent, her mother was able to make the large mortgage amount every month but after the stock market crash and the beginning of the Great Depression, it became a different story. Nowadays, nobody in the entire building has a job—there's no money—not even have enough for food! She quails when her mother sends her upstairs to ask the tenants to ask for just a few dollars on account. When she knocks, they know who it is and they just call out, "Maybe next week." It's worse when they open the door; they're embarrassed for themselves and sorry for her.

Miriam takes a deep breath, deciding not to tell Ketzel about the other, really terrible news, about her sister, the awful car accident. If she doesn't talk about it, she can avoid thinking about it herself. There'll be time some other time.

"Well, we moved uptown because my mother bought this apartment house a few years ago," Miriam answers. "Right now we've got just one paying tenant. He works on that big bridge they're building on 168th Street, the George Washington." She stops, thinking of her mother's face, the bitter furrows around her mouth, the desolate kitchen. "They're going to foreclose on her, Nehring Brothers. She's going to lose her life savings, everything."

Ketzel sighs. "That's really tough. Nobody has jobs now. We're lucky, I guess. Except Mom. It's serious; she's getting worse. You remember on that picnic how she wasn't well? That's why we left right after that. Jaime closed the house and we went to Mexico and then to Switzerland. I went to school there. Jaime took her to the best doctors but...." Ketzel's voice trails off, unsteady. "Finally, she wanted to come home. She said, 'I'll get better in New York. My comrades are the best cure.'"

They're quiet for a moment, sipping their sodas. Then Ketzel says, "Hey, what do you know, I'm a dancer now." Miriam looks up, surprised. "Remember I went to ballet school? Well, I'm finished with that stuff. I'm doing modern dance now. I saw Irma Duncan in Switzerland. I really dug it. No more tutu stuff. We wear loose togas, dance to 'The Marseillaise.' We just gave a performance at the Manhattan Opera House."

"That's wonderful!" Miriam says. "I remember when Jaime took us to see Les Ballet Russes. You raved about Anna Pavlova."

Miriam was also remembering the way Ketzel sometimes acted when they were kids, a little snobby, like that Leda Anchutina, that Russian girl dancer in their class. But Ketzel's not like that now, she thinks; she's really glad to see me. And Miriam always loved Ketzel and loved her whole family, especially Jaime, and she hopes they still remember her fondly.

"Girls, I'm sorry, I have to lock up," Mr. Goldstein says. They smile and pay and sweep out and never stop talking.

"You're coming tomorrow for lunch," Ketzel reminds Miriam as they part. "Don't forget."

Ketzel's late getting home and she speeds up the stairs. Jaime waits, pale. "You know how Fanny worries," he says.

"Daddy, don't scold. Miriam—remember her? I ran into her today. She's coming for lunch tomorrow." Before he answers, she darts past him to her mother's room. Fanny's dozing but, hearing Ketzel's voice, pulls herself up, holds out her thin arms. She's delighted to hear about Miriam, that she's coming to visit.

"Do you remember the last time we saw her?" Ketzel asks. "Six or seven years ago, that picnic up at Mosholu Parkway?"

"How could I forget?" Fanny sighs. "It was the last time we were all together. It will be nice; Joe and Sarah are coming for lunch too. They're so good to me. They have so much Party work, it isn't easy for them."

Ketzel nods, holding her mother's hot hand to her cheek. "It was a good idea we came home, Mamacita. We have family here. Now you'll get better."

After Ketzel softly closes the door, Fanny leans back. The picnic seems much longer than six years ago. Her illness, a downhill battle. She swallows tears and closes her eyes. Then I still had hope. We left New York and went on a long, impossible journey. Now it's home and the last trip.

Saturday, a quarter past twelve. Miriam hurries down Lenox Avenue. She shouldn't have taken so much time this morning, trying on different blouses and skirts. It's been so long since she saw Jaime and Fanny, and she wants them to think she's grown up, changed from a wistful little girl dressed in old hand-me-downs. She finally settled on a white pique dress her mother had remodeled, a princess style that outlines her slender waist.

An old woman slowly shuffles by her and the thick odor of her dirty body assails Miriam's nostrils. The woman's swollen hand is red from the tomatoes dripping out of the bag she clutches, full of rotten vegetables and what must be rancid meat bones The smell of garbage reminds Miriam of the old men she'd seen last winter in Central Park. Their shoulders sagged, their beards were stained, they shuffled about, useless, dejected, in old coats with fur collars, tattered pants, their homes shacks made out of boxes, tin, junked cars, and stove pipes leaning sideways. But above these dumps, on a high hill surrounded by black snow and refuse, they'd hung the emblem of America, the Star—Spangled Banner, so that it could be seen waving patriotically. Homelessness, poverty, misery are everywhere, and anger and disgust sweep through her, coloring her mood. Now, nearing Ketzel's house, she hears a man's baritone voice singing about Joshua and the walls of Jericho and her heart skips a beat. Jaime! Ketzel's already at the aerieway grated door. "You're late," she says, but she's smiling. "Come see Mama. She's been waiting all morning." She leads Miriam past the kitchen but just then her father appears, wearing a short white apron, carrying a large cooking spoon, his smooth dark face shining.

"Bien venido!" Jaime cries, hugging her. "I'm making Ketzel's favorite—arroz con pollo. You liked it, too. I remember." Taking her shoulders and looking into her eyes, he says, "A grown-up lady now. *Muy guapa—so pretty.*" Miriam is tongue-tied, but he doesn't give her a chance to answer as he dashes back to the kitchen. "This time don't burn the rice," Ketzel calls after him, laughing.

As the girls go upstairs they hear him harmonizing with a record. "Go down, Moses, way down in Egypt land …" "Paul Robeson," Ketzel says, "sings better."

The spicy odor of chrysanthemums greets Miriam as she opens Fanny's door. She thinks of the garden below where they played movie games, Fanny calling down not to be so noisy. Today, brilliant sunshine pours in, almost blinding her, bleaching the orange and blue serape on the floor. She hears a familiar low, musical voice and goes toward the window. Fanny's lying on a chaise lounge and although Ketzel's told Miriam about the T.B., Miriam isn't prepared for the thin, languid figure and the shell-like translucent face.

"Come, let me see you," Fanny commands. Taking Miriam's hand she says, "We've all come back from a long journey, Miriam dear. You're grown-up and so …" She hesitates and then finishes in Yiddish: "*Sheyn.*" Pretty. Miriam's lips tremble as she leans over and kisses Fanny's forehead.

Sitting at the foot of Fanny's chair, she finds herself telling about her sister's death and Clara's terrible grief. Words pour from her—that fateful night when her mother, eager as a young girl herself, running to the bakery to get the fresh warm rolls Bertha liked, the boyish Irish cop at the door, hesitating before blurting out the unbearable news, her mother's terrifying scream and falling, her aunt trying to jump into the fresh-dug, moist grave, the last glimpse of her sister's beautiful face—her smashed jaw making her look belligerent, as if she were angry at being dead. And her mother held up by others, her face twisted in agony, her eyes staring, empty, a wooden puppet.

"I've learned to accept her death," Miriam pauses. She's afraid she might sound uncaring. "We hadn't been that close; she was older than me in so many ways. And she was away so much. But my mother can't. She never will. Bertha was always her favorite. She was tall, beautiful, very smart. Not like me." Miriam gives a short laugh and turns away to look at the tree outside the window, it's leaves glinting in the sun. "I don't mind."

Thoughtfully, Fanny says, "You do mind, but that is natural. You lost a sister, and that is terrible. But listen, my darling, you have so much—a sweet face, beautiful eyes. People like to look at you. They like you. We love you. That's better than beautiful."

They sit without talking for a few moments. The room is quiet except for the tinkling of chimes moving at the open window. Then Fanny says, "I'm glad you came today. You'll meet Party members, good people. They work hard for the movement. Like I did when I was young and strong."

"Mama, Miriam, our guests are here." Ketzel's standing at the door. "Lunch is ready."

Fanny smiles, reaches out to take Miriam's hand. "Come, there'll be plenty of time to tell you more now that we have found you. Let's meet our friends." She rises, walking slowly, and leads them down to the dining room.

It was like the times Miriam remembered from years past. The table is set for company, the red and yellow tablecloth, an overflowing fruit bowl with golden oranges, plums and grapes, foaming pitchers of beer and soda. Four people are already sitting there when they come in and Ketzel introduces them, the older couple first. "They're Party members," she says proudly. Joe is District Organizer and Sarah is the head of the Harlem Branch." Then, turning to a younger couple she begins, "This—" but the boy breaks in, grinning, to say, "I'm Sean." He's short, stocky, in a plaid shirt three sizes too large, his elbows showing through. "And that's Gretchen," Sean says, betraying his Irish accent. Gretchen has thick, white-blond braids that she's pinned around her head and with her deep blue eyes Miriam thinks she's probably the prettiest girl she's ever seen.

"We're members of the Y C L. That's the Young Communist League, in case Ketzel hasn't already told you. Ketzel's a member, too, but she doesn't do much branch work because she's a great dancer," Gretchen tells Miriam.

Ketzel, blushing, protests. "What she means is that the Party needs us dancers and writers—giving our special talents for the benefit of the movement. Okay. Let's eat!"

Around the table they talk about current issues, what's happening with the Scottsboro case, the problems with the N A A C P and the I L D. Joe's received some criticism from the Party about the Harlem leadership and he begins sounding off about it. Working with other organizations, yet maintaining "unchallenged leadership of the Communist Party," as the Party demands, is difficult. Joe, burly, ruddy-faced, says defensively, "I'm not the most patient person in the world even though I *am* a disciplined Party member." But everyone's hungry and for a little while there's only the sound of people enjoying the good food spread before them.

While they're having coffee, breaking the silence, Ketzel says, "Joe, tell that story again, I'd like Miriam to hear it, the one you told Fanny and me—about the milk demonstration."

Joe reddens, runs his plump fingers through his sandy hair, asking "Are you sure no one will be embarrassed?"

"Nonsense," Fanny says, and smiles at Miriam. "We're all grown-ups here."

Joe doesn't need more encouragement. "Okay, here goes. About a week ago, last Monday, early, when I got up to 135th Street and Lenox, there was the usual number waiting for me at the Unemployed Council. Not the same ones; there's always plenty others, hungry, lots of kids, mothers with babies in their arms, pushing baby carriages. The crowd was pretty big, I'd say maybe even fifty. There wasn't any milk for them—hadn't been for several days.

"We usually march, a whole bunch of us, with me at the head up to Borough Hall, demand to see an alderman. Most of the time we do end up getting some relief. As we go down the streets we make a lot of noise, singing, shouting, yelling slogans like 'We want milk! Milk for our children!'"

"Aren't there cops around?" Miriam asks.

"Yeah, but mostly they don't give us a hard time. But yesterday, when we got there, they decided to ignore us. The guards wouldn't let us go in and we stood on the steps waiting. No one comes out, but finally someone does. A guy—a big, tough-looking character—he yells 'Quiet!' Then, sweet and sarcastic, he says, 'Ladies, no one here will see you today, so will you all kindly disperse.' Everybody gets mad, but we're not sure of what we'll do next. Then one woman, a big one, pushes her way to the front. She's red in the face, mad as a plucked hen." Joe stops, takes a drink.

"She starts to scream 'Maybe you don't understand, mister, we need milk—milk for our kids, M, I, L, K!,' she yells. 'Do you know what that is? Well here, let me show you!' and she pulls her sweater open so her big breasts come tumbling out. She runs up to this guy, sticks her chest right under his nose. 'You see what I mean?' she hollers. Now we're in an uproar; the crowd starts howling and laughing, can't stop. She steps back into the crowd, buttoning her sweater, but her face is red and she's laughing and crying at the same time. A minute later an alderman comes out. He talks to us nicely, tells us to go back to our relief bureau and we'll be taken care of the same day. And we were, too!"

"Sorry I wasn't there," says Sean, "just to see the look on that guy's face. It must have been funny."

"Funny and not funny." Jaime's indignant voice comes from the doorway. He brings in a big bowl of golden caramel-topped flan and sets it down hard on the table. "No milk for children, but yesterday twenty thousand gallons of milk got dumped into Connecticut Bay. Things like that—this is why we have to keep fighting."

"We're doing great work—important work," Joe says, turning to Miriam. "That is, the Communist Party is. We open up stores in neighborhoods, people meet, have coffee, we show them how to speak up, to fight …"

"I wish fighting could get me a job," Sean says. "It's almost two years now."

But Sarah says, interrupting him, "Oh, for Chrissake, let's just enjoy ourselves today. Will somebody please pass the dessert?"

Miriam laughs with the others but she's seen enough poverty in her lifetime. Although they always had enough to eat, she knows frigid rooms, dressing in front of a tiny electric heater, inadequate blazing gas jets on walls that often caught on fire. They'd lived in Hell's Kitchen, next door to a big wooden Indian in front of the barber shop window and she remembered coming home Friday nights with her mother and sister from the free concerts at Carnegie Hall when they'd have to hop over a drunk lying across the floor. In a rented room down the hall there'd always be a skinny blonde prostitute sitting on a bed, filing her nails, waiting for a customer.

Here at the Ortegas the people are feisty and cheerful. Poverty doesn't have to make people sad and sour, if they are willing to work, to change things, sharing, believing they can change the world. Not like Miriam's mother, who feels she's fighting the world alone, sarcastic and angry, watching every penny, everyone against her. Miriam wants to know, to be with these friendly people; she's warm and happy with them.

Ketzel's voice breaks into her revery. She's describing her recent dance recital. "That union hall, you should have seen it! Unbelievable—a horror! Dark, rickety folding chairs that could land you on the floor. And, to top it off, our dear radical friend, Emanuel Eisenberg—he's the dance critic," she explains to Miriam—"gives us a terrible review. He said it's just sheer, crude propaganda, with a low level of dancing."

"But everyone I know," Gretchen says, angry and defensive, "thinks Martha Graham and Anna Sokolow are marvelous. Everyone says they gonna be famous some day!"

"Hope you're right. They get great reviews but not Tamiris. She's panned a lot—even in the *New Masses*." Ketzel pushes back from the table. "But I'm happy to say that our 'Fiesta' number in Mike Gold's play about the Mexican revolution just got a rave write-up."

She jumps up, raises her arms, breaks into a tarantella. "Okay, everybody, that's enough talk. Can't sit any longer. Miriam and I are leaving." She circles the room, stamping lightly and whirling to the door, grabbing Miriam's hand. "Nice seeing you again, folks. Thanks for lunch, Jaime. We're off to the movies—the Acme. A new Russian film, *Alone*. Sound romantic? We hope. So long, everybody!"

The movie isn't at all romantic, as it turns out. It's about a young shepherd in the hinterlands, the head of a small village in need of assistance. The Soviet government sends an agent to help. But the agent is not only inefficient and lazy but corrupt as well, and at the end the villagers organize, expose him, oust him and decide they can run their own commune.

As Ketzel and Miriam leave the theater, two young men in front of them are discussing the film. "It's easy to see why they didn't show it in the Soviet Union," says one, a tall thin youth with kinky hair. "It was honest for a change. It wasn't the usual crap about the great Stakhonovite hero who saves the day—that courageous, self-sacrificing bullshit." He laughs.

His shorter, stockier companion is annoyed. "One corrupt official doesn't condemn an entire country. That's not why they don't make those movies. You Ypsils are always looking for reasons to knock the Soviet Union."

"Our comrade Stalin supplies enough reasons to knock Russia," his companion retorts. "We don't have to look for them. He can justify anything—famines, murderous collectivizations, the fiasco in China …" He stops.

Ketzel is standing in front of them, tall and blond, her face pink with anger, her green fluttery dress in motion as she gesticulates angrily.

"You—you—you son of a bitch!' she sputters. "Stalin is right. You're social fascists! You'd like to destroy the revolution."

The two boys, gape, astonished. The tall boy gulps and says, "Hey, don't take it personally. Just voicing my opinion—for whatever it's worth." Looking appreciatively at Ketzel and Miriam, he adds, "We don't want to make two pretty girls angry."

Ketzel, confused and flattered, glares at them. Miriam, embarrassed, says, "We accept your apology. Come on, Ketzel, let's go. Let's get some coffee," and begins walking away, Ketzel following reluctantly.

Later, Miriam isn't sure if she'd deliberately mentioned coffee, wanting to give the two boys an opening, but that's what happened. They walked behind the girls at first; then they caught up. "Funny," the heavy-set boy remarks, "we were just going for coffee too."

The four cross Union Square on their way to the Crusader Cafeteria. Despite the grime and cigarette smoke that render the large windows opaque and the heavy air unbreathable, everyone goes there. A big bowl of thick noo-dle soup costs only ten cents and radicals of every denomination sit in the noisy, crowded room forever, talking and arguing.

Ketzel's quiet, not sure about staying, but after a while, she relaxes. The boys are named Sydney, the tall one, and Mark. Sydney starts the conversation by discussing movies, and they find they all agree that "All Quiet on the Western Front" is a great anti-war film. They talk about directors, David Wark Griffith, Rene Clair, Eisenstein.

"Remember in the Eisenstein movie, *The Odessa Steps,* that has that great stone staircase leading down to the sea?" Sydney says. "How the baby carriage keeps bumping down towards it and you're so tense—you don't want it to end up in the water!"

Miriam shakes her head. "It was just marvelous. It kept going back and forth showing the student with the eyeglasses—the carriage—the student again. He reminds me of someone. It could even be you." She looks at Sydney and smiles and the four of them stay and talk until it's very late.

❧   ❧   ❧

Miriam and Ketzel are in different classes and it's difficult for them to meet but they keep a regular date, to meet every Friday after school. Clouds skitter across a dull gray sky, pushed by brisk breezes, trees sway, dry brown leaves circle in the air. Miriam stands in front of the candy store, waiting impatiently for her friend. Mr. Goldstein waits with her. He likes to tell his wife about Ketzel, she's beautiful, the clothes she wears, like a Russian doll, embroidered blouse, boots, a little beret—a picture!

Ketzel comes flying down the hill, her hair streaming, breathless.

"I'm awfully thirsty," she tells Mr. Goldstein, giving him her most dazzling smile. "I'll have my usual chocolate soda, double scoops, but first, a great big glass of seltzer."

She leans back with a sigh after emptying the glass. "How's everything going with you, kid?" she asks Miriam. Without waiting for an answer, she goes on. "Last night, what a great rehearsal with Martha. She has a new ballet, impressionistic. *Heretic,* she calls it. We are all in black, she's in white in front and then the group moves, all of them together, across the stage. It's a great number." Then looking at Miriam, she says, "What's with you?"

"My history teacher, Mr. Henley. A lot of the time I think he's drunk. He smells. Dirty fingernails, like he's been digging ditches."

"So what? Stop complaining. I think he's a sympathizer. Don't be so critical."

"I'm sure he is; he's always knocking the government.But he's not teaching us anything. The kids are worried about passing the Regents. They want to go to the principal." Miriam frowns.

"You better talk to those kids. It's not a good idea," Ketzel says quickly. "Listen, tell Henley what the kids want to do. Bring him a nail brush and a shaving kit. Say it's an early Christmas present."

Ketzel stands up, ready to leave, but Miriam stays seated. "I wanted to tell you about a boy I met," she begins, hesitating. "If you've got time." Ketzel, realizing she's been abrupt, says, "Sure. I'd love to hear. I've always got time for my friend." She sits down and pulls up another chair to put her feet on.

"On my block there's a bunch of Catholic and Jewish kids. Sometimes I hang out with them. There's one guy, Julian. Julian Sawyer. It's a nice name, isn't it?" Seeing Ketzel's impatient look, she hurries on. "I see him more than the others. He's a homosexual, very intelligent. We go to plays together. We went to see that play *Four Saints in Three Acts* by Gertrude Stein. He explained it to me, but I still don't get it."

"He can't be the boy you want to tell me about. Is he?" Ketzel looks at her watch.

"No. One night last September Julian comes around with a friend, a guy—tall, good-looking, gray-greenish eyes, dark-blonde hair."

Ketzel leans forward, "Now it's getting interesting"

"Yeah, he's handsome, except he's got pimples. But was I surprised! He's a great reader. He's read everything, a lot more than me, that's for sure. We talked all night. He owns a red roadster and some of us drove out to Coney Island. The others thought we were nuts 'cause we sat in the back, in the rumble seat, and just talked, about books of course. The next day I met him we kissed a lot and then we went to Brooks Brothers to pick up a new suit he was taking to Wisconsin. He's there now but he's been writing to me."

"So what's the problem? You'll see him when he comes home, won't you?"

"Yeah, but he says in his letters 'we have unfinished business to take care of.' What does he mean by that?"

"Come on." Ketzel leans over the table, grinning at Miriam. "Of course you know what he means. He's preparing you for it."

"Well, I'm not sure about that, although he writes very poetic letters. He keeps saying he's going to be a famous writer someday."

"Good," says Ketzel. "If you're going to have an affair with anyone, a famous writer will do. What did you say his name was? So I'll know it when his book comes out?"

"It's a funny name—Delmore, Delmore Schwartz. I'm not sure I want to, with him. What do you think?"

Ketzel grins. "I think he's full of hot air! Don't be a softy!"

Fanny invites Miriam often, even when Ketzel is away at rehearsals. They sit and chat in her room and when the air turns chilly, Jaime lights a fire and brings them cookies and fragrant, spicy chocolate. Often members of his organization, the National Defense of Political Prisoners, come trudging up the stairs for a meeting and Miriam watches them file by: Theodore Dreiser, the president, gray-haired, stooped over, John Dos Passos, a gentle face, Langston Hughes, handsome, with a lady friend; and, occasionally, especially when Ketzel is expected home early, a young poet, Martin Montero. The two girls think he's the best-looking man they've ever seen and discuss at length whether it's his shining, sable hair, high cheek-bones or sloe eyes that make him so sexy.

"He looks like Rudolph Valentino," Miriam says.

"No, more like Ramon Novarro, but taller, thinner, like a borzoi hound," Ketzel sighs.

When they tell Jaime how gorgeous they think Martin is, Jaime grimaces and says, "He's good-looking but he's got a sharp, malicious tongue. I know that very well."

Jaime is aware, like everyone, that Martin is smitten with Ketzel but that he tries to disguise his infatuation by adopting a careless, indifferent attitude. It fools no one. Ketzel pretends not to notice, but it's obvious she's delighted.

One dark winter afternoon, Miriam visits Fanny. It's snowing and she knows Fanny will be alone. A good time to talk, and maybe Jaime later will make them drinks. Besides, Ketzel told her they've just received a letter from Elena in the Soviet Union and Miriam's curious to hear about them.

They're mostly complaining letters, Fanny tells her. The food shortage, living in one room, sharing kitchen and bath with two other families, meager wages. But for Party members there are special privileges, better provisions, cakes and whipped cream. Last year, when Arthur was sick, Elena was given a free stay with him in a children's sanatorium in Anapa, and that was wonderful.

In her latest letter, she says that Arthur has joined the Komsomol, the Communist youth organization, and has a new friend, Volya Yoffe, a nice young boy who writes poetry. Dolmotovsky, a famous poet, thinks his poems are good, so they must be. Elena doesn't say much more except that work is hard, she misses everyone, she's lonely. She sends her love.

"I must write back soon," Fanny says. "How lucky she is to be there. Tell me, what did you think of the demonstration last week? You went with some friends, I heard."

"It was fantastic," Miriam says enthusiastically. "There must have been a hundred thousand people and hundreds of signs for 'Jobs or Wages.' William Z. Foster, the head of the Communist Party, was the main speaker. 'We know the way out!,' he proclaimed. 'We workers have to make demands, take things in our own hands.'" Miriam tells Fanny, "He's great—his enthusiasm lights up the crowd."

"Did anyone get hurt?" Fanny wants to know. "I heard cops were on horses."

"I don't think so. We all ran like hell, screaming. The horses had chests like barrels. I thought they'd plow right into us. Boy, was I scared!"

Fanny says, "Screaming! Like in Russia, under the Czar—the same."

"It was really something." Miriam shakes her head. "Fanny, why do communists feel so strong about Russia? They talk about it like it's heaven or a utopia."

Fanny fixes her pillow, sits up straight. "Because it is exactly that—a dream come true. Think of it." Her face is stern, intense. "A poor country—a big country, a tremendous country, *one-sixth of the world.* They threw over the czar!, made a revolution!, created a new society—a communist government! Do you know the words of the *Communist Manifesto*?"

She stops, taking hard, deep breaths for a moment, holding her head erect, weighing each word, slowly, passionately, with all her strength. "'From each according to his ability, to each according to his need.' Do you know what that means? Equality. Everyone works, but there are no bosses. They are their own bosses. Everyone is the same, gets the same—no rich, no poor. We're all *tovarichy,* comrades. No fears, no worries, no wars. So much love! People smile at each other in the streets. They're comrades. They hug and hold each other." She laughs. "We like to say there'll be strawberries and cream for everybody."

Her voice deepens, becomes solemn. "It will take time, it has to take time, there's hardship and suffering first, for a while, but it will happen—it must happen! The world belongs to us. 'Our people, our world, a new world.' It's a dream come true—a miracle—a real miracle!"

Glowing, exhausted, she leans back and closes her eyes. After a moment she says, in a quiet tone, "It's warm, Miriam. Please, dear, I need some air."

She lies back and Miriam goes to the window. Stirred, excited by Fanny's words, she opens it and stands a long time, looking out on the quiet street, Silence everywhere. Cold air sweeps into the room. It's snowing hard now; pearly, opalescent flakes swirl and circle in a smoky haze. The dark street and houses have disappeared, a faint light shimmers somewhere and a thick fleecy curtain obliterates everything. There's only a hushed whiteness. Everything sleeps.

She whispers to Fanny, who smiles and waves good-night. She tiptoes out.

Fanny rarely leaves her room now, but for this important occasion she makes an exception. Ketzel is appearing with Tamiris in a special dance recital. Jaime borrows a friend's roomy Pierce-Arrow and drives Fanny, Miriam, and two comrades up to Olinville Avenue in the Bronx. It's in the Co-ops, a housing development started by the International Workers Order. The Co-ops are set apart, like a little country all its own with low-story apartment houses surrounded by winding paths, courtyards, gardens and fountains. There are also lecture halls, libraries, community rooms and special places to show movies and kids with names like Leon, Vladimir and Sovietina, red scarves around their necks, run freely all over the place, in and out of each other's homes.

"They're having a fundraiser for the Scottsboro Boys Legal Defense. Make sure to come," Jaime had told Miriam a few weeks earlier when she was visiting. "Edith Segal's group is performing, too."

Sean and Gretchen are already there, reserving seats for them. Joe and Sarah, in charge, are busy trying to have more chairs brought in; they haven't expected such a large turnout. The room has been spruced up with new posters and cartoons as well as a hammer-and-sickle painting with a large picture of Stalin. Coffee, tea in a great silver samovar, sponge cake and madelbrot are piled on a long table in the rear and someone's singing a Russian song, strumming on a balalaika while kids, playing tag around the table, grab goodies when nobody's looking.

Everyone waits. When the curtains part, electricity jolts through the hall. Springing forward, whirling, stamping, beating their elbows on small drums, Tamiris and her troupe appear, pulsing, earthy, filled with wild energy.. "The body itself knows how to move" is one of Tamiris' favorite sayings.

In "Go Down Moses," the third number on the program, the lights grow dim and on the darkened platform twisting, writhing bodies depict the suffering, the agony of the enslaved negro. Then slowly the dancers rise from their knees, grappling, grasping, thrusting upwards toward the light until, finally, they stand upright—tall, free! They stretch high, higher, toward a new world. They sway, run, leap in joyful abandon. The music stops. They halt, link their arms and march in a straight, defiant line, to the front of the stage—challenging and thrilling the audience with their message: Come join us, comrades! Rise with us! We are the future!

Miriam feels as if she's on fire. She tingles, caught up in the fervor, the spirit, the excitement. For a long time now she has thought about joining the movement. She knows that Fanny wants her to, that Sean and Gretchen are anxious for her to work with them and she years to become a part of their world..

But something happened one night in Harlem, an incident that lingers in her mind, disturbing her, raising questions she can't easily answer and it's holding her back. It occurred at an outdoor meeting Gretchen had invited her to. Miriam had been given a stack of *Daily Workers* to sell while Sean and Gretchen were busy setting up the ladder, attaching the American flag to the top that was required to be flown at any public gathering under city law. A small crowd of negroes in threadbare clothes had already begun to gather. Miriam was nervous, but Gretchen was composed and smiling as she mounted the steps, attracting bystanders with her pretty face, the street light glowing on her blond hair. A few moments later Sean followed, his open face and assured, ringing voice commanding instant attention. The crowd grew larger.

"Why is it that in the richest country in the world with the highest industrial development we have the deepest worst economic crisis in history?," Sean thundered. He paused, his eyes searching their faces. "I don't have to tell you what we are suffering here—unemployment, poverty, disease. Why should this be? Could it be the fault of the capitalist system—where the rich have everything and the masses go hungry? Across the ocean in Russia, one hundred and sixty million people, one sixth of the earth, decided they wanted no more of it. They kicked out their czar. They stopped the fighting, stopped the war. Now they're showing the world they can run their country without the blood-sucking usurers and the profitmongers we have here. They have a workers' and farmers' government free from hunger and unemployment." The crowd applauded, nodding to each other. "He says the truth," someone called and a few buy *The Daily Worker* from Miriam.

A young man standing at the back of the crowd has been distributing leaflets and moving closer, Miriam sees that it's Sydney, one of the boys she and Ketzel met at the movies one afternoon. She starts over to him, waving and smiling, but one of the Y. C. L. comrades runs quickly, getting there first. He grabs Sydney, pushes him hard, snatches his leaflets and throws them in the gutter. "Scram fast," he threatens, "before you really get hurt." Sydney, outnumbered, outweighed, bereft of his leaflets, grimaces, shrugs and walks away.

Miriam runs after him and grabs his arm. "I'm sorry. He had no right to do that!," she says.

"It was stupid for me to come alone," Sydney answers as they move away. "I've been beaten up by these precious comrades before, so this wasn't so bad." Then he grins, "I'm sorry to see you're one of them. I wish you had more sense."

"Oh, I haven't joined the C P yet. I'm just thinking about it." Why does she feel defensive?

"Well, you better think about it—hard!" he says and strides away.

Later, Sean talks to her. "Keep away from people like that. They're worse than fascists. They're trying to destroy the Soviet Union. They'll never succeed, but we have to stop them from distributing their scurrilous lies." Miriam likes the way he says "scurrilous" with his Irish accent, but she's puzzled. "Sydney and his group worse than fascists?" She finds it hard to believe.

When Sean sees her confused expression he says, "You'll understand in time. Hey, you sold all the papers we gave you. We'll have to make you our prize salesgirl!" But she's disturbed. Even if Sidney is wrong, he still has a right to give out his leaflets.

Even when she was a little kid, injustice and brutality upset and haunted her. It seemed to have begun with those nightmares about Sacco and Vanzetti when she was a little girl. She's always read and now she's doing even more—*Hunger,* Gorky's play *The Lower Depths,* Frank Norris's *Chicago.* She's bought John Reed's *Ten Days That Shook with World* and thinks it is one of the most poetic, thrilling books ever written and begins to understand the meaning of the Russian Revolution, its significance, its importance. When, if ever, has an entire country risen up, defeated the enemies surrounding them and created a communist nation? This is the first time, the first glorious time—it's happening in her lifetime! Sure, there's lots of problems, many mistakes. It's easy for people like Sydney to find fault. What the Party says makes sense, though. A true socialist has to support and work for the U S S R with everything he has, his heart, body and soul. Without question.

"Bravo, bravo!" The audience is beaming, applauding, shouting, cheering the seven dancers. Ketzel is radiant; she knows she has never danced better. As she jumps from the low platform and makes her way to the group awaiting her, comrades hug her, showering praise. When she reaches Fanny and Jaime she has tears in her eyes. She throws her arms around Miriam, saying "I'll never forget this night!." Then she beckons to Martin, whose eyes are burning with fierce pride. Sparkling mischievously, extending her hand to him, she tells him, "You may kiss the queen". He ignores her hand and pulls her to him. As they kiss, a loud chord played on the paino from the front of the room, interrupts their embrace.

Frank, on the stage, is bellowing, "Everyone, your attention, please! We are happy to announce that we've been extremely successful tonight We will—we will—we will free the Scottsboro Boys! Now let's all sing together, comrades." He begins: "Arise, ye prisoners of starvation …"

Ketzel puts her arm around Miriam's shoulder; they raise their right fists with all the others. When they come to the lines, "the earth shall rise on new foundations/We have been naught, we shall be all," Miriam whispers to Ketzel, "I'm going to join the party".

Prinkipo, 1930–1932

Trosky finds his life cut off from the world difficult. He's isolated, lonely, irritable, his main channel to the outside world only through his son, Lyova. Although Zina's little boy is quiet and obedient, Trotsky wants him sent back to his mother in Berlin, claiming, "Natalya is tied down hands and feet by Sevya," and although Natalya is happy with the child, she is caught up in a web of difficult personalities and family problems.

In Berlin, Lyova is also finding it very hard to cope. His half-sister, Zina, is ill, both mentally and physically, and difficult to deal with. She loves Berlin but hates it when she hears the frightening Horst Vessel songs and the heavy boots of the Nazis pounding in the streets. She writes to her father, calls him her "Dear Ogre," and complains to him about Lyova, that bosses herr She tells Trotsky that she thinks she's having a nervous breakdown. Besides thedifficulty of dealing with Zina, is finding it very hard to cope with the many problems in his daily life; he has the burden of publishing the 'Bulletin', he is penniless, worried about his wife and child in Russia, and has a troubled relationship with Jeanne Molinier, his lover.

Trotsky has been occupied with the problems in Germany and Spain. In Barcelona, the Communist Party has already expelled several Trotskyists and semi-Trotskyist groups, as well as Andreas Nin, leader of the Trotskyist P.O.U.M., the Workers' Party of Marxist Unification. Trotsky nevertheless urges unity for all the communist ranks—to unite again against the fascists.

"A grave historic responsibility will burden those who promote the splits ...," he writes. "Heresy hunts that confuse and demoralize the workers can only bring about a fascist victory." History will prove him right only a few years later. To Remmele, a leading Communist in the German Reichstag who proclaimed, "Let Hitler take office—he will soon go bankrupt, and then it will be our day," Trotsky answers, "It is an infamy to promise that the workers will sweep away Hitler once he has seized power ... if fascism comes to power, it will ride like a terrific tank over your skulls and spines ... you have very little time to lose." But Pravda *and the German Communist paper* Rote Fahne *call him, among other things, a panic-monger and a stooge of German Chancellor Bruning.*

CHAPTER 3

New York City, Winter 1932

The winter of '32 was one of the coldest in New York City history. For six weeks, inside subway stations, hanging near change booths, there's a white flag with a red ball in the center, informing the public about ice-skating Central Park ponds. From morning until dusk, bundled figures circle the rinks; shards of sun glint from noisy, scraping blades, and trees bend like old men under the heavy crusty snow. In the subway, where the temperature never gets above five degrees, waiting passengers often spread newspapers on the cement floor to keep their feet from freezing.

Clara has three gas jets going on the kitchen stove, one heating water for coffee. The air is sour with the smell of gas and the steaming water, but Clara won't tell the super to put a fresh layer of coal in the furnace. "Let those lousy tenants give me some money," rolling her eyes up towards where nineteen apartment-dwellers have paid no rent for months. "They're knocking on the pipes! *Hub zai in dredt!* They can go to hell." She's wearing a frayed woolen cardigan left behind by a school teacher who skipped out one night.

Miriam is just getting up. She watches Kootah sitting on the table, studying Clara with yellow eyes while she sits waiting for water to boil, rubbing Vaseline on the back of her chapped hands. There's a tapping on the door. "Who's calling so early?" Opening the door a crack, Clara sees Ketzel standing there, uneasy, embarrassed.

"Come in," Clara says. "Quick—you're letting in the cold."

Clara take a step back, looks at Ketzel. She's tall, imperious, a snow queen, wearing a tight-fitting brown helmet-like hat, a long, brown muskrat coat and high leather boots.

"What brings you to our neighborhood?" Clara says. Her tone is sharp. Then she adds, "Come into the kitchen, where it's warm." She clears off a chair, pushes Kootah off the table and busies herself at the stove. "I'm making coffee. It's almost ready"

Ketzel hesitates, shakes her head. "Sorry I'm calling so early, but someone gave me a ride uptown and they're waiting outside. I'll just stay a minute."

Miriam appears in the doorway, rumpled in a flannel nightgown. "Ketzel?" she exclaims, trying to smooth her tangled hair, ashamed of the ugly room, her own disheveled appearance.

"I wanted to call," Ketzel says apologetically, "but you don't have a phone." She probably doesn't want to sound accusing, but that's the way it comes out. She adds, more gently, "I heard from one of the comrades you had the 'flu, so I got Martin to give me a ride up here." But clearly she can't wait to get out of this dismal place fast enough.

"We're giving a farewell party at my house Saturday night for filmmakers leaving for Moscow," Ketzel continues. "Jaime and Fanny told me to make sure you'd come. And bring that Knute fellow you told me about."

"Fine, I'll be there," says Miriam. "Now go—don't make your friend wait." She darts a glance at her mother—she doesn't want Clara asking questions about some "fellow."

"All right, I'm off." Ketzel quickly leaves, making her way back through the littered hallway, with gray, broken tiles.

Clara sits at the table, trying to get milk from the frozen bottle. Two inches of cream have popped to the top, pushing up the paper cover, and she's chipping some of it for her coffee. "We should be honored by a visit from such a *groyssa prietza.*" Miriam thinks that it means fancy lady although she isn't really sure but she doesn't bother to answer. It always amazes her when she visits other homes and sees people talk to each good-naturedly, without sarcasm, as if they liked each other. It didn't happen here very often. Kootah's back on the table, sniffing the sweet butter, and she pushes him off.

"Mom, don't you ever feed this cat? He's skin and bones."

"I don't see him to feed him—he's out every night. Like you, he's a bum. Then he comes home, sick.'

"Mama, cut it out—please." No matter what she says, that's the way it always ends. She knows her mother is right, at least, partially. She is out every night, but not sleeping with boys, as her mother suspects and fears. She's attending meetings, selling *Daily Workers* on streetcorners.

"Don't worry," she tries to reassure her mother every so often. "I'm not coming home pregnant." She must think I have a hundred boyfriends, "Well, I haven't. I'm not a Clara Bow. I guess I don't have 'It.'"

But now things seem to be changing, since she met Knute on that cold night. She'd been assigned by the Branch to help out with the picket line at the Foltis Fischer Cafeteria on 86th Street and Lexington Avenue. They'd been on strike for a few weeks and the future didn't look good. Management hadn't offered anything, even to sit down and talk, and strikers lately haven't showing up for picket duty. When she'd walked down from Dr. Raab's office that afternoon, the cold wind seemed to cut through her coat. At the corner, in front of the cafeteria she could see only one man walking up and down with a sign and she considered going home. But she gathered up her courage, decided she could stand the cold, and approached him: "I'm a YCLer here to help with the strike." He looked up and flashed a smile and she gulped. He was tall, wearing a cap over a thick mop of blond hair. He was the handsomest man she'd ever seen, like someone out of the movies.

He put a picket sign on her shoulders and while they walked up and down he introduced himself. His name was Knute, he said. He was a Finn, here in the United States for only a few months and afterwards, they went out for a cup of coffee. The next night, he asked her to go to the movies. Miriam wondered if she was beginning to fall in love with him. Besides being the best looking man she'd ever met, he was sweet and gentle, not like the young, crude boys she'd dated recently.

On the night of the party at Ketzel's, he wears a tan overcoat with a blue scarf that matches his eyes. He's like a Nordic god, Miriam thinks, and she doesn't mind the long walk from 156th Street though it's snowing and her feet are frozen. When they arrive at the Ortegas, they look up at the house, ablaze with lights and the sound of people talking.

"I bet there's a big crowd," she tells Knute. "We won't know many of these people. Jaime has all those intellectual friends, poets and big-shots in the Party. We're lucky to be invited."

"Good. Let's not stay long." he answers, "We'll go to a midnight movie." This is what they do, as often as they can. They can be almost completely alone up there in the second balcony, kissing and holding each other.

The long parlor room is crowded; at the far end is a large buffet with an improvised bar. Jaime has ordered food to please everyone, since there'll be almost as many negroes as whites. Ella Crowell, a buoyant lady and an experienced cook, stands behind the food table with her two teen-aged boys, beaming, helping guests heap their plates with fried chicken, pickled pigs-feet, collard greens, and sweet potatoes. Since this is a send-off for a film crew leaving for the Soviet Union, there's also caviar, beef borscht and blinis, bourbon and vodka. Above the din, the Red Army Chorus is singing "Stenka Razin" on the gramophone.

Ketzel comes flying over the minute she spies them. Although simply dressed in a cross-stitched embroidered blouse, she's still the prettiest woman in the room. After she introduces Miriam and Knute to a few people, she dashes away. Miriam looks around to see if there's someone she knows but realizes these Party people are important ones—not the "Jimmy Higginses" like herself who do street-corner meetings and distribute leaflets. While she and Knute sip their vodka cocktails, a pretty coffee-colored woman approaches them. "Aren't you the young YCLer who helped me in Harlem when I was organizing the Scottsboro March to Washington?" she asks Miriam.

"Of course," Miriam says, flushing with pleasure, flattered at being remembered. "You're Louise Thompson. This is my friend, Knute."

"Hello," Louise says. "Now come meet some of our celebrities. We'll have to make it fast, I'm supposed to give a little speech."

With Miriam in tow she approaches a group and introduces her to Max Eastman, handsome with white hair; Theodore Dreiser, chubby, homely with a receding chin; and James Rorty who gazes at her with sharp, intense eyes. She doesn't know what to say after the introductions and when she looks around for Knute, she sees he's getting his plate filled by a motherly Cora, urging him to take more because he's so skinny.

"Comrades!" Jaime's almost shouting above the din. "I'd like to introduce an outstanding worker who's involved in our fight for freedom and justice throughout the world. She's a founder of the Harlem Branch of the Friends of the Soviet Union. Now she, Langston Hughes, and twenty-two others are leaving for the USSR where they'll be making a film called *Black and White*. This evening she'll tell you a little about her past experiences in the Soviet Union, and the wonderful Russian people she met there."

Louise Thompson is a fine speaker, her enthusiasm contagious. People applaud often and Miriam understands why. She tells about a country where Negroes are accepted as people; in Russia, she says, they don't have to wear a mask, grin and lie, as Lawrence Dunbar describes in his wonderful poem. Everyone is free, equal in the new world Margaret Walker dreamed about—where they're building factories, dams and subways, making great movies, where Negroes can live a decent life, a good life. "Our color in that wonderful country is considered a badge of honor," she concludes, "the key to the city," then steps away to loud hosannas and whistling.

Jaime moves into the center. "Now, to another part of the program," he says. "I know many of you would call me a doting father, and it's true. As some of you may know, Ketzel, my daughter, has been studying with some of our greatest dancers. Tonight she's going to give us her own version of that popular ballroom dance, the Argentine tango, and her partner will be that soon-to-be famous poet, Martin Montero."

Martin swaggers through the crowd, stunningly handsome, dressed as a gaucho, wearing a wide sombrero, a poncho and studded heeled boots. The strains of "El Choclo" can be heard, at first softly, then louder. Suddenly, as if flung into an arena, Ketzel hurls herself into the center of the room. She's wearing a short, tight black dress, stiletto heels, dark silk stockings, her golden hair drawn back into a tight chignon held by a tall shell comb. She stands still, taut, challenging, her head high, her body rigid. Martin walks to her slowly. She reaches up for his sombrero, tosses it away. He curls his right arm about her, pulling her to him in a quick, sharp gesture, and they begin. He swings her around and bends her over backwards, leans over her, pressing his face close, as if he's whispering in her ear. They move into a figure eight, their feet caressing the floor, backs ramrod straight; they turn, slow, fast, kicks to the side, creating intricate patterns. Their legs twine about each other, their arms tremble, their fervor rises. The music ends abruptly; they are pale, their arms about each other in a rough embrace. As they tear apart and stalk off in opposite directions, the audience breaks into cheers and applause.

Miriam looks over at Jaime. He's running his hand through his thick, dark hair, a familiar gesture when he's disturbed, his eyes glowing with love and concern. Miriam wonders: if her own father were alive, if he would look at her that way? How lucky Ketzel is. Just then Knute catches her eye; he wants to leave. But Miriam motions to Knute that he has to wait a moment; she must say good-bye to Fanny, who's sitting to one side, back straight, regal in a dark red velvet dress and silver earrings. While Jaime is introducing Kenneth Spencer, a great Negro baritone, Fanny whispers to her, "We don't see enough of you. Come, please, even if you're so busy." Miriam promises, kisses her flushed cheek and makes her way to the small anteroom where Knute is waiting.

As they're about to open the outside door a young man pushes inside. He stops them, grabbing her. "Nicolas—it's you!" Miriam says, startled. "Where did you just come from?"

"Shush, please," he hisses. "Don't make a sound. Nobody must see me." He pulls her back into a corner of the little vestibule crowded with coats, boots and umbrellas. He's pale, wearing a thin jacket, his hands trembling, his eyes darting, watchful.

"When did you get back?" Miriam whispers. "I wanted to ask the comrades about you, but you told me not to."

"Listen." Speaking quickly, very softly, Nicolas says, "I am without papers. Please understand. About your friends—you ask me to find them. I must tell you fast. They are not in address you give me in Moscow. So people not see us talking, I meet them in market. Arthur in prison, arrested, six months. Elana in State Hospital." Nicolas stops, then adds, slowly, "Sorry I bring bad news. But I make promise to you. Now I must go." Giving her a quick kiss, he slips back down into the dark staircase, leading to the basement and the street.

Miriam feels shaky and she fumbles with her scarf while Knute helps with her coat. They descend the brownstone steps silently, but as they walk away from the house he looks at her. "Come here for a minute," he says, pulling her into the dark aerieway beneath the steps. "You're shivering. Let me warm you" and opens his overcoat, to hold her close. After a moment Miriam asks, her voice tight and harsh, "What's happened? Arthur and Elena—what could they have done? They're good people!"

"Miriam, don't worry. Maybe it's not true. We don't know the whole story." He stops, bends down, kisses her. "It's useless to talk now. Come, let's get out of here."

For days afterwards Miriam walks about troubled, questions flooding her mind. None of the letters Fanny has received from Elana up until now had any hints of trouble in them, at least not the ones she's shared with Miriam. There had been only glowing accounts of life there, especially in the early ones.

"Although food is scarce in Moscow, there's always something to eat in the clubs for Communist youth," Elana wrote in the last letter Fanny had received. "For a few kopeks you can have piroshki or butter-bread sandwiches with ham and cheese. Arthur has been going to poetry readings with a new friend, our neighbor, Nadezda Yoffee. She's much older but very nice, and she loves poetry, too. They have great readings—Essenin, Mayakovsky."

But for some time now there had been silence, which is why she had asked Nicolas, who was going back to the Soviet Union, to find out was happening. Did Fanny or Ketzel know about this? Surely Ketzel would have told her if she'd heard something. But then again Miriam hadn't seen Ketzel much during the past few months. She'd been very involved in rehearsals with Tamiris and busy with her secret love affair with Martin.

❦   ❦   ❦

Miriam meets Ketzel in Yorkville one afternoon at the Kultur Sovetz. She was free; Dr. Raab had cancelled his appointments for the day and Ketzel had time between practice and rehearsals. They liked to meet in the run-down Hungarian café, with its oilcloth-covered tables and scuffed linoleum with its back room filled wth chess players or those who simply wanted to read the *Daily Worker* or the Hungarian Communist paper. Men, mostly unemployed would sit there for hours, eating big chunks of buttered chollah for ten cents, talking and whiling away the time. Occasionally they glance over at the two attractive girls, but not for long—who had money to take a girl out these days?

Miriam really doesn't care for Ketzel's poet, but she knows Ketzel is crazy about him. "How's it going with Martin?" she asks politely.

"He's a wonderful lover," Ketzel says with a dreamy half-smile, "sweet and gentle. But he gets jealous if he thinks I'm even looking at another guy. The way he talks, he had money at one time, but since he started to write he's always broke."

She gets up to fetch more coffee. "This stuff is really vile, but it's hot," she says. She goes on talking about Martin, describing his tiny furnished apartment in the East Village. "It's so damn cold there that all you can do is jump into bed to keep warm. And that's all we do," she adds with a grin.

"You really sound happy," Miriam says, wiping a grimy fork before she starts on her strudel. "I wish that Knute and I … not that he's anxious. After I told him I was a virgin he stopped asking me to come up to his room when his landlady was out. I guess where he comes from, you have to get married first."

Ketzel thinks that's really funny. "Oh, you poor kid!" she giggles, and begins to sing "I can't give you anything but love, baby." She stops, then says, "Platonic love, that is," and giggles some more.

"Okay, so you're the expert," Miriam says. "Give me some pointers on how to get your man. Or should I read 'Advice to the Lovelorn' in the *Daily Mirror*?"

"Enough said," says Ketzel and opens her purse. She lays out a Tangee lipstick, Rimmel's mascara, a silver compact with loose powder, and an eyebrow tweezer and begins a long lecture on how to capture a male. It's as complex as a military operation, and as Miriam listens she realizes she can never carry out this line of attack.

"I don't have any silk stockings," she says defensively. "I have just one lipstick and it's the wrong color. I don't have silk underwear; it's plain, white cotton. I'm a lost cause, I guess."

But Ketzel won't give up. As she puts the stuff away, she says, "Next time we get together I'll give you a few pairs of my stockings and we'll go over to the 5 & 10 on 86th Street and buy you a whole drawer of makeup."

Soon after, though, things between Miriam and Knute happen quite easily—she doesn't need any of that stuff. But she doesn't tell Ketzel.

🍁   🍁   🍁

Vodka flows like water at Bonita Williams' house this Saturday night. She's giving a party; she's always hosting gatherings. She likes people and she'll tell you so in a large, booming voice. She's a great speaker at street-corner meetings, big, earthy. Miriam sits on a large couch sipping her bloody mary, bored, trying to look absorbed in her drink She doesn't know any of the people here. Molly and Sean promised to come but they haven't shown. She hasn't seen very much of them during the past year, even though they are all working in Harlem. They're busy with the Harlem Unemployment Council, whereas Miriam's unit is involved with selling *Daily Workers*, spreading the news of the Scottsboro Case, organizing street marches and rallies in the Scottsboro Boys' defense. There's a lot happening; only a few days ago, on May 27, the International Labor Defense succeeded in getting an indefinite postponement of the boys' death sentence and the Party held a tremendous affair at the Rockland Palace on 135th Street. Paul Whiteman, Ethel Waters and Duke Ellington had given their all before an excited audience of more than a thousand people.

All winter she's been going up to Harlem after work almost every day. The preceeding fall Molly had handed her an application last fall, saying, "They need young, intelligent people there. It'll be great experience for you." But the stifling, acrid odors from burning refuse, the great puffs of smoke and angry flames leaping from garbage cans, and the frightening, yawning tenement windows made her feel sick and she'd half-run all the way to Party headquarters. She was the youngest person in the branch, and although the twelve older white workers and three Negroes were friendly, she'd been ill at ease. She feels the same way at this party.

Sitting next to her on the couch is a thin, pale young man. He's leaned his crutch against the wall and takes a drink from one of the comrades, who has brought it to him. She recognizes him: Isadore Dorfman, who's just been in the hospital for several weeks. The police had sailed into an anti-lynching rally the Party was holding on 125th Street. When they attacked a colored woman with clubs, Dorfman had come to her rescue and had been badly hurt.

"You're very brave," Miriam tells him. "I get scared at some of these rallies. Guess I'm a coward."

"Of couse you're not!" he replies, vehemently. "Besides, it's really not that dangerous. By the way, I hear you're a good worker, not a complainer, not one of those who like to sit around and shmooze." He begins complaining about some of the other comrades; he'd been in the Party for nine years and enjoyed gossiping. But Miriam, who didn't know most of the old-timers, isn't really interested.

Finally she asks a question about something that has been bothering her. "Why did they transfer Cyril Briggs downtown to work on the Daily Worker? He was very friendly and everyone says he was one of the best people they had in Harlem for fifteen years."

"Excuse me." Dorfman abruptly, clumsily gets up, his voice cold, reaches for his crutch. "I see Louis Sass over there—got to talk to him," he says and limps away. A few feet away, he turns back and adds, sharply, "Some people ask too many questions. The Party made the decision. They assigned Ford and Davis here in Harlem because they're top men, great organizers. They felt they were needed here. And Sass, too. The Party knows what it's doing and we have no business asking questions."

I might have known not to ask, she thinks. Feeling squelched and unhappy, she resolves to get drunk. After all, people look like they're having a good time when they get 'sloshed.' She goes back, pours herself another drink and then another, talks to some people she doesn't know and who don't seem interested in knowing her. All at once her lips feel numb; she starts to feel sick. After she throws up twice in the bathroom she pulls her coat out from under the pile in the bedroom and ducks out. So much for Party affairs, she decides on the subway. Her lips don't seem to be there and her chest hurts.

The following morning she's awakened by sunlight streaming into her room. Looking out, she sees Kootah limping along the backyard fence, exhausted, blood streaming from one ear. I guess he had a great time with his pals, she htinks. She can't say that for herself. She decides that while it's exciting to sing "The Internationale," doing Jimmy Higgins work is not, even though she wishes it were. She goes to every meeting of the YCL branch, attends classes at the Jefferson School, tries to understand dialectic materialism, but *Wage, Labor and Capital* is just a bit too much for her. Selling the *Daily Worker* on 125th Street is a chore she detests; standing at a subway station or outside a movie house in the damp and cold, or even in nice weather, is not for her. She hates being a saleswoman. Most of the time she gives the paper away if someone seems interested and tries not to feel upset when they yell at her or push her arm away. But even worse is door-to-door canvassing. The Party's rule is that two people have to go together, and in Harlem it has to be with a Negro comrade. But the branch has only three Negro members. Why is that, she wonders. Why, in spite of all the successful rallies and demonstrations that the CP holds about the Scottsboro case, why don't more Negroes join the Party? But when you knock on a door in Harlem and the tenant opens it and sees two white people, as often as not, he'll quickly shut it. People aren't rude; it's just that they're not very cordial. After all, that's understandable; black and white weren't friends for a long, long time.

Her friend Esther speaks at street-corner meetings a lot. She just hops up on the stand and begins. Miriam would love to be able to do the same, but when she asks Esther "What do I say up there?" Esther answers, "It's easy—just talk about all the banks closing, the evictions. Give 'em some statistics, like unemployment in Harlem three times greater than in the rest of the country. Tell them about Russia." But Miriam can't bring herself to do it.

What she really likes about party work is going to a diner after an assignment, having coffee and talking. She wants friends and companionship, but everyone's busy. Maybe if she lived in the Coops it'd be better, but that's not possible. She can't afford it on what Dr. Raab pays her.

Last June, after she finished high school, she spent the summer waitressing in a summer camp in exchange for tips. Now she's finding being at home "the pits," as Ketzel would say. There's food at home and clothing, of a sort; Clara has altered, patched and put together a decent winter coat for her. But whenever Miriam has to ask for subway or movie money, Clara mutters, "Get a job."

"But Mama, there are no jobs."

"Secretarial jobs there are—stenographers, office workers. Mrs. Siegel told me. You could be a good secretary; you're smart enough."

The Woods School of Business on Lenox Avenue and 122nd Street has the cheapest fees and a good reputation. A thin, nervous man comes to the house to sell a course on shorthand and recommends that she learn Pittman Method. "It's highly respected and the most accurate," he tells them earnestly.

"Okay" says Clara. "For six months I'll pay."

"But Madam," he protests, "the course is not easy. It takes hard work, practice and at least nine months or a year of serious application to become a proficient stenographer."

"Six months or nothing. I won't pay more," Clara insists. Miriam feels lightly nauseated at the prospect, but she has no choice. She hates the whole thing but attends class twice a week, where she's taught how to make mysterious marks that supposedly stand for words. She refuses to study, so she can't make out what the strange squiggles she puts down on paper mean. Beside, she's busy with activities every night after she joins the Party.

In February Fanny tells her about a doctor who needs an office girl and so she quits the Woods School. Later she manages to get a job as a senior stenographer on the W.P.A (a sympathetic young examiner feels sorry for the young girl whose eyes fill when she fails the dictation test). Called on to take dictation at large meetings of important people, she makes funny squiggles and then recalling as much of the conversation as she can, she types up the minutes. Luckily, about ninety percent of the time she's able to do a fair job. Occasionally someone protests, "I *never* said that," but fortunately it doesn't happen too often.

Fanny's friend, Dr. Raab, is a dermatologist who treats patients for skin ailments. Actually, most of his patients are young men with gonorrhea or other sex-related diseases. He lives and practices in a large, luxurious apartment building on East 86th Street and needs a receptionist for only five or six hours a day—three in the late morning and three in the early evening. Kind and dough-faced, suffering from stomach ulcers, he apologizes to Miriam about the meager salary but justifies it by the small number of hours he needs her. "Also, you do have to tidy up and vacuum a little. I have a cleaning woman who comes in once a week."

She accepts the job, delighted to be working. His patients, almost all men, turn out to be very polite; they smile at Miriam and many try to date her. "I'd have to be nuts to go out with any of those guys" she tells Ketzel. "Gonorrhea! Yoikes!"

The thirty-five dollars a month he pays her is just fine, after all, she's just going on eighteen and there aren't any jobs around. Besides, her mother doesn't ask for any of her pay so she has enough to treat hungry comrades to hot dogs and coffee and has plenty of free time in the afternoon. She meets friends, goes to the Met, the Kultur Sovietz on 84th Street. After she meets Knute on the strike line she pickets every day with him. It's only natural that she's tired when she comes back to the office; after putting on her white uniform, sometimes she curls up on a sofa in the back room and goes to sleep. The outside bell isn't very loud and quite frequently Dr. Raab has to answer the door himself. He yells at her often but doesn't let her go. Later, when she quits, she recommends Ana, a German comrade, to replace her.

"Is she like you?" the doctor asks, wistfully.

"Oh, no," Miriam says, "She's very conscientious." Sometime afterwards she runs into Ana on 86th Street. Ana's looks very military in her leather jacket and boyish bob. When Miriam asks how it's going with Dr. Raab, Ana beams. "Oh, he luffs me," she says.

"Sure" Miriam answers. Smiles. "I can guess why."

❧   ❧   ❧

One afternoon in April Knute waits for Miriam at the Automat on 14th Street. It's not the cruelest month, at least not for me, Miriam thinks as she hurries up the street. She's late but feels light and happy and she knows Knute doesn't mind. He likes the atmosphere and enjoys the difference between the dingy Crusader and the Automat's sanitized atmosphere. To him it's an icon of American cleanliness and efficiency. Most everyone likes the Automat, actually. The food is cheap and good, but they like it for other reasons, too. It's white-tiled, high-ceilinged; the brass is polished bright and gleaming. All around the room, lining the walls, are small glass cubicles containing sandwiches, puddings and salads. The glass boxes are locked but two, three, four or more nickels, deposited in a slot alongside, make the doors swing open. Hot coffee and hot cocoa flow from shining gorgon-headed brass spouts and cost five cents, but hot water is free and there is sugar and sliced lemon on every counter, available to all. Many unemployed and homeless people spend warm comfortable afternoons there, reading the newspaper or visiting with friends who drop by.

Knute looks up as Miriam sits down opposite him, but his smile is a bit forced. He turns his attention to his second cup of coffee, which has spilled over. He places a napkin under it, on the saucer, fishes out a cigarette from his coat and lights it. He takes a long drag, exhales slowly, watches the smoke rise and then says, his voice slightly shaking, "Miriam, I've got to go back home—to Finland."

She looks at him. She knew it was going to happen sooner or later, but it's still a shock. "I'd hoped you could stay here ... I thought that we might ..." Miriam lets her voice trail off; she isn't sure what she wants to say.

Knute raises his cup, puts it back down. "I'm sailing out late tonight," he says. "I got bad news—my little brother is sick. They think it may be infantile paralysis," he says. "My cousin Arne—in a minute he'll be here—he told me ... I must go back."

"When you go—would you like me to go with you—maybe later—join you? She'd like to smile and say it lightly, but it doesn't come out that way. Her lips tremble; the corners of her mouth turn down.

He reaches over to her, saying, "If it were only possible, but it isn't. First of all—" But he doesn't finish telling her why because at that moment a chubby, curly-haired man appears, winding his way toward them through the tables.

"Arne! It's about time," Knute says. "Come sit down and meet a wonderful girl—my Miriam." Knute puts his hand on Miriam's shoulder and presses it while Miriam reaches up to cover it with her own. "Arne has some interesting stories to tell us about Russia. I know you want to hear them."

Arne has a warm smile. Leaning over to brush Miriam's cheek, he says, "My god, I'm hungry and I'm so happy we're meeting here. I love this place. Hey, let me get us some food,"

"But you don't know what we want!" they both protest.

"Never mind, I'll just get everything," he answers and trots off happily to the center of the room, where a gray-haired matron standing behind a circular marble table makes change, instanty throwing down the exact amount of nickels. After changing five dollars, Arne returns with hamburgers, baked macaroni and cheese, rice pudding and coffee for everyone.

"It's unbelievable," he says as he distributes the plates around the table and sits down to attack his lunch with gusto.

At last, leaning back contently, smoking a Lucky, he tells Miriam, "Knute wanted me to meet you. He's right. You're nice and pretty, just like he told me."

He takes a sip of coffee before he starts. "Maybe Knute didn't say—we're cousins but I was born here in the United States—an only child My uncle, Adolph, Knute's father, had seventeen kids with two wives. We Finns enjoy making babies, right, Knute?" Knute glares at him, embarrassed.

Arne, grinning, goes on. "I don't know if he told you. I just got back from the Soviet Union. It was most interesting! You know, my parents supported the Russian Revolution, always papers and talk about it in my home. I studied engineering here in City College. But ... the Depression, no jobs, so I decided to go to Russia, like a bunch of other Finns—thousands." For a moment his tone deepens, dry and bitter. "Thousands went, only hundreds came back, those lucky enough to have American papers."

He takes a large bite of his hamburger. "My parents tell me to look up a distant relative—Frenckell, an engineer working on hydroelectric plans, the technical director of the canal 'combinat.' I didn't know where to begin, so I headed out to where the Stalin Canal was being built. Tremendous, a hundred miles long, a link between the White Sea and the Baltic. It was unbelievable, amazing, almost entirely completed in less than two years.

"I was lucky to get a train ride with a friend of Rovio, a big shot in Soviet circles." Arne stops, chuckles. "I'm just telling you this because this train had been used by the Russian imperial family. Everything was covered in thick, musty velvet, even the toilet seats! Imagine."

"For god's sake, Arne," Knute interrupts. "I'm sure Miriam's not interested in velvet toilet seats."

But Miriam shakes her head and laughs. "Don't listen to your cousin. Just go on."

"From Povenets, we took a paddle steamer, the *Karl Marx*. Very comfortable. Such a festive occasion. Every dock was decorated with flowers and bunting and made of wood; hardly any cement was used. Even the sides of the canal were lined with it. Millions of trees, most from the great Karelian forests, long, thick pines. But we didn't see any workers and when we began to ask they said that they had been removed and put to work on the Volga-Moscow canal being constructed. We believed it, of course, until one day, almost at the end of our journey, I met an American Finn and this is what he told us."

Arne pauses, pushes aside one empty plate and begins on his baked macaroni. "Believe me, it's hard to eat and tell you this story. That men can do this to other men.... The entire crew that worked on this canal lived in temporary barracks during the winter, in tents in the summer. The workers were divided into individual crews under the surveillance of 'trusties'—you can call them prison guards. If any single prisoner escaped, the trusties knew that they themselves would be shot. They got just enough food to keep them alive. The intelligentsia and the kulaks received the least. The work norms were so high only the strongest could fulfull them. Disease everywhere, spotted fever, typhoid, scurvy raging, uncontrolled. To go to the hospital was to enter the cemetery."

Arne's voice is grim as he lifts the cold coffee cup to his lips. "The American Finn was laughing when he told me. 'You see how festive it is here on the locks? But if you go farther back you'll see a different story. Bodies of thousands of forced laborers. Not in regular graves, just buried like animals.'" He wipes his forehead, which has broken out in a cold sweat. "It isn't just what the American Finn told me. I saw for myself, at the camp at Solovetskiye. They walked around with dead eyes, without hope. In a Soviet labor camp, a ten-year sentence is a death sentence."

Knut says, "Arne, you've said enough. I think Miriam is tired." She's hardly moved during Arne's long account, but now she shakes her head. She knows she needs to hear this.

"You must hear one more thing," Arne says. "This English story, it's so ironic. In Karelia, in 1931, under Soviet rule almost all of the timber was cut by prison labor. News of this came, somehow, to the English House of Commons and there was a great uproar. 'England must not buy lumber from the Soviet Union because it is the product of slave labor,' they shouted in Parliament and they sent a three-member commission to Investigate. In Leningrad, as soon as they got wind of this, guess what they did? They removed all prison labor from the route. How did they get rid of the prisoners? Easy. They just drove them deep into the forest. Now, you might ask, where did they get construction workers? Another easy answer. They brought them in from Petrozavodsk and the collective farms. The English were told they could talk freely to the workers but they didn't think to ask them questions. Anyway, the workers had been coached to give proper answers." He leans back, wipes his face with a napkin. "But, let's face it, not even many Russian people know about the prison labor camps. They only know that millions of people disappear, vanish without a trace. No one dares to ask. People separate and sometimes they disown their own relatives and friends."

Miriam looks at Knute. "Do you suppose that's what happened to Arthur? That he was put into a prison camp? What could he have done? He's just a young boy. He was happy in Moscow, he had friends, they went to the Youth Centers, they read poetry." Her voice begins to quiver. She stops, looks at them, hoping they can reassure her. Arthur must be all right and safe somewhere.

Arne jumps up. "Let me get you some hot coffee." He runs over to the change table to get more nickles.

"Miriam," Knute says, taking her hand. "I don't know what's happened but I think he was arrested because—not because he was against the government—but because he was Nadezda Joffe's friend. Her father, a general in the Red Army, was a close friend of Trotsky. When he was sick they wouldn't let him leave Russia to get medical help and he committed suicide. This Joffe was very popular; thousands attended his funeral. Listen!" Knute's voice is harsh, his eyes shooting blue angry sparks. "No one has to be a spy or a counter-revolutionist in Russia today. If you're critical of the government—of Stalin—or be a friend of someone who is … that's all it takes."

Arne's back at the table and now he has in tow a tall young woman with flaming red hair and wide, almond-shaped eyes. Putting his arm about her waist, he says, "Miriam, I just met this beautiful young lady at the counter. She says she knows you and I told her to come over and say hello."

"Tamiris!" Miriam smiles, extending her hand.

Tamiris laughs, embarrassed by Arne's admiration. "I'm glad to see you," she says. "I know who you are, even though you might not remember me. You're Ketzel's friend. I've been trying to reach her for the last few days, but it's impossible."

Arne is capitvated by this vivacious, good-looking woman and encourages her to talk about her dancing. She's happy to oblige, sits down with them and immediately launches into a description of her new work. called "Salut au Mond," part of a "Walt Whitman Suite." "In it I try to show the problems of the Americans—how he struggles for his existence in the new world … the problems of the Chinese, who quietly accepts his fate, the Negro, who suffers from discrimination and racial prejudice." She looks at the three listeners, her handsome face glowing with enthusiasm. "But underneath, they all have the same problems and, at the end, they all unite in peace and work together."

Arne tells her eagerly, "You have great vision. I think you're very artistic."

Tamiris sighs. "Thanks, but it sometimes seems I can't please anyone. If Charles Weidman uses pantomine, they say that's dramatic flare. If Martha Graham uses stream of consciousness, that's okay, too. But I can't make artistic statements without being called obvious. Tell me, why do they say it's bad taste on the stage to have a person shot out of a cannon—a cannon made up of dancers?" Miriam almost smiles at the image but stops when she sees how serious Tamiris is.

"Is it any more in bad taste to wage horrible wars?" Tamiris goes on. "Anyway, no one can deny what John Martin says about me in the *Times*. He wrote, 'Tamiris dances gloriously. She should just cut loose and dance about on the stage in her sheer loveliness of movement.' Now I can't complain about that, can I?"

She gets up, flashing a wide, charming smile that lingers a bit longer on Arne's face. "I really have to go. Thanks for the coffee and for listening to me sound off." She calls back to Miriam, "Tell Ketzel to phone me" and sweeps off.

Arne takes his leave soon after. He knows this is the last time Knute and Miriam can be with each other.

When they're alone at last, the couple make plans for their last day; they'll go rowing in Central Park. But when they get there they're told it's too early in the season; the boat house isn't open. So they walk around the pond, holding hands, making footprints in the squishy mud. They buy apples and raisins and hot coffee and go back into the park, sitting on rocks, hugging, relishing the warm sun, the nippy, spicy air. "It's beautiful," Knute tells her. "Like you."

"I'll never forget today," Miriam whispers, snuggling in his arms, a pang in her heart.

They go to the White Castle for nickel hamburgers and sit for a long time in the little shop. Then to 42nd Street to see *Grand Illusion,* paying no attention to the screen. Afterwards it's late and dark. Knute is leaving in a few hours and has to pack up. As they kiss good-bye on her stoop, he promises he will write, his face in the shadows. He doesn't mention her suggestion about her going to Finland and she knows it's best not to bring it up. "Perhaps you'll be back as soon as your little brother is better," Miriam says. "By next spring, maybe?" she adds wistfully.

"Yes, I hope so," he answers. But she knows they won't see each other again.

Later, she lies in bed, feeling forlorn and sad, and it takes a while until she falls asleep.

France, 1933

In January, 1933 Trotsky learns that his daughter Zina committed suicide in Berlin. She sealed the windows and door of her room and opened the gas jets. Trotsky and Natalya go into their room. They stay there for several days. When the Old Man finally appears, his face is lined, his hair almost entirely gray. Never again will he wear the white suits he always favored.

That year Trotsky is offered asylum in France. He and Natalya lived outside of Paris, first at Royan, later in Barbizon, near Fontainebleau. The city itself, he is told, is out of bounds. Andre Malraux, author of Man's Fate and now a critic of the Soviet Union, contributes to the cost of hiring a bodyguard. They discuss many topics and in answer to Malraux's observation that "One thing that communism will never conquer and that is death." Trotsky replies, "When a man has done the tasks that he has set for himself, when he has done what he wanted to do, death is simple."

Meanwhile, the new task—building a new international—looms before Trotsky. Will he live long enough, be well enough? The task seems overwhelmingly difficult, the obstacles insurmountable, watching the constant bickering and quarreling among the tiny groups who want to build a new movement.

CHAPTER 4

New York City, Spring 1934

Arne's stories worry Miriam but she stays active with the Young Communist League, even working harder, to keep her mind from missing Knute. One night, although it's against her better judgement, Miriam decides to tell her mother what's she's been up to, that she's joined the Y C L.

"You're telling me something new?" Clara asks, sitting at the kitchen peeling apples for tsimmis, Shabbos dinner. "What else could I expect. You're always running around with those schoozem."

"But Mama, Communists do a lot of good, for everyhone—for the homeless, the immigrants, the Negroes." She can't resist adding, "We don't call them schwartze, like you do."

Her mother, like most immigrants in New York, thinks of black people as a lowly race, fit for hard labor, inclined to be lazy, not capable of being educated, an inferior species of humanity. Clara gets mad when she hears Miriam talk about discrimination and exploitation. "Who isn't?" she'll ask. "Too bad!"

"But Mom, it isn't only that. It's much worse. Remember when we heard on the radio about that man, Claude Beals in the South, in Florida, who was lynched? It didn't say how they tortured him to death. They couldn't say that over the air. They cut off pieces of his body"—she doesn't want to say that it was his genitals—"and stuffed them in his mouth." She finds herself beginning to choke but makes herself finish. "They hanged his body from a tree and burned it. They had a party. Everyone came for miles around."

Clara doesn't want to hear this stuff. She believes acts of violence are aberrations in America; she accepts everything, as most immigrants do. And although many Jews from Russia and Poland brought traditions of unionism and socialism to their new country, Clara's not one of them. She wants to accept America unconditionally, uncritically, even though she's never believed the stories about America being the *"goldener Medina"* She shakes her head and gets up from the table, puts the apples in an enamel pot. "Listen, but you won't anyway. It's terrible what happens sometimes, but it's not going on such much anymore."

Miriam realizes she shouldn't have brought up the lynching, the oppression and fear that still prevail in the South, the way people use words like schwartze and nigger instead of the more dignified 'Negro'. How can she make her see that the America that's supposed to be a great democracy simply doesn't exist! The white ruling parties, Republicans and Democrats, have no interest in improving the lives of the poor, the immigrants, the Italian, Irish, Russians, the colored people, in treating everyone as equals. It serves their purpose to keep sections of the population as underdogs. It's good for the economy. How else can you keep service and labor so cheap?

She's trying to explain all this while her mother adds orange peel and honey to the small pot, bubbling away, but now Clara bangs a spoon down on the stove and glares at Miriam.

"If I tell you I want you to stay from the Kommunisten, if I say I want you to study, get a good secretary job? Would you do it? Ha! A nechtigah tug! You know, you could be blacklisted for the rest of your life. It's dangerous to be a Communist. You could end up in jail. Many of them …"

"Okay, mom. Skip it." Miriam's angry. She turns to leave. "You're right. You always are. It never fails. But I'm staying in the Party." Before she slams the door, she yells back, "It's the most important thing in my life."

❦   ❦   ❦

"Why did you leave Tamiris? Miriam wants to know. Ketzel has quit her group and is now a member with Anna Sokolow. They're sitting on the stone steps of the Lewisohn Stadium, waiting for the symphony concert to begin. Their picnic basket is open and they're carefully peeling hard-boiled eggs.

"There's lots of reasons. I feel bad about it. But Anna … she's a really great choreographer and smart too." Ketzel stops to open a small jar of tomato juice and take a sip. "She's one tough baby. People say she's pretty, I don't. She's very small."

"Is she bossy, like Martha Graham?" Miriam asks, carefully wrapping egg shells in tissue paper, putting them back in the basket.

Members of the large orchestra have entered the pit and are noisily tuning up, playing staccato passages.

"Yeah, they're a pair. Sometimes, when they're together you can watch sparks flying. Demanding—don't ask. What really gets me is a number Anna's just composed. 'Strange American Funeral.' It's about an immigrant steel worker who's killed when he falls into a vat of boiling metal; its symbolic, it shows how the individual in America is destroyed by the capitalist system". Ketzel fishes out a heavy thermos with collapsible tin cups.

"Lemonade?" she asks her, filling them as she speaks. "What's great is how Anna works, she makes characters come alive, not just stick figures. Some think she's a genius."

Miriam detects a slight note of envy in Ketzel's voice but doesn't try to reply. Ketzel's probably not interested in her opinion.

"Have an apple" Ketzel says, "they look delicious," and leans back, against the cement step of the tier above, "Here comes Willem van Hoogstraten, the conductor. Some moniker, right?"

As he enters, there's warm, energetic applause and everyone quiets down. The stadium is full, fourteen thousand people from all parts of the City, have assembled to hear Beethoven's Fifth Piano Concerto, and tonight Jose Iturbi, the renowned pianist, is soloist. Although the concrete is uncomfortable, they haven't brought cushions as many old people have done.

When the concert ends, Miriam and Ketzel climb the steps to Amsterdam Avenue looking for Jaime's black Model A Ford, a recent purchase. He's going to pick them up and bring them both to 117th Street. Among the throng making its way up the hill, Miriam spies a familiar face and calls, "Sydney, Sydney, over here," and waves. He recognizes her and weaves his way over, accompanied by two young women, a short blond, the other, taller, dark-haired.

Sydney begins introductions, nods at the blond girl on his right. "This is Sylvia Ageloff, and her friend Ruby Weill." Ketzel and Miriam introduce themselves and then one of them starts talking about the concert. They chat a little, the conversations flags and the five young people stand, awkwardly silent. Ketzel, raising on her toes, her long, blue voile skirt billowing in the breeze, shakes back her long mane, impatiently exclaims, "What's taking Jaime so long?"

Sydney looks at his watch. "We'd better move along, it's after eleven already. The trolleys take forever," he says, and after brief good-byes Sylvia and Ruby leave. Ketzel, looking after them, says,"

"What's he doing with those girls. I think the blonde must be at least five years older than him."

"I don't think she's his girl friend, maybe she's a member of the Socialist Party, like Sydney," says Miriam.

"I wouldn't be surprised if they're Trotskyites. I'll bet your friend Sydney is. He sounds like one."

"You know, Ketzel" Miriam is surprised her voice sounds so angry, "If anyone says anything critical about the Soviet Union, you call him names right away. Can't people have different opinions?

"Okay, sorry. Forget it," Ketzel put her arm over Miriam's shoulder, "I'm glad you're sleeping over. I've got a lot of stuff to talk to you about."

Of course she does, thinks Miriam but why does it have to be about Martin. Their secret affair seems to have lost some of its excitement and she wonders sometimes if it's because Jaime has ceased to be suspicious, stopped asking annoying questions and appears to accept the love affair. Also, her father enjoys hearing about their successes at the Roseland Ballroom where they're often the center of attraction, doing a loose, almost wild double Lindy and a very sexy rhumba. Once in a while they win a contest and Ketzel brings home a little dancing statue to put on Fanny's bureau.

That night, lounging on her oversized, downy bed, Ketzel goes into greater detail about her love affair.

"It's not very noticeable, in fact I can't put my fnger on it. I miss the little pet names he used to call me, like Chula, Munequita or the little love songs he'd croon at night when we were in bed." Ketzel can't help a small laugh, a sad one.

"It used to be so wonderful. He'd say, just a minute, I must do something very important, before … well, you know. He'd rush to the bureau, for a little bottle of perfume, Emeraude's his favorite, dab it on my ear lobes. Now, it seems like he's in a hurry. It's rush, rush, rush even though he still enjoys it. I guess you still don't know much about that stuff. Or shouldn't I ask?"

Miriam doesn't answer. She's still upset about Knute. He was awfully sweet but careful about everything and she hasn't heard from him since he left.

When it comes to sex she remembers Delmore Schwartz, that great writer, poet or both. He'd written her two or three letters from the University that winter and she knew she'd be seeing him when he came to New York in the spring. It might be fine with him, she thought, she liked him, he was good-looking even with that acne on his face, really smart and he'd read practically every book in the world. But where would they go? Maybe a small hotel, one near Columbus Circle. But it turned out that what Delmore had in mind was somewhat different. When they met that evening in May she was freshly showered and smelling sweet with Coty's Chypre, full of anticipation. "Let's take a walk," he'd said. That's fine, she thought, okay for a beginning. She knew he'd have enough money. Just before he'd left for College they'd gone to Brooks Brothers, a high-class expensive men's store, to pick up a new suit he'd ordered for Wisconsin.

It was quite dark as they walked along Riverside Drive. He kept looking for a grassy place under a bush and at last he found one, He pulled her down beside him and began telling her how pretty she was and how he had missed her. Uncomfortable, with stubby weeds poking her backside. She began to wonder how long this would go on and where this was taking them. She found out soon enough. After a few minutes, he started to make little movements, suggesting she might pull her panties down. Comes the dawn!

"Do you think I'm having sex here on Riverside Drive under a bush?", she asked, and without waiting—"I don't want to do it here. It's crazy and besides we could get arrested!"

"Thank you very much" he scowled at her. "What did you expect." Furious, disgusted, he pulled her to her feet. They walked silently back to her stoop and he stalked off. Good-bye, my gallant poet, she should have called after him but she only thought of that later. Confused, disgusted, a little disappointed, straightening her blouse, she watched him walk quickly down the street and out of sight.

She decides to tell Ketzel about it. Ketzel listens carefully and after a minute she says Delmore's a blowhard and a nut. It's really a funny and stupid story and and she begins to laugh. After Miriam considers a moment she agrees. "I guess it is funny," and she ends up laughing too. Ketzel digs out a box of Fanny Farmer chocolates and before they fall asleep they've finished the box.

The next morning, at breakfast, Ketzel realizes that she hasn't told Miriam the whole story about Martin, something she heard from Anna Sokolow. Anna told her she saw Martin last Wednesday morning, coming out of the San Moritz Hotel in a hurry. When she called to him he acted a little funny and pretended he hadn't seen her. "I think he was embarrassed. Just thought I'd tell you though it's none of my business," Anna said.

Ketzel lights a cigarette. "I'm sure he was with a dame. You know, these Latin lovers, they think they can do anything, but women have to be chaste and faithful. I haven't said anything. With his bad temper, he'll make a nasty scene which I don't need right now".

Miriam, buttering a corn muffin, asks, "How will you find out for sure? Hire a detective or follow him yourself?" She thinks, why bother, let him go, 'good riddance to bad rubbish.' She won't miss him, she never liked him.

"I'm not going to, at this point. I meant to tell you before, Jaime, Fanny and I are going to the Soviet Union. A short trip, two weeks. Jaime wants to give her a birthday present, since she's feeling a little better now, it's a good time." Then, seeing Miriam frown, says quickly "I wish we could take you. Maybe if we go again."

Miriam is thoughtful. She wouldn't really want to go to Russia now. Since Arne told her about the slave camps, what she read about the collectivization, the millions of cows, horses and pigs slaughtered, families destroyed and the awful famine, she's not sure that she wants to. Stalin's picture is being plastered over every bare space in Russia, he's being idolized, 'our great leader' and she can't stand hero worship of <u>any</u> kind, Washington and Lincoln included.

❧   ❧   ❧

Ketzel was right about Sydney after all, Miriam discovers. She runs into him one Saturday morning the following November at an unemployed demonstration in Union Square. They're both peddling their respective newspapers and she was surprised when she saw he was selling *The Militant,* not *The Socialist Call.*

"So you are a Trotskyite. Ketzel was right after all." she tells him, prepared to walk away. Fraternization with the enemy was frowned upon and she doesn't want to be called down for it by comrades in her branch. But Miriam had often thought of Sydney since that first meeting; she was lonely, he was so easy to talk to and she didn't know anyone else who loved movies as much as she did.

"You don't have to walk away, do you?" Sydney calls after her. "Didn't you talk to me and my friends at the Concert last summer?"

"Yes", she answers. She stops and turns around. "I really shouldn't have. By the way, are your two friends Trotskyites too?"

"No, they belong to the Muste group, the American Workers Party—at least Sylvia does. It's another organization but there's talk about us joining together." Sydney smiles at her, sees he has only two papers left. "Listen, I'm about finished here. How about you? Let's go for coffee. I won't put poison in it and I know a place where your Harlem friends won't see you."

They walk to a diner and talk all afternoon This time they talk about books first and they find they both like Conrad, Hardy and Dostoevsky, except for

'The Idiot'. Sydney doesn't care for D. H. Lawrence, "too mystical for me," and likes Fitzgerald much more because "he knows how to describe the rich."

"Yes, but I still think you can't rule out D. H. Lawrence. How about 'Sons and Lovers'. Didn't he give you a clear picture of miners' lives?" she asked? "How about when he described a daisy amd compared it to the 'golden mob of the proletariat surrounded by the showy, white fence of the idle rich' … I liked that, he's very poetic."

They talk about German and Russian movies; the homosexual themes in 'Maedchen in Uniform" don't interest him but they both liked 'M', Eisenstein's 'Ten Days that Shook the World' and 'Potemkin'.

They're miles ahead of American film makers." Miriam says. "Remember the scene in 'Komradshaft' when the German miners tear down the barriers so they could rescue the French ones?"

When they part, Sydney holds her hand a moment. "Would you like to see 'Awake and Sing'? They're doing it up in Harlem in the Rockland Palace. They changed it, made white Jewish cab drivers into negroes. Kind of funny, isn't it. I can get cheap tickets, my treat."

"You don't understand," Miriam answers. "I can't go with you. Today, it was sort of accidental but …"

Sydney doesn't reply for a moment. When he speaks Miriam can see he's choosing his words carefully.

"Look, we seem to have enough to talk about without getting into politics. Right? That's number one. Second, think about this. If the organization you belong to is that rigid, so afraid of its members speaking to the enemy, to any-one who doesn't agree with them, then something's rotten in Denmark." His voice rises, heated, rough, his lips in a tight, thin line.

Miriam steps back, startled at his sudden flash of anger. "You don't have to get sore. Let it go." She's turned off and wants to get away, but when she sees the number Five bus approaching she says, "I'll think about what you said. Okay?"

She likes Sydney, eyeglasses, serious, skinny. Since Knute had left there'd been a dearth of people she could talk to, but she could also hear Fanny saying, "You're not a real communist. You don't have the strength of your convictions."

Miriam has begun to be careful about discussing the Communist Party in the Ketzel household. Whenever she brings up questions that puzzle her they're brushed aside and she's told to bring the matter up at a branch meet-ing. But there was never time there, the agenda was always full of day to day activity that had to be taken care of. Fighting for food and shelter for the unemployed, fighting to free the Scottsboro Boys were important tasks of Party comrades in Harlem and they were doing a great job, but it was confusing to some, at least to her, when they were criticized by the C P. Comrades, they said, were forgetting that the purpose of working with other organizations, like the N A A C P was "to destroy the influence of the reformist leaders, not to make peace with them." Very soon after she joined, she began to see that policy and directives came from Moscow. The rank and file had little to say, administrators and officials were moved or removed at the orders of Party officials and as negroes were mostly inexperienced, important administrative positions had to be awarded to white Party members. As a result there was often resentment, anger and chaos. Charges of white chauvinism were made at almost every unit meeting and there were more than a few expulsions. Sometimes, after a bitter Party meeting, Miriam would find herself questioning, *"Is this the way I imagined it would be?"*

❦   ❦   ❦

"Meet me for lunch," Ketzel orders her on the telephone. "Just got your phone number from your mother. I'm gonna be down on 14th Street. We're rehearsing at Sophia Delza's studio right across from your office building, at 40 fifth Avenue. Got lots to tell you."

Miriam had lots to tell her too. Her new job, three days a week at the National Social Credit organization is a tremendous improvement on being Dr. Raab's receptionist. She's paid twelve dollars a week and her hours are not very strict. She can come in anytime between nine and nine-thirty and leave about five. Mr. Nyland, slim, sharp-faced, with European manners and a soft Swedish accent, is great to work for although he likes to kiss her on her lips every now and then. She supposes it's a fatherly gesture. No matter, he's always kind and when she can't find a missing file, he doesn't scold. Writers and prominent people belong to the Social Credit organization, like Gorham Munson the writer, and Charlie Chaplin. It has been already put into practice in Ottowa, Canada and the theory behind it was that government could issue money based on national wealth. Supposedly this could solve many of the evils of capitalism, like unemployment and poverty, according to Social Credit theorists. She can't quite figure it out, it seems impractical and a lot of nonsense, but okay with her, she has a job.

"Let's meet close by," Miriam suggests. "It's so darn cold today."

"No, let's go to Luchows, my treat. I know it's a few blocks further but they have a good lunch and we can take our time."

On 14th Street the store owners have been making gallant attempts to usher in the Christmas holidays, hanging faded wreaths from lamp posts and lighting their show-windows more brightly. Five-cent apple vendors, clean-shaven unemployed young men, are on their usual corners, stamping their feet, blowing on their hands, "Pullers" stand at the doorways of their stores encouraging customers to buy long johns and watches, legless beggars on dollies push themselves along the sidewalk, and pretty models in fur coats, high up in a second floor window, go twirling about. Tempting odors of roasted chestnuts and sweet potatoes perfume the air, people, wishing they had money to spend, jostle each other in the crowded street and Miriam, passing Hearns, decides to treat herself to a pretty blouse. After all, now she can afford to pay as much as three dollars for a new one.

Ketzel has lots of news for her when she arrives at Luchow's. They weren't leaving right away for the U.S.S.R. Jaime is working on an article on Mexico for the Saturday Evening Post and also finishing up the last chapter on his book on the Klondike, called "Silver Folly." Besides he has his regular column on the New Masses. Fanny, feeling a little stronger these days, is helping him with typing and even doing some research.

"They don't have time to miss me" Ketzel gulps her beer thirstily. "But that's good. I'm glad. I've been running around with Anna's group. and we're busy as bunnies. We don't get support from the Theatre Union and we've got to take bookings from unions and labor organizations, wherever we can get 'em. You should see the small, rickety, run-down halls we have to dance in." She laughs. "The other day we accidentally knocked the piano off one of their tiny stages—we must have ruined it, what a racket when it crashed!"

Ketzel stops talking just long enough to order sauerbraten for both of them and more beer.

"It's tough for lots of the girls. They've got to work to eat. They practice at night after working all day. Sometimes they're so doggone tired, it's pathetic."

"How are you getting along with Anna?" Miriam encourages Ketzel to talk about her work. Although she wouldn't ever admit to the fact, she's just a little jealous. Ketzel's found her vocation, she's happy and she's really talented. That's more than she can say!

"Anna's beginning to be successful, she's getting good notices, and recognition. Even though she's quick-tempered, hollers a lot, drives her dancers, they love her," Ketzel says.

She grins, "Listen to this. When Anna was still with the Graham group, a rich lady (you know the type, one of those society big-wigs, patron of the arts) asks her. 'What did you do before you took up dancing? Anna grabs a peek at her, puts on an ashamed look. "I was a prostitute,' she tells her. Madam money-bags, stunned, goes to Martha. "Isn't it terrible about that poor young girl having to be a street-walker. Martha just smiles and says, 'Anna has a lively imagination' and cuts the conversation. But she was steamed!—She takes Anna aside and tells her "Keep away from rich patrons from now on!" But Anna couldn't help it, she really can't stand those patronizing rich bitches."

After she takes a hearty swig of beer she peers across the table. "Hey, you don't look so good. You're getting real skinny."

"I don't know why," Miriam answers. "I eat enough." She'd like to tell Ketzel that she's seeing Sydney but she doesn't want to get into a discussion about Trotsky. Not that Ketzel would want to listen, Miriam knows. She'd simply say, "Stay away from him." Ketzel reads very little and although she's a Party member, she's never been interested in politics. Ketzel's a hedonist, she decides, loves all the the good things in life, but no matter, she's honest, warm, fun to be with and Miriam loves her.

"Why don't you introduce me to a nice guy" Miriam suggests as they say good-by. "I need a new boy-friend". Silently she adds, guess he'll have to be a C P. member. She doesn't tell Ketzel she intends to call Sydney this week-end and see 'City Lights' the Chaplin movie, with him.

      ❦   ❦   ❦

February days are cold, gray and dismal and Miriam notes that she misses the free afternoons she had, working for Dr. Raab. Not only the comrades at the Kultur Sovzek but hanging out at the Zoo cafeteria, watching the seals leaping for fish and drinking hot chocolate. Recently, she's cut her activity somewhat in the Y C L giving excuses like having to work late or home responsiblities and she feels as if she's in some kind of limbo. Sydney's kept his word and doesn't discuss politics but he's very active in a hotel restaurant strike. She's lonely, Sydney's not around and Ketzel and her parents are busy, getting ready for their trip to Russia. and when Jimmy Carter, the organizer of her unit calls on at her office to tell her about an important meeting that night it doesn't improve her mood very much.

"Did you see the article on Austria in the yesterday's Times?" he asks.

"You mean about the attack on the Karl Marx Hof, the commune the Social Democratics have in Vienna. Yes, I read about it—it was awful," she tells him.

It had been in all the papers. Dollfuss, the Austrian Chancellor had made an unexpected attack on the workers' homes using a pretext that they had to search for weapons. The workers had struck back with heavy fighting. 140 had been killed but there had been losses also on the government side. Heavy reprisals were expected. Shock and surprise was felt throughout the world. It was the first attempt of the working class to strike back at the sweeping fascist onslaught.

"Do I have to go tonight, Jimmy? I really don't feel well," Miriam answers, she's having trouble swallowing and her head feels warm.

"Sorry you can't come but make sure you're there tomorrow," he says "The S.P. and some of the A F of L trade unions holding a big meeting to honor the Socialists who got killed. That is, they think they gonna, those fascist sympathizers. We're gonna bust it up. We're making plans tonight. About 5,000 of us are rallying up in the Bronx tomorrow afternoon and marching down to Madison Square Garden. We'll have the Red Front Band, plenty of banners and Irving Potash, the head of the Trade Union Unity League is gonna lead. Like he says, they *think* they're gonna have a meeting."

The next morning Miriam, her throat still hurting, tells Clara she won't be home until late. She hates going to this rally, expects and fears the angry crowds, catcalls and scuffling. All this sickens her but she knows she has to go. Clara, at the kitchen table, finishing her cold coffee, nods resignedly,

"You're sick but you run, run, run,"

Because she'd like to meet some of the comrades from her branch she asks to get off work early and takes the Ninth Avenue El to 50th Street. Crowds milling about, signs and placards abound, faces cold and grim. Many of them are holding the special edition of The Daily Worker put out that day, denoucing Matthew Woll, head of the A F of L, and Mayor LaGuardia, who are scheduled to appear that evening—These are "agents of fascism," the paper accuses—"they must not be allowed to speak."

Faces are intense, like bloodhounds, sniffing the air for prey and Miriam's heart beginning to pound. *Stop being a ninny*, she tells herself. Her throat feels as if it's closing, she fumbles in her purse for some Ludens Cough Drops, her head is warm and throbs. All at once she hears her name and sees a member of her Harlem branch approaching, it's a stocky young man, with warm brown eyes, and a pronounced lisp that somehow makes the most serious remark seems comic.

"Harry—Harry Milton" brushing through the crowd, sounding more cordial that she means to be but she's really glad to see him.

"Yeah, that's me, Miriam. Hey, not a good idea for you to come tonight. There's gonna be trouble, people might get hurt," he tells her and takes her arm protectively. He has a debonair, gallant manner making Miriam smile and say, "I know you'll protect me, Sir Galahad."

She's happy to hold onto him and begins to feel better already, as they push their way to an entrance but the doors have been blocked by the Socialists who are making C P members divest themselves of banners and signs before they enter. Members of the brass band who have to leave their musical instruments outside in the hall are screaming. Abuse and threats inside and outside the arena are now scalding the air making it almost impossible to hear anything except the calling and yelling of slogans "We demand a united front from below" "Social Democrats are no better than fascists."

Finally they get in. The air in the great auditorium is heavy, dense, opaque, warm with angry energy. "Harry, what's going on?" Miriam asks him as they make their seats in the upper balcony. "Why are we doing this. It's wrong. I'm not a great theoretician but I think the Party's wrong. Everybody knows the Austrian workers aren't revolutionists but they were good people, anti-fascists and brave fighters and they fought to defend themselves. We have no right to break up this meeting! It's terrible."

Harry's answering but Miriam can't hear what's he says. A battle is beginning on the platform. Clarence Hathaway, a senior C. P. official is trying to take the podium from Algernon Lee and socialists are preventing him physically from doing so. C P cadres have been posted in different corners of the tremendous hall to chant and scream slogans during the lull between speakers. The C P, as they have threatened, will not allow Woll or LaGuardia to talk. When there's a lull, Harry tells Miriam, "It'th hard to believe thith but I read that in some part of Prussia, I forget which, the C Peven voted with the Fascists so they could defeat the Social Democratic candidate."

Disorder and chaos rule the hall, the noise is unbearable, the meeting is a shambles. Miriam has had enough. "I'm leaving" she shouts to Harry and she starts to go, Harry follows. At the door a big crowd attempts to hold people back but Miriam has decided she's getting out. No one listens to her "excuse me" and when she pushes she finds she's being pushed back with screams and curses. When she finally gets to a space in the hall and begins to straighten her hat and coat, she wonders why the floor feels cold.

"Oh, God, now what," she asks herself, looking down. Almost crying, looking like a bird standing on one foot, she screams, "Harry—my shoe."

He's still making his way through but he stops, nods, yells, "Okay, wait" and dives back into the huge crowd. She can't believe it, he's back in a minute, triumphantly waving her left black pump high above the crowd.

As they stand in the hall, Harry says, "Let's wait—I think they're finishing—I hear some music." The meeting has ended, has had to end, the entire audience is singing the Internationale but the music seems to be coming from two different groups and some words are different. The Socialists are chanting their version—'the Socialist Party"—and the Communists, at the top of their voices are proclaiming that 'the International Soviet' will be the human race. "Aren't we all the human race?" Harry's chuckling and shaking his head, "at least we're supposed to be."

He insists on taking her home. "There'th gonna to be a lot of flack about this," he sighs as they walk to the subway. "The capitalist press'll ridicule all the radical, left-wing parties in the country. You know what they'll thay and it's true, the communists and socialists are busy fighting each other and we're the crathies."

On her stoop, Harry takes her hand. "I'm fed up with the Party." He fishes out a gray piece of cotton, gives three strong blasts into it and jams it into his rusty pants "I've had it. I'm gonna head for the west coast, maybe thip out from San Francisco" and leans over to kiss her warm forehead. "So long, honey. You're a sweet kid. Too bad Knute had you first."

On Friday, Clara busies herself all day, shopping, washing, putting newspapers down on the clean kitchen floor and preparing Shabbos supper, the special meal of the week. Mirim, reclining in the old beat-up Morris chair in a corner watches her mother. She's been home for the past two days, sleeping almost all the time, cuddled a flannel nightgown, taking aspirin, drinking hot tea and listening to Amos and Andy on the radio.

She likes to see Clara perform the usual ceremony at the end of the week. The room is dim now and a sabbath hush pervades the air. Her mother's face, the grim tightness gone, is now soft and gentle. She stands before the three white tapers and after they are lit, sways her body gently to and fro. Then she raises her hands, weaves them three times above her head and brings them down, cupping her eyes, moving her lips in silent prayer. After a few moments, she'll give a little sigh, straighten her shoulders and turn away to serve the evening meal.

There is gefulte fish, chicken and boiled beef and everything tastes good to Miriam who's recovered her appetite. Afterwards they talk a little, mostly about the tenants; a Hungarian student interning at Bellevue Hospital and Sam Pitt, his job on the George Washington Bridge finished, going back home, down south.

The conversation dies. It becomes quiet again in the shabby kitchen, shadows hover and the sorrowful past begins to creep in from the dark corners. In the cut-glass bowl on the scarred sideboard, white sheets catch the flickering light of candles; letters from her sister, her last words. Her voice echoes in darkening room.

Her mother says, softly, almost to herself, "It's nice you're home tonight."

Miriam doesn't answer. In a little while, as if she can't help herself, Clara goes on, "To stay home a few days you had to be sick."

Oh, mama, mama, don't! Miriam shrivels, wants to cry. She swallows, her throat tight. *Let it go*, she tells herself. *It'll pass, it always does. Wait. Give her time.* Searching for something, she recalls a melody that years ago her young mother used to sing.

"Remember that song, Mama. 'Lehrenze kinderlah, Lehrenz tierly, In der shteib ist heis'—it was about little children in a warm room?" Clara is still but in a little while she sighs, nods, and begins to hum.

Quiet again, the only sound a faint clang of the trolley on Lenox Avenue.

In a little while Miram gets up, bends over to kiss her mother good-night and Clara raises her hand to touch Miriam's cheek before she turns away and closes her eyes.

A few days later, Miriam makes her way up the Ortega stoop, invited for lunch, Ketzel, finally, has found a free Saturday. Two men, one slim, with delicate features, the other round-faced, with full lips, brush by her on their way down, unnoticing, their voices loud, waving their hands.

"What's this all about?" she asks Ketzel standing at the open door.

"James Rorty and John Dos Passos, they're the last ones." Ketzel answers. "We had a big crowd here this morning, Edmund Wilson, Lionel Trilling and a bunch of others."

She shuts the door, whispering "Be careful what you say to Fanny today. She's really upset. They're writers from 'The New Masses.' They had a hot meeting about that riot in Madison Square Garden and they're sending a letter to the Party, criticizing its actions. Some of them are going to resign."

"I'd like to meet John Dos Passos. He worked a lot on the Sacco-Vanzetti case, he's a good writer." Miriam takes off her coat, lowers her voice. "They're absolutely right. What happened was terrible! The Party was wrong. We should apologize or at least try to explain why we acted that way."

"Fat chance" answers Ketzel, thrusting The Daily Worker at her. "The Party blames the Socialists. Here, read it. It says 'the Socialist Party leaders sinned in following a purely defensive policy instead of going over to the offensive.'"

"But Algernon Lee said—the communists behaved like pigs and we …"

"No, I don't know where you got that and, honestly, Miriam, I don't give a damn about the whole thing." Ketzel throws herself down in her favorite chair by the window. "I've got my own problems. The Party will have to solve its own."

Miriam sighs, realizing that she'll be fighting a hopeless cause if she continues to talk about it, especially how she's been feeling lately, and she'd better get clear in her own mind about lot of things in the Party before she starts shooting off her mouth. She decides to let it drop. Plumping herself down on Ketzel's bed, she says, making an effort to seem interested.

"Guess you're right. What's happening? I'm all ears."

"It's Martin. Now I know for sure. Can you believe it? Do you know what that bastard's been doing lately? Fooling around with a blond bitch, her name is, get this, Cordelia! She's from the mid-west and her parents are loaded. They're coming east. Meanwhile she's staying at the San Moritz on Central Park South."

Ketzel's hands begin to tremble, her eyes tearing. Miriam hands her a hanky from a lacquered box nearby. She has a strong suspicion that Martin loves himself more than anything in the world and uses Jaime's connections to get a publisher for his poetry.

"Does he know that you know about her?

"Oh, yeah. I asked him. He says they're just friends, she's trying to be a writer. She was an English major in College and now she's taking some courses at N Y U. She's just wants him look over her stuff." Ketzel blots her eyes carefully so as not to smear the mascara. "I think I know what stuff she means and I bet she's a terrible writer besides."

"You know, Ketzel, it might be true, they might only be friends." Miriam tries to sound reasonable but she's bored with the whole thing. She's sure Martin's a liar and a cheat.

"Do you really think I can trust him? Am I too jealous?"

"Give him a chance. See what happens." Enough already, she thinks, let's get this over with, and examines the bureau for a cigarette lighter.

Ketzel sighs. "I guess you're right. I'll have to see. Damn! He's so good-looking but I guess I oughta find a guy with a stronger character."

Going to her triple-mirrored vanity she locates a medium red lipstick, peers into the bevelled mirror and beings to carefully outline her lips.

"Meanwhile, I'll just have to believe he's still my sweet, faithful lover not …" looking at Miriam and grinning "not—a dirty, rotten liar."

After she's finished making up and apparently satisfied with her reflection, she reaches for Miriam's hand. "Basta! Enuff! Let's make a movie. Garbo's at the Regent. Queen Christina—John Gilbert."

As they run down the stairs Ketzel sings, "Moanin' low, my sweet man, I love him so …"

❧   ❧   ❧

Miriam is so involved with activities that she's too busy to miss Ketzel, Fanny and Jaime who, on the spur of the moment, have left for their long anticipated trip to the Soviet Union. They want to be there for the May Day celebration. In Harlem there's a lot going on in the Party units and at a meeting Miriam hears a report on the April, 1934 Eighth National Convention. The struggle against black nationalism is a major priority, the members are told. New decisions are handed down. They don't affect Miriam very much except that there seems to be twice as many assignments in selling the Daily Worker and holding open-air meetings. She's conscientious but makes sure that she goes to the movies and occasionally makes a concert.

This night she's alone at Lewisohn Stadium. She was supposed to meet up with Sylvia Ageloff, the woman Sydney had introduced her to at the Iturbi concert, and Sylvia's sister, but at the last minute they weren't able to make it. But she can't miss Ravel's Bolero which she loves so she goes by herself. While she waits, she opens an envelope, a letter from Ketzel, just received.

Dear Miriam,

I've got so much to tell you but since we're here only for a couple of weeks, I'll spill it all in this letter so I won't have to write again.

First of all, we're staying in a beautiful hotel, right in Red Square, the National. It's beautiful, old-fashioned, red carpets, a marble bath and white bear rugs! What luxury in a communist country! We're very comfortable and will stay here for the rest of the trip.

We're running into a lot of friends. William Patterson from the I.L.D. is here for treatment, he has T B. We met Paul Robeson in the lobby with his wife Essie. He's simply gorgeous, Essie is half his size, attractive, very smart. She's seems to be turned off by what she says is "vicious shoving and the sickening smell of cabbage everywhere".

There's so much going on. They're always having celebrations and we get to many of them because Daddy knows Eisenstein. They met when he was making "Que Viva Mexico." Remember when we saw it? We just went to this great party. Eisenstein did a dance he learned at the Savoy and Litvinov did an Irish jig. Loads of great food!!

Talk about spirit. Moscow has these huge signs "We are building Socialism for the entire world" and everyone, even the little kids collect scrap metal, sing revolutionary songs. The new subway stations! Unbelievable! Gorgeous! Made of marble, in different colors, named for heroes and famous people. There's wonderful care for children, lots of nurseries and day-care centers, not like in our good old U S A. Every factory has a restaurant and the workers get cards for their meals which cost practically nothing.. No wonder a lot of Americans decide to stay here.

The May Day celebration was unbelievable, banners, flowers, people from all over the world, England, France, Spain—loudspeakers blaring—Red Square decorated with flag, banners—special seats for workers and engineers who built the new subway. On a great white horse into the square comes this tall man, in white military costume leading the way and on top of the Mausoleum presiding over all, like a god, there's Stalin with a bunch of officials. I thought my ears would split with the the shout went up, waves of roars. HAIL THE SOVIET UNION—HAIL THE RED ARMY—little kids singing the Internationale—and marching, marching, thousands of workers!

I made inquiries about our friends. It's better to write this than tell you in person. Arthur is dead and I understand, though I've not been told directly, that Alana is in Siberia. More when we get home which should be soon unless Fanny and Jaime decide to stay longer. It's okay with me because Anna Sokolow's here. She came to be with her boy-friend, Alex North. Here's hoping she asks me to join her in giving some lecture-demonstrations. By the way, I look good, at least that what everyone tells me. Been doing a lot of swimming in one of those indoor pools along the Moscow River—sun-bathing too—imagine sun-bathing in Russia.

Miss you——wish you were here. Maybe not. You're nosey and people don't ask questions here. By the way, would you call Martin? Give him my regards, tell him I'm having a wonderful time.

See you soon.

A Russian bear hug and lots of kisses, Ketzel.

When she finishes, she folds the three sheets and puts them away in her purse, not aware of what she's doing. The conductor is bowing, the audience applauding, the oboes making delicate spirals that wind in the air. But all she can see is Ketzel, surrounded by flowers and banners, and over it, like a double-exposed photograph, the sorrowful, haunted faces of Alana and Arthur.

The sick realization of Ketzel's news—her friends—gone, gone for good. She'll never hear from them, see them again. As she sits there, the lovely music sounds hollow, meaningless. At intermission, she goes home.

France, Summer 1933

Trotsky has had painful lumbago but continues to work, outling his ideas for a Fourth International, realizing how difficult the task before him is going to be. He doesn't think much of French intellectuals and writes to Victor Serge "I have been even in their homes and have felt the smell of their petty bourgeois life … We must look for new roads to the workers." He proposes that Trotskyists, wherever it is feasible, enter a mass party to recruit from their membership; the manoever is named "The French Turn".

As soon as they arrive at a village inn at St. Palais, after being besieged by reporters, there's a fire. Supposedly it is because of drynesss, due to hot weather. It appears to be accidental but, because of crowds, he's forced to hide in Molinier's car, pretending to be an American tourist!

Meanwhile, the new task, building a new international, looms before him. Will he live long enough, be well enough? He is strong physically, although since childhood he has had "chronic catarrh of the digestive tract" according to doctors. But he was healthy, vigorous, dynamic, going without sleep, adequate food during the revolutionary times, the excitement, the vast amount of work, the Civil War, the Red Army. It is only later when demands lessened, the party weakened and confused by the machinations of the triumvirate, that his health deteriorated. "At time of stress and indecision," Natalaya said, "his body breaks—lumbago, gout and the never-ending sieges of insomnia."

In Barbizon, near Fountainbleau, where the family next move, they are able to make short trips to Paris which has been declared out-of-bounds to them. He and Natalya enjoy a happy evening when Lyova and Jeanne come for dinner with a bottle of French wine in their small cottage. But it is one of his most sorrowful times, when he comes upon Van burning rubbish in the garden. Trotsky hands him the portrait of Christian Rakovsky, his oldest and dearest friend, a handsome man, with generous features, a doctor, revolutionist and up until now, his most ardent supporter and hands it to Van. "You can burn this too," he says. "Now, nobody remains."

CHAPTER 5

Summer, 1934

Miriam gets a call from Sydney in August and although she'd like to see him, she makes other dates and tries to keep busy on week-ends, going to Jones Beach, or getting a ride up to Camp Nitgedaiget in Beacon, where they'd swim in the Hudson, have Friday night campfires, sing revolutionary songs, attend Saturday night concerts, and ball games on Sunday. They'd eat communally at long tables, share the work in a huge kitchen and, even if you had money, you couldn't spend much, everything was so cheap. But one Sunday, during the fall, she goes to the phone in the candy store and dials his number. Sydney's voice comes over surprised, warm and happy.

"A movie? Okay for tomorrow night. Can't make it tonight. I've got a meeting. I'd invite you to come but I know you wouldn't."

"What makes you so sure?"

"Com'on. Miriam. It's at the Trotskyite headquarters, a place you wouldn't be caught dead in, although you might learn something."

"I'm always ready to be educated." Miriam's annoyed, peevish. She must be nuts, she thinks. "Where'll I meet you?

At eight o'clock, she waits for Sydney in front of the headquarters on 10th street. "Why am I doing this?," but she knows why.

Too many questions about the Communist Party are bothering her and there's no one she can talk to. Maybe she should stop reading critical reports and just accept accounts of the wonderful progress the country is making and the happy life of the Russian worker. She gets reports in Party meetings, reads about it in the Daily Worker, hears from visitors returning with glowing acounts of the great Dnieprostroy dam, etc. What do Trotskyites have to tell her? Will she get honest answers from them? About the Shakhti sabotage trial, for instance? Except that they weren't given a trial, those men were just convicted and executed. How about Professor Karatygin who, with forty-seven others, supposedly destroyed the meat supply. If everything is so sweet and light and hunky-dory in the Soviet Union why are so many people arrested and shot without trials? Why are these men saboteurs in the first place? Why do they want to destroy their wonderful country? Is it just because they're not allowed to voice their opinions, or their disagreements? Are they angry, disgrunted because they've lost power, the Mensheviks, Socialists, Oppositionists? Are they jealous of Stalin and hungry for power themselves?

Located on eleventh street, on the second floor of an old, dingy building with warped floors is the headquarters of the Communist League of America. Folding chairs for about twenty people are set up in rows with a table in front for the speaker; in a corner there's a mimeograph machine and a telephone, which most of the time is not in service, Sydney tells her.

A pleasant-faced man, with slouching shoulders, blue-eyed, florid complexion, wearing a thin cotton flannel shirt calls the meeting to order. He looks Irish like some of the men in Hell's Kitchen where she'd lived long ago and she notices he's missing a few fingers from one hand. He's James Cannon, one of the three leaders of the group, Max Shachtman and Martin Abern the other two. The speaker tonight, Cannon says, will be Max, talking about the Chinese Revolution. A dark-haired, stocky man then comes to the front of the room. He has high cheek bones, slit eyes and a sardonic smile. From the moment he begins Miriam is spellbound.

Although his voice is shrill, especially when he raises it, he's a magnificent speaker, dramatic, interspersing his address with cutting witty, or sarcastic remarks. He starts by describing the background for the Chinese revolution which occurred between 1925 and 1927. Although Trotsky, Zinoview and Radek resisted, Stalin ordered the Chinese communists to enter the Kuomintang of General Chiang Kai-shek and disarm themselves. At a large meeting the night before in the Bolshoi Theatre, Stalin defended his policy: 'We are told that Chiang Kaishek is making ready to turn against us again. I know that he is playing a cunning game with us, but it is *he* that will be crushed. We shall squeeze him like a lemon and then be rid of him'. But the very next day, Chiang's troops enter Shanghai and massacre the defenceless workers!

Miriam's been listening intently when suddenly all the lights go out and the room is plunged into thick darkness. She gasps and clutches Sidney arm but when everyone laughs she's relieved and blushes.

Sydney laughs. "Happens all the time. We didn't get up the dough for the electric bill this month. Trotskyists don't get 'Moscow gold.'"

At this point, Miriam thinks the meeting's over but everyone remains sitting in the dark, the audience, fired up by Shachtman's eloquence won't move. They clap, call for him to go on and after five minutes, someone finds a candle and gives it to Max. It's long and white and he holds it like a lantern, holding it high, waving it to underlining important points in his address. The scene becomes living theatre; in the gloomy room, his eyes and teeth gleam in the dancing, yellow flame and the audience, caught up in the spectacle, relishes his theatrical performance, applauding his jokes and witticism every other moment. When it ends, a great meeting, the comrades are still excited, milling about, laughing about Max's great performance. Sydney wants to introduce her to some of his friends but Miriam spies Sylvia and darts over to her.

"I didn't know you attend Trotsky meetings," she says.

"We're going to merge," Sylvia tells her. "Right now I'm a member of the American Workers Party, 'Musteites' but we're be together soon." She smiles, "What's with you? Are you still in the C P?"

Miriam doesn't answer, she's not sure just where she is right now. She changes the subject and makes a date with her to go to the Davenport. a free theater that charges no admission and has fine performances.

"I'm sorry the meeting ended so soon," she tell Sydney afterwards, as they walk towards Fifth Avenue. The street's almost deserted, littered with fruit skin. As they cut through Union Square Park, the homeless are making themselves comfortable for the night, staking out their bedrooms on splintered benches, rolling up newspapers for pillows. "I'd like to ask you a question." She's holding his arm and they walk slowly, enjoying the mild October evening. "In The Militant it said that in the election in Germany, the Socialists got seven million votes, the Communists about five million, twelve million votes altogether but still Hitler won. It's hard to believe …"

"Yeah" Sydney says. "It's hard to believe but the Socialists were weak, confused, stupid even. The Communist Party called them Social-Fascists, said they were worse than the Nazis, just like they do here and they bragged 'in a couple of years it will be our turn'. Result! Hitler walks into power, not even a pane of glass broken. In 1933 he's Chancellor." Sydney throws away the stub of his cigarette in disgust. "If you think about it, it's frightening. Trotsky wrote about it in 1930; he predicted exactly what was going to happen." Whenever Sydney talked about politics his voice becomes rough, almost angry, and even though the air is pleasantly cool, Miriam shivers.

"I'll ride up with you" he says. "Take you to your door".

"You'll get home at two o'clock" Miriam protests but he insists.

As they climb the steps to the top of the double-decker bus, Sydney beings to tell her about the strike in Minneapolis last July led by the C. L. A.

"It wasn't easy for our members to get into the A F of L. We'd been already thrown out of it and the C P as well. But we got back into through the Teamsters Union in Minneapolis, a guy, Bill Brown the head of Local 574, a real militant, wanted people like us, who know how to organize the workers and give the bosses a real fight. We set up a food commissary, organized a women's auxiliary, published a newspaper 'The Daily Organizer' that told the truth about what was really happening … Max, Jim, Goldman from New York, the Dunne brothers and Farrell Dobbs. The strike began last July, lasted five weeks … a smashing victory … Trotskyism in action … one of the greatest, heroic and best organized struggles in the history of the labor movement …"

It's interesting and she listens carefully but as she looks out on the river, its dark waters touched with rippling lights, a soft wind ruffling her hair, she can't help thinking it might be different if it were Knute next to her. He wouldn't be talking politics, he'd find a little time to be romantic. When they say goodnight, Sydney pulls her to him for a kiss. He's clumsy, a novice, she thinks, but he *is* nice. "Goodnight, Sydney, thanks," she says. "I've learned a lot tonight."

The Ortega family is home at last! It's easy to spot Ketzel, waving, radiant, a tawny fur toque on her loose hair, a matching cape swinging from her shoulders and behind her, Fanny, walking slowly, leaning on Jaime's arm. All of them see her at the same time and call, their voices high and happy. Miriam's been waiting for them while the Ille de France is docking. It's taking a long time but the atmosphere is festive, crowds chattering, arms filled with red and yellow roses, flags flapping in the breeze, the acrid smell of damp pilings mingled with smoke.

"Miriam, it was wonderful" Ketzel hugs her. "The whole trip—unbelievable. What a country, what an experience! And being with Anna and Alex. It looks like we'll be working together here in New York!"

Fanny, a small smile, tired, thinner, says "So happy to see you, darling. We'll go ahead. Be sure to come home with Ketzel," and leaves with Jaime in a taxi.

"Martin couldn't make it," Miriam tells Ketzel. "He called me to tell you he'll call you tonight." Ketzel doesn't answer. She seems to be watching people filtering down the gangplank but when she turns, her lips are trembling." Okay, that's fine—about Martin, I mean. Forget it."

After they find a cab and have all the luggage stowed in the trunk Ketzel leans back, takes a deep sigh. "Tell me what you've been doing. Besides the Y C L and working. How about guys?"

"Not much, actually nothing. Movies, Rogers and Astaire. I saw 'Battleship Potemkin' again." She doesn't mention Sydney. Ketzel is as fond of him as she is of Martin, which is very little.

"Oh, I've got to tell you about Eisenstein. Everyone used to think he was just great." Ketzel opens her purse, looks for a cigarette, takes one from Miriam. "But he's in trouble now. He was working on John Reed's 'Ten Days' but they didn't want Trotsky in it so it probably won't be released. They really dig film over there. They're always quoting Lenin … 'of all the arts, the cinema is the most important for us.'" She stops to light her cigarette, grins.

"Listen to this. I got to visit a studio where Romm was directing 'Lenin in October'. They were doing the scene when they capture the Winter Palace. The night of the revolution, the workers are wild, charging through the halls, tearing up the grand staircase. Then one of the actors, I think he's supposed to be Antonov-Ovseenko, (he's over in Spain right now) yells 'Stop! Be careful, these are works of art.' It was so funny!

"Maybe you can use it in one of your dance numbers," Miriam suggests. "I haven't done much, went to the Davenport theatre a few times." She doesn't say she went with Sylvia. "'Tartuffe' was great!" She pauses. She'd better not mention going to the Trotsky meeting, although she hasn't stopped thinking about Shachtman's talk.

"One weekend there was an unemployed teacher demonstration in Union Square," she goes on. "Hundreds of them, angry! Yelling about jobs!"

Miriam decides to stop talking. Ketzel's looking out of the window, not listening and Miriam not sure if she's crying. All at once, Ketzel says, 'I've got a fantastic idea. Let's go to Katz's. Get some pastrami and potato salad. How about it—hungry?"

Miriam's relieved. "Great!" she says. *We're better off without Martin*, she thinks. *Hopes they've split for good.* "I'm happy you're back."

Since they hadn't seen much of each other, they've made a pact to meet once a month on Saturdays for lunch, preferably at Ketzel's house so Miriam could also visit with Fanny. Ketzel's very busy, involved in production of Anna's latest work; in additon she's performing in "Four Soviet Songs."

"The music's wonderful," Ketzel tells her. "He's a great composer, Eli Siegmeister. Come early, you'll watch us rehearse."

Miriam watches in the rear of the darkened theatre. Anna's really imaginative. A group of dancers on one end of the stage reel about, their limbs loose, their heads, drooping, while at the other end, women, cluster together, jerking, as if being beaten by whips or receiving electric shocks. It's a strange and frightening picture. *What's Anna trying to say?*, she wonders, *it's just a little beyond her.*

When Ketzel appears, tired and hungry, Miriam wants to talk about the dancing but Ketzel says some other time. She wants to talk about herself and Martin. "We're together again," she says sheepishly. Miriam's not overjoyed but Ketzel's happy, so that's that.

"How about going to Chinatown? Martin is meeting me later. Should I ask him to bring a friend so we can make it a foursome?" Ketzel asks.

"I could call Sydney," Miriam says, hesitantly.

"Okay, but no politics" says Ketzel, making a little face.

When the the taxi leaves them in Chinatown they push their way through narrow, winding alleys, colorful kimonas and fans hanging outside of tiny stores, grimy streets bursting with people, and hundreds of small cheap restaurants, vegetable and fish stalls.

"They have the most wonderful kites in this Mott Street store, butterflies and dragons," says Ketzel, "I ordered a beautiful gold bracelet for Fanny and they made it just the way I'd designed it, it's their speciality."

"Look at the little Chinese kids" says Miriam. "So cute, their round, black-button eyes are so serious."

"Some Russian look Chinese, I think they're probably Mongolian." Ketzel says, "I must tell you, Russian people really love their children, they give them so much care …"

Irritation rises in Miriam. "That's stupid! People all over the world love children?" Now she's angry. "And how about kids that end up in Siberia? Do Russians love them? Oh, I guess they can't because they're political enemies."

"Okay!, Miriam Forget it!" Ketzel sighs, stops at a restaurant window. "Look at those glossy roast ducks, on hooks. Doesn't it look like they've been brushed with lacquer? Let's get a move on, the boys may be there already."

Both Martin and Sydney are outside of the Yat Bun Sing restaurant. Everyone's hungry so they order won ton soup, stuffed crabs, chow mein, fish balls and roast pork. Then Martin, a little tipsy with wine, fishes in his pocket and brings out a little box.

"Here you are my dear" he says, putting it in front of Ketzel's plate. "Something I just bought—for us—I could have bought you some bears' testicles but I thought you needed this for my sake."

Ketzel opens the box and reads the little paper on top of the tablets. "This is a love potion that many have taken throughout the years. It will strengthen your passion which may be fading and restore the ardent feeling you once had for your lover." Ketzel laughs and blushes as she reaches over for it, and Sydney looks at Miriam.

"I think I'll have to go over to Man Gar Chung, maybe they have some magic stuff to make women fall for me," he says.

"See if they have anything that can help a person loosen up," Miriam says without thinking. When they get up to leave the restaurant she realized what she said but it's too late. Sydney's face has a tight, closed look and a moment later he says he has to be somewhere and leaves.

Sydney doesn't call Miriam after that dinner but she's too busy to be concerned. She dates a comrade from the Harlem Branch and goes to a few C P parties with him. He's dense as dishwater she tells Ketzel, but he sure does a great Lindy. Sylvia Ageloff invites her to a family dinner in Brooklyn for Christmas dinner, the food's delicious (they have a great cook), but all they talk about is clothes or travel and Miriam finds it boring. There are four sisters, two of them, Sylvia and Hilda, live up on 110th Street and Broadway in a large, once elegant apartment building their father once owned.

Miriam spends a lot of time shopping for a present for Fanny. It has to be a nice one since the gift's both for Christmas and her birthday on the 26th. She finally finds a blue woolen shawl which matches her eyes and doesn't empty her pocketbook. She buys chocolates for Ketzel and a corn-cob pipe, as a joke, for Jaime. She really would like to buy him a Meershaum but by then there's no money left. She realizes that her mother's birthday's on January 5th and all she can do is buy her a card in the five-and-ten, but that will be a first anyway. In Miriam's family, birthdays weren't noticed.

Sydney's voice is almost unfamiliar, it's been so long.

"I've been meaning to call" he says. "Been too busy, lots going on."

Miriam's breathless from dashing up two flights to the phone located in the hall of the third floor. She gasps, "I'm really glad you got around to it. I've been thinking of you too."

They walk through the park, barren trees, bleak in black and white, the sun, sharp and glittering, their branches drooping under the heavy snow. "Ketzel says they're round and heavy like Isadora Duncan's arms", Miriam remarks but Sydney has no interest in modern dance or dancers. Afterwards they go to a little coffee pot on Amsterdam Avenue. Miriam wants to say something about the remark she made some months ago but before she begins, Sydney says,

"There's gonna be hell to pay in Russia now. Do you know about it? Kirov was assassinated."

"I haven't read the papers the last few days," she says. "I haven't been such a good revolutionist lately.

"You're okay with me," he tells her. Coming from Sydney that's high praise. "It just happened, a couple of days ago."

"Ketzel met him, said he's very popular, almost more than Stalin."

"He was, maybe too much for his own good. They're going insane now. Right after Nickolaev did it, he was shot along with 14 other Komsomoltsys who, they claimed, were guilty too—without a trial, of course. Then they killed 116 prisoners in jail! … We haven't seen the half of what's going to happen!"

Sydney pushes away his cup so angrily that some of the coffee spilled into the saucer. "Zinoviev and Kamenev have just been kicked out of the Party. They're gonna be court martialed. They're shipping thousands to Siberia. Of course Stalin's dragging Trotsky into this."

"But Trotsky's not in Russia anymore. How can Stalin hurt him?"

"Miriam!" Sydney shakes his head. "Of course, he can. He already has. He's lost his citizenship, he's exiled, no other country wants him. But even if Stalin can't get Trotsky, look at what he's doing, to his family, his friends."

Miriam stops walking. "Sydney, why don't we go to a movie?" When Sydney, surprised, hesitates, she pleads, "I'd rather not talk anymore, especially politics. I'm upset about a lot of stuff lately. I've got to think, get things straight in my head." Then, realizing she's being abrupt, knowing he's touchy, she kisses him. "Your cheek's cold, Sydney. Please?"

Miriam makes her way slowly to Ketzel's house. She got off the bus a few blocks before ll7th Street so she could walk, sort out her thoughts and go over what she intends to say. Other springs she'd pass by just to look at some of the pretty gardens. Today, she scarcely notices them. She's thinking of how she'll break the news of her decision to leave the Y C L. At first, there'll be kisses and hugs, "where have you been hiding all winter?," and Fanny will reach out with frail hands, look into her eyes and say "We missed you." Jaime will hug her for a brief moment, she'll get a little dizzy, as always, by his warmth and tobacco smell and Ketzel will come dashing out of her room to kiss her and say, "That's enough, Jaime, even for a princess."

How will she tell them that she no longer believes in the Soviet Union, that the working class has lost its power, that Russia is no longer a communist country, but one ruled by fear and terror. That Stalin making himself into, not a new Lenin, but a terrible dictator, forcing terrible collectivations where millions of peasants, cows, horses and pigs die. Does she dare ask such questions? she asks herself. She has seen Fanny angry once, her pale face flushed, her voice shrill.

As she passes the little gardens, odors of pink and white dogwood blossoms in a silky breeze make her think of the phrase "the darling buds of May." But there's another couplet that's more appropriate … a Shakespeare couplet … "For sweetest things turn sourest by their deeds. Lilies that fester smell far worse than weeds." It had been such a miraculous dream—the promise of socialism. Now it was disappearing—turning sour, dying … yes, festering. If she were in Russia now, she thinks I'd probably be in a prison camp in Siberia and when she reaches the front steps, she climbs the steps slowly, feeling like there's an iron bar in her stomach.

The warm welcome she expected greets her and Jaime has made flan he knows she likes. After they finish coffee, while they're still at the table and the conversation takes a lull, Miriam draws a deep breath, and decides this is the time.

"Listen," she says, her voice husky, hesitating a little. "You're my friends, the dearest ones I've ever had so … Please, I hope you can accept what I have to say and still feel the same way about me." She waits a moment. Everyone is quiet, waiting for her to go on. In a rush it comes out.

"I'm resigning from the Y C L."

Jaime and Ketzel, surprised, look at her, then Ketzel looks down at her plate.

Fanny, frowns, "What is the problem?" Then asks, "It's too hard for you, being active in the party, working …"

"No, it isn't that at all. Miriam starts, swallows, tries to keep her voice from shaking. "It's fine and it hasn't been that hard for me. The Party's been going great, the unemployed work, organizing, the Scottsboro Case. No, everything, everybody's good, working hard."

"Then, what is it?" Now, Fanny's voice is sharp.

Miriam glances at the napkin she's been folding, tries to speak in an even, calm voice, although it keep shaking, "I don't believe in the Communist Party any longer ..."

"Just what does that mean? Fanny clutches her napkin tightly her fingers white. "Just what are you trying to say? Do you know what she's talking about?" she asks Ketzel and Jaime.

Jaime shakes his head, reaches for his pack, offers it to Ketzel, and Miriam, impatient, plunges on, forcing herself to look around the table at their faces,

"What the comrades do in America, I think it's great. They're really dedicated people, like Sarah and Sean and the others. The Jimmy-Higgins, fighting for justice, the Scottsboro boys, the unemployed. But what's happening in Russia is wrong and terrible. It isn't a dictatorship of the proletariat any longer—but it *is* a dictatorship". Her voice is steady now. "You saw what they wanted you to see when you went to Russia. You didn't see the slave labor camps. You didn't see our friends, Alana and Arthur because they were dead!" She looked at Fanny, her face beginning to redden, deep anger within her rising. "What happened to them?" She pauses, "Did they ask a few questions? Or doesn't one ask questions in a Communist country?" Miriam's surprised at her sarcastic tone. How dare she speak to Fanny that way.

Jaime looks down, she knows he doesn't want her to go, the sun pouring through the open window catches the blue lights in his hair. Miriam goes on, answering her own question, she can't stop now.

"No, no one dares. Not if they want to end up in prison, exiled or shot!"

"Miriam," Ketzel's voice is pleading. "I wrote you about Alana and Arthur. Why bring it up ... for God's sake what are you trying to do?"

The other two are silent, Ketzel's face is white, she busies herself, reaching across the table for a chocolate wafer. Jaime, rigid, flickes his cigarette into a ashtray.

"We know why she's bringing it up." Fanny's hand trembles, she drops her cup, it clatters onto the saucer, breaking the deathly silence. "I can give her the answer. Alana and Arthur were friends with Yoffe's daughter—Admiral Yoffe, the friend of Trotsky, Trotsky's supporter." Fanny almost hisses the words, her face white, eyes blazing, "If you ask me they deserved what they got."

"I don't believe in fighting socialists and calling them fascists. Trotsky is right when he says that that was the way we helped Hitler to come to power." Miriam rushes on, almost garbling her words, she thinks she sounds stupid and knows she's making a vain, ridiculous attempt to convince them. 'Yes, Trotsky's did criticize Stalin but he is right ..."

"Stop. Stop. You're a little fool—no, you're a liar and a traitor". Fanny gets up, her shoulders shaking, swaying, clutching the table. "I don't want to hear anymore. You don't belong in this house. I think it's better if you leave—right now!"

"Fanny, Jaime, Ketzel" Miriam stands. "Please." She's choking back tears, angry at herself for beginning to cry. She doesn't know why she's saying 'please'—she knew it would end this way.

Jaime pushes his chair back, abruptly, his lips tight, eyes dark. "Enough! Let's finish this conversation now. Miriam, you'd better go. This isn't doing Fanny any good." He puts his arm across Fanny's shoulder to steady her.

Ketzel is on her feet now, all three of them look at Miriam, who's frozen, unable to move. Judgement's been passed. She turns, goes to Ketzel's room for her jacket, returns to the dining room, where all three are standing, silent, stunned, angry. They avert their heads and don't look at her as she halts in the doorway, her voice choking on the words, "Good-by. I love you, no matter what you think of me." She's crying as she goes down the hall. Her hand is on the doorknob but she stops and turns when Fanny calls her.

"Listen to me, Miriam." Now, the older woman's voice is smooth icy-cold. "Don't you ever come here again—you are not welcome in this house." Then, in spite of her effort to remain in control, she screams "I don't ever want to see you again—ever."

Miriam runs down the stoop, trembling. I've made a fool of myself, she tells herself. walking past the gardens and waving to the chubby Italian lady watering her pansies. I'm finished with the C P. I'll never have to go to another regimented meeting. No, that's not quite true, she admits. It was only when she had her own opinion or a disagreement with the Party line that she felt that way. So, she's been kicked out, she'll just have to accept it. Expelled from Paradise, like Eve who took a bite from the forbidden golden apple—Trotsky apple, I suppose. The analogy amuses her, almost makes her smile. But her heart skips a beat when she remembers, I've lost the Party and my friends.

At Fifth Avenue and 110th Street she decides to walk through the Park. Little kids splashing at the edge of the lake getting wet, mothers screaming at them. The air is vinegary and sweet, like apple cider. She feels chilly and walks briskly, looking for a bench so she can sit in the sun to get warm, the realization of what's just occured begins to hit her. Her friends—she'll never see them again, sit at their table, breathe their spirit, their hospitality.

Fanny—oh, Fanny. Her heart skips a beat and she stops so suddenly a little kid on skates almost rolls into her. She stands on the path, remembering what Ketzel had told her, about her mother, how Fanny's face would light up when she'd hear Miriam dashing up the stairs. She'd always felt accepted and happy in that lovely home, like a member of the family.

In her dreary fatherless home, she'd been like a little runt, like Eliza in Uncle Tom's Cabin who had "just growed" although in her own bitter, critical way her mother loved her. Fanny made her feel loved, important, her affection warming her, like the soft blue cashmere sweater Fanny'd given her for her birthday. At home, birthdays were never remembered. The sweater's in a drawer now at her house. Should she send it back?

She'll never stop loving this beautiful, high-strung, generous woman even though she threw her out. Her legs feel weak and she finds a bench, letting salty tears roll down her cheeks. It had been a lovely dream, joining the Party. She had thought the C. P. would be the answer to all the world's woes, the answer to her life. Why couldn't she have been an obedient Party member, accept what's given as the truth; everything could have been hunky-dory, thinking and analyzing get you in trouble. Looking for the truth—most members didn't, it's so comfortable, leaving theories and policies to the Great Leader, the Sun God, Stalin. She couldn't. She had to leave the Party but she hadn't wanted to lose her friends.

In a little while, in spite of her despair, hope, like a willful forest stream, trickles its way through her thoughts. Jaime, Ketzel aren't like Fanny. Their faces, even though they'd been silent, she'd seen their eyes, they'd been miserable when she rushed out. They still care for her, she feels it in her bones. Their feelings won't change.

She makes herself get up and walk quickly. Then she breaks into a jog and covers half a mile before she has to stop, out of breath. At a broken stone fountain which miraculously works, she gulps cold, sweet water. A sense of freedom start to flow through her, her mood changes, she feels as if the burden she's been carrying has disappeared and when she meets Sylvia and Hilda, her voice is strong and cheerful. They're her comrades now. She's still a communist, a real communist, one who doesn't have to be fed theory, take orders from Moscow, close her eyes, worship an evil dictator!

France, 1935

Trotsky and Natalya's younger son Sergei, a scientist, a professor at the Moscow Institute of Technology, has never involved himself in politics. But he is arrested and, in August 1935, exiled to Siberia, part of a new wave of persecution that sends thousands to concentration camps. Natalya reminds Trotsky of the 1926 meeting of the Politburo at which Trotsky accused Stalin of "applying for the job of gravedigger of the Party.." And how later another comrade told him, "Stalin will never forgive you for this, neither you, nor your children, nor your grandchildren."

Meanwhile their welcome in France is wearing out. The Communist-backed Popular Front is becoming patriotic. Newspapers shriek against Trotsky's presence in the country. There is talk of sending them to Madasgascar or Reunion Island. In the past, the sound of someone singing the "Internationale" in the street was reassuring to them; now it makes them tremble, for they do not know whether it is friend or foe.

CHAPTER 6

France, 1935

Miriam knows Sydney would like her to join the Workers Party but she's reluctant. "I want to know more," she tells him. "Maybe I shouldn't have joined the Y C L so fast."

"I wouldn't say that. You joined because you believe in the class struggle. Well, let me give you a little history lesson and bring you up to date." Sydney takes a deep breath. "At first, it was wonderful in Russia. Problems of course, big problems, but afterwards, beginning in 1920, things really began to change. First of all, people expected Germany to follow Russia's example, which would have strengthened the Soviet Union, but that didn't happen. People were exhausted from the war, terrible fatigue, Russia, a backward, agricultural nation trying to meet the challenge of an industrial world. The Party was weak, many factional struggles, they began to loose sight of real democracy, Lenin saw that happening but unfortunately he died and Stalin was there, ready to step into the breach and seize power." Sydney stops, and looks at her. "Listen, you've got a lot to learn. If you're interested, I'm happy to be your teacher."

They're on their way to a Party meeting that Sydney had received permission for her to attend. As they turn down fourteenth street, Miriam asks "Aren't we going the wrong way?"

"No, we're not. We've moved. We used to have a fancy new headquarters. We rented it around the beginning of '35, on Fifth Avenue. I don't remember exactly when. Now we're on eleventh street.

"Why did you move.?"

"It's funny when you think about it. After we merged in December with the Musteites we decided that nothing's too good for our new Party. We put in a switchboard and a lot of phones connected to small offices, all totally unnecessary. Muste used to have a great following. He was a preacher—you'll see, he still looks like one—he's tall, has a bony, kind face. His supporters were mostly Bible students, Y W C A girls, do-gooders, from the past. It was okay to give money for the unemployed, progressive issues but money for Trotskyism! No sir! They left pretty fast. Now we can't fork up the rent—as usual".

He adds, shaking his head, "I am doggone tired. We had the first session of the Plenum last night ... until four this morning and there's two more nights of it. It's about 'the French Turn' There's a big faction fight about going into the Socialist Party."

"Sylvia told me Cannon said when it comes to a political fight, Trotskyites can stay awake and talk longer than people of any other political type. Is that true?" Miriam wants to know.

"It's true," Sydney shrugs. "But if you want democracy in a Party then you have to have discussion, no matter how long it takes."

Miriam's happy to see Sylvia there when they arrive. She says she's glad Sydney brought her and motions to her to come sit beside her.

"I'm sure Sydney told you about the factional struggle. We're supporting Martin Abern. Marty, Muste and Hugo Oehler are putting up a stiff fight against going into the S. P."

"I don't know much about the whole thing" Miriam tells Sylvia. But does it makes much sense for a new Party, when there's so much to do, to dissolve itself and go into another?"

Just then, Cannon, walking by, hears her. He stops, smiles at her and says, "You'll hear many good arguments tonight why it does make sense." You're new to Trotskyism. In time you'll understand our idealogy," and moves towards the podium. He's spoken gently but Miriam feel annoyed, it smacks of condescension. He's probably right, she thinks, but nevertheless she feels irritated. Would he have spoken to a young man the same way? She doubts it. She tries to listen carefully and follow arguments but doesn't get many of the references and innuendoes members thrust sharply at one another. It's noisy, the speaker on the floor has to raise his voice to be heard. Papers rustle, members leave their seats to get coffee in the back, talk with other caucus members there, and mimeographed statements are being constantly passed around.

At eleven o'clock, Sylvia gets up to leave. "I've got work tomorrow. This'll go on till ... god know when. Are you staying?" Miriam is happy to go. She waves goodby to Sydney but he hardly notices, he's having a hot argument in the rear of the room, his face flushed, hands trembling. Democracy—it's not easy—she thinks, but it's better than the silence and acquiescence in the C. P.

Although July is blistering, unremittingly blazing, one day, when she hears a dear familiar voice ask on the phone, "Hey, are you busy?," she jolts into happiness! "If you can get off at three, how about we drive to Jones Beach? I've got another suit in my car." They meet, swim, have dinner, gossip, it's just like old times. But only about their work, Ketzel's dancing, Miriam's job at the Municipal Art Committee. It's as if Ketzel is saying, we're still friends, let's skip the politics, what Fanny doesn't know won't hurt her. But Miriam can't help asking about her mother.

"It's very serious now, the doctors can't do anything," Ketzel says, shortly.

"Would she want to see me?," Miriam asks.

"She doesn't say and I don't bring it up." Ketzel looks away.

September, 1935

Returning from a Labor Day picnic, Miriam receives a message; Fanny has died. The funeral will be private on Tuesday morning. Comrades and friends are invited to pay their respects in the afternoon at the house. Ketzel says please come. When Miriam gets there. the rooms are jammed, the air is stifling despite the fans. Taking a cold drink, she stands in a corner, hoping that she won't be seen by former comrades. Suddenly, Jaime is at her side.

"Miriam, I'm glad you came," he says. He's taut, eyes darkly shadowed, his hand on her shoulder, icy-cold. "It would have made Fanny happy. She did care for you, in spite of the politics."

"I think so," she says, almost stammering. "I always loved her, I never stopped." She would have liked to add how warm and generous she had always been, that she'd never stopped loving her, but somehow the words won't come. Tears well up in her eyes, Jaime's silent, his arm on her shoulder and they are both quiet until Ketzel comes to join them.

As she says good-by, Jaime, holding Ketzel's hand, says, "Miriam, We talk about you—often," adding, "Come for lunch, like you used to—in the old days." He manages a small smile, "We won't talk politics."

🍁　　　🍁　　　🍁

Fall and winter passed quickly, both Miriam and Ketzel busy, with little time to spend together. Finally, on a bitter day in February they'd managed, at last, to arrange a date for dinner at Ketzel's house. Puddles of rain had frozen during the last few days and light snow fallen, concealing treacherous, black ice beneath. Ketzel and Miriam, hurrying, on their way home, hungry and shivering, laughing and talking, hold onto each other to keep from falling. Miriam has to let go of Ketzel's arm to reach into her pocket for a handkerchief and then—it happens. Ketzel slips and before Miriam can grab her, Ketzel falls backward, hard, hitting her head on the pavement with a loud crack. Miriam bends over her shrieking. Ketzel doesn't move. Then, a moment later, she shudders, blinks and scrambles to her feet.

"I'm okay—fine. I don't need any help." When they get to the house, she says, "I don't want to worry Jaime. Let's say I took a tumble." But her face is white and when Jaime sees her he becomes alarmed and insists on calling the family doctor to check her out.

After Dr. Morris's visit, and everyone's reassured that Ketzel's okay and just has to stay in bed for the next several hours, Jaime busies himself in the kitchen, preparing some food. He calls to Miriam to "come and get it."

"Ketzel just loves this, doesn't she."

"Ah yes, she's my princesita" Jaime smiles and as she grasps the handles of the tray, he presses her hand,

Dinner over, hearing Jaime's voice busy on the phone in his study, she climbs upstairs to the third floor. It's so strange to be back in this house again. Many things are different now with Fanny gone but the familiar warmth of the dark wood panels with its cinnamon smell still lingers. She remembers Jaime and Fanny, so much in love. Fanny once told her, Jaime liked to say he had captured "the fairest in the land" but Fanny knew she was the lucky one. Will something like that ever happen to me?, Miriam wonders. Probably never. Down in the garden the red maple stands, leafless, snow-limned, like a sentinel, when they were little kids playing Robin Hood and Maid Marion, Arthur always wanting to kiss Ketzel. Oh, Arthur, poor Arthur, what a brave little kid he was, trying to be Zorro, like Douglas Fairbanks.

The slate twilight seeping into the shadowy room matches her nostalgic mood. Turning away from the window, she spies an old oval-shaped radio squatting on a table. Happily, she finds a Cuban band on the dial and soon the strains of a familiar rhumba fill the room, "El Manisero," 'the Peanut Vendor.' She hums the words, then, unable to resist the beat, using tiny steps, keeping the upper part of her body stiff, as her Latin friends taught her, she sways, dreamily.

"May I have this dance, Senorita?" Miriam turns, startled. Jaime's standing at the door and she stares at him, embarrassed.

"You've been watching me." Blushing, pulling down her black sweater over her skirt, she looks past him, "It's getting late, I think I'd better leave." Her words tumble out, "Tell Ketzel I had to go."

"No," Jaime shakes his head, "Miriam, stay, I could use a little company tonight." He comes close and holding out his arms, he asks, "Ketzel says you're a good dancer." Teasingly, "You'll have to prove it." Without waiting for a reply, he curls his arm about her waist. For a moment, Miriam is still, her feet seem rooted to the floor, but then, the music and his closeness prevail. Trembling slightly, looking up at him, she nods, puts her hand on his shoulder, her body yields and they turn and sway together.

When it ends and another piece comes on, Miriam feeling she should say something, begins "I ...", but Jaime puts his finger lightly on her lips and sings, "Cuando se quiere de veras/Como te quiero y a ti/Es imposible mi cielo/tan separados vivir", and he and Miriam slowly move to the plaintive old love song. The room seems to change, the rosy, dusky light flickers on dark glowing floors. When it ends, still holding her in his arms, his voice husky, Jaime asks, "Did you understand the lyrics, Miriam?"

"Yes, of course," and although she realizes she'll sounds like a little girl, she adds, "I took three years of Spanish in High School. I should. Remember you helped me study for the Regents?"

"Of course." Her answer disturbs him, he'd been moved by the longing, sentimental song. Why does she mention school, reminding him of how young she is. He says, "Of course. You were a fine student."

When she doesn't reply, he adds, "Fine in many ways," and then, yielding to an overwhelming surge of tenderness, he bends and kisses her.

Miriam springs away, almost pushing him, her head spinning. Jaime's silent, dazed by his impetuousness. He murmurs "I'm sorry, I shouldn't have done that," but she doesn't answer.

Whispering, "I have to go now" she walks past him, runs down the two flights to the coat rack in the hall vestibule, shaking, heart racing, cheeks flushed. Jaime has followed and takes her coat from her. Holding it as she slips into it, his puts his hands on her shoulders and whispers, "Please don't go. I'd like to explain".

"No." Keeping her voice steady, Miriam says, "Not now. I have to."

Jaime goes to the door, blocking her way. "I must talk to you".

"Okay. Tell Ketzel I'll call her." Brushing past him, heedless of the slippery ice, she runs down the steps,

Jaime stands at the head of the staircase, watching her, annoyed with himself. It was just a kiss—wasn't it? In his study, he fills his pipe with fragrant tobacco, leans back, trying to still his agitation. No. If he were really honest with himself he would admit it. After Fanny's death and long before it, he had thought many times about Ketzel's friend, the small girl with dark, curly hair and fringed grey eyes, so intense, "a Trotskyite." She was wrong about so many things, confused about politics, how things really work, unrealistic, her thinking simplistic but so alive! But it was not just a kiss, was it?

Miriam rushes down the street, not knowing where she's heading. She only knows her mind's in a whirl and she's still shaking from that brief encounter. She scarcely notices daylight fading fast, although it's only four-thirty in the afternoon. The snow is falling lightly, the street silent except for the muffled sound of a passing car. She has to go somewhere she can sit down, her knees won't stop shaking.

She counts her change, she has enough to get into a movie. It'll be warm there and she can think. At the Regun they're showing "Duck Soup." She decides quickly and finds herself sitting in a half-empty theater with musty, cold seats, Chico's jabbering in Italian-English and Harpo tooting his horn, the scene almost as crazy as the one upstairs in the attic an hour ago. Would anyone in his right mind imagine that a middle-aged man, (Jaime must be about forty-five years old) would make a pass at a young girl, less than half his age, the dearest friend of his own daughter? But Jaime isn't just a middle-aged man, he's someone she's secretly adored ever since twelve years ago. Was that just a playful kiss or does he really like her. If it was just an impulsive thing, why didn't he say so? But he did want to explain. Why didn't she let him? Why did she rush out like a confused little kid.

When the movie is over, she knows she can't go home; she wants to see him again, at least so that he can see she's a mature woman, not a baby. After all, it was just a kiss. Should she call him? What will she say? She goes into a dimly, lit candy store on the corner, ignoring the curious gaze of a round, swarthy woman, bundled in a thick brown sweater, knitting behind the counter, and calls the Ortega house.

"Jaime. It's me, Miriam."

"Miriam." She hears relief in his voice.

"How is Ketzel?" She feels stupid, asking the question. She's sure she's fine, sleeping soundly.

"She's okay." His voice is impatient. "Where are you? You rushed out so quickly, I was afraid you might fall, like she did?"

Miriam hesitates. She knows he will tell her to come back to the house and yet she says, "I'm two blocks away. I went to a movie. I just called to say I shouldn't have run out like that. I'm sorry. That's all."

"I accept your apology," his voice now bright and happy. "It's too late and cold to go home now," he says, authoritvely. "You'd better come back. I'll have a hot drink ready for you." He tries not to sound anxious. "Come."

Her hands and feet are almost frozen by the time she runs up the steps. "I went to the Regun," she says as she takes off her coat and follows him into the kitchen where steaming chocolate, his special recipe, waits for her on the stove.

"I guess the movie was funny, but I just couldn't get into it," She tells him, watching him pour the hot liquid into heavy mugs.

"One has to be in the mood for the Marx Brothers." Jaime says, without thinking. Sitting opposite her, leaning back, sipping his black coffee, he says, 'But sometimes, they're so damn crazy, you can't resist. Remember, in 'Duck Soup' when Groucho hold up a paper—he's dealing with some important people and he tells them, 'Why, this is so simple, a child of ten could understand it'. Then he whispers to Chico 'run and get me a child of ten. I can't make heads or tails of it.'"

Miriam laughs. "How about in 'Animal Crackers' when Groucho says 'We'll search every room in the house and then the house next door" and Chico says 'what if there isn't a house next door; and Groucho says 'then we'll build one' and starts to draw up the building plans. Ketzel laughed so hard that time she got a stomach ache."

"You kids were a handful when we took you to the movies," Jaime runs his fingers through his hair. "Do you remember that summer when it was so very hot, and you insisted, of course it must have been Ketzel, that we had to go upstairs to the so-called 'roof garden' even though it was raining."

"You used to buy us 'Charlotte Russes'—the little cake with whipped cream and the cherry on top. Ketzel always had to have another because she finished the first so fast." Miriam, her eyes clouding. "Mostly I remember all the nice things when I was a little girl Fanny did for me, even later, when she was sick."

Jaime gets up. He's not sure he wants to talk about Fanny. "Do you want more chocolate. If not, let's go into the living room. I'll make a fire."

Watching Jaime working at the fireplace, Miriam snuggles into the velvet down cushions, her confusion and dismay of a few hours ago completely vanished. Outside, she can see the heavy black branches bending under wintry blasts and in the room the soft, golden glow of lamps, the shadowy patterns from the fire playing on the walls make her feel confident and contented. Is this what she needs, she wonders. Why did she panic when Jaime kissed her? She's a big girl now, isn't she? She was able to stand up for her political beliefs with Fanny, even if she hadn't done the best job expressing them. I can't believe he really likes me, she thinks, but if he does, it's wonderful, it's so easy, it's so nice being with him.

Jaime sits back on his haunches and they're both quiet, watching the shooting flames, red and gold ants creeping along the logs.

"Miriam, I know it was sudden, when I kissed you this afternoon. I'm sorry." He turns towards her, his dark eyes searching her face. "No, honestly, I'm not sorry. There've been many times in the past I felt like it."

Sudden delight darts through her but she murmurs, "Jaime, you've always been nice to me, like everyone else in the family … I didn't think …"

"I know you didn't. I didn't either … then." Jaime jumps up, stirs the ashes, and goes to the window, pulls the heavy curtains together. "Why don't we change the subject", he says and comes to sit on the floor besides the couch, leaning back to look at the fire. "Let's talk, maybe for the first time, not about movies or politics. About you. I heard that you have a new boy-friend."

"There isn't much to tell. I felt bad when Knute, I think you met him, went back to Finland. He still writes to me, not often, especially lately. Now, I'm seeing Sydney." Miriam stops. Should she be open and frank about herself? Why not? "Sydney's nice, I like him, especially his politics, but he's moody. and he seems lonely at times." She laughs, "Even when I'm with him …," she stops, surprised at what she's just said.

Jaime frowns, then says, his tone gruff, "You know how I feel about Trotskyites. But that's beside the point. You really don't know him very well. Do you think it's a good idea to keep seeing him?"

"I'm not sure." Then, wanting to change the subject, she asks, "What about Ketzel and Martin. I guess you know about them."

"It's almost three years they've been together," Jaime says. "And the truth is, I don't like him. I think he's got a mean streak in him but there's nothing I can do." He pauses and then says, "I want to tell you about Fanny. We had a wonderful marriage. We did quarrel once in a while because I felt she gave too much of herself to the movement, even after we had Ketzel. Though I'm as devoted to the Party as she was, I wanted her to be more of a housefrau but she insisted on being active and going to work until she had to stop. I guess that's the Latin in me ..."

His voice is unsteady and he clears his throat. "Her illness was terrible for both of us. You weren't here at the end." He reaches for a cigarette in the pocket of his robe and lights it, taking a deep pull. "Let's talk about something else now. I'm alone and have to go on living. I want to go on living. Tell me, Miriam, do you think of me as old? Look at me. Forty-six ... I feel like a young man."

As if to demonstrate, Jaime selects a heavy log from the stack, rapidly and skillfully placed it on the blazing fire.

"In my country, it is young. We still make revolutions ... We make them at any age," he laughs.

"Jaime" Miriam says, watching him move about the room. She doesn't want to hear about his age or Fanny or revolutions. "Tell me about Mexico when you were a little kid and all the wonderful things you did on the hacienda."

He's happy to oblige and, sitting next to her on the floor, in his lightly accented, musical voice, he tells her about his family, the estate that he and his sister still own and operate and the little white pony, Zapata that he learned to ride on.

The fire begins to ebb, the room becomes chilly. Jaime looks at Miriam, curled on the couch, almost buried in the down cushions. "I think you're getting sleepy. Wait now ..." He goes to a closet in the hall, takes down two woolen blankets, a red and yellow sarape and warms them before the fire before he covers her. As he leans over, he says, "Sleep here, tonight, chula. It's warm in this room. Ketzel will be happy to see you in the morning."

She catches hold of his hand for a moment. "Jaime, wait. I want to tell you something" With a timid glance, she says, "I'm not sorry you kissed me." He smiles, hesitates but walks to the door. When he turns back for a moment, he finds she is looking at him with the clear-eyed gaze he has always found so enchanting.

"Good night" she whispers.

"I'm so glad you're here—Jaime convinced you to sleep over, right? I've got so much to tell you." Ketzel gleefully babbles on in her high, silvery tones as she stands in the doorway, pulling on her Indian flannel bathrobe. "I'm starved, aren't you? Let's have breakfast. Where's Jaime—is he up yet. I smell fresh coffee." She charges into the kitchen as Jaime rushes out.

"You girls will have to fix yourselves something. Coffee's made. Have an important meeting this morning. I'm off," he says. As he dashes past the living room, he calls "Good morning, Miriam. Hope you slept well." Quickly pulling on his galoshes, donning a leather jacket and woolen cap he darts down the front steps.

As they sit at the kitchen table, covered with a coarse white cotton cloth, embroidered with red, yellow and blue cross stitches, Ketzel describes the new, exciting ballet she's beginning to work on.

"I had wanted to tell you about this when we got home yesterday, before I took that stupid flop! It's about this poem Martin wrote and just got published, It's called 'The Fire.' About that terrible fire in a dress factory in 1911 when one hundred twenty-seven young girls died. Some burned to death inside but most of them had to jump out of the windows because the fire exits had been locked. They didn't want the girls to go out on the fire-escapes for a breath of air when they had a break! It's an awful story but it can become the basis of marvelous dance piece. If I'm capable of choreographing it! I'd love to get Louis Horst to write the music. That's if he isn't too busy with Graham these days. But if not, I'm sure I can get Alex North to do it. Wait a minute, let me get you a copy of his poem. You haven't seen it yet, have you?"

All the time Ketzel's going on, Miriam's only half-listening. *She's thinking of last night, remembering Jaime's kiss, so unmistakeably warm, his finding her attractive and—with a shudder of delight—desirable!*

"Here it is, hot off the press." Miriam's amused at Ketzel's slang. She loves peppering her conversation with what she thinks are colorful expressions. As far as seeing Martin's poem, or any of his work, it couldn't have happened. Martin didn't like her, had never really liked her, tolerated her, at best. After Fanny had exiled her from their home, he was delighted to cut her dead whenever possible. When some loyal members of the Y C L (of which he'd had been a member until his twenty-first birthday) told him about her critical remarks about the Soviet Union and Stalin and her resignation from the Party, he'd sneered, "That stupid little ignoramus—who does she think she is. Good! Glad Fanny kicked her out. The Party doesn't need her kind." Miriam decided it was just as well not to mention this to Ketzel. She and Martin had enough problems in their relationship. Miriam takes his poem and reads.

> THE FIRE
> *I died*
> *Seventy five dollars for my life*

Mama, they gave you seventy-five dollars for my life
I died
But I will never die again
It will be different from now on

Listen—listen
Let me tell you how it was
Late in the afternoon
We were tired—too tired to talk
Murmurs—machines humming
cloth rustling—needles singing
clicking
stitching castanets
T H E N

SCREAMING—SHRIEKING
F I R E!!!!!!!
BLACK SMOKE
FIERY FLAMES
BLAZING CLOUDS
HELLISH SICKENING FUMES
RED AND BLACK COBRAS COILING UPWARDS
EVERYWHERE—ENGULFING—
FOREST OF FIRE
EVERYWHERE—

T E R R O R—H O R R O R—P A N I C—
 R U N—E S C A P E—ESCAPE
N O
 NO
  NO ESCAPE

DOORS ARE LOCKED
WE WILL DIE

WE ARE GOING TO DIE
GOTTENU—JESUS—GOD

We cannot breathe—we are choking—we are dying—

TRAPPED—STRANGLING

ENGINES—FIRE ENGINES
COMING—WITH LADDERS
SEE—THEY WILL SAVE US
LOOK BELOW—We are too high

  AN INSTANT—A TINY MOMENT—HOPE
  P L U N G I N G
  SMASHING
  DEATH—
  Still—silent

THEY CANNOT REACH US—We are too high

    We must jump!
  We will be killed
  JUMP—THEY HAVE NETS
  HERE—JUMP INTO THE NETS
  J U M P—

  BLACK BUTTERFLIES
        CIRCLE THE AIR
  Someone says "she is not dead"
  "NOT YET" I answer
  They do not see
  BUT I HAVE ARISEN—FROM THE STILL BLACK SKIRTS ON
      THE GROUND
  I SHAKE MY FIST-
  I TELL THEM—
  I will not die to satisfy your greed

We will not die
We will organize
This will not happen again

It isn't bad, just ordinary she thinks, but she tells Ketzel, "It's very good and I see what you mean. It could be made into a great dance piece, there's action—death—rage. Someone can recite it on the side of the stage while the group dances it. I've seen pieces done that way."

While she says this, she notices how the sun slants along the length of the table, catching the amber pot of honey, the oranges in a bowl, the gold of Ketzel's hair, the excitement sparkling in her eyes. How sad it is that isn't Fanny here, to see her beloved daughter, creative, so beautiful. There's so much sorrow in the world, things that just naturally, accidentally happen, my sister dying in a car crash, Fanny's terrible illness … Why do we murder—why do we kill? In America, the electric chair, capital punishment, shooting down demonstrators in front of the White House, workers, strikers—and in Russia, the land of the great revolution, what is happening there?

"Do you know you just shivered?" Ketzel looked up from re-reading the ending of the poem. "What's with you. How'za about we get out this morning. It looks glorious! There's skating on the lake!" Although Miriam starts to say something about listening to Dr. Morris, a few hours later, they're in Central Park, on the ice, waltzing to the strains of "The Blue Danube."

Norway, 1935

A German comrade manages to obtain asylum for Trotsky and his wife in Norway, where a Labor government has just been elected, but red tape delays their departure. "The French government demands that I leave in twenty-four hours," Trotsky writes to the Norwegian prime minister, "I am sick, my wife is sick. The situation is desperate ..." Finally they are given a six-month visa and allowed to leave.

"Quiet, rugged, handsome Norway!" Natalya writes enthusiastically. They are living with friends, Social Democrats. Trotsky works on his book, The Revolution Betrayed. *On weekends they picnic in the country. But news begins to reach them of the mass expulsions from the Party in the Soviet Union, the imprisonment and executions of Oppositionists.*

Then, in August, even as the fighting in Spain intensifies, Stalin puts Zinoviev, Kamenev, and othe leading "Old Bolsheviks" on trial, charging them with "terrorism" and sentencing them to death. The leaders of the alleged conspiracy, convicted in absentia, are Trotsky and his son, Lyova. The same month, members of the Norwegian fascist party invade Trotsky's home, seeking evidence that he has violated the termms of his visa. Despite Trotsky's vigorous efforts to defend himself, pressure from Stalin turns Norway's Labor government against him. At the end of August, Trotsky and Natalya are put under house arrest and urged to move to another country, if they can find anyone who will take them.

CHAPTER 7

Spring 1936

Years later, in a reminiscing mood, Miriam and Ketzel agree that 1936 had been a 'humdinger', one of the most turbulent years in their lives. Miriam can never forget the warm night in July, when the Civil war in Spain erupted; and Ketzel remembers the same night, her first really accomplished performance.

Up until that time Ketzel had felt she was a good dancer. Yet, she would often say to Jaime, "I'd love to be able to be creative" She had little interest in politics, she lived in the present, movement and rhythm necessary as air to her. But after that July evening, she said "I'll never forget the first performance of 'The Fire.' After three enthusiastic curtain calls, my life changed!"

Working with Martin, together they had managed to create and produce a dance piece, amazing their friends, as well as themselves. Two years earlier they had fallen passionately in love. It happened one night when tired, she'd decided to leave Anna's house early As she opened the door a tall man, with fine, acquiline features was standing there. Afterwards he said "I was astounded. I was looking at one of the most beautiful girls in the world and I couldn't even say hello!" He took her home, they sat close together in the taxi. He suspected she would have gone to his place that same night.

For the first year they couldn't get enough of each other. They adored each other, enjoying, as well, the whispered murmurs of admiration when they'd enter a room—"Don't they make a stunning couple." After some months, they decided to collaborate on a dance piece, her choreography, his poetry. There was was often a problem, one that Ketzel would refer to as "Martin's wandering eye.' "Remember, Martin, the pretty girls are here to dance—only!." But while they worked, their passion to create, the excitement of theatre kept them together.

Miriam, Sylvia, Hilda and Ruby wait outside of the Majestic for Ketzel and Martin to appear. Miriam knows Jaime will be with them too, glowing with pride. It's been several months since that January night and he's called her twice at work, asking her to have lunch with him. She's refuses but longs to see him, the little melody they danced to like a music box tinkles in her heart. Something might happen in the future and thinking about him weaves like a bright thread though the dull fabric of her days. Meanwhile, she goes to meetings with Sydney, begins a course at Hunter College.

While they wait at the stage door entrance, Hilda tells Miriam about a union meeting called for the following week. "The A. F. of L. is trying to set up a union of white collar workers, the Bookkeepers, Stenographers and Accountants Union." Miriam's saying there isn't much sense for W. P. A. workers join a union, they're just temporary jobs …" when Ketzel, Martin and Jaime come out. There's kisses, warm congratulations and after a few moments Martin takes Ketzel's arm, saying, "Sorry. We'll be late, our friends are waiting for us at Luchow's."

Just as they're getting into the cab Sydney comes rushing down the street. He's perspiring, eyeglasses bobbing, his white shirt clinging to his damp chest. "It's here—the Civil War … Spain," he yells.

Martin grimaces, pulls the taxi door shut, says sharply to the driver, "Go."

Miriam and the others, stunned by Sydney's words, wait for him to catch his breath. He gulps, pulls off his glasses, wipes the damp rims before he speaks. His hoarse voice trembling, he says, "Franco's invaded Spain! Azana knew he was coming, did nothing—the socialist party, the communist party and the Popular Front government did nothing but—listen to this—my dear comrades"—Sydney raises his right fist in the air and shouts so loudly that everyone in the crowded street hears and turns to look at the excited young man. "The workers of Barcelona did! The people of Spain have taken power!"

The group is silent for a moment; Sylvia and Hilda are embarrassed at the outburst, theatre-goers look at them curiously. "It's hard to believe!" He can't stop. "The workers seized power! Azana wanted to make a deal with Franco until the last moment. He tried to keep the invasion of Seville, Navarre and Saragoza a secret—so the government could refuse to arm the workers. But in Barcelona," Sydney chuckles, "the workers raided sporting goods stores and took guns—they went to construction jobs, got sticks of dynamite, some friendly Assault Guards got them government rifles. The same thing's happening in Madrid." In Valencia they're grabbing kitchen knives and pulling up the cobblestones, in Malaga they're firing on reactionary headquarters ..."

He pauses, takes a breath, his eyes snapping with excitement. "Things are happening so fast—changing every moment—we're witnessing a revolution!"

The three girls are still, for a moment. Then, Hilda and Sylvia begin asking questions; what's going to be? what action will the Party take? will we send volunteers? Miriam takes a deep breath, joyful lightness sweeping through her. There's hope again!

For the next few day, everyone talks about Spain, the capitalist press and radio carry daily reports of the fighting. But after a few days, interest abates somewhat and news of the fighting is often relegated to inside pages. But great excitement continues in the socialist and communist press abroad and at home there's tremendous enthusiasm for support of the Republicans. Meetings are held in many cities throughout the country, money is raised for supplies, and on December 26th, ninety-six inspired young army volunteers, the first contingent of the Abraham Lincoln Brigade, mostly communists and communist sympathizers, set sail on the S S Normandie. They are headed for Albacete where they will meet up with the Internationale Brigade, volunteers from England, France, Germany, Italy and Poland. Dr. Edward Barsky, of Mt. Sinai Hospital in New York, a handsome dedicated Party member, has gathered a corp of doctors, nurses and medical assistants, to go. The Socialist Party has set up its own separate group, named after its leader, Eugene V. Debs, and on a corner of Union Square, the Rosenbergs, Ethel and her husband, Julius, committed Communist Party members, sing Spanish Republican songs while he passes a hat for contributions.

Ketzel calls Miriam at work. "Great news. We've gotta meet for lunch. Right! It's fantastic about Spain. Martin wants to go, the Party may send him," her voice rings out in happy chimes. Miriam answers quietly, makes the conversation short. She's not supposed to make or receive personal phone calls although she's on the switchboard most of the day. She doesn't want any trouble in her new place of work.

She loves being on the W.P.A. It's the best job she's ever had and her salary of $21.57 weekly is the most amount she's ever been paid. Being in an office on the thirty-second floor of the new R C A Building at Rockefeller Center is an additional plus. Lunchtimes she goes down to watch skaters on the ice rink while she munches nickel hamburgers. A high society lady, Mrs. Henry Breckinridge of Virginia has been put in charge of The Municipal Art Committee and Mayor LaGuardia is its honorary chairman.

Miriam's already committed a faux pas which had the entire office amused for several days.. One morning everyone had been told that the Mayor was coming to visit and late that afternoon, the entire office still waited for him. Bored and disinterested, Miriam's reading at the quiet switchboard, lost in Edgar Allen Poe's short story, "The Tell-Tale Heart" when, all at once a high-pitched squeaky gabble pierces the air. She jumps up, startled; in front of her is a scary, stumpy, dark apparition under an enormous black cowboy hat.

She screams, "Who are you?" The gnome looks amazed. Mrs. Breckinridge storms out of her office, furious—"You don't know who this is?" she screams, then smiling graciously, she tells the gnome, "Come in, Mr. Mayor—we've been waiting for you."

Later, as Miriam expects, she's called into the office and told she's not hired to read at the switchboard.

As part of Miriam's job she's assigned to work in a beautiful, Italianate stone building, on East 67th Street, which was built as a small museum by Thomas Fortune Ryan, a millionaire, now loaned to the Committee. Every two weeks Mr. Landgren, Miriam's boss, hangs a new show. She gets to meet some of the artists as they come trudging in with their canvases under their arm, Chaim Gross, the Soyer brothers, John Marin, Kuniyoshi, Chagall and others. "I think I've learned a lot about painting," she told Ketzel after she'd been working at the Gallery for several months. "After we put up the pictures, I walk around, looking at them like the critics, Howard Devree of the Herald—Tribune and some of the others. The next day in the papers when they talk about which are good; listen to this, I've picked out the same ones."

Ketzel and Miriam are to meet at twelve in the Central Park Cafeteria Zoo at 65th Street. Benches and tables with umbrellas overlook a seal pond and people gather at noon, watching the sleek black mammals leap gracefully through the air, catching the fish tossed by their keepers. Waiting for her friend, a warm breeze ruffles Miriam's skirt as she sits under an umbrella at the Zoo Cafeteria. All at once, Ketzel arrives, her cheeks flushed, sputtering with delight. "I must read you this review before anything else," she carols.

"This is what John Martin, the dance critic of The Times said. 'Last night, a truly inspiring and freshly innovative dance program was presented at the Majestic Theatre, a collaborative effort of Elizabeth Ortega and Martin Montero. Mr. Montero's poem "The Fire," a moving, dramatic work, has been adapted and, one might say, transformed into a remarkable spectacle that resulted in a standing ovation for the two artists. Picture a sewing factory, women working, like caged animals to a frenzied, staccato rhythm and at the end, women, trapped high on the edge of the building—before they take their final flight, like great butterflies, to their death, The audience is electrified—in complete empathy with the awful plight of the victims … One of the best dance and theatre pieces we've seen in a long time."

Ketzel slaps the paper on the table and stands. She raises her thick hair falling about her shoulders and holds it up so that the air can cool her neck. The light wind wraps her white, pique tennis dress about her long, slim torso and pointed breasts. With a joyful grin, she exclaims, "Now—that's what I'd call a review! Martin is walking on air. Now, hear this!," her voice rises, trilling—"I have another piece of good news! I'm getting married".

Miriam starts to say something but Ketzel cuts her short. "I know what you're going to say—he hasn't been exactly faithful!" She looks down at the table, rearranges her knife and fork, adding slowly, "I think he's changed, beginning to grow up. After all, he is twenty-eight years old. Jaime might say that he's a little too old for me but seven years difference isn't so much." Miriam, watching the seals, thinks what about twenty-five years?

"Well, it won't be for a while. At least a few months. We've got too many engagements. Afterwards we might go to Spain," Ketzel adds.

As Miriam walks back to work, she tells herself to stop having foolish pipe dreams, just 'cause he kissed you. She crosses against the light, a driver yells at her, "Watch out lady," and it makes her smile. I ain't no lady, I'm twenty-one years old. Jaime's twenty-five years older but he's strong, so alive! During the rest of the day, a popular song—'It was just one of those things, just one of those crazy things', insists on drifting through her mind.

Miriam plunges into activities, meetings, fund-raising affairs, attending rallies, especially those against the embargo, the 'Non-Intervention Pact' the United States, England and France signed, agreeing not send any help or war materiel to Spain but everyone knows that Hitler and Mussolini are aiding Franco, sending him fighting troops, planes and amunition, scarcely trying to hide it.

One evening in September, Miriam arrives home, late and exhausted from a demonstration at City Hall to find Harry Milton sitting on her stoop, shabby and hungry but she's glad to hear his familiar lisp. Finishing his second cup of coffee and a box of Oreo cookies they reminisce about when they'd last seen each other. "Wasn't it two years ago—that awful rally in Madison Square Garden after the Stalinists broke up the Socialist meeting." Miriam says.

"Yeah," Harry laughs, adding sarcastically, "The next year, they might decide the Socialist Party is 'kosher.'" He takes another cigarette, apologizes, "I'm smoking up your entire pack," and inhales deeply. "Since then, I shipped out a few times from the west coast, nothing much. I'm gonna go to Spain. Maybe it's my one chance to do something heroic—fight the fascists, to help the revolution. I wanna thee Barcelona." His face, once chubby, is thin now, his eyes shining.

"Wars are horrible," Miriam says thoughtfully. She looks at him intently across the table, clasping her hands. "It makes me sick to think about it. I don't think I ever could shoot someone, kill a person." She hesitates, then, "Yes, I could. If I'm angry enough, if people—children—are tortured, murdered ..." Her face is flushed, her eyes stormy. "Yes! I could!"

Harry laughs, squeezes her hand, grins. "You're a good kid, Miriam. You'd make a good fighter."

As she gets up to make him more coffee, she says, "We have to get started early in the morning. I'll call a few comrades. You need clothes and heavy shoes. Winters in Spain are very cold."

The next day she calls Sylvia to talk about raising money. After they talk Miriam asks, "Look, we could have a dinner party. I'd make spaghetti. Would it be okay at your house?' Sylvia quickly agrees, she's not much of a cook, she knows Miriam's competent and can take over the main responsibility.

She's has been at Hilda's and Sylvia's place a few times. It's on the upper west side in a large apartment house—one of those buildings from pre-depression days with elegant lobbies, great spacious rooms and baths, a maid's room near the kitchen. Hilda, Sylvia and Ruth had a privileged youth, attended private colleges, travelled to Europe. Although they dressed simply, their clothes were expensive and comrades wondered at first, wondered how they came to be in the party. But during these times, besides workers and unemployed, there were many others who were attracted to communism—students, writers, artists, intellectuals. They understood that capitalism created poverty, unemployment, waste and war and that there had to be radical economic and social change.

"I'll take care of making all the food," Miriam volunteers, and shops and cooks all day, preparing meatballs and spagetti. Sydney arrives in the afternoon, ostensibly to help her. He's already gone to the liquor store to buy a few bottles of Chianti—his contribution to the party. He works as a 'runner' for a wall street firm, Salomon Brothers and Hutzler. A relative used 'pull' to get him the job, and his salary of eighteen dollars a week has lots of people in the party envying his steady income. But having a regular job doesn't help his usual mood. Sydney's been depressed since he's no longer the acting organizer of the New York Chapter; he'd been filling for Joe Carter. Miriam had hoped they'd decide to have him stay on in that position but it didn't happen. He hates being a "Jimmy Higgins" but doesn't know how to go about setting up a caucus, or taking a political position which would raise his esteem as a theoretician and he doesn't have that 'cronyness' ability, the arm around the shoulder congeniality, that attracts a group around him.

The dinner's been a great success and Miriam sits in the kitchen, cooling off, sipping a little wine, talking to Sylvia when Hilda comes in, bringing dirty plates. "Those comrades from the Bronx, including that guy, Ben-the-Ape, sure can eat," she exclaims. "So did those others who live near here. Who are they?"

"Sam White and George Black—two brothers," Miriam tells her. "Not very original names but they both like my cooking. Maybe I've got myself new profession ..." She hears loud angry voices coming from the foyer and darting out she sees a group surrounding Martin and Harry—facing each other, raised fists—Martin, his black eyes, slits of cold rage, Harry, red-faced, towsled. yelling, "Right, I <u>am</u> going to Spain! I'm fighting for a *revolutionary* Spain—you wouldn't understand that!"

Martin, screaming, lunges at Harry but Sydney quickly slips between them, holding him back. "We don't want you Trotskyites—you scum—fascists," Martin spews, his words thick with hate. "We don't need you—stay away—I warn you—all you bastards ...'

He drops his raised fists, yelling at Sydney. "You too. You son-of-a-bitch." To Ketzel, her face taut, he shrills "What in hell did you bring me here tonight?" He makes for the door, pulling her with him.

The stunned group hear her say apologetically before they hear it slam, "I didn't know who'd be there. Miriam said it was just a fund raiser ...".

Miriam, embarrassed, remains cool and grins, "Well, that's a good ending. We raised fifty-five dollars for Spain. Let's drink to that!" Everyone troops back into the living room but Sylvia remains in the foyer, her face a map of annoyance and agitation.

In her deliberate way she says, "Really, Miriam, I think you might have shown better judgement, inviting those two. I know Ketzel's your friend, but Martin …!"

Miriam says nothing. *She's right of course*, Miriam thinks, *but none of us are so smart about choosing our friends*. A few years later, with a twinge of irony, she recalls Sylvia's remark … "You might have shown better judgment."

CHAPTER 8

New York City, Fall, 1936

A few weeks go by before Miriam hears from Ketzel. She isn't going to make the first move after that scene. Perhaps our friendship is over. We're far apart politically and if she marries Martin …

Harry leaves for Spain a few days later, promising to write often. Between work, night school and meetings she doesn't have much time to dwell on the incident. But one day, when she finds a letter on the kitchen table, which looks as if it had been there for a week, she's delighted. Without looking at the return address she knows it's from Ketzel.

The letter is stained; it looks like it has been sitting in the kitchen for days. "Why didn't you tell me this came?" she asks her mother, trying not to sound angry.

Clara shrugs and turns away. Nowadays she acts as if Miriam's life and activities are of small concern to her and it's hard for Miriam to accept how little, apparently, she matters to her mother. She's going to have to get out of the house soon.

In the envelope there's a check for twenty-five dollars from Jaime.

Ketzel writes,

"Miriam dear, Let me apologize for Martin. He's got a lot on his mind these days. We expect to go to Spain but we're planning to get married first. Of course, you'll be the first to be invited——Martin said so. He's really sorry he stirred up such a fuss, although he won't admit it. When Jaime gave me the

*check he said 'This is for Harry and give Miriam a kiss for me.' I guess he feels
like a father to both of us."*

Miriam, her eyes glowing, tucks the letter away to read again.

Harry's first letter doesn't arrive until almost two months later. Miriam
brings it with her to share with Sydney. It's a mild evening at the end of
November, and she's meeting him in Union Square Park, withered leaves,
faded yellow, still clinging to dusty trees.

"I just got a letter from Spain!" she tells him, pulling him to a bench,
"Harry. I haven't opened it yet." Sydney loosens his tie, required dress in his
Wall Street firm, leans back to listen.

Oct. '36

Dear Miriam,

*I'm in Barcelona after a long, hard trip. Everyone's very friendly, we're all 'com-
paneros', they wears blue jeans and canvas shoes, like a national uniform.
There's thousands of different parties, unions and organizations, the U G
T——Socialist, the C N T, the anarcho-syndicalist, the P O U M, (Andres Nin, the
head, he was close to Trotsky but they had differences) and the P C E, the Communist Party which is getting bigger by the minute. In every store front you see a
sign saying it's been taken over by a union or a political party.*

*I hang out on Las Ramblas. It's a great, wide street with trees leading down to
the sea, a statue of Columbus high up on a column. The companeros have been
showing me how to use a "poron," a large glass bottle with a spout that shoots
out a jet of wine. They tell me I learn fast. I'll be going to Albacete for training
any day now. Will write soon.*

Have to stop now. Salut, Harry.

Miriam sighs. "That's it, a skimpy letter. I guess he's busy practicing with a
poron bottle."

"That's not fair," Sydney bristles, "Harry's a brave, militant guy." As they
walk towards the Workers Party headquarters, he adds, "I should be there, but
with my lousy eyes I'd be dead in no time."

"So far, there's enough volunteers," Miriam says. "They're volunteering from all over—Germany, England, France, Holland. Besides, there's lots to do here."

At the headquarters, they find only Hilda and a few comrades have shown up so they decide to call off the meeting and adjourn to the Crusader. Shirley Freed, just back from Spain, who was scheduled to be the speaker of the evening, comes with them.

They put two tables together in the rear away from the crowd and Shirley begins her talk. She's about twenty-four, a plain, broad face, with flashing quick brown eyes, tall, square-shouldered, energetic, enthusiastic.

"I'd better tell you a little about myself first. My mother was a descendant of Isaac Serveter, a famous rabbi during the Spanish Inquisition, but she wasn't religious. She and my dad, both dead now, came here about 1899. On Saturday night they'd go to the Russian Club here for lectures and poetry readings, dances and they'd always take me with them, even though I was just a little girl. They were friends of Emma Goldman, anarchists, and when I heard that she'd been invited by the F A I to come to Barcelona, I decided to go too. I'm a trained nurse and as soon as I heard they were needed in Spain you couldn't stop me! The only reason I'm here right now because I had to see my uncle—he's very sick."

"I got there in August. Barcelona was so beautiful I couldn't believe it! Loud speakers were on all the time and when you walked down the Ramblas there were little booths under the trees, flowers, trays of red ties, handkerchiefs with the hammer and sickle. Everyone wears badges with insignias of their party or union, almost everything's collectivized, no charge for taxis; gas, electricity and coal free, no tipping in the restaurants. It was so wonderful, I kept telling myself this is what a communist society looks like. Listen to this, here's something funny." Shirley stops, smiles, takes a sip of coffee. "On Sundays they'd stop the war, the Fascists hold Mass all day long so there's no fighting, and the lottery's still going on. Imagine! On every corner an old man or woman call out what's left for the next day's drawing—and they're still having bull fights too, whenever they can."

"My friend, Justin and I ate with the Militia in a big hall; noisy, steamy, everybody laughing, enjoying themselves, the food and wine good, plentiful. In Barcelona, at least at first, when I got there, you could go anywhere in the city to eat."

Shirley looks around at their rapt faces. "Some of you are Jewish, right? There was even a Jewish restaurant; chicken soup, blintzes, in a small hotel. All the hotels have been taken over by trade unions and political organizations. The C P has a big one on the Plaza de Catalunya with two big pictures of Lenin and Stalin hanging out in front."

"Demonstrations and gatherings went on all the time, usually at the Grand Price Theatre. It'd be blazing with lights, red drapes, flags, posters, hammers and sickles. Emma Goldman spoke at one of them, she's a fantastic speaker, full of fire, dynamic. She's not exceptionally good-looking, I'd say, but when it comes to men, well, how should I put this … she likes 'em."

"Andres Nin spoke there in September. He's the head of the P O U M, the Workers Party of Marxist Unification, the main, anti-Stalinist, Trotskyist group. He's short and heavy with thick eyeglasses, very popular. He got lots of applause but I heard nasty rumblings in the hall while he talked. It came from the C P of course."

"They never disappoint us!" Sydney says, and Shirley nods in agreement. "But at the end everyone sang The Internationale and marched down the Ramblas together, the F A I, the U G T, the Anarchists, the P S U, and the Communists."

"That's what it was like in the beginning, in July. Now in November it's already changing. Although the workers still have power it's only on the local fronts. At the beginning, workers took over the factories, the mines, the means of production and although the government in Madrid was at the top, in July, the main power was in Catalonia, controlled by the workers, the 'Central Committee of Anti-Fascist Militias.' You could say there was almost two governments. But after the invasion, when the fascist armies began making headway, the country was in a state of flux and a regular army was needed. Azana, the head of the Popular Front, which included the petit-bourgeois, the socialist and communist party, put officers of the Army in direct command."

Shirley stops for a moment. "It's really hard to describe the situation. The Anarchists and the P O U M, the most radical political parties, didn't have a clear vision of what was imperative—a clear program. They didn't realize that they needed to form their *own* government—that it was wrong to enter into an alliance with the bourgeoisie. They had to remain independent. But now what's happening is that they're being pushed into the Popular Front and stripped of their own power. In September, Alexander Orlov came from the U S S R to take charge. You know what that means? Who'll call the shots now? Don't answer." Shirley smiles sadly. "Of course. Who's helping Spain; giving or rather I should say, selling them guns? Someone put it this way the other day.

He said 'the revolution was defeated at the first cough of a Soviet airplane.'" Shirley pauses, looks at the serious faces of the Comrades and shakes her head.

"We've always wanted a revolution, a real revolution. But that's not the C P line. Dolores Ibarruri, their spokesman, says over and over—'the revolution taking place is a bourgeois democratic revolution.' It's *only* about defeating fascism. Although the C P says that the most important thing is to defeat fascism, we know that they're more afraid of a workers' government that can defeat Franco—but will destroy Stalin as well."

Afterwards, Sydney stands, stretches, trying to assume a nonchalant air, "Yeah—Remember how excited we were? But as usual, the Old Man had it right. He knew what would happen as soon as the P O U M entered the government." He raises his finger and quotes: "'The worker's party that enters into a political alliance with the Popular Front, renounces the struggle against capitalistic militarism and capitulates to it.'"

Miriam, struggling against a wash of sadness, murmurs, "We had such great hopes; now, just a few months later, it seems to be disappearing but the workers won't give up their land and the collectives so easily, will they?" To her own ears her voice carries a desperate note.

Sydney grimaces, "I'd love to believe it won't happen. Anyway, my hat's off to Harry." He stands, fishes out a pack of Wings, lights a cigarette, his hands trembling. "He's a brave guy, fascists in the front, Stalinist bastards in the rear and cooties in the trenches." He smiles and Miriam can tell he's trying to cheer both of them up. "I heard the red lice are as big as small lobsters, just like in World War I. They've probably been waiting for this one. Can you imagine little red lobsters in your pants—or is it bloomers girls wear?"

Shirley, her face flushed, her eyes shooting anger, has overheard him, "I'd like to find some humor in what's happening. But there's nothing positive in being so facetious."

"Sydney didn't mean to be rude," Hilda chimes in. Sydney, abashed, murmurs an apology.

'No, it's okay" Shirley says, softening. "Listen, I know your heart's in the right place. Anyway, I'm leaving tonight." Getting up she adds, "Going on with the fight." She looks around and smiles, "Before I say goodby, let me give you an anarchist salute." Facing each one in turn, she grasps his or her wrist and encircles it with her warm, wide hand.

"I'll never give up the struggle. I'm sure you won't either. *Avanti!*" and she briskly weaves her way out through the crowded table.

Sydney calls Miriam the following week. "Would you like to meet for dinner? I miss you when I don't see you around." Well, it's one way of showing affection, Miriam reflects. They make a date for the following night to eat at a little Polish restaurant, 'The Ilinka', a favorite of Miriam's. As they pass the busy corner of 14th Street, throngs of women shoppers are entering and leaving 'Kleins', the department store on the corner, renowned for clothing bargains. The unemployed still sell apples on street corners but there are fewer than than there used to be and people's faces seem slightly less harried.

The little Polish restaurant on Second Avenue is dimly lit, uninviting from the outside. Through the steamy front window they can see Emil, a stout man in a grimy apron, scooping out immense mounds of mashed potatoes and chunky wedges of pork, while calling to the two waitresses to "get a move on."

Miriam, happily breathing the pungent odors of sauerkraut and caraway asks Sydney, "Doesn't it smell great? And the food's as good as Luchow's."

"Here comes Miss Sadie Tucker," Sydney says as a large, blonde woman approaches, smiling warmly, embracing Miriam. After she ambles away Sydney begins telling Miriam about a meeting of the City Executive Committee he attended the night before. "When we went over plans for the future we decided to set up branches in different boroughs of the City. I'm delegated to find a headquarters on 125th Street that's decent and affordable and they want me to be the organizer there."

Seeing Miriam's pleased expression he stops her before she can speak. "No. Don't congratulate me—it's going to be a tough and probably thankless job but I'll be in charge. Now, here's where you come in. I know you've been thinking of joining the Workers Party and if you want to …" He stops, nervously to take a sip of beer, then continues, "We could take an apartment together so it would be easy for us to work in the neighborhood." Reaching across the table for her hand, he adds sheepishly, "If you want to—or if your mother insists—we could get married."

Miriam startled, laughs. "Sydney, I'm overwhelmed! I guess this is a proposal." But she's not really surprised, she's anticipated that sooner or later he was going to ask her to live with him. She likes him a lot and respects his intelligence, but a lot's missing, even if she's not sure what it is, if it's with her or him. And she's afraid of his quick impatience and irritation with small details, like having to wait for her when she's a few minutes late. She recalls a happy, more light-hearted romance with Knute. And then there's Jaime …

"Sydney," Miriam says, slowly. "I'd been thinking of getting out, getting my own place, I love my Mom but she's so bitter and sad these days." She stops, thoughtfully buttering a piece of chollah. "Let me think about it a while. As for Harlem, I'm glad they made you organizer. Maybe they're starting to recognize your ability."

"Oh, right," Sydney waves away the compliment with a slightly cynical grin. "They didn't have such a hard decision to make, not too many people are ready to move up there."

Later, while they're having coffee, Sadie plunks herself down at their table even though Emil is hollering at her to "get off her fat ass and do her job." "I don't mind him," she tells them. "He keeps trying to get me to go upstairs to his room." Sadie likes movies too and recommends the one with Ginger Rogers and Fred Astaire, on 14th Street, and then she adds, looking at both of them. "Maybe you two should get married already." Miriam smiles at her but Sydney looks away, annoyed.

As they leave the restaurant, Miriam opts for "The Gay Divorcee" but Sydney wins out and they see "The Thirty-Nine Steps." When it's over Miriam declares: "That was the right choice. It was fantastic—when the woman and the train whistle scream together—unexpectedly, I almost jumped out of my seat."

While they wait at the bus stop, Sydney says: "Think about what I asked you. I'm not what you'd call a romantic guy but I'll try." And before she boards, he bends down and plants a kiss on her cheek.

Some weeks later something happens which make her come to a decision. Although she's busy with school and work, when she's asked to help out in an affair to raise money for Spain, she can't refuse. The party's being held in a brownstone on 117th Street, on Ketzel's block, and she's put in charge of preparing refreshments. She arrives early that night and looks around at the large kitchen located in the back of Philip Rosenblit' home, Ketzel's block. It's a well maintained brownstone, with elegant glass doors and shining brass knobs. *Not like the one Mom and I lived in, neglected and shabby.* She recalls her own backyard full of little yellow dandelions she watered every day. She thinks back, amused, she was such a dumb little kid, she never knew they were weeds that people pulled out of their gardens. The host of the fundraiser is Philip Rosenblit, a close friend of the Ortegas and she can't help wondering if Jaime will be there.

Miriam's asked Sylvia to give her a hand at the party but she hasn't shown up yet so she begins work by herself, fixing potato salad, cole slaw, arranging platters of ham, roast beef and chicken. As she chops celery, she hums 'Ay Carmela' along with the music coming from the upper floors.

All at once, a voice, husky and low, murmurs her name. It's Jaime, he's standing behind her and his hands are on her shoulders. She whirls about—his arms around her. Again he whispers "Miriam ..." but he stops and steps away. He's looking past her—to the garden door. Someone's come in.

"Philip!" he says.

"Didn't you hear me?" Philip asks, standing in the doorway, "I was in the shed." He looks at them, a little surprised, his arms full of bottles of home-made beer. "We're running short. Give me a hand upstairs."

Jaime goes quickly to help him, "The last batch you made was excellent," he tells him. As he passes Miriam he says, "Sorry, I can't help you with the food. When Ketzel comes I'll send her down."

Alone, Miriam, cheeks flushed, legs shaking, makes her way to the kitchen table. There's a little wine glass half-filled with Sherry, and she sips it slowly, admonishing herself to cool down. Voices and noises from above, more guests arriving, she hopes someone's coming down to help her with carrying up all these dishes—she doesn't want to go up there right now.

A little while later, sweeping in a cloud of cold air, bundled in winter coats, Hilda, Sylvia and Ruby, arrive in a gay holiday mood, chattering, ready for the evening's entertainment. Miriam, irritated, but resolving to remain calm, looks at them for a moment before she says, "Sylvia, weren't you supposed to be here early to help me?"

Sylvia prickles a bit before saying, "Ruby was anxious to meet some of the literary celebrities and we promised we'd pick her up."

Miriam tells herself there's no point in picking a fight. She turns to Ruby saying, "Well, Ruby, I heard that Lillian Hellman, John Dos Passos, Martha Gelhorn and a lot of other celebrities are going to be here. Anyway, everything's ready so there's nothing left for you to do. Go, enjoy. Ask Dr. Rosenblit to send someone else to take up the food."

When they leave, Miriam begins tidying up the kitchen, not sure of what's she's doing. Shaking, she stands at the sink, washing the same bowl over and over. She can hear the Negro Choral Group upstairs lustily opening the evening's entertainment with their first number, 'Railroad'. Suddenly, she can't bear to be there another minute. She pulls on her coat and and speeds out of the kitchen door.

In the dark street tiny white flakes circle lightly in the lamplight and she stops to lift her face for their touch. She remembers Jaime's hands on her shoulders. "*It was like the first time! Except now I know I'm in love with him!*

That's why I turned—why put my arms around him. I didn't even know what I was doing. When he murmured my name ..."

She starts to run. She runs all the way to 110th Street to the bus stop—almost flying, hugging her purse close to her breast as if it contained a precious secret.

The next day Miriam expects that Jaime will call her either at work or at home in the evening. Every night she tears up to the third floor, the pay phone is two flights up in the hall—every time she hears a ring. But it's silent the entire week. After ten days of anxiety and longer, she can't stand it anymore. She calls Ketzel. "I haven't been over for a long time, I could make it for lunch Saturday."

"Great." Ketzel answers. "There's plenty of food here but we'll have to fix it ourselves. Jaime's in Mexico. He left suddenly. He's acting mysterious these days. Says he's bringing his sister to the wedding. Right! but he didn't have to go to Mexico just for that. Anyway, can't wait to see you."

Miriam hangs up and a few days later she cancels the Saturday date with Ketzel. Going to that house now doesn't make any sense and she doesn't want to see Ketzel the way she feels.

She goes about all week, crushed, alternating between feeling rejected and angry. *Why is he acting so myserious. Am I making too much of a kiss, a caress?* After Knute left, he stopped writing. He'd told her once that she didn't know anything about men. Maybe he's right. How could she know about men? Her father died when she was only three. She sees it happens all the time in the Party. A comrade'll come on strong to a girl, pile on the compliments. After he gets her in bed a few times, he usually flits away. How could Jaime be so cruel? She thought he was different. Why did he leave just like that? Did our embrace mean nothing to him?

Women flirt too but then it goes deep and they fall in love ... end up getting hurt. Is our society to blame? Does it warp men's ability to be honest? Would it be different under socialism. Will men be faithful in a different society, not play games, really love? Maybe men aren't capable of real affection, maybe they're born fickle! *I guess it wasn't love,* she concludes gloomily. *He just wanted to kiss me again.*

She's isn't surprised when she catches a heavy cold, runs a temperature, and has to get into bed. Her mother guesses the problem has to do with some "comrade" and refrains from questions or remarks. Instead she goes to the outdoor market under the train at 116th Street, picks out an old chicken and makes a good soup for Shabbos. Miriam eats the soup, cries herself to sleep, recovers, goes back to work after the week-end, deciding that there's been nothing more than a light flirtation between the two of them and that's that.

A few days later she resolves the situation. She comes home one evening and finds Clara in an easy chair, exhausted as usual, her hands folded in her lap, her fine, light hair straying from hairpins.

"Mama," Miriam plumps down on the sagging couch and hugging her old velvet pillow, plunges in. "Sydney, you remember him, don't you, well, he asked me to take an apartment with him. He came here once and you were glad he's Jewish even though you said he's too thin, smokes too much. I think you liked him, well, a little anyway. We're not planning to get married—that is, unless you insist. We'll be working for the Party so we'll have to live in Harlem."

Her mother, who's just had an argument with Tyrone, "der schwartz super," doesn't seem to be listening, but after a moment, passing her hand across her forehead, wearily, says, "Go ahead. I'm not surprised. I knew you would move out, sooner or later. The first mistake in your life it won't be." She looks over at her daughter and shakes her head. Then she adds, her voice softer, "It's good you won't move far away. Maybe you'll come over once in a while, you'll spare an evening."

"Of course, Mom," Miriam says, relieved. "Of course I will." Then, "Things'll straighten out for you soon." Trying to sound cheerful though she knows it's inevitable, she adds, "Mama, try not to worry so much about the house. I'm sure you won't lose it. The Nehring Brothers won't foreclose, they'll give you time."

After a few moments, she says, "Wish me luck, Mom."

"Sure," sighs Clara, who's been sitting quietly, "Someone in the family should be lucky."

But Miriam still isn't certain about what she wants to do and holds off talking to Sydney about their living together. Something stops her. She knows she's still hoping Jaime will call her when he returns, even though it's clear he isn't going to.

It doesn't take long for Miriam and Sydney to find headquarters for the Party. There are vacancies everywhere. 125th Street from the Harlem River to the Hudson is poverty stricken, littered with garbage and old newspapers that flutter against the sky like great dirty-white hawks. Most empty stores are not even barred, broken windows gape into deserted streets. It's easy to locate a vacancy, there are hundreds. They find a large room in a dingy building with a small, filthy toilet in the hall for a monthly fee they can afford. Comrades bring folding chairs, a battered desk and a Sterno stove from the local Salvation Army. They clean and sweep the floors, scrub the toilet, arrange the furniture. After they finish working one Saturday afternoon Colay, Gonzalez and Franky crack open the bottle of cheap Chianti and toast their new project with jelly glasses.

"To the Harlem branch of the Workers Party of America, to a new Fourth International—to victory in Spain—to our Comrade Trotsky ..."

While they raise their glasses and voices, Miriam looks out of the unwashed windows onto the forsaken, windswept street; her mood, like the fading light of dusk, is sad, tinged with melancholy and only faint hope. *We're so small, so alone, surrounded by enemies on all sides ... it seems so depressing here. Will we be able to get people to come, to listen to us, to convince them? It doesn't seem promising. But what's the alternative—do nothing?*

She turns to Sydney, smiles at him, touches her wine glass to his and sings, along with the others, the last words of the Internationale, *'tis the final conflict, let each stand in his place.'*

Norway, Winter 1936

The Norwegian government, afraid of losing the coming elections, orders Trotsky to sign a statement pledging not to interfere "directly, orally or in writing, in political questions directly or indirectly in other countries..." How can he remain silent in the face of what is happening in the Soviet Union, in the world? He refuses to sign, and he is silenced. While he is being held incommunicado, Stalin's allies point to his silence as proof that he cannot answer the accusations coming from Moscow.

Then, in December, a way out: through the efforts of the renowned Mexican painter, Diego Rivera, Trotsky is offered asylum in Mexico. On December 19th the tanker Ruth *sets sail, carrying Trotsky and Natalya. They are leaving Europe forever, the cemetary of their daughters and so many of their hopes.*

Trotsky writes to Lyova how thrilled they are to be in Mexico. He and Natalya marvel at the rich produce of Mexican earth, the soft warm air and the sunny, blue skies. Also, American comrades are already there to begin work as secretaries and guards.

CHAPTER 9

Winter 1936–'37

The latest news from Spain is worrisome, frightening. There's furious fighting on the Saragossa front and around Madrid. Russia's sending some ammunition, but not enough and making sure that none of it falls into the hands of the P O U M or Anarchists fighters at the front. At the end of October the fascists are bragging that it will be just a matter of days until they're in Spain's capital. Newspapers carry headlines like "Madrid—Doomed City" and "Franco Ready for the Kill" and on November 6th the Popular Front Government is transferred to Valencia and it looks as if Madrid will fall the following day.

Miriam's disheartened. She decides to call Ketzel whom she hasn't seen for a long time and they arrange to meet for lunch at Rumplemeyers on 59th Street, opposite Central Park. She's always wanted to eat there when she was a little girl; and after skating on the lake, her nose and fingers frozen, she'd watch and envy the rich kids troop in there for hot chocolate. And how desperately she'd wanted regular ice skates that came attached to their shoes instead of the kind she had that had to be screwed on, on both sides, and kept falling off. Her mother had promised to buy her a pair but then bought her another pair of roller skates because they cost only a dollar!

By the time they meet, events in Spain have changed. Her mood elated, she waves to Ketzel from down the street and runs to hug her. "Madrid is saved!" she cries. "They turned the fascists back. It just happened!"

"I know," says Ketzel. "Let's celebrate."

At first they talk and laugh, Miriam's spirits high, enjoying everything, in this upperclass tearoom—the gentile atmosphere, the thick carpets, her dainty cup of hot chocolate shining with mounds of whipped cream … as delicious as she'd imagined and she can even have two—if she wants 'em.

In a little while, during a lull in their conversation, Ketzel turns to Miriam, almost pleading, "I hardly see you these days, Miriam. It seems like we're drifting apart. You're so busy with meetings. Politics are important but …"

Miriam looks out of the luxuriously draped windows facing Central Park. A cold rain has sudden begun, splattering across the sidewalks, lashing the trees, men holding onto their hats as they scurry down the street. Her mood changes and she'd like to answer Ketzel coolly, dispassionately, but she knows herself.

"It's hard, Ketzel," she says slowly, clasping her hands tightly. "What's going on in Russia … the horrible rotten lies about Trotsky. They'd almost be funny, if it weren't so tragic … Zinoviev, Kamenev, all three accused, a bunch of others too." She hears her voice rising now but she can't help it. "As if they actually plotted to kill Stalin! It's crazy, it makes me sick! But it doesn't bother you! Why? Why doesn't it? Why can't I convince you?"

"Look, Miriam," Ketzel's voice is soft, persuasive, reaching across the table for her friend's hand. "We both love justice—we want to make the world a better place, but people see things differently, and they act differently. Why can't you accept that?"

"I can't. No! Not terror, phony trials, murder."

"Fine. Let's drop it!" Realizing she sounds annoyed, Ketzel pauses a moment and Miriam can see she's making an effort. "Please, Miriam, let's not fight. Look—I've got to tell you about my idea, you're always the best audience in the world—the most fun—usually." She giggles, "Oh God. There I go again."

Miriam sighs, then can't help a breaking into a little smile. She appreciates Ketzel's attempt to keep things pleasant but it isn't always easy. "Okay, go ahead," she says, resignedly, "Let's hear it."

"A new idea—it'll make a great ballet. It's about La Pasionnaria—the great woman leader! It's in all the papers, how she's fighting in Madrid. 'No Pasaran.' She's fantastic! fiery!—inspiring. Can you just see it? Throbbing music as they're tearing up cobblestones, making themselves into a chain, passing them from hand to hand, piling them into barricades. The soldiers at the Segovia Bridge start to retreat, she faces them, screams: 'Come back—across the bridge is our enemy—We must save Madrid.' They stop—make a circle around her—shout 'No Pasaran!' and fire until the enemy turns and runs."

"Then, for the finale—this can be so dramatic—the streets of the City deserted, empty, quiet—the 11th International Brigade arrives—frightened people creep slowly from their homes. 'The Internationale' begins softly and then swells, louder and louder—the people gather in the square around the bedraggled, victorious soldiers ..." Ketzel pauses, takes a deep breath, smiles. "What do you think?"

"Yes," says Miriam, dryly, she's listened to all this as patiently as she could but she can't help saying, "It's good. Think of all the old guns you can use as props—the ones the Anarchists got from from the Soviet Union. Very colorful! Be sure you include Durruti. The C P had to send for him even though he is an Anarchist—a leading Anarchist, a military leader at the Aragon front. They needed his ability so he was sent to Madrid with a hand-picked force. He's just been killed—no one's sure how it happened. Why not make him one of your heroes?"

"For God's sake, Miriam. Can it! What's gotten into you?" Ketzel glares across the table. "This isn't like you. Is something wrong? What's your problem?"

Miriam looks down into her empty cup. After a moment she glances out of the window and says, "It's stopped raining. Let's take a walk—get out of here."

As they walk up along the Park, towards the Sailors and Soldiers Monument, buttoning their coats against the cutting, wintry breeze, Miriam says, "My mom's miserable these days, I'm not any consolation for her. I'm thinking of getting out," and tells her about Sydney's proposal.

"He's a nice guy." Ketzel's thoughtful, "I guess it'll be a good arrangement. But are you going to be happy with him. What *I* think you need is a love affair—a real one."

Miriam laughs, a little dry sound. She wants to talk about Jaime but she doesn't dare. They've stopped near the Subway entrance at Columbus Circle when, impulsively, she says, "I must show you something," and opens her large pocketbook. "Our English class had this assignment, we had to describe a dream. See what my instructor wrote on my paper? 'I would say this is very Freudian. You deserve an A.'"

Ketzel reads it quickly, goes back, reads it again, slowly. "Wow!—this is good. I love it. You're on a speeding train, speeding very fast, black birds outside, rapping their sharp beaks against the glass, wanting to capture you—carry you away on their great dark wings. You want to let them in but the window's stuck, you can't open it ... and you watch them fly away.." She stops, looks sharply at Miriam. "Whoa, I get it. Not very subtle. Who's the guy? Something's been going on! Tell me about it!"

"Ketzel, you're nuts!" She snatches the fluttering papers, putting them back in her purse. "The only one so far was Knute and he left, gone with the wind. A long time ago. You can't mean Harry Milton!"

She shakes her head and laughs, "No thir!" And that ends it.

A few days later, Miriam calls Sydney. "I'm taking you up on your offer." She tells him in what she hopes is a casual, yet affectionate tone, then, adds, seriously, "It might work out pretty well. We'll try—right?" *He probably expected I would say yes*, she thinks.

He's silent for a moment. Then he says "That's great. Would you have time to look for an apartment? Remember, it can't be far from 125th Street. I think I can get some comrades to bring over my furniture, whatever you'd like to keep, to our new place. Once you find one."

Already, he's giving me orders, Miriam thinks, amused. "I'll start looking as soon as I can but I'd like to wait until the end of my school term, if that's okay with you," she tells him. She's not sorry she's delaying their move together, she needs more time to get used to the idea.

They meet one night on 125th Street to check out the new place. Walking east towards the Hudson, passing the famous Apollo Theatre, now bare and dark, the colorful billboards and flashing signs long gone. During Christmas break Miriam found a small three room apartment in a run-down four-story building with a creaky elevator that tended to make unscheduled stops between floors. It has more than enough windows, light, appeared free of large cockroaches and was affordable, fifteen dollars a month, it's main attraction is that it's on 116th Street, close to their work in Harlem. The only furniture they have so far is a small table, three chairs and a double bed, but the janitor in Clara's building has promised to bring them an old couch and two easy chairs as soon as he can borrow his uncle's truck. On the table filled with two apples is a lovely red decorated bowl from the Soviet Union that Rose Karsner, Jim Cannon's wife, gave them.

Franky's father, who has a heavy Italian accent, a warm, stout, man with a large mutton-chop mustache, has decorated the little piney fir tree in their railroad apartment on 103rd Street off Lexington Avenue. He's a lonely widower and while he fixes steak, fried potatoes and salad for their Christmas eve dinner, he puts on Galli-Curci and Caruso singing arias from Aida and La Traviata. Afterwards, Sydney and Miriam pick up Franky's pretty Italian girl-friend, Beady, who lives down the block and all four of them go to a midnight movie.

It's late when Miriam and Sydney take the elevator to their apartment. They can still smell the fresh paint but the bed's ready.

She wakes after Sydney's left for work and makes coffee with milk from the outside on the window sill. As she sits, sipping the hot liquid, she decides she needs to buy some oilcloth to cover the chipped table …

My new home. My own place. It's a big step … Funny—I don't feel nervous. I hope it's the same for Sydney … Sydney, Sydney, my new partner. I don't think I'll ever really know him, but I think he cares for me … he tries to be gentle and considerate … loving. Their first night together—more or less what she'd expected.

After she rinses her cup and starts to scrub the stained sink with Dutch Cleanser, she begins to feel domestic and hopeful about their future. Quickly, they settle down into a pattern of work, their office jobs during the day, Party work at night, courses at Hunter for Miriam, meetings almost every night for Sydney.

She's amazed at how hum-drum and ordinary life can be with Sydney—even when they make love. There are no surprises but she hadn't really expected any. As time goes on, she becomes aware that the only time Sydney becomes animated is when they have company, friends or comrades. She's happy when friends or comrades come over, even spend the night, because then there's conversation in the house. Otherwise it's quiet. When they first met he'd seemed to take a genuine interest in what Miriam thought, about books, movies, about herself and how she felt. But soon Sydney seemed to pay her less and less attention, and an affectionate embrace only meant he wanted to go to bed. *Well, okay,* she tells herself, *it's a home, my home.* She enjoys fixing dinner, it's cheaper than eating out and besides, she likes to cook.

On a February night, she's busy at the stove when Sydney gets home. He asks why she's bothering, they'll be late, they're supposed to be down at the Hippodrome early, to help out. Miriam realizes she's forgotten the big public meeting the Party's putting on that night! Trotsky's speaking on the recent Moscow Trials by telephone from Mexico. It's been planned for a few weeks and a large crowd, several thousand people are expected to turn out.

"How could you forget about something like this?" Sydney yells. "It's an historic event! We sold over a thousand tickets!"

"I guess I got the dates mixed up," Miriam's meek. "But the guy bringing the couch and chairs is coming tonight. He called me a week ago. There's no way I can reach him. I'll just have to stay home but you can go."

"For god-damn sure!" he slams out. A minute later, he sticks his head through the door. "If the Comrades wonder what happened to you I won't tell them you forgot something like this. I'd be embarrassed to admit it."

Miriam's upset even after the couch and chairs arrive and make the empty room look a little homier. She can scarcely wait until Sydney gets home, ready to make an apology, but his grim face stops her.

"How was it?" she asks, hesitantly.

"It wasn't." Sydney says. "No, I shouldn't say that. Let me put it this way. We did hear Trotsky for a few minutes but that's all. Max Schactman read the rest of the speech." He smiles sheepishly, rubs his eyes and says, "Make me some coffee, I'll tell you.

As she gets the coffee ready, he begins describing the evening. "We had a great crowd, someone said it was more than sixty-five hundred people, seemed like every radical in New York was there, besides Angelica Balabanoff and a lot others. It started late. We waited a long time—problems with the phone lines we were told. Finally, Cannon began, gave a great introduction. Then Trotsky's voice came on. We heard him for about five minutes, but right after he said 'I am ready to appear before an impartial Commission of Inquiry and if it decides that I am guilty, I will place myself in the hands of the executioners of the G P U' ... he's cut off!"

"What happened?" Miriam asked.

"Well, we waited some more but after about fifteen minutes we're told there's some trouble with the phone lines that can't be fixed and there'll be nothing more from Mexico tonight. Everyone's upset. There's bedlam for a few minutes but it quiets down when we hear that Trotsky sent a copy of his speech and it'll be read by Max Schactman.

"I wish I had the text here. It was great. The Old Man said he'll set the record straight, he'll prove every single charge false and expose the political meaning of this gigantic frame-up. What a roar from the audience! Afterwards, we all stood up and sang the 'Internationale.' Outside there were some Stalinists, the usual crap from them, but also there was lots of cheering and yelling, 'Long live Trotsky!' in the street."

"And I missed it. I'll never live this down." Miriam moaned, "Did Sylvia want to know where I was?"

"Sure." Sydney answers. "I told her the truth, but I didn't say I got mad at you." He drinks the last of the coffee. "You're forgiven, honey-chile." He stands and puts his arms about her. "Let's go to bed."

Ketzel arrives at the great circular information desk of the Grand Central Station in the middle of the marble floor, and discovers she's fifteen minutes early for her appointment with Jaime, Adelita, her aunt and Martin, who's meeting her here. It's hard for her to stand still so she practices dance movements, lifting her torso and straightening her spine. When she looks up at the high, blue ceiling twinkling with the constellations of the zodiac, she thinks: *This place is gorgeous with all this exquisite marble! I wouldn't mind getting married here, especially when they unroll the red carpet for the 20th Century Limited.*

Everyone arrives finally and they take a taxi up to 67th Street, off Central Park, where they have an appointment for dinner at the Cafe des Artistes. Ketzel looks at her father, Jaime looks thinner, tired, his trip to Mexico hasn't done him much good. She knows he was at the Hacienda helping Adelita, but he's often not there when she calls. And when she did get him on the phone he sounded evasive, almost mysterious. But there are other things on her mind and before turning her attention to the meal, when she glances about the beautifully decorated dining room with its gilded mirrors, soft lighting and magnificent murals, she has a sudden idea.

Turning to the others she asks: "What would you think of having our wedding party luncheon here? Isn't it a great idea! Look at all these magnificent, sexy, naked wood nymph murals by Howard Christy Chandler—very appropriate don't you think?" Everyone laughs, Martin, pleased with the suggestion, quickly agrees. Jaime looks troubled. "Adelita wants to pay for your wedding party," he says, "so I don't think it should be very expensive."

Adelita breaks in quickly. "No—no—no. Please, the money is not important. It's a wonderful idea."

Martin is letting Ketzel and Jaime assume responsibility for the wedding. He's busy writing an article on the Spanish Civil War and also making arrangements to go to Madrid after they are married. He's been asked to come and anticipates a new, possibly remunerative assignment. This is a good period for him. His writing is going well. Several pieces have been accepted by the 'New Masses' and 'The Daily Worker', and he's now a member of the League of American Writers; Dashiell Hammett likes his stuff, especially his articles about the Trotskyists. "They are subversive and deceitful—which is hardly surprising since the same qualities are typical of Trotsky himself," Martin wrote.

His personal life is going well too. He and Ketzel have settled down into an calm relationship. At twenty-nine, he's even more attractive, chiseled features touched with the sensuality of a coiled snake. In addition to the little he earns from writing, Martin relies on teaching Latin dancing in a little school in the Village. He knows Jaime doesn't like him very much but he adores his daughter and goes along with whatever she wants. Over dinner that night in the Cafe des Artistes, Martin turns his charm on Adelita and she tells him about the hacienda she and Jamie own jointly. He's impressed by this delicate, aristocratic lady, intrigued by how different she is from Jaime, whose high-cheek-bones and straight black hair reveal his Indian heritage.

"There are only a few great haciendas remaining that make pulque from the maguey plant," Adelita is saying. "People don't drink pulque, the way they used to. Personally, I don't like it very much—it tastes like a cross between beer and buttermilk," her tapered fingers smoothing the dark hair pulled back in a heavy bun, held with a silver clasp. "The estate is so large we used to have a little trolley to go around it. We're fortunate, we have one of the few profitable ones left; during the revolution many were burned down ... enough of this," she says, with a warm smile, "you must come and visit soon."

"We will—won't we, Martin." Maybe after we get back from Spain." Ketzel says, going to embrace him and then leans over and to kiss her aunt's smooth cheek. "Now, let's choose a menu for the wedding."

❧   ❧   ❧

June arrives with jaunty gusts, blossoming trees and yellow daffodils. It's Saturday and everyone who doesn't work seems to be in Central Park. Martin watches a little boy dashing ahead of his father with a red and white sailboat he's going to launch in the Conservatory pond, tennis players hurrying by to public courts. Hansom cabs with artificial flowers stand waiting for customers and tired nags are patient as drivers brush down their coats and hang little straw hats from their ears. For out-of-town visitors and honeymoon couples it's their first sight of Fifth Avenue as the horses clip-clop down the wide street. And it was just yesterday, Martin remembers, that he and Ketzel stood before a Justice of the Peace in City Hall and were made "man and wife."

"Thank God, that part's over," he thinks, and increases his pace to the Cafe. He wants to make sure the tables are arranged so that there's enough space for dancing as well as for the Mariachi band. Knowing that it will please Adelita and Jaime, Martin's hired Mexican musicians, dressed in traditional tight jackets and wide sombreros, to play and sing native folk songs. And Ketzel will be wearing a new gown she copied from Frida Kahlo's self-portrait. In the Cafe des Artists there are banks of flowers everywhere, giant tea-roses Ketzel adores, luxuriant ferns, the air heavy, sweet and damp, great canvases of Chandler's wood nymphs, sensual, gossamer-dressed women cover every wall, and gilded mirrors are lit with golden light.

Trudi Schoop, a comic Swiss-born dancer "the female Charlie Chaplin" whom Ketzel adores, enters first, bouncing into the room followed by two blond, blue-eyed dancers, May O'Donnell and Dorothy Bird, stunning in their light summer dresses. Then comes Anna Sokolow, small, intense; Tamiris, flaming red hair, almond-shaped eyes; Martha Graham, regal sculptured head, high cheek-bones; Doris Humphrey, delicate, graceful; Jose Limon, the head of a Greek god, the body of a graceful bull; Lucas Hoving, long limbs; and Michio Ito, slim, agile.

Thirsty, hungry, they flock around the bar, downing drinks, hors d'oeuvres of caviar and shrimp to the strains of 'Perfidia' and 'Begin the Beguine'. All at once, the music stops and Ketzel appears, her red-gold hair woven into braids winding about her head, an embroidered blouse, full long skirt and long silver onyx earrings. She makes a stunning tableau and everyone spontaneously breaks into applause.

The music starts up again, the liquor flows, the guests crowd around the sumptuously laden buffet table, and amid the noisy popping of champagne corks the newly-wedded couple is toasted every five minutes. As the afternoon wears on, people relax, tell stories that flow even faster than the wine. Mary Garden, older than most of the dancers there, a friend of Jaime's, makes them all laugh when she recounts her retort to John Martin, the cold, brilliant critic of the New York Times. "You critics are like enuchs," she told him. "You know all about it but you can't do it."

"When I was starting out, I'd get off from work so damn tired but then I'd have to run off to practice! I had to work—or go hungry—there was no way I could just be a dancer and study dancing," remembers Anita Alvarez.

"It seems it'll always be that way for us, for painters, for anyone in the arts," says Sophie Maslow.

"But what makes it worse, is jealousy between the artists." Jose Limon, sitting nearby with Pauline Koner, adding in his precise English, "We should be able to work in harmony, support each other in our endeavors, not indulge in the rivalry and back-biting that prevails in our field. It makes me very sad."

At another table, Anna Sokolow relates an encounter with Irene Lewisohn, interested in improving the life of the east side youngsters. "She'd come to the Neighborhood Playhouse wearing a sable coat, carelessly throw it over a hot radiator and have her maid hand her a finger sandwich. You can imagine how we felt, some of us who didn't even have enough money for lunch that day. Sometimes, when we'd meet at her house on Park Avenue, she'd describe a project she was interested in and then, in a kind of slow, imperious way she'd had, say to us: 'Now—be creative.' Imagine! We'd get fifteen bucks a week and that was supposed to keep ourselves going."

Ketzel, after visiting her guests at each table, joins Miriam and Sylvia, who've been enjoying the spectacle from a corner. They know only a few of the guests and Ketzel, lingers, telling them about the different dancers. Just as she's getting up, saying, "Excuse me, I must go have a twirl with my new husband," Jaime approaches, holding out his hand to Miriam.

"Would you like to dance with an old man?" he asks, pulling her up and taking her to the tiny dance space before she can answer. The band is playing a familiar song and as he puts his arm about Miriam's waist, he whispers, "Do you remember this song—'Cuando se quiere de veras?'" Miriam nods, looking up into his face. Trembling a little, she sees he's flushed and a little drunk. They move together, slowly, not speaking. Then, Jaime bends down, "Why did you go to live with Sydney?" he mutters.

Miriam, at first, startled by the question, can't believe what she's heard. Then anger rises within her, what right does he have to ask her that? She whispers furiously: "How can *you* ask me that?" Then, a second later, "I could ask you about Mexico, couldn't I?"

"Miriam …" Jaime begins, helplessly. He realizes hazily, that, in his muddled state, he's started an exchange that's ending up badly. Miriam says nothing, waiting for him to go on but he realizes there is too much that needs explanation and he can't explain anything, not now.

When the music ends she says, "Thank you. I enjoyed the dance," and hurries back to her table. She sees Sydney who has just arrived and links her arm through his. "You must be hungry," she says, her voice somewhat shaky. "The food's great and there's plenty left."

The party begins winding down but as the musicians move to put their guitars away, Adelita, a vision in a light green lace dress, a glittering comb in her high-piled luxuriant hair, a filmy shawl draped about her shoulders, stops them with a request. They start to play and Adelita begins an old nostalgic song "Cancion Mixteca," her voice high and sweet. Ketzel comes to her side, takes her hand, then Jaime joins them and all three sing: "Que lejos estoy del cielo donde nacido" and when they reach the lines "y ahora yo vivo sin luz, sin amor—and now I live without light and love." Jaime looks directly at Miriam who, embarrassed, murmurs to Sydney, "It's been nice but let's leave soon. Okay?"

Ketzel's busy saying good-bye to all of her guests, giving them small bouquets, but she stops Miriam. "Wait for me. I've something to tell you." When the room's empty, she tells her. "We're leaving for Barcelona. Martin has letters of introduction to some Russian officials and I'd like to do a few performances to help keep the morale high. Keep in touch with Jaime while I'm gone. I know he's going to miss me. You know how he is!"

Adelita, takes Miriam's arm, making her promise to have lunch with her before she returns to Mexico. Jaime, standing a little off to one side says nothing and then finally leaves with his sister. At last when Miriam and Sylvia make their exit, their arms filled with flowers, Sydney brings up the rear, full of twenty-year old rum, ready for a nap.

For Sylvia it's been a delightful afternoon. As they're getting ready to leave Miriam remembers to tell her about Harry Milton and she says, "The last I heard he was going to the Huesca front with George Orwell and another guy, Goff. I haven't heard anything for a long time though and I'm …"

"It doesn't make any sense to worry," Sylvia interrupts. *Oh right!* Miriam thinks, *She always has such sage advice.* Then Sylvia adds: "I've been thinking of going to England with Ruby." She sounds wistful. "I could use a little excitement in my own life."

"Me too." Miriam says. "I wouldn't mind going to London or Paris or anywhere—right now."

"You've got me for excitement, honey-chile." Sydney interjects, putting his arm about her, swaying slightly. "What do you say we go to Bear Mountain tomorrow with Harold and Rhoda?"

Miriam looks at Sydney gratefully. Her head is still in a whirl. "That's a swell idea." She smiles at him. "I'll pack us a picnic lunch. I'll wear my new playsuit."

Coyoacan, Spring and Summer, 1937

When Trotsky's ship arrives in Tampico, he and Natalya are welcomed by a delegation that includes Max Schactman, Diego Rivera's wife Frida Kahlo, and an emissary from Mexican President Lazaro Cardenas. The following day they're transported to Cuernavaca and move into Kahlo's house, the Casa Azul. Some American friends are there as well, ready to serve as secretaries and guard the exiles twenty-four hours a day.

From the moment Trotsky arrives he sets to work creating a Commission of Inquiry before which he can defend himself against Stalin's charges of terrorism and treason. In March the Commission of Inquiry into the Charges Made against Leon Trotsky in the Moscow Trials is formed, headed by the eminent philosopher John Dewey. The Commissions' work is complicated by the polarized politics of the Left. John Dos Passos, Max Eastman and Normal Thomas are among those supporting the commission's work but its opponents include George Bernard Shaw, Theodore Dreiser and Andre Gide.

Trotsky gets everyone working and soon the house hums with activity, typing, translating. It resembles the old days, including all of its tensions. One day when a paper is not ready for him, Trotsky leaves the room, slamming the door so hard its small panes shatter onto the floor. This "Commission of Inquiry" entails assembling evidence from archives and newspapers, obtaining records—an almost insurmountable job.

Undaunted, the 80-year-old Dewey travels to Mexico to lead the inquiry, which proceeds under armed guard. After a month of testimony and research, the commission rules the Moscow Trial to be a frame-up and Trotsky ends the hearing by talking about the tragic degeneration of Bolshevism. "I do not despair," he says. "Three revolutions made me patient … The experience of my life, in which there has been no lack of success or of failures, has not only not destroyed my faith in the clear, bright future of mankind, but, on the contrary, has given it an indestructible temper."

CHAPTER 10

Summer, 1937

Miriam calls Adelita a few days after the wedding luncheon and sets up a date for lunch. College is over for the term and she's restless and at odds with herself and the world. Also she's afraid Jaime will come with his sister and she's reluctant to see him. Her feelings for him are in a turmoil and she'd rather avoid him. She's trying to create an equilibrium in her life—a peaceable routine of work and activity. Also, she's anxious about Ketzel's going to Spain, but Ketzel never seems to worry about her own safety. "I'm a special person," she liked to say. "I'll always have good luck—Fanny told me I was born in a caul like Hamlet and it'll protect me." Miriam's amused, oh, yeah, she thinks?—but she knows there's no point in arguing.

The day is relentless hot, the City bakes and in the Central Park Zoo the huge gray polar bear lies panting in the shade. But when Miriam arrives in Yorkville, the Kleine Konditorei is cool and dimly lit, and sounds of ice tinkling in frosty glasses greets her. Jaime, silent and dark, is already there with Adelita, who looks approvingly at Miriam, who arrives, a little breathless, in a pretty light blue voile sleeveless dress, beads of sweat outlining her curved bow-shaped upper lip.

"The reason I wanted you meet me here was because I thought you might want to see this part of New York," Miriam says, brightly, ignoring Jaime's grim silence. "It's a small city, with its different shops that sell sausages—imported beer, black pumpernickel ..." She stops to give her order to a tall blonde waiter at her side, his eyebrows and his pencil raised.

"It's changing a lot now," she goes on after the waiter leaves. "The Nazis hold marches almost every night, demonstrations, open-air street corner meetings. They're tough and mean and they'll beat up anyone who dares invade their territory. Even so, a foolhardy bunch of us Trotskyists (she notices that Jaime winces slightly) or Communist Party members (she throws a little smile in his direction but his face is impassive) hold a street-corner meeting. Sometimes it can be pretty scary."

The luncheon is somewhat quiet. Jaime doesn't talk much and eats little, mostly sipping imported lager beer and puffing his pipe. Adelita regrets having to leave New York so soon, saying, "I hate to be going but there is business with the hacienda I must attend to," and then begins asking Miriam about herself, her work and her ambitions. When it comes to a career, Miriam tries to explain.

"I'm not sure what I want to do. I don't know yet. After seeing my mother wring her hands every day worrying about money, I'd like a secure job, but that's ..." She pauses a moment, asking herself why she should tell anyone about her needs. "One thing I do know, I'll always be active in the radical movement." With a mischievous glance at Jaime, "Even if it isn't in the Communist Party." Jaime's face remains blank.

Adelita reaches for her pack of Fatimas, leans over to Jaime for a light, says, "I think you two will have to tolerate a moderate liberal like myself. I support Lazaro Cardenas, our president. He's a fine man, amd I admire him."

"I do too," Miriam breaks in, enthusiastically. "He's a real person—in fact, the only friend that Trotsky has—in Europe and elsewhere. I'm sure you know Rivera convinced him to invite Trotsky to Mexico."

"Aren't you forgetting someone else? A famous Mexican artist, David Siquieros." Jaime's tone is dry, irritated. "He's in Madrid, right now, at the front, fighting the fascists. Yes, Mexico is the only country in addition to the U.S.S.R., sending ammunition, planes and supplies to Spain."

"*Bueno!* Let's not talk politics today." Adelita taps her teaspoon lightly on her coffee cup. "Miriam, you must come to Mexico and perhaps you'll visit your friend Trotsky. Bring a friend if you like. And Jaime, you must come home soon now. I think you know why."

The luncheon doesn't last much longer. Standing outside, under the restaurant canopy, saying good-by, Jaime says quietly to Miriam,

"I'll phone you this afternoon. There's something I'd like to talk to you about."

She looks surprised. "I guess I didn't mention I'm leaving today for two weeks on vacation. We have that place up in the country. I'll be back at work Monday, two weeks from today."

"Then when you return." His effort is to be off-hand but his intensity gives him away. "Let's make it definite, I'll call you that morning to make sure you haven't forgotten."

Miriam can feel a blush spreading across her face as she turns to Adelita, saying "I'm going up to Mahopac, catching the 3:30. We have a little bungalow up there, six of us, all comrades." She laughs, "I'll bet they're in the lake right now."

Adelita's suprised. "How is it with such hard times in the United States you're able to get away in the summer—isn't it very expensive?"

Miriam chuckles, "Not really. Not this one. I'd say our place is very rustic—primitive really! We have to use a pump in the kitchen sink, the ice-box has a broken door, and the toilet—well, there isn't any to speak of. But it's cheap, about fifty dollars for each couple for the whole season. In the spring, one of us, it's usually Sydney, buys a car. He's a good driver. He buys a Model A Ford for about $100—sells it for about fifty or seventy-five dollars so we manage to have a summer for very little money …"

"An excellent arrangement—I admire you young people." Adelita hesitates a moment. "You're idealistic and enterprising." Her white glove pats Miriam's face, lightly, "It's too hot to kiss you but I'm happy we had a chance to know each other." She sweeps to the curb where Jaime's hailing a cab. "Now, I'm serious," she calls to Miriam as a taxi pulls up. "You must come and visit me in Mexico.

Miriam arrives in Mahopac later that afternoon. Sydney's waiting at the railroad station.

"Guess what?" he says. "A surprise visitor. Harry Milton, just back from Spain, he looks terrible, nervous as hell. Sylvia met him today up at the head-quarters and brought him with her. We can put him up on the couch or he can sack up at the Ageloff's place."

As the jalopy circles the pond Sydney brings Miriam up to date. Harold and Rhoda have just had their weekly quarrel, Beady's back is bad, as usual, and Franky's brought up lots of meat from D'Agostino's, so they're all set for the week-end.

They eat out-of-doors in spite of the mosquitos, enjoying the light breeze rippling across the water. Harry's quiet during dinner, his no-longer chubby face lined with fatigue. When he finishes, he walks to the water, takes the creaky rowboat tied to the dock and stays out a long time, mostly drifting with the current. When he returns he finds the comrades have taken blankets and unfolding them on the grass, under the tree, waiting for him.

"I guess you guys want to hear about Thpain?," he asks, with a half-sigh.

"Sure do, Harry, only don't start yet, let's wait for the others to get here," says Harold, who heads back to the third bedroom, which is the barn he shares with Rhoda. She wants to get married but his mother objects, he can do much better. It doesn't even have to be a nice Jewish girl, she says but she should have either money or a good career. After all, he's an accomplished musician, plays viola in the Metropolitan Opera orchestra, studied with William Primrose.

"Okay, we're here!," Hilda's voice rings out; the contingent from the cottage on the hill has arrived and Sylvia, Daisy and Shyke, all Workers Party comrades, come trooping in behind her. It's beginning to get dark but they've brought their blankets and pillows and quickly make themselves comfortable.

"We're ready, Harry." Sydney says and everyone quiets down.

"Remember I wrote you from Barcelona—I guess it was sometime around December." Harry says, standing on the front step of the cottage door, so everyone can see him. "I'd been with Mary and Juan Brea but they left just about that time and I thigned up with the Lenin Division, guys from different countries, the International Brigade, good guys. Mainly all they cared about wath fighting Hitler and Mussolini and defeating fascism.

Shyke, resting his back against Daisy's knees, calls out, "Not the Stalinists! Win the war against fascism—okay but you gotta keep the status quo … keep the bourgeoise in power."

Harry goes on, "Right! At first the Thtalinist were small but they got big very fast after they convinced all the anti-fascist parties to join the Popular Front. By the end of '36, the Popular Front had the P O U M, which was the most revolutionary and anti-Stalinist, the U G T, a socialist trade union, and the C N T, also a trade union, but mostly anarchith. At the beginning, the radical parties had their own militias, but when they thtupidly—and I must say, thtupidly, joined the Popular Front, which included very conservative members of the bourgeois government, they were disbanded. If you want to know the truth, the thtalinists were more afraid of a revolution than of fascism. More than anything they wanted a good relationship with England and France and once they were in the driver's seat, they deliberately wrecked any kind of a revolutionary movement."

"At the Aragon front." Sydney's voice comes from a dark shadow where he's propped his back against a tree.

"Right." Harry answers. "What did the the P O U M army get—9000 men were armed with—guess what—American Winchethter rifles, the type Custer used on the Indians! Military junk! They used 'em during the Civil War in Russia. That's what Russia charged thpain for—460.5 tons of gold—$518 million dollars—old guns, some 80 years old! But it's only fair to say they did send more up-to-date ammunition, planes and machine guns later on—to the other fronths. But not at the Aragon front—we didn't get them, just a few old, unreliable machine guns."

He stops for a moment, his hands trembling. He says, "I could use a glath of water or thome of Miriam's lemonade," and makes his way into the cottage, stepping carefully over three pairs of legs.

Rhoda stands up. "I've heard enough. I'm going to bed."

When Harry returns, carrying a cold drink and some cookies, he sits down on the bench vacated by Rhoda.

Harry goes on. "Anyway, I've gotta tell you about the great guys I fought with."

"You were with George Orwell—you showed me a picture of you two together." Harold says.

"Yeah," says Harry, "he looked like a scarecrow! A ragged leather jacket, a woolen cap, no soles on his boots and this Frenchman, Benjamin Peret, a poet, a friend of Andre Breton also was with us. The Spaniards are funny, brave fighters, they're not afraid of dying but when they'd hear the bugle call at 8 a. m. they'd yell like hell!—the only reason to be bugled awake early in the morning is if there's an enemy attack. Also they didn't wanna fight if it was raining."

Harry pauses, takes a deep breath. "We never had enough of anything. Twelve overcoats for 100 men, thin shoes, 'alpagatas', those rope thandals, not enough tobacco, candles, and most important—firewood! God! it wath cold up in those mountains, howling wind, cold rain pouring into the trenches got into your bones! Firewood, we needed it desperately, the mud in the beet fields, huge lumps so slippery you'd fall right into icy puddles. One horrible night we were on a deserted barn—I'll never forget—the floor was covered with human bones and filth and rats crawling over you." Harry passes his hands over his eyes. He asks. "Are you sure you want me to go on?"

"Look, why don't you take a break now?" Franky says. "But we want to hear about when you were arrested and how you got out."

"I've gotta stretch," says Shyke. "I've got a charlie horse."

Everyone gets up. Some of them walk down to the pier and watch the tiny wavelets changing from purple to dark blue, listening to frogs' mournful grunts across the water and their depressed mood doesn't lighten. When they've all straggled back, Sylvia asks Harry, "Would you rather continue tomorrow?"

"No," he says, gruffly, waiting for them to get settled. "I'd like to get it all off my chest. Finally, I did get to see some fighting—it was at Torre Fabian. Our plan was to raid the territory so the Fascists would have to move troops from the other side of Huesca, where the Anarchists were attacking again. I have to tell you about Kopp—my Commandante—God, how I admire that man! If he's thtill alive. Lots of stories about him. We ended up in jail together." He stops to laugh, clears his throat. "But I'll come back to that later on. He'th a fat guy, an engineer from Belgium, made gun powder secretly for Spain. When they discovered him he beat it and took a lorry filled with guns and ammunition with him. We had some of the horses from the Spanish Cavalry—they were beautiful! He loved to ride and he'd be up in front on horseback leading the troops carrying a black and red flag. A lot of the 15 and 16 year old kids rode too. I hate to say this, but they rode some of those poor horses to death. I was wounded during that raid, took a shot in the shoulder but it wasn't too bad. Finally, near the end of April, I got back to Barcelona."

Harry pauses, takes a handkerchief from his pocket and wipes his forehead.

"We heard that a lot of things changed in Barcelona in a short time." Sydney says. "Is that true?"

"It's rue! The Assault Guards were brought back, armed police forces, like in Puigcerda, attacked Anarchist strongholds and that was the beginning of the end. I gotta say, ther*e wath* a lot of fighting between the anarchists and the P O U M. The anarchists had no clear cut program. For instance, in April the P O U M paper, "La Batalla," published 13 points for victory. They wanted the *government* to call a delegated congress of worker's and peasants' syndicate that would become the government itself! Tell me, does this make sense? Would the government itself call for an organization to supplant itself? Nin—the head of the P O U M, although a very sincere guy, Trotsky really liked him but they had political differences. He's juth not a revolutionary leader." Harry stops, looks down, seems to be examining his bare feet, then when he looks up he says bitterly:

"Let's face facts. The longer the Popular Front controlled by the Stalinist thays in power, the greater the danger we lose everything, including the war. The Comintern now has men in all the strategic spots. The S I M, and the G P U are polishing off anyone—everyone who's not an errand boy. Nin was arrested in June. They couldn't force him to make a phony confession. It looks like they've killed him already." His voice shakes, he stops a minute.

"I saw what was happening and decided to get the hell out. On May l9th I was arrested in Port Bou. They brought me back to Barcelona and a hundred of us—Kopp, me and others got thrown into jail, a long, damp, stone room, no beds, no blankets, a thin piece of bread, rice, potato soup. We orgainthed a hunger strike, managed to get thome news out. After four days, the joint Plenum of the Anarchists and the Youth pathed a resolution demanding our immediate release."

Harry sighs, shakes his head. "It took a long time, I was let go finally. I couldn't find out what happened to Orwell and Kopp."

There's silence as everyone tries to digest the implications of what Harry told them.

"That's it, comrades?" He looks around. "Where's my thneakers. Can't remember where I left 'em."

"Are you okay now, Harry?" Miriam asks. "This whole thing …?"

He grins, "Physically I'm fine. I don't think the hunger strike was the worst thing for me." He's found his Keds and bends over tying them. "I've taken off some weight so that's good."

He walks away a little and looks out at the lake. "I have trouble sleeping. When I finally fall off it's the same thing over and over again." He pauses and when he continues, his voice is shaky. "It's something that happened one night on a hill, where we were fighting. There were these twelve little kids, nice kids. They belonged to the Youth League of the P O U M—maybe thirteen years old and they had guns. They'd been posted about 40 yards from a Fascist parapet. I saw them at dusk, lying on the grass. When dawn came up they were still there and they knew they could not move until the next night. They'd pulled up grass and earth to cover themselves and they had to lie there absolutely quiet all day long. If they moved, just an arm or a leg—they'd be shot. I couldn't wait until it got dark, I had to go and see how they were. I crawled over—before I knew it I'd almost crawled over one of the bodies. They were there—dead—seven of them. Dead. Only five had managed to creep away."

He clears his throat. "I have this dream—over and over. The kids lying quiet, their eyes are open. I keep telling them—'don't move—don't move'—but I know they're dead!"

❦   ❦   ❦

The weekend passes quickly. On Monday morning Sydney, Franky, Harold and Shyke pile into the Model A Ford, Harry stays on for a few more days. Miriam, Sylvia, Daisy and Beady, left behind, busy themselves, cleaning the bungalows but devoting most of their time to tennis, swimming and sun-bathing.

During the following two weeks, Miriam and Sylvia spend more time together. Sylvia's just received a letter from Ruth, her sister, who's in Mexico, working as the Old Man's secretary and Miriam can't help feeling a little twinge of jealousy. To work for the Old Man—what an honor! and to be in Mexico! Pearl Kluger, another Party member (with an atrocious Bronx accent) had been chosen to take notes at the Dewey hearings and now Ruth's down there. *The Party's like everywhere else, Miriam thinks resentfully, it's the same, you've got to be pushy—you have to make yourself known to get somewhere.*

Although Sylvia's an agreeable companion, Miriam's a bit disappointed to find her rather staid and pedantic. Not surprisingly, Sylvia doesn't care for Ketzel. "Ketzel's too critical. I feel like she's always judging me. You're different, you're much more accepting." Miriam knows she, herself, is plenty critical. For example, she doesn't like Sylvia's friend, Ruby, very much. Something about her seems phony, she's just *too* pleasant but she would never say so. Is she a coward or just diplomatic? She isn't sure.

One warm evening, sprawled on beach chairs, facing the lake, Miriam asks Sylvia if she's going with anyone.

"Not right now. I wish I did," Sylvia admits, fanning herself with a pleated Chinese fan. "When I was younger in college, I had some dates." *Maybe when she was nineteen, Miriam thinks. She might have been more attractive but now that she's over twenty-five ... Not that she's plain, just not particularly noticeable, small, dark-blond, with regular, neat features, and small blue-gray eyes, hidden by spectacles, reminding Miriam of the Ogden Nash couplet "Men never make passes/at girls who wear glasses."*

"There doesn't seem to be much on the horizon—at least for me," Sylvia adds with a rueful smile. Miriam can understand why; popular girls in the movement were, for the most part, dynamic, colorful and what some might call promiscuous; tough competition for an ordinary looking, conventional female like Sylvia.

Then thoughtfully, Sylvia murmurs, "You're lucky to have someone, Miriam, even though you don't seem to be"—she interrupts herself with a light laugh—"in love."

"I'm not. He's nice but maybe I was too impulsive. We did have to be in Harlem to work to sette up a branch. And besides, I really felt I had to get out of my house." She stops. She'd have liked to tell Sylvia about Jaime but doesn't know how to begin. She's afraid she'll sound foolish, perhaps childish, so deciding to change the subject she says, "How's Ruby these days? I haven't seen her around much." Not that Miriam cares. *There's something stiff about Ruby. Stiff—that a funny word, but it seems to fit her.*

Sylvia responds quickly. "Okay, fine, I guess. She's really a sweet girl. She makes travel sound so inviting, she keeps talking about going to England. I'm seriously thinking of going with her." She hesitates a moment. "I can't go this year—maybe next—who knows? Maybe we'll meet some nice men over there—we can't seem to find any here—at least I can't."

Lounging on the canvas chair, in the deep shade of an leafy, gnarled tree, Sylvia's heart-shaped face is wistful.

Coyoacan, 1937

Although fifty-eight years of age, Trotsky still has the erect carriage of his youth, his sharp blue eyes and keen look giving him an aura of a much younger man. It's almost inevitable that Frida Kahlo and he would become lovers. His relationship with Natalya began very shortly after his marriage to Alexandra Lvovna and the birth of their two daughters; there had also been rumors of other, more fleeting dalliances. Although a stickler for propriety, old-fashioned, courtly and often charming and witty in the company of women, he had always had a lively interest in sex and in the past when a woman responded to his advances, he'd tend to make a direct, coarse proposition. He is not the romantic lover, who woos with soft words and flowers; sex was usually a matter of honest lust.

Trotsky and Kahlo are two of a kind: highly charged, creative, immensely talented and skeptical of convention. From early in their marriage, Frida and Diego Rivera had both been unfaithful. From the moment Frida Rivera greets Trotsky at the pier, his interest flares. She is bewitching, seductive. and she in turn is drawn to the magnetism and glamour of this older man, this hero. All during the Dewey trial, Frida sits very close to "El Viejo", 'old man' or, as she nicknames him affectionately, "Piochitas," 'little goat'.

Passionate love letters and secret meetings ensue. Rivera seems unaware of the goings on but Natalya is depressed and jealous. Trotsky's various secretaries tolerate his sharpness, his impatience and "lordly manners" but his betrayal of a woman who has devoted her life to him makes them question: Has all that he's been through caused him to lose his balance, his moral sense?

After three months, Frida and Trotsky end their affair. They both recognize that if it continues the resulting scandal could be disastrous. Frida is relieved—she tells a friend "Estoy muy cansada del Viejo"—I am very tired of the Old Man." Trotsky continues to write her ardent letters and briefly entertains the idea of making love to Frida's sister, Cristina. But eventually coming to his senses, he turns back to Natalya with tears and apologies, calling her "my only one, my eternal one, my faithful one, my love, my victim."

CHAPTER 11

New York City, Summer-Fall 1937

During the next two weeks Miriam tries not to think about what Jaime had said about calling her that Monday when she returns to work—how will she feel if he does call and she sees him that night? Ketzel has told her he's been hard to reach and he may be seeing a beautiful young woman, a close family friend.

As Monday's date comes closer, she nervously thinks about what she should wear and settles on a sleeveless, princess-style dress of white sharkskin that gently clings to her waist. With white sandals to match, she looks attractive but she knows she's no match for a Mexican beauty Jaime once mentioned. Is that why Jaime is being so mysterious about what he's doing in Mexico?

Sydney, who's elected to take his week's vacation during this hot spell to catch up with some reading, observes, as she boards the train:

"You look great." Somewhat unusual for him, she thinks, he hardly ever notices her appearance.

"What's the occasion?—It can't be the dentist, he's a little too old for you."

"Thanks" Miriam answers, pleased but also a bit guilty. "No man's too old for me—if he's a good one." Her quick answer surprises her, though it has no special significance for Sydney, who shrugs and waves as he drives away. Why did she say that, had Jaime's age bothered her?

As the train clatters on, she ponders on Harry Milton's news about Spain. The revolution's almost dead, Andres Nin murdered by the Stalinists haunt her thoughts. She makes a determined effort to turn her thoughts away. What's the sense of brooding about what now is the almost inevitable defeat of the Republicans in Spain.

Instead she thinks about Jaime. Will he call?—will he meet her after work today. What is she going to say to him? What if he tells her he cares for her? Of course she can say she's attracted to him—which is true, she decides. But what if he says he loves her? Will she tell him she loves him? Does she? He's twenty-five years older, sophisticated, a writer, with literary friends, successful. She's always worshiped him but he's Ketzel's father. Should she stay with him tonight? Every time he's near—she feels a pull—he does too. *Like animals must feel before they make love.* It's crazy. She must be crazy. She wishes she knew what the hell she wants! She must be really stupid. It was foolish to move in with Sydney … she wasn't sure how she felt about him but she went ahead. Now here she is—getting involved with another man before she doesn't know how she feels about the first. Does she know what she's doing, what she wants? Why doesn't she grow up before she get's herself involved again?

Jaime calls at 9:30, and quickly Miriam makes a date with him for the evening. At 5:15, when she leaves Rockefeller Center, he's already there, waiting under the marquee of Radio City Music Hall. A new film, starring Charles Donat and Marlene Dietrich, called 'Knight without Armour' is being advertised with glamorous pictures of Dietrich as a Countess in pre-revolutionary Russia. At first she doesn't see him, blocked by hordes of tourists swirling about, but when she finally spots him her heart jumps, his honey-dark smooth skin, the white shirt open at the neck, an attache case under his arm. He's probably just come from the Colliers' office.

The moment he sees her, his serious, almost troubled look fades from his face and with a warm smile, he comes quickly to her. He bends to kiss her but she turns her face slightly so that he can only brush her cheek. He drops his hands. "I'm really glad to see you, Miriam—I'm not sure you are."

"That's not true. Of course I am," Contrite, annoyed with herself, shakey inside, she reaches up and kisses on his cheek. "Where can we go? It's awful today—somewhere cool."

His good-humor is restored by her little caress. "I know you like to eat out-of-doors so I made a reservation at the Claremont Inn—125th Street—on the Hudson," smiling at her. "They have a terrace. Flower gardens—fresh breezes from the river."

The white-framed green trimmed manor house with colorful awnings is almost empty when they arrive, the terrace deserted, too early for music and dancing that will follow later in the evening. Now, there's only one couple in a far corner, looking deep into each other's eyes. After ordering iced tea and salads, Miriam and Jaime lean back, looking at the stony cliffs of the Palisades opposite and a red tugboat, struggling against the current.

At first the conversation is light. Then a silence falls. Jaime reaches across the table, "Miriam, how about us?—What are we going to do?"

Finally, she manages, after hesitating, looking at him with open gaze open, fluttering, confused,

"Jaime, I'm not sure I know how I feel—honestly."

Jaime interrupts, impatient—"Maybe you aren't sure—I can understand that—we haven't been alone together for a long time." He stops, realizing that he sounds upset at her answer. "Perhaps I better remind you!" He turns his head, gazes at the deep flowing current and then looks at her. "You can't have forgotten last year—when Ketzel bumped her head. We talked for hours that night. It was wonderful, for me at least. And I thought for you." His fingers tighten around hers. "Then at Philip's house—you turned to kiss me. We were embracing when he came and interrupted us. Is that how you act when you're not sure?"

"Jaime—that was so impulsive—I didn't think …"

"You knew what you wanted. Don't deny it." He stops and reaches for his cigarettes, takes a deep drag, exhales before going on. When he speaks again his voice is soft. "Wasn't that the real you, the one who responded to me?"

"Please Jaime, let's drop it—let's leave it for now. I was being infantile and foolish—whatever I did. I'm trying to understand it myself …"

Silence. In a moment their food arrives. When the waiter leaves Miriam lifts her wine glass, says softly, "Let's drink a toast—to the revolution—to comradeship." Jaime raises his tumbler, adds dryly, "To love."

They turn to their food, talk about Ketzel, the wedding, Adelita, her job, now that the W P A is closing.

"It's really such a shame to close up this wonderful art gallery," Miriam says. "I bet a lot of them will be famous someday, Soyer, Chagall, Kuniashyi," adding with a laugh, "Maybe I can get a job as an art critic after the project folds up."

The sky is becoming pewter-gray, the sultry air lightening, little whisps of breeze, freshening the air, hint of impending rain. They linger at their table, holding on to the relaxed mood. Across the river, a huge circle of lights on the ferris wheel of Palisades Amusement Park shimmers in the dusk.

"You know, I almost forgot to tell you, but I brought with me a letter from Ketzel, from Barcelona. She asked me to show it to you—you know how busy she gets—she doesn't always have time to write." Jaime reaches for his case, and while Miriam reads he walks to the end of the terrace.

Dear Daddy,

I am sitting outdoors in a little cafe called Cafe de Las Ramblas, writing you. The chairs are really hard but it's charming and old-fashioned with little marble-topped tables. You remember you once told me what Cervantes said "Barcelona is the flower of the beautiful cities of the world, the honor of Spain ..." He was so right! In the town square, on Sunday, people do the "Sardana", a lovely folk dance. Everyone joins in; they pile their bags in the center so they can put their arms over each others' shoulders. I love this City!

Things are almost normal, people say, although there're great shortages of necessities, olive oil, tobacco, even bread. If you have money (the same old story) you can get anything you want. The revolution seems to have come and gone (they didn't even hold a May Day parade) except there's lots of tension and fighting between the different political groups. I keep away from that stuff, I've enough politics in my dance group. I leave that kind of thing to Martin.

I've become friendly with a very attractive older woman, Caridad Mercader. Magnificent flashing eyes, active C P member. So are her sons, Ramon and Luis, very good-looking boys. They're on the front lines now. Despite everything that's going on——or maybe because of it?——there's a lot of romance in the air. Caridad is having an affair with a Russian general, Ramon has a Danish girlfriend, a nurse who took care of him when he was wounded, La Pasionaria has found herself a truck driver who likes French cigars and silk pyjamas and we hear that Hemingway has got himself a blond newspaper woman.

Are you working hard? What about your novel? I hope you're not lonely. Call Miriam, take her to lunch, only DON'T TALK POLITICS. Stick to books and movies. Show her this letter so I can kill two birds with one stone.

Te quiero

Ketzel

P S We'll be leaving for Madrid soon——will write

Miriam sighs, the letter is not reassuring, sisterly, as if Ketzel feels that Miriam's almost like another daughter to Jaime. After reading the letter again, she puts it away and goes to join Jaime and takes a cigarette from him. They watch the Hudson River Day Line boat, ending its voyage, slowly making its way down the river, returning to port.

"Ketzel certainly has no shortage of gossip," Jaime laughs. "Her letter sounds like Spain is a great place to find love."

Miriam can't help saying dryly. "It looks that way. Great for journalists and Russians, but not so healthy for oppositionists." When Jaime sighs and looks away, she adds hastily, "Let's skip that for now."

She touches his arm. "What shall we do? Should we take Ketzel's advice and go to a movie?" Then, in a moment, noticing his look as he turns to her, her heart missing a beat, she adds, "Maybe that's not such a good idea. We could take a ferry ride, right here. Take the boat over to the Palisades and come back. We used to do that when we were kids."

He smiles, "I'd like that," pressing her arm to his side. "But you'll be cold."

"Then I'll have to borrow your jacket." She looks up at him with a little grin and as he kisses the top of her head, making their way to the pier, a thrill runs through her.

The boat churns its way to the Jersey shore and back to the New York Harbor, half empty. Jaime drapes his jacket over Miriam's shoulders and they stand at the prow, watching the dark gray foamy waters divide, pressing close to each other. Clouds drift over the round hazy moon and little white saucers, cast by fog beams, dance on the rippled water. Somewhere, unseen, an accordian is playing and a wobbly voice sings "O Solo Mio."

"Remember the poem by Shelley about the moon?" Miriam asks. "You read it to us when we were little kids. When I found it in my poetry book in high school and I memorized it. 'And like a dying lady, lean and pale/Who totters forth, wrapped in a gauzy veil/The moon rose up in the murky East/A white and shapeless mass.'"

"Yes, I remember, Miriam," he says. "I used to watch your face when I read it."

She doesn't answer. It's quiet again except for the dusky wail of fog horns across the choppy water.

They dock and as they walk down 125th Street, Jaime asks, "What now? Where do we go from here?"

He would like to tell her that he's waited so long for this night, it can't end now … but meanwhile she's slipping off his jacket, handing it to him.

"Thank you, you're very kind." Her voice warm, teasing, but under the lamp light, her face is troubled. "Jaime, I don't know where we can go now—it's getting late." And after a moment's hesitation her reasonable self beginning to assert itself. "I'd better go home. There's work tomorrow."

"Okay—if that's what you want." Trying to sound offhand, not succeeding. "Let's get a cab—you 'll be home in a jiffy, as Ketzel would say."

"No—wait." She doesn't the evening to end—not so quickly. "Let's walk home—it's not very far—not even a mile."

He doesn't answer, takes her hand and they walk down the wide street, mostly deserted now except for an occasional hobo staggering along, a sunken-eyed cat sniffing an over-flowing garbage can.

"Not exactly Lover's Lane," Jaime mutters.

"No," Attempting to recall a little of the light mood a few minutes ago, she says, "I remember when Ketzel and I were little, it was so bright, crowded with gay people. We'd go up and down the street, window shopping, stopping at the Apollo, looking at the pictures of the big Negro stars." She chatters brightly, holding his arm, looking up into his face.

"Let's walk more quickly—I'm sure you want to get home soon," he answers gruffly, and they don't talk until they've reached the apartment house on ll6th Street. The small entrance is dark, the heavy air laden with the smell of garbage. The elevator rattles its way up to the fourth floor landing, Miriam fumbles for her key and when she opens the door, stale air rushes out at them. Jaime follows her into the kitchen. he pulls a chain and the electric bulb dangling from the ceiling bursts into a blinding glare that bounces off the cracked, dingy plaster walls.

"So this is where you and Sydney live," he says.

"Yes—this is home." Embarrassed, sarcastic. "Everything we need—a chipped, metal table, two old wooden chairs—just right for luxury dining—our deluxe kitchen is even complete with dirty dishes in the sink."

Jaime starts to say something but she goes on, "It's awful and ugly—but I'm lucky we can manage the rent."

"Miriam, stop! Don't you think I know about being poor? I'm Mexican. I am a revolutionist—remember!" Then, his voice low, he says softly, "Chula, I'm not looking at where you live. How can that matter to me? I'm looking at you standing here under this light, a lovely girl." He comes closer. "Please, please don't stay tonight. This isn't a safe neighborhood for a woman to be alone. I'll worry if I leave you here."

"You want me to go home with you, I guess." Blurting her words looking up at him. "And I want to too, Jaime, but I don't know if it's the right thing to do." She feels her cheeks redden but she can't help plunging on. "I don't know if it's the right thing to do. I'm not sure it's a good idea."

Jaime looks down at her, laughs and lightly hugs her. "Look, just come home. You can sleep in the guest room on the top floor—the one with what you used to call 'the nosy tree.' I'll stay below, keep my distance." Then, seizing upon her hesitation, he takes the keys from her hand, goes to the door which is still open. "Please, Miriam." She nods with a faint smile.

It doesn't take long to find a taxi to the house and Jaime runs up the brownstone steps but Miriam stops, to look up at the wide brownstone bannisters curving out at the foot of the stairs. *They are like arms opening wide, welcoming me,* she thinks. *They always did, even after Fanny threw me out.*

Jaime insists on making some iced tea, while Miriam goes upstairs to Ketzel's room. She slips off her damp dress and finds a dark blue terry-cloth robe which she wraps about herself before joining Jaime in the kitchen. They sit with the rear garden door open, eating Uneeda Biscuits with butter and strawberry jam that Jaime finds in the cupboard. Jaime talks about the house needing quite a bit of work; he's been neglectful about necessary repairs but soon their conversation peters out and he goes to the doorway, lights his pipe, and stands looks out into the garden. Miriam, finishing her drink, realizing she's got to take the next step, takes a deep breath and stands up.

"Time to say good-night, Jaime. I'll find my way up—I know it pretty well." She gives him a brief hug and makes for the stairs, afraid to linger.

"What about a good-night kiss?" Jaime holds out a restraining arm but she ignores it, laughing "We'll make it a good morning kiss tomorrow." Gathering up the long robe that threatens to trip her she calls back "Good night, sweet prince, parting is such sweet sorrow," and quickly mounts the basement steps. *How dumb can I be?* she thinks, *mixing up Romeo and Juliet with Hamlet? That's what I get for trying to be poetic!*

She lies a long time in the wide double bed on the top floor listening to the muted ticking of a little clock and crickets beyond the thick grass below. A soft breeze flutters the curtains, the branches of the nosy tree rustle, its leaves casting moving shadows on the walls.

It's been a long time, almost two years since she loved him. But it goes back much further. It must have been since she was a little girl—the first day when Ketzel brought her to this house and she walked into the kitchen. He was there, a slender man wearing an apron, standing at the stove and when he'd turned and smiled—dark brown eyes—shaggy, shining hair, she'd thought—*he's so nice—he's so beautiful.* And then his voice when he said hello so rich and creamy, like poured chocolate. It began right then. He was always so good and gentle to her, so kind, and this house became a refuge for her. She'd visit Ketzel—even when she knew she was at her dance class. Jaime'd say 'wait for her' and he'd make hot cocoa just for her, talk to her and listen while she talked about the books she was reading.

When she sat with him she'd longed to touch his hair and when he'd get excited, a lock of his shiny hair would fall over his forehead. She'd want to reach over and brush it away but of course, she didn't dare.

Sometimes, he'd put his arms around Ketzel and her—he'd say, "My two girls," and Ketzel would reach up to hold his hand and she'd longed to.

Tonight they had been so easy with each other. Tonight, on the ferry—standing behind her, holding her close, his arms about her waist. She could feel his thin, hard body as she leaned against him—his lovely smell like soap, tobacco and sweat, sweet, like fresh cut grass. It felt so right, so good, so wonderful.

He's sitting downstairs by himself, she thinks. She punches the pillow, wider awake than ever. They don't agree politically—they're on different sides, but she knows that he's the kindest, gentlest person in the whole world.

Impatient, she swings her legs off the bed. She goes to the long, oval pier-glass mirror and raising her arms, stands there looking at her naked body. The golden glow of the little bedside lamp lights the delicate lines of her neck and shoulders, the almond-white of her legs, her slim waist. She raises her arm and traces with a finger, the arc of her small full breast down to a rosy-tipped nipple.

She thinks of him, so near and a magnet inside her pulls her to him. She thinks of his hands thrusting into her hair, his lips grazing the curve of her neck, his legs entwining hers. Her thighs have become heavy, her throat's tight, and her desire for him so great, she feels dizzy. With an effort, she turns towards the bed, shaking her head, and makes herself lie down.

Then, all at once, she jumps up and runs from the room.

Her heart beating wildly, she stops at the doorway of Jaime's study. Silent, she stands and watches him. His back to her, he sits under the light of his green glass desk lamp, twirling his front lock of hair, deep into a manuscript. *Well, evidently he's able to work, she thinks. He's not dying of unrequited love.* Maybe she's the only one who is and she's slightly amused. *You're a little crazy, she tells herself.*

Then she whispers, "Jaime." He turns and sees her there, her slender body like a white shining lily, encased in blue. He stares, astonished as she shyly holds out her arms. His face bursts into surprise and delight and she knows this is right. In an instant he crosses the room. Later she tells him, "I think you flew."

❧   ❧   ❧

At nine-thirty the next morning, Miriam hears noises in the kitchen, Jaime's making fresh-brewed coffee. She races downstairs, frantic.

"Oh, my God, it's so late. I was due at the office a half-an-hour ago."

"I hope you'll forgive me, querida." He's busy, looking for a potholder. "I called up and told them you were not feeling well, you couldn't be in today. Fortunately, Miss Croxdale wasn't in either. Sit down, querida, huevos rancheros, special, for us."

'I have to kiss you good-morning first."

"Absolutely, the coffee can wait."

Later, after they've enjoyed breakfast with good appetites and light hearts, Jaime asks,

"What shall we do—now that I have freed you? How about the beach? We'll lie in the sun, get tan and buy hot-dogs with sauerkraut." Jaime grins across the table. "First we'll have to go buy you a bathing suit."

"It sounds great. Let me think if I can."

"Why can't you! I thought we would have this day for us?," his voice tinged with annoyance.

"At last week's meeting we were given a Branch assignment, told to make it if possible," Miriam explains. "I really should go … the Nazis are having a big demonstration in Madison Square Garden on Friday, we're giving out leaflets in Yorkville tonight."

Jaime puts down his cup, starts to speak—stops—then begins again. "Listen, Miriam—we have to talk."

"I know, Jaime." She's serious, a little frightened. "We have to."

"No, I don't think you do know. I want to talk about us." He gets up at the door, lights a cigarette. He stands there, looking out at the garden.

"Many times, Miriam,—all that long period when we didn't see each other, many things went through my mind. Even then, I knew I loved you and I thought, I hoped, you cared for me." He comes back, stands at the table, looks at her.

"Now that we know, we discovered last night," he says. "I want us to be together. Do you want to—is it possible?"

Miriam puts down her cup so quickly it clatters on the saucer. She looks up at him, her eyes shining, tells him shyly, "All I dreamed about in the last couple of years was—that you'd be in love with me. Now, it's happened." She pauses, "About Sydney. I'd really hate to hurt him. But, I think, we both knew it wasn't very serious and it probably wouldn't last very long. But what about Ketzel?"

Jaime sits down, reaches for her hand, "She'll be fine. She loves you." But … Miriam hesitates, "The age difference …"

"Ketzel is intelligent enough to accept our age difference. She's sophisticated enough to know that there's always been such relationships. You wouldn't know about it but about 1926 there was a Peaches scandal, she was only eighteen years old—Browning was old enough to be her father, or take your President, Andrew Jackson. He married a girl more than twenty-five years younger and had a big family—"

"Okay, Jaime—that's enough." Miriam laughs. "Did you do research in American history so you could argue the point? You don't have to convince *me*."

Jaime grins. "Not really. It just came to mind. Anyway,—what do you say—Can I write Adelita and tell her to come to New York or shall we go to Mexico and be married there?" He leans over, kissing her but she stops him.

"Jaime, please listen. You're forgetting something very important. You're forgetting why I left here a few years ago, why I was thrown out."

"No—I haven't." He goes to the stove to refill his cup, then looking sharply at her, he says, "Miriam, I've thought a lot about this. I know how dedicated you are politically and I respect, I'll always respect, your opinions. You and your comrades are wrong—insane—but that's beside the point. You have to drop the Workers Party, the Trotskyites. It's important to me." Jaime pauses, remaining at the stove, his voice strained, "I've thought about this a great deal. You don't have to belong to an organization. Just be an ordinary citizen for awhile—so we can be together."

"Whoa, stop right there. Just what are you asking me to do—forget politics?" She begins to tremble, her voice unsteady. "You want us to get married. I want that too. But let me understand this. You're saying I can go to work or be a housewife—maybe even have a baby—stay home and cook but no politics—especially the kind you don't agree with. Do you expect your wife to shut up about her political beliefs when they differ from yours?" Her voice has become sharp with sarcasm. "Maybe you'd like to have a large family. They're now giving 'heroine rewards' in Russia for women with lots of babies." She clasps her hands so hard they're white. "What about you? What are you going to do? Of course, you'll still have your writing—your career and of course you'll still be a C P member. How would you feel if I asked you to give up being a Stalinist?"

Jaime winces, flushing, "I wish you wouldn't use that term. Yes, I'll still remain a Party member. There are many reasons for my doing so—but the main one is that I do believe in the Party—and its leadership." He's defensive, he knows, and it annoys him.

Miriam stands up. She's angry now, her voice loud and sharp. "Just which leaders do you believe in? Isn't that a good question? Are there any left? Your great leader, Stalin, is killing off all of them and I do mean all of them—all the old Bolsheviks—the generals—Zinoviev—Kamenev—Tukachavesky—sending them to Siberia, putting them in front of a firing squad."

Jaime's turned away, looking at the red geraniums on the window-sill as if the solution to their dilemma might be hidden somewhere amid the petals.

"The phony trials, the terror in Russia." Now she's yelling. "People are afraid to talk, afraid that they'll be taken away in the middle of the night—even your own friends—what happened to Alana and Arthur?"

"Enough!" Jaime shouts, glaring at her. Miriam stops, afraid she's going to burst into tears.

Then, after a minute his voice hoarse and bitter says, "This isn't getting us anywhere."

The room is deadly quiet. Miriam thinks, *this is unreal, it can't be happening.* She sits down again at the table and looks at Jaime, at the stove, lighting a cigarette, his hand shaking. Her head down, she looks at the white cloth, seeing nothing, drained, empty.

Jaime, his face impassive, takes a deep drag, waiting. She knows he wants her to deny what she's just said, he wants her to reassure him that everything will be as it was ten minutes before. But she can't. It can't be.

"There isn't anything more I have to say." Getting up, wearily like an old woman, she leaves, slowly climbing the stairs.

She knows she should leave, get out of that house but instead throws herself on the bed, unable to move. She hears no sounds from below. A half-hour later she forces herself to dress, get her things and makes her way down. As she nears the front door, Jaime, who's been waiting in the hallway, grabs her wrist.

"Just let me say a word—please!"

Dazed, she looks at him. In just fifteen minutes, a wonderful night, an unbelievably happy world that bloomed like a morning glory has faded and gone. Jaime's a stranger now, his face ashen, his eyes dark, not the man she adored, the sweet, warm passionate man who had held her through the night …

Jaime says, "Why can't you trust me."

She waits until she can answer in what she hopes is a calm, reasonable statement. "It's mistake. You really don't know me, Jaime! You don't know how I think and feel—not really. I love you. I've always loved you. But I've grown up now and I think about the world and what happened—what happened to the wonderful dream that's now being destroyed by Stalinism but you … you're still in love with the little girl you took to the movies and I think that's what you want me to remain forever."

Jaime's mouth tightens into a sharp thin line. "Miriam—that's not fair! I told you—I respect you completely … you're an adorable, wonderful young woman but you tend to judge on the surface. There's so much you have to learn …" Jaime hesitates now … speaking softly, "So much I can't tell you. I want us so much to be together … Try to see it my way. You make political opinions too hastily made with too much emotion …"

"My political opinions?" Now, anger surges. "And to tell you what you already know, I don't respect yours. You and your Party have thrown away all regard for humanity—for people—for—" She pauses, choking, trying to keep her voice steady. "All you do is worship the Soviet Union. If someone doesn't he's a traitor and deserves to die. Well, that's not for me. I believe in truth and freedom. Keep your wonderful god Stalin—and your Party! Now let me go." Miriam pulls her arm from his grip, opens the door. Trying to escape the drumming in her ears, she dashes down the front steps.

Hearing Jaime behind her she doesn't see the iceman in front of the house and crashes into him. His dripping block of ice falls from his shoulder and smashes onto the sidewalk. He looks down at the damage, begins to curse in broken English, overriding her frantic apologies.

Jaime, standing, surrounded by shining slivers of ice already beginning to melt reaches into his pocket and produces five dollars. He murmurs in his best Italian, "Please take it, the lady is very sorry." The iceman's face broadens into a happy smile. He nods and says in heavily accented English, "Lovers' fight," then mounts his wagon, gently flicks the reins and his scrawny horse clops away.

Miriam want to go but can't move, her legs are like stone. She wants to be somewhere, hiding in a corner, like Kootah, her cat, after a bloody night, pain tearing her apart.

Jaime steps toward her. Neither speaks. As if all that had occurred in the past few minutes hasn't happened, they reach for each other. His arms hold her so close she can scarcely breathe. Fervently, they cling together.

When they pull apart, Jaime reaches for her hand. "Miriam, don't go. You aren't giving me a chance—you're not trying to understand. Don't let it happen …"

"But it's happening. It had to." When she looks up at him, sees his soft brown eyes full of love and pain, she can't bear it another minute. "I'm really sorry, I love you." She's crying. "I'm so sorry for both of us."

Jaime pulls her to him again. She reaches up and brushes away the lock on his forehead. He bends, searching again for her lips but she turns her head. Her legs trembling, swaying, she forces herself to walk down the street. At the corner, she glances back, Jaime has not moved, his eyes still follow her.

On Fifth Avenue she hesitates before she makes her way to Mount Morris Park. Still shaking, she sits on a bench. Now it's over, once and for all. He couldn't see the truth although he'd said long ago that truth was the most important thing in the world. She remembers once, long ago, when Ketzel was about ten years old and she'd asked her father what color her eyes were, he said they were the most beautiful green he'd ever seen.

"What about Miriam's?" Ketzel asked him. "Come here, Miriam, let me look" Jaime told her. They'd been in the kitchen, drinking hot chocolate, after skating on the lake in Central park.

"Come," he says, softly, smiling. She stood in front of him, frightened and shy, holding her head and body rigid but when his fingers cupped her head and gently tilted it, a surge of delight went through her.

"Your eyes," he had said, looking deeply into her small face, "Your eyes are like deep pools, "'aquafirs,'" water that springs up from layers of rocks that deep down in the earth. When you look into their depths, the light is so clear, so translucent—it's as if you are seeing the very center of the universe."

He would have gone on but Ketzel interrupted "You haven't said her eyes are pretty! Are they or aren't they?'

Jaime laughed. "Ketzel, mi amor," he said, "Miriam's eyes are gray, not pretty like yours but they are so thoughtful, as if she is always looking for the truth."

The truth. But, of course, no matter what she could or might have said, to him today, it wouldn't have made any difference. Jaime is a diehard Stalinist, he and his friend down the street, Rosenblit. He swallows falsehoods because he wants to believe them, he *has* to believe them.

Isn't it great luck, a metallic taste like iodine, in Miriam's mouth rises in her mouth, almost choking her. Jaime—this wonderful man she's simply crazy about—but he's blind, refusing to see the truth. Why does it have to turn out this way?

Her body feels like an empty husk, her face like yellow paper, her lips dry and salty. The August sun is full in the sky, brilliant, blazing through the parched leaves of the oak above her. She's baking. Dazzled by the glare, she staggers to her feet. She doesn't realize she's crying until she tastes the salty tears trickling down her cheeks.

When she arrives at her apartment she lies down and sleeps all afternoon. She knows she has to go to Yorkville that night to do an assignment, distributing announcements of an open meeting being held next week. Ben the Ape, homely, brilliant and sarcastic, especially with the women, is meeting her there—comrades are never allowed to do these things alone. She goes to meet him and for more than an hour, until their supply is exhausted, they hand out leaflets to weary workers looking forward to home and dinner.

She scarcely notices Ben's wisecracks which usually get under her skin. The emotional see-saw of the past twenty-four hours have left her exhausted and numb, and after Ben leaves her, annoyed at her indifference to his barbs, she stands on a corner, not knowing what to do. She realizes she can't go back to that hot, empty apartment tonight, she can't be alone, she has to be with someone. She calls Rhoda but there's no answer. Then Sylvia.

"Where were you today? I've been trying to get hold of you," Sylvia says. "It's Ruby's birthday. She's brought all kinds of goodies."

"I'm not sure I can be good company." The thought of a party—tonight! "The heat's got me down and Ben was annoying as usual."

"We have lots to eat—I bet you haven't had supper yet," her gentle voice is persuasive. "Miriam, come. If it gets too late you can sleep over. I know you're alone this week—my place is probably a little cooler than yours."

Their large apartment, furnished with plush sofas and easy chairs, is airy and dim—the blinds drawn to keep out the blazing red sun setting across the river, and now she's a little glad she decided to come after all.

"You look tired. Are you okay?," Sylvia asks when Miriam arrives. Her solicitude touches Miriam and her spirits begin to lift a little. She takes off her shoes and sips cold sangria. Everyone, including Ruby, greets her warmly. *These are my comrades*, Miriam thinks. *My friends—people who value truth above every-*

thing—who don't permit unreasoning faith or hero worship to blind them to reality. She needs them. especially tonight.

After they blow out the candles on a white cake decorated with pink and yellow roses and sing happy birthday, Miriam sprawls on a couch and listens to Ruby. Tonight even Ruby is included in Miriam's feelings of warm comradeship.

"I'm staying with some relatives temporarily," Ruby tells her. "I want to get some kind of work in New York. Meanwhile I'm taking evening courses in N Y U. That's how I met Sylvia and now we're good friends," her smile a bit smug. Miriam notices her self-assurance, she seems to know just what she wants. It's a trait that Sylvia lacks, Miriam observes, and that's why Sylvia's attracted to Ruby. But Ruby doesn't seem to be very knowledgeable about politics and so when everyone starts to talk about Trotsky's counter-trial in Mexico she just listens.

"Don't you just love it," Rhoda's saying, "when these great writers, Romain Rolland, and Dreiser say Trotsky has no business trying to defend himself, that he's giving 'aid and comfort to Fascism.' It's just their excuses to avoid looking at what's going on in the Soviet Union. They're such cowards." Rhoda shakes her head, her disgust not slowing her attack on a large bowl of fruit salad.

"Right," Hilda says. "And what about Andre Gide and H.G. Wells—talk about 'weak sisters.'"

"Thank God for people like Carlo Tresca," Esther says. "I met him just the other day in Union Square. Oh, I just love those sexy Italians! That big black hat and wide scarf. I told him that we appreciated his support." She's unable to resist adding, "He told me that I was a very pretty lady." She laughs, everyone grins. Esther's beautiful and well aware of it, Miriam thinks. At our street-corner meetings crowds gather fast when they see this gorgeous young woman on a small wooden step-ladder, shaking her fist at the injustices of the capitalist system and even if they don't agree with her they listen and buy our paper.

Then inevitably, the conversation turns to the war in Spain.

"Is Ketzel still there?," asks Sylvia. "Last I heard she was a hit in Barcelona. But it's so dangerous there."

"Ketzel's a hit anywhere she goes." Miriam answers, getting a refill of Sangria. "She just wrote. She and Martin are probably in Madrid by now. She said it seemed like the revolution had come and gone—no May Day parade, even. And there's shortages of most everything—but not for the folks with money." She takes a big gulp of her drink and her voice becomes harsh. "The Russians are no dopes, they're getting their money's worth supplying the old guns for millions of Spanish gold! But they have to work hard! Killing 'Trotskyites' isn't easy. But it isn't hard," Miriam interrupts herself. "Wiping out oppositionists—phony trials, firing squads, Siberia. And our dear Stalinists here, in America, raising money, loyally supporting them, closing their eyes to what's happening—the writers in The New Masses—publishing lies about what's really happening there—getting young kids to volunteer for the Lincoln Brigade fighting against fascism but saving Spain for bourgeois democracy and above all—to save Stalinism ..."

"Oh, right! The democracies!" Hilda interrupts, shrilly. "God bless 'em, America, France, England. Supplying oil and other stuff to Franco and Mussolini. Oh hurray for the democracies of the world ... 'Democracies of the World Unite, you have nothing to lose—'" She stops. "But maybe World War II."

"And while we're cheering the democracies, let's raise the glass for Stalin and his murderous cohorts—in Russia and in Spain." Miriam waves her empty glass. "May they all rot in hell!"

There's silence. Then Ruby suggests, "How about if we talk about something a little more cheerful. After all, it *is* my birthday."

"For God's sake, it's so hot in here." Miriam's face is flushed, she mutters, "Sylvia, don't you have another fan?"

"I think you ought to stop drinking," Rhoda says. "It's not that hot in here now. You've had enough tonight."

The party ends shortly afterwards. Sylvia, realizing that Miriam's in no condition to help her clear up, escorts her to one of the bedrooms where a large old fan's whirling noisily away. After she softly closes the door, Miriam, unable to tolerate the dress clinging to her sweating body, pulls it off with trembling fingers. She wipes her forehead with a damp towel, trying to hold back the aching memory of the night before—the lovemaking and the sweetness.

"It's over, it's over," she keeps repeating, and sobs until she falls asleep.

Coyoacan, Fall 1937

With the excitement of the hearings over, things settle down in the Blue House. Despite the welcome Trotsky and Natalya have received in Mexico, despite the findings of the Dewey Commission, concern for their safety remains paramount. Rivera has seen to it that windows facing the street are bricked up, and staff members assist police on night duty. The Communist press rants against Trotsky constantly, and Stalinist-dominated labor unions hold street demonstrations almost daily demanding that the exiles get out of Mexico.

One morning, at dawn, strains of a marimba band playing outside their bedroom window awaken them. An all-day celebration begins—Trotsky's birthday and the anniversary of the October Revolution. People come and go, friends, workers, union members bringing simple gifts, even live chickens with their legs tied together. There's music and feasting from morning till night and at the end Trotsky makes a simple speech of appreciation for their affection and hospitality.

Trotsky relaxes with Diego, even seeing him without an appointment, admires Diego's imagination and his ability to understand people. In discussing Mexican politicans with him Trotsky begins to see that things and events might be viewed differently from the way he thinks. On his part, Rivera admires Trotsky's courage, his tremendous talent as a writer and orator, and respects his stern convictions. They will remain friends for almost two years, despite the ups and downs in their relationship.

Trotsky needs and seeks exercise, challenges that nature, an impersonal enemy, provides. He must always walk fast, never amble or stroll. All the security sometimes makes him feel as if he is under house arrest. Occasionally, when he's given the loan of a horse, he will tear away, riding fast up into the rocky hills, almost losing his companions and aggravating his guards who have a hard time keeping up with him.

CHAPTER 12

Madrid, Fall 1937

Ketzel can't stop yawning. She stands on the balcony of the Hotel Florida, looking down on Plaza de Calla covered with pinkish-gray pebbles. They chose a front room because it faced the square. Unfortunately it also faces the German batteries, seventeen blocks away, near Mount Garabitas.

At dawn two tremendous blasts of shrapnel shook the building, one of the them splitting open the hot water tank, steam clouds billowing up along the halls. Guests spilled out of their rooms in bathrobes, dragging their suitcases and mattresses, and as Ketzel and Martin rushed out of their room they bumped into John Dos Passos. Apparently he'd been shaving; there was still some foam on his face. In front of them, heading for the lobby was Ernest Hemingway with his arm around the journalist, Martha Gellhorn, followed by the author Josephine Herbst, all in their robes. When Hemingway greeted Herbst with a cool "How are you?," she opened her mouth but couldn't speak, and Saint-Exupery, standing by the staircase in a blue satin robe, asked everyone coming down, "Voulez-vous une pamplemousse?" Apparently he'd received a large supply of grapefruits from somewhere. Later at breakfast, downstairs, which was lively, they talked about the hit; the movie theatre showing Charlie Chaplin's "Modern Times" had been completely destroyed.

Back in her room, Ketzel notices the rumpled bedclothes. The sheets piled up at the foot of the bed look like a stormed Medieval castle, she thinks with a wry grin. When she and Martin returned last night he'd put his arm about her and whispered "Let's have a little party of our own." She was wearing a nun's habit, complete, from the chemise underneath to the skull cap, but that's not how she felt last night. He hadn't been so amorous for some time and Ketzel wondered if that gorgeous, blonde girl-friend of Hemingway, with her sexy walk and long legs, had fired him up.

After three years of being with Martin, it was still easy to lose herself to his kisses. It was fortunate for her that the women they were closest to in Spain—Tina Modotti and Caridad Mercader, beautiful and passionate, with lots of experience, were older, otherwise she might have had competition. *A half Jewish-half Mexican girl like me can't hold a candle to red hot Latin mamas,* she thinks. But that isn't necessarily true, either. How about Frida Kahlo?—she's like me—Mexican and Jewish. She sure gets around, but that's because she's tremendously attractive—to men and women alike, she's heard.

A few moments later, Tina knocks at her door. In a long skirt and a dark red serape Ketzel's taken aback by her ravishing beauty, faded but still there. A poet once described her as having "a liquid look as dark as antique honey" except that now, at forty-one, her face is deeply lined and her magnificent dark eyes heavily circled. In Mexico she'd been a photographer, Edward Weston's lover for a while, and then expelled in 1930 for revolutionary activity.

"I see you're not quite ready this morning but I'm here with my Leica, Ketzel." Tina, looking about the disorderly room, says impatiently, "Can we get started? I've an important meeting in an hour."

I don't think she likes me, Ketzel thinks. She probably considers me a dilettante, not an ardent Communist like herself. Now, she's doing me a favor by taking some photographs for my dance recital. It could be Caridad twisted her arm.

Ketzel has already dressed for her sitting with Tina, wearing a nun's habit that Caridad's loaned her. It's complete with a chemise that covers a tunic, a neck scarf and scapular, her luxuriant hair hidden under a skull.

"Where on earth did Caridad get this outfit?," Tina wants to know. "Tell me what this is all about. Come, let's go to the window," positioning her there so that her profile is outlined against the light.

"Caridad was a novitiate as a sister in the Carmelite Order," Ketzel explains, sitting very still, lifting her chin a little.

"Let's try you in another pose. I'd like to take you looking out of the window—holding one arm high as if you're signalling someone—Your back should be rigid—as if there's danger—yes—that's good. Good."

"About this nun's habit—I'm choreographing a new dance. I'm awfully excited about it," Ketzel tells her. "I heard Carl Orff's music, someone just brought us the record. It's brand new! Hot off the press. Fourteenth century, Benedictine monks stuff. 'Carmina Burana.' Knocked me for a loop! Sexy music … really thrilling! Wait—let me show you something." Ketzel jumps up, begins to move around the room, bending her head, putting her hands together, praying, "I won't do the beginning—it's very slow and solemn—the nuns are doing their devotionals but then it starts to build up and here's where they do some really erotic dancing to fast, loud choral music—I have them twisting and whirling in a sort of frenzy—it's really wild and incongruous in those long, black garments. Of course it's mocking the Church, which should go over big nowadays. I've just started to work on it." She stops, and sits down. "Look, I don't want to make you late."

The older woman says, "That's okay, but I'm really busy and must leave soon." Ketzel has the impression that she's really not interested. She may be thinking about own personal problems and she's already had plenty. Right now she is married to Vidali, whom she fears and hates. He's a powerful leader in the Communist Party, and it's rumored that when they all were in Mexico, he was the murderer of her beloved Julio Mella,

"Let's finish up now." Modotti says, looking at her impassively, "Important Party work is waiting for me."

That night, Ketzel and Martin walk through the deserted streets of Madrid. "The quiet before the storm," Martin says. "Before the nightly bombing begins. Look at this Plaza Mayor, the most beautiful in the City—built in the seventeenth century—almost destroyed." Just then a street car with muffled red lights noisily passes and then it becomes quiet again. "Hungry people, dying soldiers." Ketzel murmurs sadly. "How long will it go on—and we aren't winning—."

"The other day Koltzov said something. He said it like it was funny, but …" Seeing her questioning look, he explains, "He's that big-shot correspondent for Pravda—he's got a sharp tongue, very witty and Hemingway really likes him, says he's going to put him in a book he's doing on Spain. Right now he's in favor in Moscow but I heard a story, something's happened. When he in Moscow the last time Stalin asked him if he has a revolver. Sure, he answered. Then Stalin asks, 'Are you going to shoot yourself with it?' Koltzov's says he's trying to figure out what that remark means, but of course he must know his days are numbered."

"Oh," says Ketzel, "That's awfully funny, isn't it." But they've reached their destination and as she pushes open the heavy door of the Capitol Hotel she says, "God, smell the ether." In one corner of the grimy, faded lobby are four litters of wounded soldiers who have just been brought in. Ketzel starts to move towards them but Martin pulls her back. "No, let me go," she says and walks over.

One of them is a young boy, about sixteen, the entire bottom of his sheet covered with blood. "*Mein fuss—mein fuss.*" he mutters, turning his head from side to side. Kezel bends down, reaches for his hand, whispers "Hello," to him and smiles. He tries to smile back for a moment, his eyes filling with tears. Martin, his face stiff with annoyance, says, "Ketzel, let's go. We'll be late. We can't do anything for him," and walks to the door quickly, making Ketzel follow.

The dining hall is crowded, filled with heavy smoke, loud voices, aromas of smoked meats and rum, but there's little laughter or hilarity, an undercurrent of uneasiness prevails. As they stand near the door, Martin whispers to Ketzel. "This evening is very important to me. Caridad is going to introduce me to General Kotov—he might have an important assignment for me. Don't spoil it."

"Why didn't you tell me this before?"

"What difference would it make. Now, wait here and I'll go over to get us some champagne."

Martin hurries off. A few moments later a small man with cold eyes, bald with a beard and mustache, approaches Ketzel. Looking into her eyes, taking her hand, he says in heavily accented English "I see a very beautiful girl alone and that is not good. Let me introduce myself. I am General Kotov." Before she can respond Caridad and Ramon are beside her. Caridad kisses her warmly and Ramon nods, a faint smile on his thin lips. "Not my type," Ketzel thinks. "But he's handsome with large, strong features. Likes women. Caridad said he just had a romance with a Danish girl."

"Ah, I see you've already met Martin's wife," Caridad says to the general. It's apparent from the way she greets him that this mature woman, mother of five children, is very much in love, dizzy over him like a school-girl. Ketzel wonders, "Why? The heavy brows and full lips, the icy eyes and everyone says he has a wife and kids in Moscow? Caridad must know. Guess he's good in bed. Not my cup of tea for sure!," and manages a charming smile as they move to the lavish buffet. *Not like in Barcelona*, Ketzel thinks, *seems like great food and Russians go together!*

Over coffee and Grand Marnier, Caridad turns to Ketzel and says, "Ramon and I are hoping you'll come with us to Barcelona."

Ketzel's almost too surprised to answer immediately. She looks at Martin quizzically and then responds slowly, "We'll have to talk about it. I haven't thought about going back to Barcelona and ..."

Martin interrupts. "I was going to—later." Turning to Kotov and Ramon, "I certainly will get there. We haven't had time to talk about it."

When they've left and are out in the street, Ketzel turns furiously to Martin. "You know I have no intentions of going back to Barcelona. I expect to meet my group in Paris. What plans have you been making without telling me?"

"For God's sake, keep your voice down." Martin's face is dark with anger. Then, sarcastically, "You sound like a fishwife from the lower east side. Now, let me explain." He begins to speak slowly, measuring each word. "You should be proud of your husband. General Kotov and General Orlov, he's Chief of N K V D, and some others, Siquieros, the Arenals, want me to attend a special training school in Barcelona. There's very important work to be done—getting rid of the Oppositionists—the troublemakers. Now what do you think of that?" He can't help pride seeping into the last sentence.

Ketzel takes a deep breath. She knows her quick temper and she doesn't want her honeymoon to end up badly so she tries to answer in a mild tone. "I don't know anything about those generals, except that Caridad's in love with Kotov. But why are the Soviet secret police involved? What's the important work they do?" In spite of herself, her voice rises.

Martin kisses her cheek, deciding to placate her. "Let me explain, Ketzel. There's been a lot of sabotage—anarchists, Trotskyites. This school teaches how to find them, root them out and deal with them." He can't resist adding that he's been given secret information not too many are given privy to. "That's how they were able to take care of Andres Nin." He's almost bragging.

Ketzel stops walking, looks up at him, saying "Who's Andres Nin? No. Don't answer. I don't want to know anything about the Trotskyites."

Martin, thinking he might have said too much, puts his arms around her, holds her close, kisses her and says, "Forget it. All that's important is for you to understand how important this is for me. And how much I love you."

They go back to their room, make love and the upshot of the discussion later that night, is that Ketzel will postpone working on the new ballet; they will go to Barcelona for a short time, then she will go on to Paris where she'll meet up with some of her troupe.

"Didn't we handle the problem in a mature way?" Martin asks, embracing her in bed.

The next morning, Ketzel, too lazy to get up, stretches contendedly, reviewing the past evening. She and Martin seem to be able to working out most of their problems. But some of those people—they give her the creeps. There's a smugness about them—they're just a little too arrogant and cocky. But Martin's happy with his new job and although it could be dangerous, she's glad for his sake. She forces herself to get out of bed, she must get going, and as she's carefully applying her mascara, she wonders—*What did Martin meant about taking care of that man—Andres Nin—whoever he is—or was—if 'taking care of someone' means what she thinks it does. No,* she decides, *I'm not going to think about that—it's not for me. I don't want to get into it. I can't stand it.*

Miriam scarcely notices the changing leaves that year although autumn is spectacularly beautiful, the trees flaunting their gold and vermillion banners against chilly, blue skies. The last evening with Jaime haunts her dreams and fills her waking thoughts.

Even Sydney, usually preoccupied with his own depression, notices her gray mood. In answer to his question about what's troubling her, she says it's about war in Spain, which is true enough, even if it isn't the whole truth. Although Sydney had given up, deciding victory was hopeless, Miriam continues following reports in The Times and the New York Herald Tribune hoping against hope but the news is mostly bad. Although there had been a victory in Belchite after terrific fighting and horrible losses of men in October, the Franco forces had launched a counter-offensive and finally on the nineteenth had taken Gijon, Aviles and Oviedo, succeeding in completing the capture of northern Spain. Germany and Italy are continuing to supply Franco with all his needs, including Italian "blue-arrows" while the blockade of the other European countries is successfully destroying the Republicans' cause.

Sydney's got his own reasons to be unhappy. He's been laid off from his Wall Street job and works in an electrical appliance store, on 59th Street, near the Queensborough Bridge, selling vacuum cleaners. It pays poorly and he hates it but he and Miriam manage without too much trouble on their combined weekly income of forty dollars. She often makes fish or beef liver which cost only ten or fifteen cents a pound and the butcher sometimes throws in a few marrow bones for soup. "It's good," Sydney answers when she asks him how he likes the dinner, but he can't hide a lack of enthusiasm, he's never hungry. He never cares about much except the movement. Sometimes she wonders about the enthusiasm he'd displayed during their first and second meeting, had it been entirely genuine? Had it been to attract her attention, to sell himself? Now that they were living together he had become withdrawn and depressed. Only politics held any interest for him and when they had a free evening together they'd end up going to the movies on Broadway and 145th Street. *Perhaps now I'm getting to know the real Sydney,* Miriam thinks wearily.

Harry Milton comes for dinner one night. Since his return from Spain, he's given several talks around the country on his experiences, and is on his way to Chicago where he and another comrade will address a Socialist Party meeting. Seated at the kitchen table, waving his fork, he compliments Miriam. "Betht beef thtew I ever had." And after he devours two large helpings and washes it down with the bottle of cheap wine he'd brought, he begins to speak about the latest developments in that country. When Sydney asks about Andreas Nin, the leader of the P O U M, who's been missing in Barcelona and there's been a lot of publicity about it lately, his usual cheerful expression changes.

"Yeth, I heard. Nin used to be a good friend of the Old Man's and they corresponded a lot when Trotsky was in Alma Ata, but they had political differences. The Old man was kind of impatient with him—called him a Menshevik, especially when the P O U M went into the Generalitat. When Stalin began his witch-hunt, with the phony trials, saying that Trotsky was a Nazi—Hitler's agent—well, you know the story, they did the same thing in Spain to discredit any opposition to their taking over the government. But they couldn't get honest, good men like Nin and other comrades to confess to any treason—or anything. Well, that thon-of-a-bitch, Antonov-Ovseenko, the Russian Consul General in Barcelona, had Nin taken to Alcala de Henares where they used their thpecial Soviet techniques to get him to talk. When he wouldn't—he had nothing to confess, they got this other thon-of-a-bitch, Vittorio Vidali, Contreras, to plan a 'a Nazi attack' to 'liberate' him. They took ten Germans from the International Brigade, put Nazi uniforms on them and had them attack the house where he was imprisoned. They spoke in German and left behind train tickets like he was a Nazi agent planning a getaway. They put him in a closed van—caried him off. There's no question. He was killed somewhere along the line."

"Harry, it's so awful—so terrible. When will it stop—will it ever stop?" Miriam puts down the coffee pot so abruptly that the brown liquid spills over on the stove.

"How are the comrades doing in Chicago?" Sydney glances over at Miriam—time to change the subject. "Are the meetings still going on 'till 2 a. m.? The important thing is, are we making any headway in the S P. Will we have gotten some new members after we're kicked out of the S P?"

"It looks that way. Cannon seems very optomistic about that—and about our future too." Harry's somber face lightens. "The Minneapolis comrades feel great about what's happened—they've got a very strong position in the labor movement and they're planning the December convention so that the trade unionism will take priority before anything else; they don't want it to get into a discussion of the Russian question."

"Yeah, I heard that," Sydney says. "It's good news but Jim's pessimistic about New York—the membership here. He says we've got a defeatist attitude and I can't say he's wrong."

"Well, if you ask me, guys like Burnham don't help the situation very much." Harry frowns, "For my money, he's a shilly-shallying intellectual—and a snob. He looks down on some comrades but in spite of that, listen to this, I heard Cannon's offered him the job of national secretary in the Party ... a couple of times ..."

"Aren't we supposed to have an election for that?. Aren't we supposed to vote on who's going to be national secretary?" Miriam at the ice-box, taking out some cheddar cheese, interrupts sharply, "What gives Cannon the right to offer him that position?"

"You're probably right. It would seem to be an abrogation of democratic procedure. Why don't you bring it up at the next Party meeting?" Sydney has that little slightly mocking grin that always annoys her. "Are there some crackers in the house—saltines, maybe?"

Between work at the Municipal Art Gallery, Hunter College and Workers Party meetings, Miriam is so busy she often feels like she's a mouse on a treadmill. On rare occasions she goes go up to l56th Street to see her mother. Clara has seen her worst fears realized; her long struggle to hang onto the apartment buildng on 156th Street ended late in the summer when the bank foreclosed. Clara hardly seems to react, she's used to hard knocks. Now she's managing someone's else's building on 151st Street, living in a three-room apartment that she gets in lieu of pay, and rents out two of the rooms to cover expenses.

When Miriam does go to see her mother she deliberately assumes a cheerful air; she doesn't want to add to Clara's troubles, and at the same time she isn't eager to admit that living with Sydney hasn't worked out very well. Her mother doesn't think much of Sydney, and even though Miriam has come to agree with her, she doesn't want Clara to know it. Occasionally, friends notice she isn't her usual cheerful self but there isn't anyone she can confide in; comrades are just too busy, with Party work and the rest of their lives. *Everyone has their own problems,* she tells herself.

One night at 116 University Place, she meets with Hilda at the headquarters of her branch, one that'd been expelled from the Socialist Party. There'd been several expulsions, all over the country. *No wonder we were so busy this past year and a half,* she thinks. Since the Trotskyists couldn't have a press of their own while they were in the S P (they'd put a ban on our publications) a great system had been worked out. A "personal" letter, from one comrade to another, discussing new issues and the resolutions, was mimeographed and distributed all over the counry. All of the Trotskyist factions got necessary information, were able to organize better and succeeded in making good headway. But after the Socialist Party instituted "Gag Laws" it was decided to call it a day, time to get out of the S P. Practically all of the young people who were really serious and capable of becoming proletarian revolutionists had been recruited; the comrades had been in constant touch with the Old Man in Mexico who was doing everything in his power to help. It's over now—in December there'll be a convention of all the expelled branches in Chicago ... *She'd love to go, but it's out of the question.*

"What's with you these days—I haven't seen you at any of the B S & A U meetings," Hilda asks.

"There's lot of reading and also writing assignments in this English course and they pile it on." Miriam answers wearily. Then, wanting to change the subject, "How's Sylvia? How come she's not here?"

"Busy with Ruby." Hilda's tone was slightly sarcastic. "A lot."

"If she's going back to Chicago she could attend the founding Convention? Think of it, on New Year's Day there'll be a new Party ... The Socialist Workers Party of America!"

"Right," Hilda answered, her voice amused. "I remember when we had all those debates about entering the S P a few years ago. You were against the idea, weren't you?"

Miriam, smiling sheepishly, recalls. "All I can say, Hilda, I had more nerve than brains. Some others, better theoreticians than I am, like Stamm and Oehler, opposed it too. But I felt it was dishonest and that it would hurt, not help us and I was wrong. It was a good move, but I'll never forget how benevolent and patronizing Cannon was when I made my little speech. He said he respected my honest opinion—I was a young comrade. Although he didn't say this I knew it was also because I was a female. You know the petty bourgeois attitude of our comrades, we women make good gofers."

Miriam stopped a moment and beckoned to Sydney, who had come in late. "Where was I?—Oh, yes. He said, 'Since Comrade Miriam is not politically experienced she can't understand these necessary tactical moves.' You know how musical his voice is … it's almost like he was singing those kind, understanding words.Then, when he spoke, he quoted Trotsky about the 'French Turn' … 'our tiny group needs to get some flesh on our bones' … since we weren't a real Party yet, we weren't violating any principles of Marxism.' When he finished, I crept back to my seat thinking I'd never do anything like that again. They talk about equality and socialism, but our comrades do still have petit-bourgeois attitudes towards women. The funny thing is, he really meant to be gentle and kind."

"Well, he was," Sydney said emphatically who'd been listening to most of it. "You had no business getting up there and exposing your political ignorance."

Miriam wanted to say something but decided against it. Sydney's right in a way, she wasn't as politically knowledgeable as she'd like to be but why did he have to say it like that. Sighing, she turned to Hilda, saying "Tell Sylvia to call me at work—I'd like to see her."

Hilda answered, "I'll tell her." Turning to Sydney, she said, "We know we can't all be Rosa Luxemburgs but we can try."

A week later Sylvia calls Miriam and and makes a date for a movie. "'Let's go see '*Madchen in Uniform*.'" It's supposed to have very fine photography, has a sad ending—supposed to be very good—banned in Germany." They agree to meet Friday night on 14th Street in front of the Consolidated Edison building. When Miriam emerges from the subway she walks slowly so she could look at the tall building brightly lit, the high tower, the great clock illuminating the sky. She loves Union Square with its crowded streets, throngs of women bargain hunters pushing into Klein's and Ohrbachs apparel stores, the hot-dog stands and the "shlocky" stores selling five dollar wrist watches that rarely worked.

This is my 'home town, my people, she mused. *Seems like I've walked down this street forever.* Even before, when she was nineteen and worked in the Social Credit Office, she'd walk down Fourteenth Street for unemployment demonstrations, for union marches and for Socialist, Communist, Trotskyists, all kinds of radical meetings. She and Knute would come here, holding hands, kissing under a tree. And she had walked here with Sydney too but never with Jaime! Oh, Jamie, Jaime!

Since it was Friday and she's just cashed her pay check, she goes into Kleins and buys a pretty tan pongee blouse for $1.99. *I won't tell Sylvia where I bought it,* she decides. Sylvia shops in stores like B. Altman and Arnold Constable. But Miriam knows that plenty of bourgeois ladies from Westchester come to this store, grabbing up bargains. They're the same ones who go mornings to Westchester Square in the Bronx, looking for houseworkers. Negro women, standing in small groups, almost like a slave market, would get twenty-five cents an hour to clean their fancy homes.

As she passes a striped umbrella stand, she finds the spicy aroma of a Nathan's frankfurter irresistible. *It'll be a long time before we eat so I'd better have one,* she tells herself. The warm smile of the push-cart man helps lighten her mood, especially when he heaps a double scoop of sauerkraut on the bun.

Sylvia apologizes in her gentle way when they meet. "I know it's been awhile, I'm so glad to see you. Hilda's bringing Bunny and she and Ruby'll meet us after the movie. Ruth couldn't make it. She's been busy since she got back from the Dewey hearings."

After the movie which they both enjoyed and felt that it dealt with the problem of homosexuality in a very sensitive way, they head for a cafe on 5th Avenue and Twelve Street where the others are waiting.

"You know," said Miriam, as they study the menus. "A couple of our comrades, Morris Miller and Ed Findlay, were beaten up right near here, on Seventh Avenue and Twelfth Street when they were giving out leaflets for Cannon when he was running for Mayor. They really got roughed up."

"A pleasant topic for meal time conversation," Hilda observes.

"Just thought I'd mention it—don't you appreciate that I brought it up before we started eating?" Miriam says, trying to hide her annoyance.

As she sips her iced coffee, Miriam, feeling she hasn't been very friendly towards Ruby, turns to her and asks, "Are you going back to Chicago before November? Henry Beatty and Harry Milton'll be speaking there."

Ruby smiles, shakes her head. "Yes, I know. I told my friends to be sure to make it." She hesitates, then adds, as if making up her mind, "I don't expect to go back to Chicago for some time. I like it here, especially because I've met nice people—."

"But you did say you're thinking of going to England to visit your sister next summer," Sylvia said. "You told me you'd like me to come with you." Miriam thinks she sounds a little anxious.

"Yes, it's definite I'm going and I expect you're coming too. Don't disappoint me. Maybe you and I could even get to Paris for a week-end," Ruby answers, smiling at Sylvia.

"Too bad Ruth isn't here tonight. I wanted her to tell us about the Dewey hearings." Miriam feels there's been enough of that conversation.

"Yeah, but she told me quite a bit," Hilda responds. "Everyone expected Trotsky and Sevya to be exonerated but some of the testimony was so false—so phony—it turned into a joke." Hilda laughs. "Listen to this—Sedov was supposed to have had several meetings with this accused guy, Holzman, in the Hotel Bristol in Copenhagen in 1932." She pauses, dramatically—"There's just a little trouble with this scenario—Sedov was in Berlin—never got to Copenhagen and" she pauses dramatically—the Hotel Bristol was pulled down in 1917!—there ain't no Hotel Bristol—at least there wasn't in 1932. Where's my iced tea?" She picks up her glass and sips it thirstly.

"What I don't get is how anyone can take the Stalin charges seriously," says Bunny. She and Miriam know each other from countless meetings and open-air meetings, her real name is Beatrice and she's very young. "All these famous people … The American ambassador to Russia, even; I don't get it."

"I think they know damn well what they're doing," Hilda says. "For example this guy, Carleton Beals, a university professor and a real rat—Ruth was furious. Right from the beginning he tried to pull all kinds of tricks. He attacked John Finerty, who's a great lawyer and distrupted the meetings any way he could. But they got wise to him and thank God he resigned."

"Does Ruth think he was a G. P. U. agent?" Miriam asks.

"Beals? Maybe not actually an agent from Moscow, but … look, he didn't even want to give the Commission his new hotel address. And Ruth says he was always hanging arounnd in Mexico City with people everyone knew were Stalinists."

"There seem to be spies and agent provacateurs everywhere these days," Bunny comments.

"Joe Carter was joking the other day. He said 'The governments of the Soviet Union and the U S A,' supply us with new members all the time." Then, adding thoughtfully, Miriam says, "Well so far, here, we haven't much trouble. But I wouldn't take a trip to the Soviet Union, not after …" She stops, thinking about Alana and Arthur and all the other horror stories she's heard.

"Oh, I don't think we're in any danger. We're not important enough for Stalin to go after us," Sylvia reassures, then adds, "It's horrible, though. We shouldn't have to look over our shoulders, suspect everyone, even our close friends. I don't want to do that, I never will."

Ruby nods her head in agreement, "Yes, you can't live that way. You have to trust people," she says earnestly. Then she looks at her watch and jumps up. "I'm awfully sorry, but I've got to run. Thanks for letting me join you. It's been very nice. I hope you'll let me know when you get together again. And Sylvia, I'll see you soon."

"Boy, what a formal speech," Miriam comments after Ruby's gone.

"I really don't think so," Sylvia answers defensively. "She just has better manners than many of our comrades

In a few moments the group breaks up and scatters in different ways and although Miriam should walk west to the 7th Avenue Subway she decides to return to Union Square. She wants to be alone. There are few passerbys and the darkness and quietness soothe her.

These girls with their travels and their week-ends in Paris, she muses. *I'm just a plebian at heart—I like working-class neighborhoods,* she muses. *But why was I so cranky tonight? Is it because I don't feel loved and needed? No, it isn't that. It isn't just love. I think Jaime loves me. Then, why couldn't I accept him and love him back? And keep politics out of it. Why is it that truth is, for me, the important thing in the world. But Jaime is putting his loyalty to a country—supposedly a Communist country—before truth. That's 'patriotism.' I hate it—that blind, stupid devotion! '... the last refuge of a scoundrel' That's a quote from someone—I think someone said it was P.T.Barnum. But Jaime's not a scoundrel.* The memory of his warm hands on her waist, pulling her close, kissing her eyes, her mouth, surges through her ... *You're a fool,* she tells herself and heads for the uptown subway entrance.

Mexico, 1937–38

Natalya tries to keep the household at an even keel but tensions run high and the cast of characters is constantly changing. One of Trotsky's secretaries returns to the United States in August; another, Jan Frankel, goes back in October, while Joe Hansen arrives in September. Jan Van Heijenoort, yet another secretary, stays on and in November his wife Gaby and their young son arrive. Gaby tries to help Natalya in the kitchen but friction erupts into anger one day and the women begin shrieking at each other. Hearing the screaming from the kitchen, Trotsky charges out of his study, raging, shouting "I'm going to call the police." The next day Gaby and her little boy head back to France.

The pressure on the Trotsky household continues to grow. Ignaz Reiss, a member of the Soviet secret service, disillusioned by the trials, the purges, the witch-hunts, the assassinations, decides to run. He contacts Sneevliet, a Dutch Trotskyist, asking him to pass along the warning that Trotsky's son, Lyova Sedov in Paris, is on Stalin's death list, along with Trotsky himself. A short time later, in Switzerland, Reiss is murdered.

Realizing that Lyova is in serious danger, the French police assign a special guard. There is talk about Lyova coming to Mexico but Trotsky advises against it. There are many Soviet G P U agents disguised as Spanish War refugees, and calls for Trotsky's expulsion continue to be raised. Trotsky says he doesn't want his son to have to live as he does, in a "semi-prison."

CHAPTER 13

Barcelona, Winter 1937–38

Ketzel is waiting for Tina, Aurora and Ada to join her for coffee. Although there's been a bombing a few hours before, a heavy one—unusual in broad daylight, people in this noisy, crowded cafe in Barcelona, on a Sunday afternoon, seem to have forgotten it, at least for the moment. Besides soldiers in worn and faded uniforms dragging from their shoulders, there are older men, children in neatly patched old clothes, young pretty dark-eyed girls, plump matrons and gray-haired grandmas holding small babies. Little ones run about, ducking under tables and everyone is drinking, mostly bottled lemonade or black coffee that comes with a small paper filled with coarse sugar.

Three soldiers have just come in and are standing at the doorway, looking for an empty table. They stand in the door way, shrunken with fatigue, their eyes clouded, looking for an empty table and Ketzel, after a moment's hesitation, beckons them to come. They thread their way, the air is thick, gray with cigarette smoke, and a nasal harmonica is softly whining 'Avanti Popolo'.

"Estoy esperando por mis amigas pero siempre hay puesto para tres guerreros valientes," she tells them. When they hear their native language (they were sure she was Scandinavian or English) they smile gratefully, shyly take seats and accept cigarettes and coffee.

About fifteen minutes later Tina arrives. She's thin, pale, tense, her smooth black hair severely parted in the middle. Two women are with her, one, dark haired with small pert features, the other, somewhat older, blue eyed with brown, wispy hair.

The soldiers jump up to to greet them. Manuel, who's gone to University in Madrid, knows this is proper. Tina introduces everyone, the men grin, delighted with additional female company. Jose, who's no more than nineteen, curly-headed with full lips and black eyes, looks at Yolanda, the younger one, impulsively blurts, "You look just like my wife," and when she smiles at him, he leans across the table to kiss her cheek. Everyone burst outs laughing, his face turns pink. The table is so merry that a chubby baby, on his grandmother's lap, bounces, chortles and claps his fat little hands.

Tina says, "Ketzel, I told you about these women and I wanted you to meet them. They've been through some awful experiences—they're so courageous—these soldiers can tell you." She looks at the men, speaks to them in Spanish.

Ada's face begins to change color, she hates compliments. "Let's change the subject," she says. "I'd like to tell you a funny story but I'll have to speak in English. Though I've been in Spain more than a year, I'm not very good."

As they order, she continues, "We were working in this hospital in a huge natural cave, near Bisbal de Falret, a Catalan village. It was awful, very cold, damp—hardly any light. Some of the soldiers had never even seen a doctor—in most villages they have 'curanderas'—they use herbs to cure the sick."

Tina, who's been translating, cuts in, "She nursed the men with so much love and tenderness they called her 'Abuelita'. One afternoon, at a staff meeting, she says, "You know these wounded boys like me so much they call me 'Florita—little flower'." Everyone's quiet, they don't know how to tell her the truth but a young fellow, a stretcher-bearer laughed and said, 'they call you abuelita—abuelita means little grandmother—you're like their granny.' When Ada heard that, she ran out crying, 'I'm going back to England.' But after a little while she came back and they were all very quiet. 'No," she said. "I am not going back though you call me granny. You are my family and I love you."

An old man in overalls brings a large bowl of rice and beans and a loaf of bread to the table; the soldiers eye it hungrily but hide their grimy hands under the table. Although Ketzel's just had lunch, she tears off a chunk of bread, "Tengo hambre" she says, grinning. The men look at each other and dig in.

Yolanda says, "I guess it's my turn. I worked in an old water mill, near Tuerel, that had been turned into a hospital. A great problem was the lice, it was a real torture. It was so cold we couldn't wash—we'd scratch and scratch. Then I had a bright idea. I'd pinch a little ether we used for anesthetics and we'd sprinkle it around—on the pillows, bedclothes, almost everywhere, before we went to sleep. But one night, an English nurse, Lillian, comes running to me all excited, yelling, 'What on earth are you doing? Everyone smokes here—we could all go up in flames!' That was the end of that—from then on we just suffered with the lice."

When Ketzel finishes translating everyone laughs and drinks. Then, the older soldier says, his voice, tired and grave, "I must tell you in Spanish. I do not know funny stories." He passes his hand through black hair, now gray and thick with dust. "This was in Madrid, when I was there, in the slums behind our lines, where the poor live—they came out, to take care of us, carrying the last of their little possessions—their few chickens, blankets, mattresses, tomatoes—they wanted to give us everything. They sewed on buttons for us, washed our clothes, as if we were their own children. But the enemy was bombarding with sadistic pleasure and in our trenches, about three hundred yards away, we could hear terrible cries of agony. We carried from the ruins the little dead bodies of the children who, just the day before, had sat on our laps …"

Ketzel shakes her head, her eyes filled with tears—the terrible waste, the little children … the little children …

There is silence around the table … even Tina who has listened almost impatiently …

In a little while, the youngest boy shakes his head. "Basta, no more now." Then, fishing in his knapsack says "Mi novia," and gives them a photo of a plump girl with lively brown eyes and full lips with two little girls in white dressed for Sunday school. "We'll be married in the spring" he says proudly. Then, everyone takes out pictures—sweet-hearts, mothers, wives and babies. While they're passing them around Ketzel finds Martin's photo.

"Oh, My! Yours? … so handsome!" Ada squeals.

"Here's some others," Ketzel says, handing them around. "This one is of Martins's friends, Siqueiros, Contreras, Mercader and Arenal. I call it my 'Rogues' Gallery' photo!"

"Let me see that!" Tina grabs the picture from Ketzel's hand, her eyes flashing. "Who did you say this to—that it's a rogues gallery? Did you show it to anyone?"

"I sent it to my father. When I wrote him last week. What's the big deal? It's just a joke." Ketzel frowns.

"I hope that you didn't tell him he could use it in one of his magazine articles. That wouldn't be good publicity," Tina says sternly.

"What? Well, No, I didn't. I didn't think it was necessary. No, he wouldn't, he's too busy …" Ketzel's faintly apologetic. "Anyway, I was just kidding, that's my American sense of humor."

She reaches for the picture, but Tina waves her away. She opens her purse, drops in the picture in it and snaps it shut.

"Fine, you can have it" Ketzels says unnecessarily. She's strange, that Tina Modotti, Ketzel thinks, with an interesting past. She was very beautiful when she was young, talented in photography and worked with Edward Weston in Mexico. She joined the Communist Party and recruited Frida Kahlo into its folds. When she met Jose Mella, handsome, brilliant, escaped from Machado's Cuba, they fell madly in love, married and were crazy happy until one day, about a year later, he gets shot dead as they walk in the street. Ketzel looks at her face, she's a tough and bitter woman, her husband Vidali, otherwise known as Contreras, rumored to be a Soviet assassin, is known as a man with blood on his hands. She decides to let the whole thing go, it's not important, it's just a photograph. And Tina's a little strange.

At the table, the talk begins to flag, they drink a little more, lines on the men's eyes grow deeper, they haven't slept for twenty hours, they must leave. They apologize and as they stand to leave Ketzel makes them take her two packs of Chesterfields.

"Buen suerte, vaya con Dios—we will meet again soon," they promise each other.

"First we win the war!"

They raise their fists and the little baby at the next table does the same. They say "sabemos vencer or morir!" The men hug the women, they kiss farewells. As they pass the table, one of them picks up the baby, holds him close for a moment.

At the door, they look back, and once more raise their fists and the women wave back, their eyes filling with tears.

Tina doesn't mention the photo again and Ketzel forgets about it. She's very busy, her dancers have arrived, thrilled to be in Spain, in spite of the bombing and shortages. The two performances in a small theatre end with audiences standing and singing "Los Quatro Generales."

"Come to our little good-bye party," Caridad says. "Ramon is leaving soon—he has a special assignment in Moscow." Her son looks serious behind his tortoise-shell, rimmed glasses, his swarthy, large-featured face glum, plainly not enthusiastic about his new job. Caridad is very handsome this evening. Her iron-gray hair is piled up and fastened with a jeweled comb and she's wearing a fitted black dress which flatters her tall, heavy figure. She kisses Ketzel warmly, she's taken her under her wing. The party turns out to be pleasant and lively in spite of a remark Ketzel overhears, "Any assignment's better than being called back to Russia …"

Later that night, Ketzel, wrapped in a fleecy robe, standing on her balcony, can't sleep. She and the girls had danced so well and the excitement of the performance still thrills her and then the party afterwards.

Caridad's idea. She is warm and very friendly but Ketzel's not sure she likes her. A few nights before Caridad had the women in stitches when she described her love affairs with Thorez and Duclos, C P leaders in France. She didn't spare many details—how they looked naked and other juicy details! *Even though she's sweet to me,* Ketzel thinks, *she frightens me a little.* And Kotov, with his piercing eyes, dark brows! But Caridad's nuts about him. They're both ardent C P members, she and her son, Ramon. She won't talk about Pablo, his brother, killed at the front—he was romancing an anarchist girl, and so got sent to a shock battalion, a sure death sentence. The story is that she could have stopped the transfer but didn't try. She may be idealistic, like all Communists but she also seems pretty cold-blooded. *She told me herself, she shot twenty men. "They were enemies, Trotskyist spies."*

She shivers, wrapping the robe tightly about her. God! So much suffering! When Paul Robeson sang 'Ol' Man River' at a recent performance here, he changed the words to fit the occasion! Instead of 'Ah'm tired of livin/an'skeered of dyin' he sang, "I'll keep on livin/And keep on tryin." Good advice!

Better go back to bed, snuggle up to Martin. She has a feeling that the issue of the snapshot will come up again; Tina's not one to let a matter drop if it has anything to do with the Party or Contreras—Vidali. Although they quarrel often, Tina's fiercely protective of her husband; surely she must have told him about the photo.

When Martin comes in at midnight from an editorial meeting, he's scowling, his face dark, she senses there's going to be trouble.

He starts in, "What on earth did you think you were doing, taking a picture like that?"

Ketzel's at the vanity, removing a cold cream mask—her nightly ritual, trying to be casual, she closes the lid of the Pond's jar. "What picture? What's the problem?"

"Calling it 'A Rogues' Gallery.' What in hell does that mean?" He throws his hotel keys onto the glass-covered table. It makes an ugly cracking sound.

"It means absolutely nothing! It's just an expression when guys take a picture together. I was being funny—that's all!"

"Listen, let me tell you, Madame," Martin spits out his words, "that, number one, it isn't funny and number two, we are not in America, we are in Spain, fighting a war—with enemies everywhere. I don't think you understand that—*Madame!*"

Ketzel wheels around from her image in the triple mirror of the vanity to face him. She starts to tremble, her face tight with anger. "Don't call me madame. I'm a comrade, remember!"

"Then you should remember that we are in Spain, fighting a war, with enemies everywhere"

Her anger rises. "It could be Russia with all these Generals and officials running the bloody show here."

He pounces on her, grasping her shoulders, forcing her to look up at him. "You are impossible—what you say is stupid and disgusting." But realizing he's over-reacting and frightening her, he drops his arms and flings her away. "I'm going to take a shower," he yells but slams the bathroom door hard.

Ketzel climbs into bed and picks up her copy of Madame Bovary. But she can't read. She feels betrayed by Tina but also by herself. How could she have made that remark about Russia? She feels tears prickling her eyes. Did she really think the Soviet Union shouldn't be helping the revolution? Didn't she know how angry this would make Martin—and they're still on their honeymoon?

But he's in a better humor when he emerges, tingling, swearing about the icy water and whistling an aria from *La Traviata*. Redolent with 1711 Eau de Cologne, he gets into bed and tries to put his arms around her but she shrugs him away.

"Listen, I won't call you Madame again. I'll leave that to Flaubert." He picks up her hand, brushes it with his lips. "Ketzel, dearest. You have to admit your attitude is different from the others: Siqueiros, Mercader, his mother. They're heart and soul for this war in Spain, just like you. But they're doing what they have to—sometimes they are brutal even to people you like—who are close to you."

Ketzel raises her eyes and looks at him, unable to control the corners of her mouth that insist on turning down. He sees she's been crying. "I don't know what to think." She shakes her head. "I feel that I'm useless here. I can't do what Caridad and Tina do. I couldn't in a million years even though I'm a loyal communist. It makes me sick!"

"No, no. You mustn't say that." Martin puts his fingers lightly on her lips. "You've made everyone happy here—with your dancing—giving them courage." He's lying next to her now, his arm about her. "But, you might be right, *querida*, you're just too tender-hearted. It's because you're an artist—that's your metier!"

Martin strokes her hair. "I know you want to go to Paris. Maybe we can in a few months but I can't leave now. I'm needed here. How about if you go back to New York now by yourself? I'll be finished soon and I'll join you there."

Ketzel says nothing for a few moments, trying to absorb his suggestion. *This is turning out to be a helluva honeymoon,* she thinks. Then she tells herself, *Don't be a baby.* She's upset but she's not going to act childish. "Would it make it easier for you if I did that—went home now?," hoping that he'll say he wants her to stay, to be with him.

"'I want you here but I think it's better for you to be back home. Think of it, a decent hot shower. I'm just kidding, but you could use a change from all of this bloodshed and bombing—and Jaime will be happy you're home, even though he and Rosenblit might be busy with important Party work."

She's quiet. Maybe he's right after all, returning to comforts, soft sheets and real coffee, the picture is attractive and she can use time in New York, catching up with some of the work going on with Jose Limon and the Humphrey-Weidman groups. Snuggling up to him, she says, "You know, it isn't such a bad idea. If it's better for you, I'll leave in a few days."

He wants to tell her something else but he waits until the day of her departure. Embracing each other before she boards he says, "Give my love to Jaime; tell him I liked his article in Colliers. Look," he adds, "I hope you won't mind but I don't think you should see Miriam anymore. The Party wouldn't approve. It's better that way—right?" Ketzel doesn't reply. She's bought a gift for her dear Trotskyite friend in New York and she intends to give it to her in person. She smiles and hugs Martin again.

Miriam's on her way to a Socialist function but this promises to be a happier occasion, more exciting than the endless ones that have been going on for the past two years. No wonder the Socialists tried desperately to keep the Trotsky-ists off the floor during their Party meetings, trying to limit the debates that run on endlessly.

This evening there's to be a report on the Convention just held in Chicago. The 'French Turn' has been a success and many Socialist Party members will join the new party to be celebrated on New Years Day, l938.

She stops at the door, inspecting her new outfit. Maybe this isn't appropriate for a working-class meeting, she thinks. "It's is too elegant." She sighs, pulls off the maroon woolen jacket with the beaver collar and dashes back into the bedroom for the black sweater and leather jacket she's worn all winter. She's not sorry she bought the outfit, especially when she considered how cheap it was. She'd gone to 'Loehmann's' up in the Bronx—known for fantastic bargains, a bare and dismal place with long metal racks of marked-down prices. The jacket had cost one-tenth of the original price because of a jagged tear but Clara, skillful with a needle, repaired it so well nothing showed.

Ever since that night with Jaime, even though it was a long time ago, Miriam had felt as if nothing was going right. She'd grown to hate her apartment, she couldn't help seeing it through Jaime's eyes, ugly, dirty and dangerous. Then, it happened, as it did to most inhabitatants of poor neighborhoods, they got robbed.

On a Sunday morning, as usual, Sydney goes to get the newspaper and rolls for breakfast. He comes back breathless …

"I was sure my wallet was in my pants pocket, I always kept it there," he gasps. But when he went to pay for the bread, it wasn't there.. Neither was his two weeks salary, Miriam's pay, a little radio, a new pair of scissors. During the night intruders had simply climbed down the fire-escape from the roof, entered softly through the window and had just as quietly left with their boodle. The thought of some stranger watching her while she sleeps makes Miriam's skin creep but she tries to laugh when she talks about it.

Sydney bolts the windows shut, leaving only a few inches on the bottom and top. With no air, and a few fans the bedroom is an oven—but for now they tell themselves it will have to do and it works for only a short time. On Saturday evening in October they go to a late-night movie wih two comrades who lived just a block away, brothers, they called themselves 'Black' and 'White.' They were in a good mood as they walk home, rehashing the romantic story, Black is talking about Claudette Colbert's gorgeous legs as they reach their flat. Then—Miriam screams …

"Oh my god, Oh no! Not again!" Their apartment door is swinging wildly, hanging from one hinge, like a wounded animal and in the dark the living room looks like a madman gone berserk.

"Stop it, Miriam. Shut up!," Sydney snaps. "We should be used to this by now," he mutters. Grim with disgust, they carefully make their way into the living room, weaving between the debris. In the bedroom drawers had been turned over and flung aside; the bureaus gaped like toothless crones. Sydney, standing in the center of the living room, can't help saying, "Jeez—a perfect job."

Miriam steps through the chaos to the closet. "Everything's gone, Sydney, all our clothes, my new winter coat, your overcoat, your suit, your only suit." She begin to sob, "It's awful. I'm scared. Where can people live these days.?" He puts his arms about her, trying to soothe her. "We'll have to find another place."

It takes a few days before Miriam is able to find a little humor about the robbery. She'd concealed a twenty dollar bill beneath a cake box, the weekly food allowance and it was still there, untouched! "Lucky our robbers didn't like cake. Must have been on a diet."

They spend that Saturday night in Black and White's apartment. A week later Miriam decides what she has to do. She must talk to Sydney about moving, and maybe about moving into her mother's apartment.

Watching him as he takes bite of crisp bacon and mops it up a small circle of egg yolk, she says, "Sydney, my mother has two vacant rooms in her new apartment—you know, the one she just moved to—on 15lst street, between Broadway and Amsterdam Avenue. Do you think it would be okay for us—how do you feel about it—I mean, about us moving there? She's going to rent out those rooms anyway." She feels defeated, movng back in with Clara but she can't stay in that vandalized apartment. At least at her mother's, she'll feel safe.

"Miriam …" Sydney hesitates, "look, if it was up to me I'd still stay here but you're really scared—I know it. I saw your face that night. We have to get the hell out of here."

"Would you want to go there this afternoon, to see if it's okay. My mother probably'll be home. I can get the keys …"

His answer is, as she's expected, he leaves decisions about everything but politics to her. "No. It's not necessary. If you think we can be comfortable there, just go ahead, whatever you do is fine."

As the subway rumbles up to the 145th Street station and she walks to 151st Street, a poor, hispanic neighborhood, passing a large Woolworth's and a movie house, seedy, run-down apartment houses and bodegas, she rehearses how she'll approach the subject with Clara.

Her mother, anticipating her visit, has set out farmer cheese and rye bread. As she sits down and rests her rough hands on the kitchen table, she emits a small groan.

"What is it, Mama,—the arthritis?" Miriam spreads the crumbling cheese, trying to keep it from falling off the bread, bracing herself for a sarcastic reply.

"Why do you ask questions? Do you care?"

"Oh, Mama, please, for God's sake." *What am I doing here?* she thinks.

They're both quiet for a moment and then Miriam says, "Look, Mama, I'm sorry you not feeling so good." Reaching for another slice, "This is delicious bread—Is there a new bakery in the neighborhood?"

Clara sips some tea and in a little while she begins to talk. She likes the neighborhood, the people are friendly. She tells her about a dress she's making for a meesa (she's so homely, you wouldn't believe) young woman who's getting married. "But she's paying good money," she says proudly, and then goes on to describe the tenants and the excuses they give when she comes for the rent. "It's noisy, too. Saturday nights, I don't sleep until three …"

At last Miriam summons her courage. She finishes her tea and says, "Listen, Mom, how about if we were to move in with you, Sydney and I? I know you've got the two rooms empty now." No response so she continues, "We've been robbed twice. I guess you were right, Mom. I'm afraid to come home at night when I'm alone. At least you'll always be here." She stops, realizing it sounded cold, almost calculating and she isn't disappointed when the expected "I told you so" comes.

"I told you moving there was a bad idea," Clara says. "But you had to get away from me. You go to some dirty apartment in a terrible neighborhood, just to get out of my house."

"Listen Mama, I didn't move away from you, there were a lot of other reasons." Her mother's quiet, Miriam feels tears welling up in her eyes so she adds, "Maybe you don't want us."

"I didn't say that," Clara answered quickly now, a note of apology in her voice. "You can move in—it's alright with me. If you can afford—you'll pay twenty dollars a month." She glances at Miriam, a sharp look. "I'm surprised you're still together. I'm not stupid." She takes a deep breath. "Okay, I got keys. Here," and takes some from the pocket of a shapeless housedress. "The front room has a nice brocade couch. Mrs. Carlson left it behind—she owed me plenty … a real nofki." Her voice trails away as she pulls herself up from the table.

"Let me know when you're coming." She says, moves her head from side to side. "It hurts me, between the shoulder blades. I'll go lay down a little. Five o'clock in the morning I had to get up, check the furnace. The super, that schwartze, is a bum. Okay," with a sigh. "So you'll move in next week."

Leaving, Miriam takes her mother's hand, the odor of Kirkman's carbolic soap still clinging to it. "Mama, I'm sorry you have to work so hard. I don't help you enough. I know I should," and at the door, when she kisses her, she's surprised when for a moment, her mother holds her close.

The next day is a Saturday and one of the comrades who owns an aged, rickety truck helps them move their few belongings and three pieces of furniture into Clara's apartment. "I think it's going to work out fine," Miriam tells Sydney. "And listen to this, we're going to have a telephone in the apartment. Mama and I are going to share the cost—it won't be much."

Sydney is not as elated as Miriam. "We don't need it. Let's face it, we don't have that many friends." Although he tries to be offhand Miriam knows he's depressed. Other than the few comrades with whom they spend summers with in the country they don't have many and there's little family.

"But honey, we have each other," Miriam says cheerfully but Sydney just shrugs.

The phone proves a great source of comfort to Miriam. On a Saturday, Ketzel, just returned from Spain, calls her and they talk for almost two hours, catching up—successful performances in Spain, parties new friends, new projects. Ketzel doesn't mention her father and Miriam's relieved. Just before they hang up Ketzel says, "Oh, by the way I've brought you a present, I think you'll like it."

The following Tuesday, a frosty chill in the air. Miriam, on her lunch hour, waits for Ketzel on the esplanade of the R C A building, looking down on the rink below. Among the ice-skaters a few expert males are doing fancy leaps and twirls but the majority are young women with round bottoms and shapely legs, in tight velvet jackets and tiny, flaring skirts. After twenty minutes Miriam resorts to buying a salty pretzel from a street vendor then stamping her feet and covering her aching ears, she decides to go back to the office. As she turns to go, she hears running footsteps, feels a hand on her arm. It's Jaime, panting, holding a package.

"Miriam, I'm glad I caught you." He's breathless. Their impact is like a ringing clash of cymbals and they stand still. His eyes are tender, dark, her cheeks pink, like the inside of a conch shell, they look at each other. The City, the honking taxis, the noisy tourists, all fall away—they hear nothing.

"Ketzel couldn't make it at the last minute," he says. "They called a special, last-minute meeting and so I offered to take it to you—as a special favor to

Ketzel, of course." He thrusts a box in her hands, grins and Miriam, her heart soaring, smiles back at him. Then, Jaime bends, circles her waist, and lifts her to him. She's light as a bird and he kisses her hungrily as she clings to him, holding him close.

After a moment, she whispers, "I'm frozen—let's get inside." Holding hands, they run up the street to a corner drug-store to where it's warm. They find two empty seats at the counter and over bowls of pea soup they look again at each other. They talk about Ketzel's trip to Spain, problems at the hacienda in Mexico, Hunter College, the robberies, everything but themselves. The conversation falters, stops.

In a few moments, the man behind the counter impatiently asks them, "Anything else?" When they don't seem to hear him, he whips out a pencil, writes a bill and hands it to Jaime who takes it without a word.

Miriam turns away. She clears her throat, then whispers, "I think I'm running late, I have to get back," buttons her coat, jumps off her stool. "Tell Ketzel thanks, I'll call her tonight."

Jaime doesn't answer, he remains sitting at the counter. Hesitating, trying to summon a smile she says, "Thank you—thanks for bringing my present." But when she nears the store exit she comes back. He's still at the counter, looking down into his empty coffee cup. Standing close, she touches his shoulder.

"Jaime. I still feel the same," she whispers. "It'll always be the same for me."

Turning away, she opens the door. Now he's right behind her. Out in the street, he holds her shoulders, his mouth tight with anger, trying to keep his voice down but he can't. "Do you realize how stupidly you're acting?," his voice harsh. "I know you love me—isn't that the most important thing?—Can't you come to your senses? Things are not as simple as you think they are—or that you want them to be … they're not just black or white. I'm leaving, going home to Mexico. It might be for a very long time."

Miriam shakes her head, swallows hard, keeping her eyes averted, manages to say, "You don't understand, you'll never understand," and hurries down the street. She doesn't look back.

Mexico, Summer 1937

Although the report on the Dewey hearings has been published in the Fall, Trotsky is still very busy, supplementing the evidence he presented to the Commission. The immense pressure of the work has left him in poor health, with severe headaches and high blood pressure. But it has also manifested itself in a strained relationship with his son. There are many differences between them: Trotsky is dissatisfied with Lyova's management of the Bulletin of the Oppositionists and suggests that he transfer it to New York and the comrades there. Deeply hurt, Lyova complains about his father's attitude to his mother. He's exhausted, burdened with work, worries about his parents and frightened for his own life,

He takes his father's criticisms very much to heart. but even more than that, he is depressed and despairing, unable to bring himself to face the betrayal of the old Bolsheviks he knew and admired as a child. Their phony confessions and their degradation is almost more than he can bear. And even Lenin's widow seems to be supporting the validity of the accusations! They must know what they are saying is madness!

CHAPTER 14

Winter 1937–38

Miss Croxdale throws Miriam a cold stare when she flies back into the office. Typing up the Municipal Art Calendar for the week she makes dozens of errors. Somehow she manages to get through the day. Just before she goes home, in the ladies room, she opens the box from Ketzel and gasps with delight. Inside is a beautiful Russian peasant blouse, made of heavy white cloth and thickly stitched in red and black wool. It's magnificent, the most beautiful thing she's ever owned.

"Great to have rich girl friends," Sydney says when she gets home and shows it to him, but she can tell he's pleased. He's really kind and generous, she thinks, even though he's always so depressed and not really capable of loving anyone. She wishes she loved him, *then at least one of us would be happy,* and she's glad he suggests a movie after dinner. She can sit in the dark and go over what happened with Jaime, something sad. It had taken all her self-control that afternoon to keep from breaking into tears.

Has she been a self-righteous, little prig? Thousands of people are Communists, supporters of the Soviet Union, people in the entire world believe what's happening there is wonderful and good … and right! The Trotskyists have only a thousand members, mostly in New York, a small group! So what makes us right? Why can't she be convinced that Russia is still a great country building socialism—that Stalin is just a temporary evil—if they get rid of him, the revolution will prevail. But she can't. Stalin's a monster no matter what many people say, destroying what Lenin and Trotsky fought so hard to achieve—why can't Jaime see the truth—why is he so insistent she leave the Trotskists—rejects what she says—is he more deeply involved with the Communist Party than he lets on? Ketzel says he acts so mysterious at times. But it can't be, he could never be involved with the G P U—that's ridiculous. No matter how hard she tries, questions gnaw away at her.

Ketzel manages to meet her for lunch the following week in spite of her heavy schedule. "Oh, my god, you look absolutely stunning!," she cries, hurrying towards Miriam. "I picked the right size even though I was thousands of miles away. We're going to Alice Foote MacDougalls—made us a reservation since you got a half-hour extra for lunch." Miriam sees approval in Ketzel's eyes, Ketzel wants her to look more fashionable; she hates "third-period Stalinist" apparel—especially the leather jackets.

Ketzel wants to go to the "Sevilla." "The decor is phony but the food is good." It's part of a fancy coffee-house chain, decorated in the peasant style of a country, like Spain or Italy, each one done in romantic style, with blue canvas skies, facades and balconies, flowers everywhere. That, plus waitresses in immaculate white aprons and frilly caps make these restaurants a favorite of bridge-club ladies and tourists, but Ketzel insists.

"You know why I got you that blouse?," Ketzel says after they order. "No, why?" "It's gorgeous—that's enough for me," Miriam answers. "Remember that Russian doll of mine that we always used to play with? When I saw this it reminded me of that doll, how you loved her. I had to get it for you."

"You're right—she had a little blouse just like this." Miriam squeezes Ketzel's hand, blushing a bit. "I think it really does looks good on me." "Okay, let's order and then I want to hear more about Spain. You were in Madrid with all of those famous writers—Hemingway, Dos Passos—"

"It was great meeting all these people, although I really didn't get to see them very much. I got to spend more time with Caridad Mercader. She's older but so dynamic, fiery, bigger than life. But, you might say, a little unstable, too, if you remember my letter."

Ketzel stops to pour olive oil and vinegar on her green salad. "I like Ramon too, but not as much. He's tremendously bright but too sarcastic at times. Scares me a little. he's had a strange life. He was a bell-boy in a Barcelona Hotel, then worked at the Ritz in the kitchen. 'I was very good at carving meat,' he once told me."

"Maybe a little conceited?" Miriam's busy with her Chicken Kiev.

"He's a very dedicated Party member. As soon as he was old enough he joined the C P and got himself arrested. They made him a Lieutenant after he was wounded at the Aragon front. He's got a right to be conceited. Siqueiros is crazy about him."

"Siquieros, the Mexican muralist, painter, too. My boss in the Municipal Art Gallery told me about him."

"Oh, he's great—adorable! His nose is kind of long, acquiline, but with that curly black hair and light skin and when he wears an a wide brimmed hat he's …" Ketzel, her salad plate empty, turns to her favorite dessert, golden flan, topped with whipped cream. "But he's also a genuine revolutionist. He says that creativity and politics are inseparable."

"I'm eating like a pig," she goes on. "I'd better stop. I'll be dancing five hours this afternoon," pushing away the tempting dish. "The only one that I absolutely could not stand was this guy, Contreras, real name Vidali. Tina, the photographer I told you about? He's her husband. He frightened me, disgusting, with those squinty eyes and fleshy mouth." Suddenly, she stops, takes another bite of flan. "I'm talking too much. What's with you—but, *por favor*, skip the political stuff."

Miriam's happy to oblige. It's the pleasantest hour Miriam's spent in a long time. She always feels young and carefree when she and Ketzel are together. But at the last moment, when they're parting, a remark by Ketzel throws her back into reality, reawakening the familiar gnawing pain and weird suspicions.

"Jaime's left for Mexico, very last minute—he was in a lousy mood. Says it's important," Ketzel says as she heads out down the subway stairs.

Back in the office Sarah Jane, her co-worker, bleached blonde, large-bosomed, can tell there's something on Miriam's mind. She's helping her sort out the pictures for the next exhibition at the Municipal Art Committee's Art gallery on 65th Street.

"You walkin' around heah like sumthin' the cat dragged in—for a coupla weeks now. Wanna tell me about it?" She has a soft voice, a delicious accent. If anyone has experience in love affairs, it's Sarah Jane, married twice and kids by a third. Miriam's tempted to tell her the whole story. But she bites her tongue, smiles and shakes her head. She knows Sarah Jane wouldn't be able to understand why politics can interfere with love—according to her nothing should ever interfere with love. Miriam knows she ought to talk to someone about how she's feeling. Rhoda, Hilda, Bunny? No, Somehow she wouldn't feel comfortable with one of them, trying to describe the mess she's gotten herself into. What about Sylvia? Sylvia! She's a good friend, a social worker, a therapist. She'll see her this Sunday when there's a Party meeting at the headquarters and make a date with her.

This Sunday the discussion on the nature of the Soviet State begins at one o'clock, and by three it becomes a factional dispute, soon reaching its peak, the rhetoric spouting like an open hydrant on a hot night in Harlem, although the hot air is a lot less refreshing than cool water. Two groups, one led by Burnham, Abern and Shachtman, the other by Cannon, Gordon and Clarke have been at it for hours. By six o'clock, to everyone's relief, there's a call for an adjournment for dinner, and Miriam, Sydney, Sylvia and Hilda and other rank and file members troop out to look for an inexpensive meal while the leaders remain behind, meeting with their respective caucuses discussing further strategy.

The four of them end up at the Automat on Irving Place; Sylvia and Hilda claim the Crusader Cafeteria is just too dirty. Miriam agrees to go somewhere else although the stuffed cabbage at the Crusader is very tasty. But she doesn't say anything. She knows the two girls aren't going to return for the evening meeting so there may be a chance to get Sylvia alone.

"Look," Sydney begins, although he's impatient to return to the headquarters. "You Abernites have to agree that Burnham is nothing but a petty-bourgeois professor who's against Bolshevik organization and discipline." Sydney continues after they've all returned to the table with their filled trays. "Naturally he's influenced by his environment. On the other hand as Cannon says, 'he resists being taught anything by our international comrades.' I think Jim is absolutely right."

Hilda's eyes flash as she leans across, putting down her knife with a clatter. "Why can't you admit that Cannon's acting like a Stalinist—the only difference is that he accepts, yes, I'd say, swallows everything, and I do mean, everything, the Old Man says—without question!"

"Trotsky is brilliant and a great leader," Sydney shoots back. "How can you deny that?

"Of course, we all think so," Hilda says. "But what he says now should be taken more as a guide to action—he doesn't have real knowledge of the American scene—only what's told to him. That's not his fault, but we can't take everything he says as gospel."

"Hilda, don't get so excited. You're not going to convince these die-hards," Sylvia says. "I don't think anyone is convincing anybody of anything. Your food's getting cold."

Miriam, swallowing a spoonful of rice pudding, says, "I don't get either faction's definition of Russia's government. Burnham and Shachtman call it a bureaucratic collectivist state, Cannon says it is a degenerative workers' state. I don't think it's either one." She pauses, but seeing Sydney is about to interrupt her continues quickly. "But it's not a workers' state either … Russia doesn't belong to the workers anymore—it belongs to Stalin and his puppets. That's my opinion."

Sydney grimaces, ignoring what she's said. "I love it when Cannon calls Burnham 'a perpetual talking shop.' But it doesn't go just for him—Abern and Shachtman are no slouches either."

"And I love it when Cannon insults comrades." Hilda glares at Sydney. "How can he use terms like scabs and strike-breakers about party members?! How about words like sniveling and stinking!"

"That's his working-class sense of humor! This isn't some ladies' tea party," Sydney fires back.

"Please, that's enough," Sylvia says. "We've already sat through five hours of this. Why don't we talk about movies. I just saw 'The Informer." It was power-ful—the music too.. made it even more dramatic."

"These discussions happen to be very important," Sydney says, sharply, ignoring Sylvia. "We have to clarify our position. We're heading into World War II sooner or later and as Bolshevik Leninists we have to know where we stand. Is Russia a worker's state? If she is, do we support the war—what do we tell our comrades—the ones that are gonna get drafted?"

"Sydney, I have to tell you—you're absolutely right—for once you're abso-lutely right—it's a helluva question or rather a bunch of questions and God knows, when and if we can answer them...." Hilda picks up the check on the table. "We'll be talking about this for a long time to come. Let's call it quits for tonight."

After dinner, Sydney, disgusted with the women's dismissal of the subject, hurries back to the meeting and Hilda departs for Brooklyn where she has a date. As Sylvia and Miriam wait in the almost deserted, dreary subway station for the uptown Broadway train, Miriam begins, hesitantly, "I'm glad I got you alone, Sylvia. I'd like to talk to you about something, just you and me. It's rather personal, and for once Ruby isn't around."

Sylvia frowns. "I thought you liked Ruby. She's good company. Besides, I think she's lonely."

"You're probably right. After all, she doesn't know many people in New York." *How stupid to mention her, why is she in New York anyway?,* Miriam thinks. Just then a train pulls in and they ride in silence for a little while before Sylvia turns to Miriam.

"I have an idea, come home with me, Sylvia says. "It's only eight o'clock. Sydney'll be stuck there ... the meeting'll go on until two in the morning."

"Thanks, Sylvia," Miriam says. "I'd like that."

When they get to Sylvia's apartment she puts up the tea and while they sit in the spotless, white kitchen, waiting for water to boil, Miriam wonders how to begin.

"It's about a man, isn't it?" Sylvia has a wise look on her face.

"What makes you think so." Miriam tries to smile, flicking her cigarette lighter.

"Is there anything else? I'm a few years older than you, still waiting for the real one to come along. So, what's your story? Is this about Sydney?"

"No," Miriam says. "No, I'm afraid there's someone else. Promise me you won't tell anyone, not even your sister. The problem is—the problem is—he's a Stalinist, really into the Communist Party. But he's wonderful and I'm in love with him. Is that crazy?." Relieved, she flicks the ashes from her cigarette. Just saying it out loud makes her feel better.

Sylvia gives her a curious glance, "Miriam, how could you?" She opens a tiny red tin trunk marked "Swee-Touch-Ne" and takes out two tea bags and puts them in a Limoges teapot. "Didn't you know this when you met? Question number two, how far has it gone? Of course, I'm assuming Sydney doesn't know about it."

The kettle's boiling now so she carefully pours the boiling water into the teapot and takes delicate cups from the cupboard. "I hope you like 'Lorna Doones', and puts some of the cookies on a flowered plate.

"You know, Sylvia, it just kind of happened. I've had close contact with this man (Sylvia will think it's someone at work, which is fine with Miriam), and I couldn't help seeing him often. We've spent only one night together but I know he loves me and I really do care about him—a lot. But we can't agree about anything political … so … what do I do?"

Behind her glasses, Sylvia's pale, blue-grey eyes cloud with sympathy. "Miriam, I think I know you pretty well. Politics are very important to you. How can you love this guy, if that's the way he thinks? He's not married, is he?"

Miriam shakes her head. "If it were that, things'd be a lot simpler."

"Why didn't you recognize what you were letting yourself in for? You knew he was a Stalinist early on, didn't you."

"Yes," Miriam admits. "But somehow I didn't think it would matter. It does, though."

"He probably didn't take your political views seriously, either. It sounds like you let your emotions carry you away."

Miriam gets up and walks to a window, opening it. There's noisy laughter down the street, coming from three young boys, probably students from

Columbia University. They've just emerged from an Italian restaurant and probably have had a little too much to drink. They're having a good time, not thinking about consequences. Is that what she did? She realizes she made a mistake, she didn't need a scolding, she feels discouraged, this is going nowhere.

She steels herself, and in a couple of minutes she comes back and sits down. "I'm listening Sylvia, go on."

"If you'd been more cautious you might have seen you were heading for problems and a real heartache." Sylvia sips her tea, and busies herself arranging cookie crumbs on her plate into a neat circle. "If you want my advice, try to forget him. Get away somewhere, a change of scenery, don't see or be near him for a while. Could you do that?"

"I don't know." Miriam says. "Maybe. The W P A's closing down soon and I'll be out of a job, so I'll have some freedom. It's lucky Sydney's still working, we'll still be able to pay the rent." Her face brightens. The idea of getting away from New York, from Sydney, from her mother, suddenly sounds very appealing.

"Maybe I could take a trip?" she muses. "It might just be possible, Europe or Mexico—visit the Old Man like some of the other comrades are doing."

"It's a good idea." Sylvia says. "As a matter of fact, I'm taking a trip soon, myself. Ruby and I are going to London to visit her sister and then maybe Paris." She glances at Miriam apologetically and adds, "Just the two of us. She doesn't want anyone else."

That's fine, thinks Miriam. She doesn't like Ruby and wouldn't even think of going with her. Although she doesn't want to discuss her problem any longer, in a way it's been helpful. She's already decided what she wants to do and leaves an hour later, kissing Sylvia warmly, feeling lighter and happier.

On the way home she starts to think about who she might go with. One of her comrades, maybe Hilda or Bunny. About money, she's got that savings bond for one hundred dollars she's been holding for a rainy day and this could be it. Reviewing Sylvia's advice, getting away, that bit of advice was good. But she's so preachy, all that talk about being careful. Would Sylvia be so cautious if an attractive guy came her way?

❈   ❈   ❈

The Forty-Second Street Library's warm, the odor of dry parchment mingles with the moist heat from sizzling radiators and Miriam hurries to the reference room on the third floor; the brown, lamp-lit rooms, the lemony oil smell of the long tables, a sanctuary for book-lovers, students, all refugees from the roiling life of the city. From the moment she enters tranquillity sweeps through her, this is where she does her assignments, research for her term papers, browses, dreams.

In her college work she finds that the required readings in Victorian literature surprise and sometimes amuse her—surprised that Cardinal John Henry Newman in his "Idea of a University" should be concerned with human happiness and that William Morris, a mild socialist who invented the Morris Chair (which is comfortable!), made a nutty observation that "in America all luxuries are dear except oysters and ice!" But she finds herself nodding in agreement with Morris when he says "human nature demands of civilization that it be interesting.... what really dissatisfies in America is the want of the interesting." Of course, she finds no mention of the basic problem; they're no Marxists, but their placid dissertations and beautiful writing have a calming effect upon her.

Anger and depression return when she leaves the building and reads the headlines at the newstand outside; the news about the war in Spain. In December there had been some hope of victory, the Republicans had captured most of Teruel. But now in February Franco has launched a terrible offensive and in spite of heroic fighting, under brutal conditions, in weather below 17 degrees, the Republican army, fighting along the Alfambra River, is losing ground.

"Why aren't people, the workers in the trade unions, Jews—the Jews who Hitler wants to exterminate completely—why aren't they running in the streets, demonstrating, yelling about what's happening?" Tightness in her throat, anger rising. "Why is there such apathy? Orwell found the same frustration in England. Don't workers know that sooner or later there'll be war and they'll be in it too and many of them will end up dead? Our government will be fighting, not because Hitler's killing all the Jews but because we must protect capitalism, in Europe and also in Japan. Since America needs oil, tin and rubber that's in southeast Asia, we'll get into war with her as well.

Here in America, workers aren't really concerned with Spain. For them 'the bell does not toll,' as John Donne wrote. But they *are* concerned about jobs, wages, living conditions in the U S and they're organizing in the South and pulling sit-down strikes in the North. Of course the government's on the ball too, so they create sops to placate the poor and dilute unrest and militancy—the Tennessee Valley Authority, mininum wage laws. They'll throw up a few low-cost houses, set up a W P A, but when and if it becomes necessary they'll pass laws that fine workers for striking and also make them illegal. If that doesn't stop them, they'll bring on the guns and the militia. Right now the Depression is easing a bit and there's less unemployment, although much of that is due to the growing war industry and here, in New York City, they're spending a little money, just enough, to keep the unemployed, writers and artists alive, eating and not making too much trouble. Miriam concedes that there's a lot of good stuff around. Just a few days ago she and Sydney went to see "Pins and Needles", a clever, satirical musical done by the Ladies Garment Workers Union.

As she waits across the street from the two great stone lions of the 42nd Street Library, she thinks, *I guess we manage all right in America, in spite of the defeat in Spain and all the horrors around the world—including those that our own country is responsible for. We think we're the greatest country in the world—and I suppose we are—but that doesn't mean there isn't a lot that needs to be changed. If only I knew how to change it. It so damn difficult.... overwhelming ... You can't let yourself become discouraged,* she tells herself—*it's a luxury you can't afford.*

Fall–Winter, 1938

Although Lyova is ill, troubled for some time, by an inflamed appendix, he delays the necessary operation. He's been very happy about the favorable verdict of the hearings, and in a letter to his parents in early February he sends them proofs of the latest Bulletin, outlining his many plans for the future.

But he must undergo this operation, it has now become imperative. He decides to enter a small private clinic run by Russian emigre doctors, even though he's been warned to avoid any Russian contact in the wake of Reiss's assassination. For the first few days, Lyova seems to be recovering smoothly and completely. But on the fourth day he runs a high fever, becomes delirious, screaming with excruciating pain, and within a few hours he dies.

Casa Azul learns about Lyova's death when an American news agency calls. Trotsky had stolen away surreptitiously to stay with a friend so that he can get some peace and work on his essay "Their Morals and Ours." Van Heijenoort fetches Diego Rivera and together they go to Trotsky and break the news. Trotsky looks uncomprehendingly at them, then an anguished cry fills the room. He motions them away; he wants to be alone. Only later does he open the door, his face expressionless. He wants to hurry back to the Casa Azul. "I must tell Natalya," he says.

Aferwards Trotsky and Natalya close their bedroom door. They don't see nor speak to anyone for eight days. When Trotsky emerges he can barely speak. His beard is long and straggly, his eyes swollen. Sergei is in Siberia and now, for the third time, a child is dead.

CHAPTER 15

New York City, Winter 1938

One night, on a slushy, sleeting evening in February, comrades are called to a special membership meeting at Party headquarters. When Miriam and Sydney enter the headquarters, somber faces greet them. "What's this about?" Miriam asks Sylvia, who's saved a seat for them.

"Terrible news," Sylvia whispers, her face drawn. "Trotsky's son just died. Just listen now and be quiet."

Max Shachtman comes forward slowly, carrying a sheaf of papers, his shoulders hunched as if he were chilled. He starts to speak but his voice clouds and he stops.

He begins again, "Comrades, you might have heard this news already ... It's the saddest message I've ever delivered in my life ... Lyova, Trotsky's older son, has just died. He was in a small Russian Hospital, outside of Paris, where he was operated on for appendicitis. There'll be an official inquest because many questions have been raised by his wife, Jeanne, as well as his parents."

He pauses and then looking out at the audience, everyone sitting silent, stunned, he asks "Do you have any questions?"

A comrade from the back shouts angrily. "You bet we do. What in hell was he doing in a Russian Emigre hospital? Was it an emergency?"

"Yes and no. He had been suffering for some time with appendicitis but kept postponing it. He wanted to bring out the Bulletin with the verdict of the Dewey Commission and send it to his father first." He pauses. "Shall I continue?"

Comrades are becoming more agitated, some drumming the floor and calling out. "What in hell are you doing, Max? Tell us what happened. We want to know."

Max sighs, "Lyova had been suffering for some time with appendicitis and his friend Etienne and he both decided it would be better if he went to a small Russian clinic rather than a French hospital, where they figured the G P U might easily find him. On the night of Feb. 8th he got another attack, he was in terrible pain and decided he had to go and get it over with—it was supposed to be a relatively simple operation. He wrote a letter, gave it to Jeanne, she was to open it only if there was 'an accident.' He was operated on that night ..."

Schactman stops, he can't go on. A twisted grin creeps across his face; he looks down at the papers in his hand. Everyone is quiet waiting. Everyone praying, hoping against hope, like children who always want the happy ending.

"The operation was a success," he continues. "Right after the operation, he was recovering well. Etienne visited him, Jeanne too, but no one else. They talked about politics and organizational matters. But a few days later they found him in the hall, half-dressed, raving feverish. They operated again, it didn't help—he was in excruciating pain, they tried blood transfusions. Everything was useless."

Black jumps up, "I can't believe this! Where were the French comrades ..."

Shachtman continues, after scowling at the interruption. "Although Etienne and Lyova had decided they would allow no visitors, it would have been very easy for an agent to get in and poison him. The chief surgeon hints that Lyova may have been suicidal, a crazy idea nobody believes. The staff claimed they didn't know he was Russian, although when he was feverish he was screaming in that language."

Schachtman pauses, unable to go on. "Comrades," he says, "We sent condolences to Trotsky and Natalya in Mexico as soon as we got the news. We'll take a short break now." He leaves, a shadow of his normal ebullience.

A few moments later, Cannon comes forward. He sits at a table, with his customary glass of cold milk (prescribed for stomach ulcers) in front of him. His normally florid face now pale and expressionless as if grief has wiped it clean, his voice so lows that the comrades have to move close to hear him.

"Comrades, I know you want to know about Trotsky and Natalya." Jim stops to take a sip of milk. "Right now, they are seeing no one. They're closed in his room and the staff hears them, crying and talking and crying. Now their third child is gone and Lyova was the closest to them. In all of their struggles throughout the years he had shared so much, so faithful, devoted, loving ..."

Cannon stops and looks over at the window, after a deep sigh, goes on. "On one occasion when I visited the Old Man in Mexico, he sat with me, and told me about Lyova, how he depended on him. He knew the ordeals that Lyova had had to endure, the endless lies, the desertions and surrenders of friends and comrades that hurt him, the tragedy of his sister's suicide and at last the trials which shook him to his very core."

Jim stands up, and moves close to the comrades. His face flushed, he thunders, "Whatever the truth, and I speak in Trotsky's words now, whatever the truth about the direct cause of Lyova's death, whether he died exhausted by these ordeals or whether the G P U poisoned him, in either case, it was they and their master Stalin that are guilty of his death." He pauses. "There's nothing more I can say at this time. Thank you, comrades." He steps down and shuffles to his office, not speaking to anyone.

The comrades, break up into groups, rehashing what they've heard, expressing sorrow, suspicion, and anger. In a little while, there's a half-hearted attempt to hold a regular business meeting concerning organization and finance but it breaks up early. Everyone just wants to get home.

It is one more tragedy in a time that seems filled with tragedies, and life goes on as usual. Comrades go to work, eat, sleep, make love and on Saturday night, go to the movies although now they're not given a free dish anymore. Miriam keeps up her round of work, school, politics, but now the idea of trip somewhere far away gives her something to look forward to. Ketzel's not going back to Spain and begins working on a new ballet which she hopes to present in Paris. She calls Miriam, "I'm coming to your house again tonight. Your mother's going to make some costumes for me."

Unlike other dancers in the field, Graham, Limon, Sokolow, Tamiris, who have to work or be funded, Jaime's generous allowance gives her freedom to create and even pay a small salary to a few dancers. She usually performs in a troupe but she enjoys freedom to do as she likes, from time to time linking up with other groups. *She's privileged,* Miriam thinks, *but no one can say she doesn't take her dancing seriously.*

Clara loves to sew for Ketzel. Dressmaking has always been enjoyable for her and now collaborating with this young woman is turning out to be more pleasurable that expected. Her attitude toward Ketzel is very different from that wintry day years ago when all she saw was a haughty, beautiful young woman.

Now, she tells Miriam, "That Ketzel, she's smart—got a good head on her shoulders. She could make lots of money in the business world. Too bad, she wants to be a dancer."

Ketzel comes often to the apartment on 151st Street and the two women work together in the evening. Miriam sees Clara letting herself joyfulling reliving the past, when her daughter, Bertha, her beloved first-born used to bring home a dress (she'd borrow one overnight) from Milgrim Brothers and the two would work together, copying the design. Under the lamp, their heads bent over the kitchen table, one, white-haired, the other, burnished gold,—the cutting fabric, the smell of warm cloth pervading the room, the old treadle sewing machine clacking away. Miriam's heart aches, she wishes, *if only this could last for you, Mama—a long time. Yet, at the same time, she can't help wishing a little of the tenderness and softness could have been there for her.*

As far as Jaime's concerned, she's able to keep him out of her daytime thoughts, but these days she tends to be moody and irritable. She's tried to find a closer connection to Sydney but can't seem to plug into his inner feelings. When she tried to talk about their friends, why they liked some or resented others, he'd turn a deaf ear. She knew he wanted people to like him; he'd go out of his way to do a favor for even a casual acquaintance, but he'd find it impossible to develop a close relationship. "I'm not interested in that kind of petty stuff, it's not important is it?," would be his usual answer, and the end of their conversation would be silence unless she brings up something connected with world affairs or Party politics.

After living with him all these months she should know that he is sloppy and uncooperative. There's no sense in asking him to please not throw his socks on the floor. But she can't help herself. "There's no Maggie in this household to clean up after you," she scolds. He just doesn't seem to care so she decides not to pick them up, and one Sunday morning when she counts eleven dirty socks on the bedroom floor, she begins to yell.

Grasping her shoulders with his thin hands, looking into her eyes, Sydney yells, "Miriam, it isn't only my sloppiness. You're cranky nowadays." He lets her go. "Maybe we're not good together anymore."

She can't explain, she can't say everything that really on her mind but, of course, there's no reason to shout. "A lot of things are bothering me, Sydney. My job's over soon, what's happening in Spain, the Old Man's son murdered, our having to move in here. You're right. It isn't just your socks on the floor." She goes into the kitchen, puts up coffee and starts to cry. She wants to say, "There's a big hole in my heart and I don't know how to fill it," but a few minutes later when she sees him picking up his socks, she says, "I'm okay, really, Why don't we eat out tonight? The new Cuban restaurant on 146th Street is supposed to be good."

A few weeks later just when she's telling herself that she's over Jaime, he calls her at work. Miss Croxdale storms into Mr. Landgren's office where Miriam's taking dictation and yells, "Miss Gold, I have a phone message for you. You know you're not supposed to get calls at this office. Mr. Ortega wants you to call him back. Don't let it happen again." Miriam waits till after four and everyone's gone. She wants to sound cool and unruffled but as always, when she hears his voice, she finds it hard to start speaking.

"Miriam, darling, I'm sorry I had to call you at the office. I didn't think it was wise to call you at home." Hearing the lovely musical timbre of his voice her heart quickens. "I want to apologize for the last time, it wasn't right."

"It doesn't matter," Miriam manages to say. "I know you find this as difficult as I do." "Jaime, listen, please—please." Oh God, why did she have to say this. "What would be the sense of our trying to be together?" She swallows, it's so hard to say these words ... "Nothing has changed. We're too far apart ..." Her voice dies away.

Jaime, impatient now, "Yes, I know that. And at least right now, it can't be helped. For different reasons. But you know I love you. And this isn't doing either one of us any good. Ketzel tells me you're not looking good these days, you're thin and pale ..."

"I'm okay. Really." She can't control words now, they spill from her lips. "I do want to see you, Jaime, I want to see your face, to be with you ..." She's crying now. "Being with you that night—Wait ..." She struggles to stop, telling herself that once and for all she has to handle this in a mature fashion. Steadying her voice and wiping her eyes, she goes on, "We disagree, Jaime, we can't resolve those disagreements. There are other factors too." She pauses now, afraid to continue. Jaime, quick-tempered, will probably think what she's going to suggest is ridiculous. But she takes a deep breath and continues, "I've thought about this. Maybe for a while we could write to each other. In that way, we can keep cool, not fly off the handle. And who knows, in time, something might happen. Please wait a little while. Maybe something will change. One of us might begin to see things differently or ..." She's thinking *Stalin might die, things in Russia might change,* but she's afraid it might sound childish or ridiculous and she doesn't dare.

In a sarcastic voice he asks, "Oh, so this is what you propose; we write letters instead of seeing each other? Love letters like … Heloise and Abelard. Would that satisfy you? Well, my dear, it's absurd …" Miriam doesn't hear the rest. There's a sound at the outer door—someone's entering the main office. She jumps up, "I'll have to hang up now. I'll …" She hangs up and dashes out to find Mr. Landgren looking for his umbrella on the coat rack, puzzled to find her still there.

In school, that night, she decides to continue the conversation in writing. She writes:

Dear Jaime:

I think I'm much better at writing term papers than love letters. They are not a viable substitute but under the present circumstances, I can't think of anything else to do. I'm not going to try to convince you of anything because I think, among other things, you're a lot smarter (and older) than I. And, while I'm on the subject, I think you're the most wonderful guy in the world.

Please let's keep in touch this way, don't worry about me. I promise to eat more and keep healthy. You do the same. Maybe something will change. Let's be patient, please.

Love, Miriam

P.S. This note sounds cheerful but I'm not, really.
P.P.S. I'm enclosing an excerpt from an article on "Socialism in One Country" which you might not have read. Please don't be angry at me for sending it.

In two days, Miriam receives a response, mailed to her at the office. Ms. Croxdale hands her a letter without comment and a blank face. After all, receiving mail isn't prohibited by W P A rules.

Miriam dear,

Yes, I am angry at your sending me the article. It was totally unnecessary. I know the Trotskyite position on socialism in one country and all the other political positions of this renegade and his followers. Your hero ignores the tremendous advances the U.S.S.R has made over the past fifteen years, becoming, under the worst, most difficult circumstances, the second highest industrialized nation in the world. Throughout the world Stalin is respected for his leadership, Rolland, Barbusse, Aragon, Shaw; here in America, Dreiser, Lamont, Beard and so on and on. And they are not only supporting Stalin but also condemning Trotsky.

Enough of that. When I think of our relationship, it reminds me of a certain species of bird called Swifts, the most aerial of all, flying almost one-hundred miles an hour. They live their entire lives in the air, mating in the atmosphere. Are we like them, zooming above the earth—coupling in the blue sky. That's just fine but like other species, we have to live on the ground, and be grounded in reality. I hope you can come back to earth some day, before it's too late.

I wish you the best. As for myself, nothing more can be said right now. I have some important business which must be taken care of. I will be leaving the city shortly. I don't know when we will see each other again.

As always, Jaime.

At the bottom of the neat typed, handwritten, added at the last moment were two words, "te quiero." *As if he didn't want to write them but couldn't resist.*

Although she'd steeled herself for Jaime's response, it stills upsets her. She rereads the note in the rest room of Hunter. Two girls putting on make-up at the sink, look at her and one putting her arm around her, asks, "What happened—did you fail a course?" Miriam looks at her, her eyes swimming. With trembling lips, attempting a little laugh, she answers, "You might say that. Yeah, I've just been given the gate."

Sylvia and Ruby have finally made plans for their trip. There have been several delays but at last they're able to coordinate their dates and Miriam gets a call from Sylvia that she and Ruby are sailing on the Ile de France and would she like to come down for the going-away party. Miriam can't make it—there's no way she can take off from work—but she wishes her bon voyage.

"I saw your friends this afternoon," Ketzel says as Miriam comes in after work. Ketzel has once again been invited to stay for supper. While Fanny's dishing out the chicken stew Ketzel adds, "I was at the pier today saying good-by to one of my dancers."

"Yeah, I knew they were going." Miriam says, slumping into a chair at the table. "Is there enough left over for Sydney and me?" Miriam can't help feeling a little jealous. She rarely makes dinner for her and Sydney.

"I made plenty," Clara answers quickly. "You know I do."

"I'm leaving for Paris next week," Ketzel says, between bites of chicken. "Martin wants me to come. He's doing an article for the New Masses about the Spanish refugees flooding into France and he's got something else very important he can't tell me about. Frankly, I really don't want to know." She nods to Clara, holding the pot on her hip, to fill her plate. "It's delicious. I'll take another leg, if there's one left."

"I've heard about the Spanish refugees," Miriam shudders. "France doesn't want them, they're put into horrible internment camps—even left on the roads to die and of course, German and Italian soldiers can't go back to their own country where they'll be killed. The whole thing is so dreadful!"

"Eat," Clara interrupts harshly. "You want it to get cold?" She's not concerned with Spain's misfortune—that's across the ocean and this is America. She's come to this country to escape pogroms and war, and she has enough of her own tzouris.

"Okay, mom," Miriam sighs, exchanging a glance with Ketzel. "Ketzel's right—the chicken's delicious. Can I have a little more gravy."

Mexico, 1938

After Lyova's death, Trotsky and Natalya are in constant touch with his lover, Jeanne. They know that she, also, is heartbroken. Trotsky invites her to come with Lyova's son, Seva, to Mexico. "I love you greatly, Jeanne," he writes. But she refuses. Trotsky angrily insists that Seva be sent to Mexico even if Jeanne refuses to come. He resorts to the law with the help of his friend in France, to get his grandson back. One day, Natalya comes crying to Van, saying "L. D. has accused me of siding with Jeanne and the others against him," Van tries to console her but can't help thinking that Trotsky is speaking to her "in the most cutting and brutal terms." It's only a short time since their son's death. The legal case drags on for more than a year. When the courts rule that Seva is to be given into his grandfather's care, Jeanne takes the little boy from Paris and hides him.

Throughout the summer of 1938 Trotsky is busy preparing a Draft Programme for the founding congress of the Fourth International. Comrades who have managed to escape from Russian prison camps have sent reports of the horrors taking place, but most of the persecutions, tortures and murders have been carried out in secret. The fact that so many are charged with being Trotskyists leads him to hope his movement is succeeding, that in the course of the coming war Stalin will be overthrown and the Bolsheviks will recapture the Communist Party. He doesn't realize that the Russian earth is so soaked with blood it may never recover—or if it ever does, it will take decades, perhaps centuries.

CHAPTER 16

September, 1938

Summer heat ravages the streets. Parched workers are happy to see night fall; thick air, like wet gray wool, covers the city. Friday night, the kitchen is empty and silent except for the whirring of an electric fan. Snatches of tunes, 'Perfidia', and 'El Manisero'—The Peanut Vendor,—steal through the open window, mingling with the slapping of rubber balls and the chatter of mamas clustered on the stoops, their wide bottoms spread across Spanish newspapers. Children gather about a pushcart that contains a large cake of ice, surrounded by bottles of colored liquid and for two cents a Lily cup will be filled with fresh shaved ice doused with red, green and orange syrup, sweet and cold!

Miriam's glad to be alone this evening. Her mother's at her sister's house and Sydney's at a meeting. She needs this time to be alone. Sitting at the kitchen table she looks at the three letters before her. They've arrived at various times during the past week but her mother forgot about to give them to her. Before she leaves for the week-end she hands them to Miriam, with a apologetic grimace.

She looks at the letters and reads the oldest first. It's from Sylvia, postmarked Paris and dated August 19.

Dear Miriam,

London was wonderful. We had a very short visit with Ruby's sister and decided to go right on to Paris. Ruby made reservations for us in a charming hotel, Hotel

Cluny on the Left Bank. It's full of old-fasioned charm and very clear. Paris is gorgeous.

Ruby and I get along very well, although she was a little miffed when I divided the shelf over the sink in the bathroom to divide our stuff.

We're just taken a ride on a bateau mouche that must have been 100 years old with hard, uncomfortable seats! But we enjoyed it anyway.

Will write more soon,

Love, Sylvia

Miriam can just see Sylvia and Ruby, in dainty summer dresses, sitting stiffly on an old Seine excursion boat, sailing by the Notre Dame Cathedral. Now for Ketzel's letters. She opens the earlier one.

ॐ

Miriam dear,

It feels great to be in Paris again. I feel so light here. I wonder why? Maybe it's because there isn't the same kind of pressure in the New York scene. There's no question that "our own City" is the center of modern dance. "Paris talks and New York does," they say.

Meanwhile, I've been having a helluva time, although everyone here, the whole continent, is praying for peace, trying to appease Herr Hitler by throwing him pieces of Europe. Anyone savvy knows it won't work. But for the moment, I'm relaxing, going to shows, having great meals.

Caridad is here and we're gadding around. We went to see Maurice Chevalier and Josephine Baker twice. She's a mediocre, acrobatic dancer but has this fantastic long black shining body! She does cartwheels on the stage, naked with a pink flamingo feather between her legs and she's sings too, has a sweet, thin voice. The Casino revue is great, beautiful nudes, clever and satirical. Maurice is the hit of the show; he does a German love ballad in Hitler's voice.

I'm not sure how long we'll be here. Martin is very busy and I'm just enjoying myself. Caridad is going to Moscow soon; then, to Mexico with her boy-friend, Kotov, aka Eitingon. I'm not supposed to know their plans and I don't want to. Ramon's in Paris right now. He was at a gathering of Frida Kahlo's that I wasn't invited to. I heard, although they're keeping it a secret, that he's seeing some girl, an American, but it's hush-hush. David Siquieros is here too. I met him at Ger-

trude Stein's new apartment where she keeps a collection of 131 paintings. Imagine!

Tina Modotti, Caridad and I had lunch at Prunier's last week. Caridad insisted on treating——expensive, but the oysters were delicious. I think good food is wasted on Tina——she doesn't even know what she's eating these days. She's so screwed up, scarcely talks, a zombie and I think it's because of her husband, who, as you know, is a horror. Not only is he vulgar, farting and pinching women's behinds, but there's a dark, evil side to him behind his vulgarity. It's rumored when Tina heard about someone's death she blurted——"I wish it had been Contreras——he's an assassin, a villain. He deserves to die." How can she live with him?

Enough of this gossip. I hope you're okay. It's not easy for Trotskyites (I wish you weren't). Not that we Communists are popular everywhere but we have our own country, our Homeland.

Your friend Sylvia is here——she called me the other day. You gave her my phone number, remember? She's by herself; her friend Ruby left almost as soon as they got to Paris. It seems a little strange, she persuades Sylvia to go to Europe and then off she goes——suddenly. But before she disappeared Ruby introduced her to a guy, and now they're seeing each other. That's Paris for you. Write me.

Love, love, Ketzel

Miriam puts all the pages together, stuffs them in an envelope. My two friends are in Europe, in the greatest City in the world and I'm Cinderella who wasn't invited to the ball, sitting in the kitchen.

Another from Ketzel,

Dear Miriam,

I just wrote but I couldn't wait to tell you the news, so here's another letter. Remember I told you about Carolina, an old friend of the family in Mexico? That is, she isn't old——she's the daughter of an old friend and we've known her since she was a kid. She's our age and very beautiful!——"the cat's meow"!

You'll never guess what my dad has done. I'm in shock myself. He's gone and married Carolina! Just like that. He called me and told me but didn't say much except, "I hope you'll wish us the best." I knew she had a crush on him since forever and I guess she's a fast worker. She's a nice girl but from the way he talked about her I'd never have guessed he was in love with her. I have to tell you, I'm not very happy aout the whole thing. But it's a fait accompli, so there you are.

Hope you're okay——working, busy, active——as usual.

Miss and love you, Ketzel.

Miriam sits, unable to move. The letter is still in her hand and she's unable to put it down. What did you expect—she keeps asking herself—what did you expect when you turned away from him that freezing day when he pleaded so hard. She begins to shake her head, refusing the reality.

It's really over—once and for all—finished—finished—she pulls deep breaths into her frozen body. Then, at last, beginning to cry, she puts her head down on the kitchen table and lets a flood of tears burst through.

In a little while a small evening breeze steals in, cooling her flushed cheeks and she makes herself pull off her dress and climb into the shower letting the tingling drops refresh her. Remembrance of that sweet, ardent lovemaking that misty summer evening comes stealing in and she whispers, *I'll never forget that night,* she tells herself. Then, she adds defiantly … *And neither will he, no matter who's he's married to!*

She dries off, gets dressed. She asked him to wait but he hadn't. Perhaps it was the girl—she's heard Latin women know all about how to catch a man. Tears start to come again and she tells herself to cut it out. *You've wasted enough time feeling sorry for yourself.*

Outside there are shouts and screams. She peers through the open window and sees two old men standing by a car with a flat tire, yelling at each other in Spanish. One is waving a heavy wrench as if he'd liked to kill the other one.

"I've got to get out of here." She's been thinking about going to Mexico but she hasn't made any definite plans—why hasn't she? Bunny's interested in going, too, she picked up the idea right away. She won't see Jaime, of course. But she can meet Trotsky and some of the comrades around him. Perhaps it will give her new energy for political work and take her mind off her own problems! To see the "Old Man" to hear his voice, would be thrilling! Her job's ending sometime in November and she'll be unemployed, free as a bird! She picks up the phone and calls Bunny.

"Great!" Bunny squeals, "Leave it to me—I'm starting on it today—I'll find the cheapest way we can make it! We're off!"

❧   ❧   ❧

A few weeks later, Hilda visits The Municipal Art Gallery on 67th Street. The W P A is expected to close very soon. and these are the final weeks before the Art Project closes down.

"It's not just the artists are so good," Miriam tells her, "but the building is beautiful—Thomas Fortune Ryan, a millionaire, built it. My boss, Marchal Landgren told me about him. Mr. Landgren's very artistic, has all these boy-friends, drives me crazy with his derogatory remarks about women. He's about six feet five and very, very skinny. When I look at him I can't imagine him without clothes on."

"No," says Hilda, "and I wouldn't want to try. Hilda, looking cool in a neat, navy blue print dress with a white color, agrees with Miriam about the gallery. "It's very European, the white sandstone entrance and a lovely garden on Fifth Avenue." As they stroll about the light, high-ceiling room viewing the mostly realistic paintings depicting the mean streets and towering skyscrapers of the City, she comments, "They're really good artists—Yasuo Kuniyoshi, Marc Chagall, Reginald Marsh. Look what they're selling their paintings for—twenty or thirty dollars!"

"You should see them when they come in. Old pants, dirty sneakers, lugging canvases under their arms. But they're happy to be working.!"

"Why don't you buy one—at least," Hilda asks. "I'll bet a lot of them'll be famous some day and sell for a lot of money. Look at this 'A Nickel a Shine' by Raphael Soyer. It's so good, you can really see the kids …"

"I haven't got much money," Miriam interrupts, "just a hundred dollars in the bank from when my mother cashed in my insurance policy." Miriam moves away, trying to squelch a feeling of annoyance, thinking she's probably right about buying a picture but she needs to do something right away. "I'm not buying anything now. I can't. I want to go to Mexico soon and I'll need every penny."

"They're very good," Hilda answers, somewhat snappy. "Too bad. But I know you need money when you travel." She crosses the room to look at a Chagall again, "I bet his stuff'll catch on."

Hilda leaves soon after. "Oh, by the way, I meant to tell you," she says as they stand at the bus stop on Fifth Avenue. "I just got a letter from Sylvia. She's met a guy, Jacques, through Ruby. He sounds like a dreamboat—tall, dark and handsome. Loaded too, it seems. Is that a bus coming now? With a peck on

Miriam's cheek, she dashes away. "When you go to Mexico, be sure to give my best to the Old Man."

Pechora Camps, Fall 1936–Spring 1937

Despite the vicious cruelty of Stalin's concentration camps, they have become the training grounds for the Trotskyist opposition. The hold hunger strikes, demand better food and housing and inspire everyone with their defiance.

In the Pechora camps a thousand men go on strike. It is rumored that one of them is Sergei, Trotsky's younger son. The action lasts 132 days and the camp administration, on orders from Moscow, yields on all points. In the following months, with spirits raised, the Old Bolsheviks dare to hope there might be a partial amnesty since it is the twentieth anniversary of the October Revolution.

But the terror returns with unmitigated fury. The Regime, realizing that this kind of militant action might spread, isolate the prisoners, creating a camp within a camp, guarding the inmates, night and day.

A roll call begins. Every morning, about twenty prisoners are taken on a march. Shots are heard in the distance. Only the guards return. Every day. Women and children too. One day, one hundred are taken. As they make their way, the remaining prisoners sing The Internationale. It is almost complete—the annihilation of the anti-Stalinist Bolsheviks.

Trotsky knows how awful the terror can be but he cannot guess or visualize what is really happening and he still hopes. He does not know that a whole generation has been wiped out—all drowned in blood and only he remains.

CHAPTER 17

New York City, September 1938

Several weeks later another envelope, a thick one, arrives from Paris. This one is from Sylvia. Up 'til now, she's just gotten little bits and pieces from Hilda—telling her Sylvia's staying on—and she's got a boy-friend! Miriam opens it, curious, excited.

Paris, Sept. 3, 1938

Dear Miriam,

Please forgive me for not writing to you sooner. I've been so busy with so many things that I just didn't get to it before now. And also, I wasn't sure when I would be returning home.

I'm sure you're puzzled why I've remained so long in Paris. Well——I've met some-one.

Ruby introduced me to him. His name is Jacques Mornard! Miriam, I can't believe this is happening to me. I think I'm in love. Jacques is everything I have ever dreamed of in a man. He's Belgian, very intelligent, speaks several lan-guages, English, French and Spanish. He's good-looking, dark eyes (wears glasses), curly hair, strong even features, slim, a little above average height, comes from a good family, his father's a diplomat or something, well-to-do, has plenty of money to spend.

Is it unbelievable? Almost! At the beginning, I kept thinking that it's only a passing fancy on his part and it won't last. But it looks like, for both of us, it's becoming something real and deep. At times, he tends to be a little moody and withdraws into a shell but it doesn't last long. Maybe that's why he likes me, I'm even tempered and easy to get along with.

We're having a wonderful time! Since money isn't a problem, we go to good restaurants like the Polidor, lots of atmosphere. small wooden tables, a tin ceiling, handwritten menus. Sometimes we'll go to the Tuilleries Gardens or walk along the Seine and brouse at the bookstalls.

I must sound like a school-girl. I haven't written to the folks back home, but you can understand how I feel. Since I'm running out of money and should be thinking of going home, Jacques suggested that I write some articles about child psychology for a publication called "Argus." He knows people there and thinks he can get some of my stuff published. It may be a possibility. Right now I don't know when I'll be back. When I talk about leaving Jacques makes it so hard for me. He takes off his dark shell-rimmed glasses, and says plaintively, "Please don't leave me".

I'll write soon again. Give everyone back home my regards,

Love, Sylvia

Miriam finishes the first letter, puts the second one aside. She leans back in the old, comfortable armchair her mother covered with chinz and closes her eyes. It's midnight and Sydney's already asleep. He never went to bed this early but he had a lot of wine at dinner. She's really happy for Sylvia,. Her new man sounds wonderful. It's not unusual for a handsome, desirable man to fall for a plain girl. It happens every day. After all, she's not beautiful, although Jaime told her she was. That night he must have whispered it a thousand times. She closes her eyes seeing his dark face on the white pillow beside her ... No, she's not going to think of him. She picks up the second letter from Sylvia, this one with an October date.

Dear Miriam,

Yes, I'm still here in Paris and I just noticed I never sent off the first letter. Just couldn't tear myself away and besides I wanted to stay for the Fourth International meeting at the Rosmer's house.

Jacques and I have been together practically every day except once, in July when he had to leave Paris suddenly to go back home. His mother was badly injured and her chauffeur killed in an auto accident. It was the same time that Klement, who had been one of the Old Man's secretaries, a while back, disappeared. A few weeks later they found his body floating in the Seine. Everybody in Paris is talking about it. People are saying it could have been the G P U., carved up his body and cut off his head! It was such a neat job, they say it must have been done by an experienced surgeon——or a butcher. It make you shiver!

I tried to tell Jacques about it when he got back to Paris but he didn't want to hear about it or discuss it. He had trouble with the military, they detained him because he had refused to serve in the army. Anyway, I hardly listen to him when he tells me about stuff that doesn't concern us. I'm surprised at myself sometimes, for being so much in love, I'm acting like a little girl. We've been enjoying ourselves and I won't bore you with the names of restaurants, but we did go to see Josephine Baker at le Jockey Club and to Porte Maillot in the Bois. It was so romantic! We sat looking out at the tiny lights in horse-chestnut trees along the lake, holding hands.

Jacques isn't political at all. When I wanted to attend the Fourth International meeting he said that he would go with me but wait outside. I wanted to introduce him to Max and the Rosmers' (the meeting was held in Perigny) but he wasn't interested.

The meeting opened with sad homage to three Trotskyist martyrs, Lyova, Klement and Wolf——all murdered by Stalin, they were made Honorary Presidents. Zborowski, 'Etienne', Lyova's closest friend looked very depressed——he helped Lyova make those arrangements to go to that Russian Emigre hospital and I think he feels responsible for what happened but the Committee didn't. He was made a delegate!

We'll be in New York very soon. I expect to come back in February and Jacques will follow in a few weeks. I can't wait to introduce him to you and my family. Incidentally, have you seen Ruby by any chance? She disappeared right after she introduced me to Jacques and I haven't heard from her since; isn't that strange?

I'll see you soon. Love and comradely greeting to everyone.

Sylvia

No, Sylvia, Miriam thinks, *I haven't seen or heard about Ruby and I couldn't care less. I never liked her, she was too damn sweet. This Jacques sounds too good to be true. But maybe Sylvia's just lucky. She certainly sounds happy.*

She gets up and goes to the kitchen. A good cup of tea—that's what I need right now she tells herself, and stands at the chipped black and white gas stove waiting for the kettle to boil. The street below is so quiet she can hear Sydney's light snoring through the open bed-room door. She knows Sydney's even more unhappy than usual. He hates his job and even his political life, the only thing that really means anything to him, is full of disappointment. He desperately wants to play an important role in the Workers Party but it's becoming clear that's not going to happen. He'd first become political at the University of Wisconsin, where he'd been more committed and better armed intellectually than the ordinary student. Here in New York others in the party were at least as clever as he was, often brilliant and amazingly articulate—men like Max Shachtmen, Sidney Hook and Felix Morrow—and Sydney was swept to the sidelines in the competitive milieu. Nor did he have the easy-going, affable manner required to build a caucus around his "positions," a kind of politicking found in a Marxist-Leninist movement.

She remembers an August day when they were first living together, when they'd gone up to the Workmen's Circle summer camp and after breakfast people began discussing the Soviet Union. Someone asked a question, Sydney sood up to answer it and before long he was conducting an hour-long political seminar. When he finished, there was enthusiastic applause, and his face was flushed and so happy. Now sometimes she looks at his grim face, at the way he sits by himself at meetings and her heart aches for him.

She pours steaming water over a small strainer filled with tea leaves and takes a Fig-Newton, telling herself to stop feeling sorry for Sydney. His self-pity won't get him anywhere—neither will hers. She thinks back to Sylvia's letter, to all the people who died trying to defend Trotsky and what he stands for against those who would destroy him.

Think of those two brave, wonderful people living in exile, far from home, their children and friends, dead, murdered. Every day of their lives must be full of fear. Yet they are cheerful and hospitable, carrying on from day to day. Sternly she asks herself, *What have you got to complain about?*

It seems like a stroke of incredible luck when Bunny finds the advertisement seeking two passengers to share the expenses of driving from New York to Mexico City. She phones Miriam and they arrange to meet with the driver, Mr. Conseco, a plump, balding Mexican businessman with a pencil mustache. He assures them that his Packard is in tip-top condition for a long trip, and tells them that his niece, Marisela is coming along to share in the driving. He and Marisella will take turns so that they can travel non-stop and save on staying overnight in motels. The car's backseat is roomy and the two Americanas can sleep back there whenever they want. The three shake hands on the deal.

The night before they're set to leave, Miriam and Sydney have dinner dinner with Bunny and her boy-friend, Alvin, a member of the Lower East Side Branch. All of them had met a few months before and Sydney had observed to Miriam, "Wow, that Bunny, she's really stacked." Sydney didn't usually take notice of looks but Bunny is strikingly beautiful, with smooth olive skin, liquid brown eyes, melon firm breasts and a tiny waist. She's the same age as Miriam, bored with Alvin, not political, an 'accidental Trotskyite' you might say, eager for new adventures, especially those with the opposite sex. Miriam was hesitant about her company, but having someone to share expenses is necessary and she seems easy-going and pleasant. *She's looking for a fling and that won't be hard with her looks. But what am I looking for?*, Miriam asks herself.

The night before, getting ready for bed, Sydney hands Miriam a small book. "Put this in your satchel. I just got it for you today." She's pleased, he doesn't usually think about giving presents.

"Thank you," she says, giving him a light kiss.

"It's a diary. I know you won't have time to write often. This way I'll have something to read when you get back. I really want to hear about the Old Man. Maybe you'll even get a short meeting with him if he's not too busy."

"Sydney, what if he asks me about dialectical materialism! I don't know much about it. I never did finish that course at the Workers' School." Miriam stuffs an extra lipstick into her bag. "I know what I can do. I did read 'My Life.' I'll tell him I think it's wonderful, and I'll take some Militants that have his articles."

"Miriam," Sydney says with a little smirk that always annoyed her, "He's not going to give you a test." He adds, "He won't expect a young comrade to know everything. Don't worry." Then, slowly, "Be careful. It's dangerous in Mexico. Remember what happened to Klement, even though it was Paris, not Mexico."

"Oh, my God. That was so gruesome," Miriam shudders, closing her eyes, blotting out the image. "His head cut off, the body chopped up like he'd been tortured. How can people do these things?"

"They do." Sydney's hand trembles as he lights a cigarette. "They do them all the time."

"But why should the G P U bother with people like me—or Bunny? We're not important, we don't matter."

"When they're out to get someone, they'll use innocent people, and kill them too, if necessary. Be careful, stay with the comrades and guards," he stops.

"Even there. How can we be sure? The Old Man's gotten more than a few warnings about people in his own household. Who can you trust … The Party is thick with spies." His voice harsh, he snatches the Times from the bed, goes into the living room and throws himself into the easy chair under the lamp. A little while later, he calls to her, his voice soft.

"Miriam, finish packing, and let's go to bed. You have to be up at four."

CHAPTER 18

Mexico, February 1939

On a dim, gray morning Bunny and Miriam kiss their two men goodby and pile into the back seat of Mr. Conseco's Packard. It turns out to be eight years old and has seventy-five thousand miles on it, and his "niece" Marisela, is a thirty-five, pretty, zaftig and loving young woman who sits so close to him in the front seat that it's hard to tell where he ends and she begins. But, after all, no one really cares.

It turns out to be an unforgettable automobile trip. Starting out, the foursome stock up on food and drinks as much as possible so they will only need to stop every few hours for gas and bathroom breaks. It seems a great plan and what's more, a very low-cost way of getting to Mexico.

Bunny is so happy to be off that as soon as they head out she begins singing. She knows all the words to songs like "On the Sunny Side of the Street" and "If I had a Talking Picture of You." Mr. Conseco chimes in with tangoes like "Caminito Adios" and "Aquellos Ojos Verdes" and his niece, who has a very low, growly voice, just likes to hum along. Miriam sits quietly and listens, preoccupied with thought of Sydney, home, Jaime. After the first day at least two of the four passengers end up sleeping at one time and quiet decends upon the car except for the hum of the Packard's engine, reputed for efficiency and durability. Except for minor iritations, like Marisela who takes thirty minutes every time she goes to the bathroom, and Mr. Conseco, who snores so loudly that nothing else can be heard, the passengers get along well.

After five days of riding they're happy to see that they're within one hundred miles of Laredo, Texas, where they'll cross the border into Mexico. But a few miles later, Mr. Conseco asks, "Did you hear that funny noise." "I think we have a little trouble," he says and pulls onto the side of the road. He walks down to the nearest gas station, a few blocks away, and when he comes back, he's frowning. "I talked to the mechanic. He says he thinks we have major trouble with the engine, she's leaking oil. We should be able to make it to Laredo but there we must check the motor. It may take several days."

"I knew it was too good to be true," Bunny thumps the lumpy pillow in the motel room where they end up that night. "I think he wants to dump us. He knows we can't afford to stay here for a week until the car is fixed."

"Maybe he just want to spend a week with his niece before he gets back to Mexico City and his wife. After all, it must have been very hard for him to sit that close to his niece for five days and just drive." Miriam grins. "At least we didn't pay him in advance for the whole trip."

She asks at the motel desk and finds out they can get a bus to Mexico City, on a Transportes del Norte, second class, the next morning for eight dollars. "We'll be there the next day," she tells Bunny, "it's about a thirty hour trip."

Bunny groans, "Okay. Okay. Fine. Now just let me get into a shower."

"I knew it wasn't too good to be true," says Miriam and reaches for her knapsack to record the misadventure in her diary.

❦   ❦   ❦

Miriam's Diary. Mexico, Winter 1938

Hotel Lincoln, 42 Avenida
Revillagigedo, Mexico City.

What a trip! "Second Class" did they say? More like the second ring of Hell. The seats and the arms rests (ha ha) were made of iron. Of course, we stopped anywhere along the road (that's what a second class rural bus does) wherever a passenger's waiting. We picked up a man with three chickens, an Indian with two baskets of mangoes and a baby on her back, a young girl with a heavy sack of onions, and an old man with a old billy-goat. We were lucky there was room in the back for him and for the most part we were high in the mountains so it's cool and not so smelly. Rest rooms—unheard of. Lucky for us, we found tall cactuses.

Towards evening, all of a sudden, a kid in the back starts to yell. "Pare—Pare!" He makes the driver stop, dashes out of the bus and comes back with an immense, fat, wriggling rattlesnake. "It's still alive," I scream. "You can't bring it in here."

"*Es muerto,*" *he insists, and puts it on the floor, under his seat in front of me. I try to stay calm.*

Meanwhile Bunny is flirting with a uniform up front and pays no attention to this or the fact that we're whizzing around narrow hair-pin curves at forty miles an hour. If we meet another car … I look down, I guess it's about six thousand feet. Winking lights show there's a village down there and that's also how far we can drop any moment. But I doze off anyway. Suddenly, I'm awake! Something has grabbed my shoulder. I know it's the snake and he's attacking me. I scream so loud that everyone, including Bunny, who is now sleeping on the General's shoulder, wakes up. Everyone, that is, except the snake which is dead, really dead this time. It was the kid who tapped my shoulder—just wanted to know what time it was. Why? What in hell difference did it make?

Finally, eight o'clock next morning, Mexico City. After a nap (two hours!) and a shower at our hotel, we went, with the help of a guide book, to Insurrgentes Sur (a bus depot) and then to Coyoacan. The town square is very old with a Dominican monastery and the Church of San Juan Bautista, 1583! Cobbled, quiet streets, mostly seventeenth century mansions with beautiful doors and iron gates, purple bouganvillea and pink geraniums everywhere.

Trotsky's house is on Avenida Londres, only a short walk from the bus stop. It was loaned to him by Frida Kahlo, a beautiful artist who got badly hurt in a horrible trolley-car accident and in whose house Trotsky and his wife are staying. From the outside all we could see were high walls, painted blue. I didn't say anything to Bunny but I felt apprehensive. I couldn't help remembering the angry demonstrations against Trotsky in Mexico City by Toledano, a Stalinist, head of the Confederation of Labor, and all the threats against the Old Man.

When we rang the doorbell at the 'Blue House', two men appeared with their hands on their gun holsters, looking grim but after we handed them our letters of introduction from the Party Office in New York they smiled and relaxed.

"*We didn't hear anything about you coming. That's why we looked so surprised,*" *Charlie Cornell, now cordial and warm, one of the house guards, told us. The other guard, a young, slim Mexican named Melquiades, who knows only a little English just smiled. We're invited tomorrow at four o'clock after Trotsky feeds his rabbits and chickens.*

Sanborn's on Madero—what a place! It's a store, a cafe, a restaurant, it's gorgeous! It's in an old courtyard, enclosed in glass, originally a 17th century mansion made of tiles, gorgeous ones. Imagine, Orozco has a mural in the ladies room! We had delicious ice-cream sundaes heaped with whipped cream. They say some

Americans never leave Sanborn's except to sleep. We'll have to go to the one at Reforma and Fragua where there's beautiful Tamayo murals and a great comida.

Wednesday—Hotel Lincoln

Walked to the Zocolo and up to the roof restaurant of the Hotel Majestic for a view of the great square. Coffee, nothing else. We're going to run out of money soon! There's so much to buy—everything's so beautiful, especially the silver jewelry, serapes, huipiles, (tops made of wool) and pottery. We bought food for lunch, only cheese and bread and fruit that you can peel, like oranges and bananas. We don't want to catch Monteczuma's revenge.

Back to the Blue House at four o'clock sharp, warned that the Old Man was very strict. Before the guards let us enter, Charlie and Melquiades searched and patted us down. They blushed, we didn't. Bunny enjoyed it! Waiting to greet us was Natalya and Jean Van Heijenoort, secretary to the Old Man. Van is tall, well-built and blond, with a broad handsome face and a good command of English. Natalya is sweet and frail, she trembled a little when she kissed us.

"We'll have tea in a little while when L.D. is finished. Let me show you around." The house is beautiful and spacious, U-shaped, the rooms curving about a courtyard garden that had an orange tree, rose bushes a sculpture and a miniature pyramid holding a thatched temple in its center. Finally we went to the hutches. The Old Man was just finishing his afternoon chores, and as he put a rabbit back in his clean cage and pulled off his white, I felt a kind of awe in his presence, his expression is so sharp! He's handsome in a distinguished kind of way, with a wide forehead, bushy white hair, a small goatee, eyeglasses, and he speaks so precisely.

Tea was simple, no danger of over-eating at this table. We were kept busy answering questions about our trip and I kept reminding myself that we were sitting at the table with one of the most famous men in the world. When I described the bus trip and the rattlesnake, Trotsky was amused and said that snakes have tasty meat and that the boy would get a good amount of pesos for the skin.

"You were right to be frightened about the hairpin curves," Van said. "It's fortunate that that road is paved now," and he went on to tell us about a trip to Guadalajara they'd taken recently. The road was simply a great mudhole and their car kept getting stuck. Finally, Trotsky got out and took charge. It was so deep he sank up to his knees in red-brick mud, and was spattered from head to toe, includng his bushy hair. He organized everything, ropes, campesinos, drivers and they pushed the darn car, mile after mile, until they finally arrived. "He really

enjoyed that trip," Van told us and Trotsky added, with a faint, reminiscent smile, "It was just like Red Army days—like a Russian Road."

As we were leaving, Trotsky said he would like to talk to me about my work in the Party and also about what's going on in New York. He asked me to come on Thursday at ten o'clock and of course I said yes, thank you, but I'm dreading it.

Van asked us to go for dinner tonight in a very inexpensive place. Bunny has already started to make goo-goo eyes at this handsome guy and he's already falling for her. We said fine but Dutch treat and he agreed, fast. Nobody has any money here.

Thursday—Hotel Lincoln

I made sure to be up by seven o'clock, on time for my appointment. Not that I'm sleeping. Mexico City is a noisy place. You hear cocks crowing all night long. Millions of hungry mutts roam the streets—no dog-catchers here. The chambermaids come in at six o'clock and while they slosh their mops in the halls, they give each other a blow by blow description of what happened last night. They don't talk to each other, they yell, even if they're two feet apart. Then comes the pan dulce man, the tortilla man, the leche man and a few other delivery people. They yell too.

Melquiades opened the door for me when I arrived. He reminds me so much like Jaime, slim, dark, but much younger. I wish he spoke more English or my Spanish was better. We waited in the little courtyard, until Trotsky came out and smiled approval of my punctuality.

He waved me to a seat beside his work-table, and when I sat down he was so warm and congenial I felt calm and relaxed. Maybe that wasn't such a good idea because I chatted away freely, revealing myself, as I really am, a not very politically mature person, and I started to get an uneasy feeling that he was already a little disappointed in me.

First of all, he asked me how I came to be a Party member. That was easy. I told him how I had left the Young Communist League and joined the C L A with Sydney, Burke Cochran, Frank Visconti and a few others when they got themselves expelled from the C. P. Then, how we set up a branch in Harlem and the miserable results we had. I thought I was being funny when I described our first winter's experience; after distributing hundreds of leaflets announcing an open forum, we'd get an audience of about two or three homeless men and a prostitute. They'd drink coffee, sleep through the meeting and the prostitute would leave as soon as a customer showed up. I laughed but he didn't even crack a smile.

So I went on to tell about the second winter which was just as bad. We tried to organize a small pickle factory, at the foot of 125th Street, but the workers *wouldn't talk to us outside the plant and no one came to our meetings. That experience left us 'as sour as the pickles,' I quipped, but I didn't get a smile. We gave up trying to work in Harlem. Sydney and I joined the Bronx Branch but lately, I told him, we haven't been very active—we've some personal problems. I dwindled to a stop, not getting any encouragement. He looked serious and I think he was bored and slightly disappointed..*

He decided to change the subject, after making a note on a pad. "I am sure you are aware of what's been happening in New York with the discussions on the nature of the U S S R," he said. I nodded and was about to say something but he went right on. I'll try to remember what he said. Sydney would like to know this. "Our membership has become primarily petty-bourgeois, a result of our success in entering the Socialist Party … If the party is to stand and grow, great changes will have to be made and made soon, else we face a grave crisis."

"I'm not sure I understand, what changes have to be made?," I asked. I felt warm, confused, like an idiot. "I know we have to get into a factory and work—really become a part of the working class." He took off his glasses, wiped them and gave a little sigh before he went on.

"What I and Jim Cannon are saying is that it must become obligatory for bourgeois members to connect themselves with the worker's movement, to reshape their activities and their lives. But even before that, what has to be made clear is the political line of the Party. Not, as one certain group would have it, the 'organizational question.'" He adjusted his spectacles and looked directly at me.

"I'm afraid I'm not very interested in factional struggles but that's what seems to be what the entire agenda is at these meetings," I said, sounding defensive. "Cannon and George Clarke are good comrades but sometimes I don't understand what they're arguing about, or how important it really is. For that matter, Max Schactman too, whom I like very much.. Do we have to get involved with these factional struggles? Are they necessary? Won't they destroy the Party?"

He answered me rather forcefully. "It's necessary to call things by their rightful name," he said. "Documents and what seems like endless discussion are important. In New York, like in any petty bourgeois …" He stopped and then, he got a little sarcastic, "As for my friend, Max Schachtman, he lacks a small thing, a proletarian point of view …"

I must have squirmed, feeling embarrassed and unhappy, not knowing how to continue, but then the Old Man got up. "I think we'll finish now," he said patiently, embracing me, a patient look on his face. It was strange but I couldn't help noticing, at that moment how straight and powerful his body is, although he's about sixty years old.

"*I hope when you return to New York,*" *he said as we went to the door,* "*you'll participate more in the on-going discussions, not only on the political program of the party but on the doctrines of dialectical material. I suggest that you speak to Comrade Wright. I think he would be available and happy to lead such a class. Now, let's go into the garden. Natalya and your friend, Bunny, should be there and we'll take some pictures. I want to autograph a picture for you before you leave.*"

I can't sort out my feelings about the interview. I'm sure he was disappointed in me. I know I'm not very keen politically. Hegel said, "*Nothing great in this world is done without passion.*" *Do I have that revolutionary passion? But he doesn't think I'm hopeless, he did encourage me to study.*

Later we took some nice pictures in the garden. They both were warm and friendly and invited me to go on a picnic with them sometime next week.

Friday,

Bunny came in very late and turned on the light. She just had to talk about Van, of course. Looks like it's love at first sight for both of them—they went for each other like a ton of bricks! He's married and has a son, looks like nothing will stop her, she's determined to get him. After we put out the lights, she started to tell me about some stuff about the Old Man. It seems he had a love affair with Frida Kahlo. She was probably attracted by his world-famous reputation, came onto to him pretty strong and, like Barkis, he was willin'. Diego didn't know about it, at least that's what they think. Who cares? But I hope it didn't hurt Natalya, although I'm sure she knows he really loves her. The whole thing just proves he's human. Romance at any age, I say!

Hotel Lincoln—Thursday, one week later

I've been running around so much that I just haven't had time to write. So here goes a whole week's activities. On Saturday, we went to the Merced market. It's tremendous, everything jam-packed together, babies, wrapped rebozos, lying next to whatever mother's selling. I've never seen so many different kinds of chiles, luscious mangoes, watermelons, little bananas. zapotes and all kinds of medicinal herbs. A "curandera" (healer) showed us a fuzzy green moss that will remove fat from kidneys. So far, we've been lucky, no diarrhea. What we have been eating late in the evening is chicken soup from all-night stands, it's absolutely delicious, big hunks of chicken, safe too, because it's boiled.

On Sunday, we went to Chapultepec Park. It's very beautiful, old trees, paths named for poets and philosophers, fountains, lakes, rowboats. There are puppet shows, a monkey act and even a loup-de-loup in the modern section. Castle Chapultepec, originally an Aztec fortress, is now the Museum of National History, the murals by Orozco and Siqueiros showing bloody broken bodies and Karl Marx carrying a copy of Das Kapital. Wow! We wanted to go on to the Diego Rivera Museum but we were just too tired.

Hotel Lincoln—Tuesday

Finally, a free day. Bunny went out early this morning saying she'd see me about six o'clock so I'm off on my own. I got a letter from Ketzel with a fifty dollar bill. She got my hotel address from Sydney. It's kind of risky to do that but that's Ketzel. I'll buy a few souvenirs, go to Sanborn's for lunch. I hate having to watch every penny and we need money to get back home.

Someone told us a cheap way to get to the U. S. Take a train down to Vera Cruz and get a boat. We'll have to check it out. Bunny's going back with me but returning soon to be with her Van.

There's such poverty in this beautiful country, people sleeping in doorways, hungry, homeless children, blind beggars with pock-marked faces, women with paper-thin cotton rebozos, the nights are cold, skinny children with dirty faces. Pyramids and poverty in a country of green valleys, mountains, deserts and white beaches In my history book, I read about Morelos, the "grito" of the people, Hidalgo, the gentle priest, Juarez, so serious, Zapata on a white horse, and macho Pancho Villa. It's the same cry for land, freedom, the end of church domination that we heard in Spain ... Spain! Lost! Lost! Under Franco, drenched in blood.

Better shake off this mood, get dressed, enjoy this beautiful sunshine and go shopping for a few, inexpensive souvenirs.

Hotel Lincoln—Saturday

We finally went on the picnic. As usual, perfect weather, air like cold lemonade; we brought oranges, bananas and a coconut, Trotsky looked handsome in a white cap and a blue peasant shirt, Natalya, plainly dressed in a simple dark dress and sweater. There were three cars, the first with two guards, Otto and Harold with Andre Breton, a visiting French poet, the third, Mel with Bunny and Van. I was in the middle one, sandwiched between Trotsky and Natalya with Charlie driving in front.

After a few words, there was silence. I'm not good at small talk and neither are they, apparently. Dinner and evening hours are more cheerful but here it was different. We were in the wide open, the terrain was mostly dry, arid land and open *field except for clumps of trees here and there. I was really scared, we made a perfect target for any assassin but Trotsky and Natalya were cool as cucumbers.*

An hour and a half later we pulled up on the side of the road. We took our stuff from the car and stowed it under some trees where, fortunately, there was a lovely spot beside a clear, running brook. Trotsky took off quickly with two guards behind him into a field, with Natalya bringing up the rear. Thinking he probably was off to find some 'visnagas', relieved and thankful, I wandered off by myself to a field that looked as if it covered with white snow but turned which turned out to be beautiful small, star-shaped white flowers.

"Se lama 'Estrellas de San Juan,'" Mel said, who'd been walking behind me, and we picked some for our picnic table. During lunch Van, Bunny, Otto, Charlie and I talked about the Party and all the comrades who had come to visit the Old Man. Van asked me about the latest in the factional struggle. He said he thought the Old Man was disappointed in Shachtman, felt he was flighty and inconsistent, and in a letter to Cannon described him as "the floating kidney in the organism of the Party."

Finally, Trotsky and his retinue appeared and we all got out our cameras and snapped away. Everyone seemed ready to call it a day pretty soon, and this time I sat with two guards, Mel and Jake. I was much more at ease and may even have dozed off a little. The next thing I knew was "Estamos aqui" and we were back at the Blue House.

Since Bunny was going off somewhere with Van, Mel was designated to take me back to the Hotel. On the way back, I practiced my Spanish with him. I told him I wanted to learn the words to a beautiful Mexican song that Jaime, Ketzel and his sister had sung at the wedding. By the time we got back, I knew the first four lines of 'Cancion Mixteca.'

No more entries in her Diary. When Miriam gets up to her room that night, she knows she can't write in it, at least for a while. Sydney might not feel very happy reading about Mel. And what would he think if he put down her thoughts about Jaime whose only a few hundred miles away but now forever lost to her. She snaps the book shut and puts it in her suitcase; she'd tell him she mislaid it, or Bunny had it under her junk and only found it when she was packing for home!

Mel's waiting for her as she runs down the steps from her room on the second floor. When his smooth Indian face looks up, smiling, she feels light-hearted, playful and pretty in an embroidered peasant blouse and a long cotton skirt.

She wants to know more about him so he tells her, with the aid of her dictionary, about his family and about President Cardenas, the expropriations of the railroads and the revolutionary history of Mexico.

"We go some day to Xochimilco, floating flower gardens, quisas Domingo proximo?," he asks. "The canoes have tables and chairs, we have a picnic."

The next night they take a trolley to Plaza Hidalgo in Popotla. "In this little plaza," Mel tells her as they approach it, "this old ahuehuete tree se llama 'Arbol de la Noche Triste', the tree of the sad night."

'Why is it called that? Doesn't look like anything special," Miriam says, as she walks around it.

"Cortes, the Spanish conqueror of Mexico, was here, under the branches, llorando—crying—the Aztecs—defeat him, Julio. But he returns—this time wins—a fierce battle." Mel points to the iron fence surrounding the tree. "From the Inquisition in Spain. Cortez brings torture here."

"Enough! Enough history!" Miriam walks away, she covers her ears. "No quiero mas! There's been too much bloodshed lately and I'm sick of it—bloodshed, murders—war! Forever—now and in the past. Let's go."

Mel, taken aback, stands there, gazing at her. Then he puts her sweater he's been holding around her shoulders. "Lo siento, perdoneme," he says gently. "It was in the past. Now, we are peaceful." He smiles, "Only small, peaceful revolutions!"

Miriam, shaking off her disturbed mood, smiles at him and takes his arm, saying, "A friend of mine, a Mexican, once recited a poem to me, an old Nahu poem about Conquistadores and I memorized it. It goes like this ... "Nothing remains but flowers and sad songs/Where once there were warriors and wise men.'"

It's late when they arrive at her hotel and they linger in the deep shadows near the entrance; small fingers of moonlight filter through the trees, the night air is heavy with with fragrance.

"Manana, por las noche?," he asks and she nods. There's a silence, then Miriam says, teasingly, "In my country—en mi pais—boys kiss girls good-night," and she moves close to Mel, lifting her face.

Just then, a taxi pulls up and a well-dressed man and woman emerge, obviously tourists. They glance over, see them standing close together, then disappear into the hotel.

Alone again, Miriam asks, "Melquiades, sabes esta cancion? Besame, Besame mucho?," and she sings the second line—'Como si fuera esta noche la ultima vez, "as if this night were the last time," but she doesn't wait for his answer. She puts her arms around him and he bends down to her.

❦   ❦   ❦

Bunny recognizes quickly what's going on. "It looks like you're going to see him every night," she says, amused, tart. "I guess it's okay. I'm with Van so much that you'd be pretty lonesome otherwise." Miriam doesn't bother telling Bunny she isn't lonesome, Bunny's not the greatest company.

"You're right about Mel and me," Miriam tells Bunny. "He's very intelligent but he is young and he hasn't been with many girls yet."

"So what's the big attraction?," Bunny wants to know.

Miriam, pressing a white sharkskin skirt, puts the iron down. She looks at Bunny who's putting on make-up, a forty-five minute production. "He's beautiful, like an Aztecan prince come alive, slim and graceful. When I look at him I think of a deer, with those warm brown eyes, his face, the high cheek-bones, his hands, the way they move."

"Wow, you really dig him!" Bunny finishes, puts away the Rimmel's mascara, dabs powder on her nose and stands up, tightening her bodice which pulls in her waist, pushes up her breasts. "He is kind of cute, but not my type, that's for sure. Now, take Van, he's really good-looking, a European—a big difference between him and your poor Mexican, even if he's so good-looking, which I don't see. I know you talk some Spanish but you two don't have much in common, a nice Jewish girl like you." Miriam doesn't bother to answer. Bunny wouldn't understand.

"Oh, by the way," Bunny says, her hand on the knob. "I found out about going back—we have to go to Vera Cruz. The S.S. Orizaba—they used it during the war and this is its last trip. We can go steerage very cheap. How's that for a good deal?"

"I guess we haven't much choice—we're almost out of dough," Miriam answers. "What's steerage like? Did this travel agent tell you?"

"He tried to talk me out of it. It'll be rough—the accomodations are very primitive—he means awful—although the food is the same as what regular passengers get. But I insisted, we just don't have the dough."

Miriam has to agree. Bunny's anxious to get back to New York so she can split up with Alvin, get some money together, get back to her beloved Van. As for herself, she's not sure how she feels about going home, she's not sure about anything right now.

She thinks back to the night before. Mel's hotel room was bleak, numbing cold, the cotton sheet and faded blue blanket on the bed too skimpy to keep her from shivering. Lying beside Mel she tried not to disturb him. After they'd made love, he'd fallen into a deep sleep and turned away, leaving her to think longingly of her comfortable hotel room, with woolen blankets. Why on earth doesn't she pick herself up and go back to the hotel? Is there an unwritten law that you have to spend a whole night together? Except she can't, she's in a strange city, doesn't even know where she is.

She tip-toes out of bed, gets dressed in the dark, slips back under the covers, pulls them up to her chin. A little better, she sighs and tries to fall asleep but her thoughts won't let her. Something had set the evening awry, and recalling it she clutches her pillow so hard that Mel stirs.

From the moment last night when they'd entered the flyblown hotel with a dim light over the entrance, she'd been dismayed. Why bother locking it, she'd thought, but the real shock came when Mel unlocked the door to their room.

It had been totally dark as he walked in ahead of her looking for the light for the chain and it came like a blow—the sight of the swinging naked electric bulb hanging from a frayed wire! It was like the one in the her kitchen—with Sydney in Harlem. She stood in the doorway unable to move, the yellow-gray light from the small bulb swaying to and fro, mezmerizing her. In the middle of the room was an iron bed, with two pillows, nothing else except torn curtains fluttering from soiled windows. A metallic, sour taste, like the copper penny she'd once sucked, flooded into her mouth, and nauseated she hears Mel's concerned voice asking her, "Que te pasa—what's wrong?" It brought her to her senses and she answered him as soon as she could utter … "Nada, nada, It's okay."

But the sight of the dirty room under the swinging light had thrown her into reality. It was all the same—the ugliness, the desolation of poverty. Alongside of the beauty of Mexico, the sable-haired natives, the searing blue skies, the lovely music, the lazy charm, there were the open sewers, the tiny fingers of emaciated babies, clawing dried breasts of dull-eyed mothers, little kids with stick-thin arms crying "penny—mister—buy Chicklets—buy Chicklets." Poverty—everywhere and what was she doing here with a gentle young boy who had enchanted her with his Aztec beauty …

Mel was quiet. When she looked into his eyes she saw bewilderment. With a rush of tenderness, for him, for both of them. she embraced him again.

Toward dawn, she moved suddenly, and startled, Mel turns, surprised to find her dressed in bed, beside him. "Tenia frio," she explains. He smiles, kisses her and in a little while they fall asleep, their arms about each other.

The day before their early morning departure, Bunny and Miriam go to the Blue House to say good-by. Trotsky and Natalya are waiting for them in the garden for tea. At the table sits Albert Glotzer, who had been in Prinkipo as Trotsky's secretary, and has come for a visit. Miriam looks at the animated faces, people talking, laughing, enjoying each others' company and thinks of the courage and strength of these two people. After all they're been through they just keep going on with their lives. They just keep going on with their lives. Someone begins to talk about about how much work it is to move, to set up another home, and Trotsky remarks, "In the thirty-six years of living together, whether in a Geneva mansarde, a flat in the working-class district of Vienna, the Kremlin and Akhangelskoe, Alma-Ata, a villa in Prinkipo, Natalya worked in each one, hammering nails, fixing cords, hanging things up ..." He pauses. Everyone is quiet, surprised, he rarely talks about Natalya, but it is wonderful to hear. He was going on, "She never ceases to amaze me ..."

Then, Natalya speaks up, embarrassed, relieved, her voice cheerful, "Our old friends, the Rosmers, are coming soon—bringing our grandson Seva! Albert, you remember the little boy you used to read to, when we were in Prinkipo?"

He laughs. "Of course, that's not the only thing. How can I ever forget the hunting expeditions we went on." Turning to Trotsky he says, "I had to follow you, picking up the bloody birds you shot down. I didn't like that sport, if you can call it that. But I must admit the wood-cock we had for dinner that night was the best meal we ever had on the Island."

In a little while, Miriam says, "We really must go now. We've got packing to do and we're leaving early tomorrow morning." Trotsky gets up and the good-byes begin. Bunny reminds the group she'll be returning soon and Miriam says she'd also like to come back, perhaps next year, if possible.

As she waits for Bunny to make her interminable good-byes, looking at the faces of these two courageous and loving people, she remembers a story Trotsky described somewhere ... about an archpriest, Avvakum, who had also been exiled. It was about their journey in Siberia, how the rebellious priest and his faithful wife stumbled on together, their feet sinking into the snow. The poor exhausted woman kept falling into the drifts and she began to reproach her husband, asking him 'How long, archpriest, is this suffering to be?' and he said, 'Markovna, unto our very death.' And sighing, she answered, 'So be it, Petrovich, let us be getting on our way.'

It's the same with these two, Miriam thinks. Trotsky wrote "… never did Natasha reproach me—even in the most difficult hours, nor does she reproach me now, in the most sorrowful days of our life, when everything has conspired against us."

Natalya hugs Miriam and Trotsky encourages her to work hard in the Party. "I will, I will" Miriam answers, and looks into his sharp blue eyes, seeing his energy and spirit, unshakeable, as always. But she notices, also, the sadness, the awareness of how soon his life can end.

Melquiades accompanies her to the door. They're alone, and as they linger by a mock orange bush, waiting for Bunny, they embrace. "Voy a escribirte," she whispers. His arms tightens, he murmurs, "Te quiero. Espero que si"

"Are you glad to be home?," Sydney asks as they push their way through the throngs on the pier, people waiting for passengers to disembark. Alvin has already grabbed Bunny, anxious to see her alone, and they disappear in the crowd.

"Chalk up one reason, the only one, for going steerage, we get let off first," Miriam says dryly. "Yes, I'm glad to be home. Thanks to S S Orizaba's iron beds and racing rats (she and Bunny had been the only two passengers on the lowest deck) I didn't sleep three nights."

Sydney hails a cab and she settles into the seat, sighing with relief. "What a nice treat, Sydney." She looks at his face. He looks used up, as if he'd shrunk, his gray, worn overcoat hanging loosely on his shoulders.

"Not enough sleep for me either," he says. "I've been getting home late. There's a lot of stuff going on in the Party. The situation's getting worse and we're heading for a split." He goes on telling her about the frequent, late-night meetings in which witty sarcasm and not-so-witty insults made up most of the agenda, and he can't resist telling her about a remark made by Cannon. Jim had been away and when he got back he was confronted and held responsible for certain problems. "My God," he'd said, "The seven little Trilbys—(Burnham, Shachtman, and the Abern clique) they're all innocent, of course,—and who's the Svengali—me!"

Miriam grins appreciatively, her mind elsewhere. She'd been worried about how'd she feel when she saw Sydney but now that they were sitting, side by side, it's the same as always, a dullness, a sort of hopelessness, about them and their relationship. She remembers … Jaime and Mel … are they out of my life? What's going to be?

"I'll tell you all about my trip when we get to the house," she promises, "but I'm just too tired now." Their taxi speeds up along Broadway, passing Columbia University, and enters the bodega-lined streets of Morningside Heights, now fairly quiet. She's quiet, musing, *if it were summer, strains of music—'The Peanut Vendor' or 'Perfidia' would be filling the air—*

"… but how safe are they now—really …," Sydney's talking about the Old Man and Natalya, "with those god-damn Stalinists so strong, and G P U agents all over the place—they're like spiders hiding in closets." She hasn't heard a word he's said.

CHAPTER 19

New York City, February 1939

The National Social Credit Association calls Miriam a few days after she returns and asks her to come in for two or three days a week for some typing. It's not a full time job but the pay is not too bad and Sydney doesn't seem to mind, they're able to manage, they spend very little. Movies are cheap—some are still giving away dishes. They get a pretty flowered plate each time they go and have almost enough now for a full set. Party dues are based on their income and there are lots of good cheap restaurants, especially on the lower East Side where they seem to be most of the time.

Anything she does seems to be okay with Sydney. He's sort of detached and, at times, almost indifferent to her. She would have worried about him except that he doesn't appear depressed and eats well when he's home for dinner, which isn't too often. He works late three nights a week and drops over to the headquarters afterwards for the endless discussions going on there.

One night, a few weeks later, on her way home from work, after she's just been paid, she passes a small liquor store on the corner. Her mother used to enjoy a little nip of schnappes especially at night, but wouldn't think of spending the money herself. She'll get her some, she decides and when she asks the stocky Puerto Rican for a small bottle of Courvoisier he runs for an apple-picker to get one down, then wipes off the dust with a damp rag.

After dinner Miriam says, "Com'on Mom—let's have a drink. Get some glasses." Clara, with a wry grimace, brushes a damp whisp of hair from her forehead, dries her hands and drops into chair. "Gut," she says, after the first sip. Miriam begins to tell her about Bunny's romance with Van and other amusing things that happened during her trip, making sure to avoid talking about Trotsky, about the tragedies in his family. Clara listens attentively, saying very little, smiling at the story of the snake.

I really love talking to my mother like this, Miriam thinks. *Better buy more schnappes.* All of a sudden her mother rises, waves her hand impatiently as if to say that's enough of this nonsense—a waste of time—trips, vacations. Then, realizing she's being abrupt, mutters, "Thanks for a nice treat," and wearily shuffles out. Miriam sighs. Her mother probably had never had a vacation. A beautiful girl, married at nineteen, maybe for love but mostly for security—women had to be with a man. Almost from the beginning, things fell apart. In an rare moment she once confided to Miriam, "He was too much for me," and as Miriam found out later when her mother blurted it out in a bitter moment, her father looked for his sexual satisfactions elsewhere, even with her aunt, her mother's sister. No wonder romantic stories have little appeal for Clara.

Miriam's putting the bottle up on the shelf when the phone in the living room rings and as she picks up it up, Ketzel's voice, high and clear sings out, "Miriam, honey, it's me—your old pal. Listen kid, I'm coming home."

Miriam catches her breath. "Ketzel. I don't even know where you are."

"That's okay. Sometimes I don't even know myself. Right now I'm at the hacienda with Jaime and Adelita but ..." Ketzel pauses a moment to steady her voice, and after a little cough, goes on, "I'm not doing so well—I haven't told anyone here except Jaime. I need to see a good doctor. I'm coming home."

"That's fine—I mean I'm glad you're coming back but I'm sorry you're sick. Is it serious?" She sits down so suddenly that the phone falls on the floor and she almost misses Ketzel's response as she picks it up.

"I don't know—I feel lousy all the time, my period never stops, I'm bleeding a lot." Her voice falters at the last three words and Miriam can hardly make them out.

"What does your doctor think it is—what's causing it?"

"He acts as if he knows and wants to operate. But, Miriam, I'm scared. I want to see Dr. Kulka, you know, my gynecologist—the one Martha Graham uses. He's smart and sweet. I have an appointment for next week, I'll be back on Thursday. Will you meet me at the airport—please?" Ketzel sounds almost pleading..

"Sure—sure. Just give me the flight information" All at once it strikes Miriam that Martin hasn't been mentioned but she decides not to say anything, there are probably good reasons Ketzel's husband isn't coming with her.

"Miriam—are you there? Listen, I'm putting Jaime on. He'll give you the information and he wants to say hello."

"*Ola*, Miriam" Jaime voice comes over, smooth, copper-toned. Miriam feels an involuntary twing, then silently scolds herself. "How are you?" he asks, and doesn't wait for the answer. "I'm so glad you'll be with Ketzel. Look, she didn't ask you to do this but I am. After the operation … It looks like there may have to be one, could you stay with her a few days? If you're with her, she'll really be happy and get better quicker."

"Of course." It seemed so easy for him to ask her to do this. It was as if he were making love to her, his voice, as always, affectionate. But she can't allow herself to think of that. *Ketzel is sick, she's my friend, she needs my help.* Her answer is short.

"I told Ketzel I'll stay with her as long as she needs me."

"Wonderful." Sensing some sharpness in her voice, he becomes business-like. "Okay, now let me give you the information. I'll be calling every day after she gets to New York, so we'll be talking again."

❧   ❧   ❧

The airfield is covered with slosh and mud, the wind crisp and sharp. Ketzel pauses a moment at the top of the little staircase leading from the plane, her long hair whipping across her face. Spying Miriam, she flies down, catching her in a bear hug. Miriam looks at her friend's face. She's thin, it makes her look older, but tells her, "You look beautiful, as usual," and they talk non-stop all the way to the brownstone.

The house is dark, outlined by a violet and purple sky, soft lights gleaming from the windows. Miriam, looking up, remembers how as a little girl, with hungry eyes, she'd dash up the steps, anticipating the warm welcome, the mingled odors of cinnamon and Christmas tree, the sounds of plates and pots in the kitchen, the blazing fireplaces,

Ketzel pauses, too, thinking of the carefree days she'd spent here. A warm, safe world then, shielded from outside turmoil, a world that revolved about her. It's different these days. Now she can't handle most of it, rivalry among dancers, back-biting from friends … her husband!

"Doesn't Sydney mind your staying with me. You've been away for almost a month and now you're here?'

"He said it's fine, he's got plenty to do. He's in the Cannon faction, they're busy almost every night of the week, but that's political stuff and you've no idea what I'm talking about. Anyway, I know you're not interested."

"I'm not." By this time they've arrived in Ketzel's room and she throws herself on the bed, closing her eyes. "Politics aren't important to me. I get upset about other things. Martin, for instance."

"Yeah—tell me about Martin." Miriam sits down beside her. "I wondered why he didn't come back with you."

"We're on the outs, that's why and he doesn't know where I am. We had a big fight about four weeks ago and I flew to Daddy at the hacienda. You know, with this bleeding for the last few months—I couldn't dance—I had to cancel several performances and I was in bed a lot alone all day."

Ketzel's voice breaks and she starts to cry. "I'm a big baby, I know ... It wasn't pleasant," she whimpers, "being holed up in a Paris hotel with cold meals sent up to you while everyone is out wining, having a good time or planning something they don't want me to know about. Martin was out with Caridad, her general, Siquieros and Contreras practically every night. Then, he'd come back to the room with a bouquet of flowers and French perfume—big deal!"

Miriam doesn't know what to say. She hates Martin and not only because he's a Stalinist. "He's macho, like many Latins," she tells Ketzel. "Probably acted like the others when he was in Spain. Of course your father's an exception. Do you think Martin loves you—really?"

"I'm sure he does even if ..." Ketzel stops herself from going on. After a moment she saiys "Look—what guy likes a sick wife?—he's usually very patient but he felt very hampered when I was laid up in bed—wanted to paint the town with the others. The main thing is with us that I've got to get better," her voice urgent, "and soon."

Dr. Kulka's office, on the upper east side, is furnished with ordinary waiting-room furniture—unpretentious, Miriam thinks. So is Dr. Kulka, small, pleasant, a refugee with a charming Viennese accent, considered by dancers in Ketzel's circle to be one of the best in New York. "So," he says, "Ketzel—goot to see you." He kisses her and smiles warmly. "Who is my patient today?"

He's with Ketzel a long time and Miriam is beginning to be alarmed, when she emerges, radiant, from the inner office. "Miriam," she bursts out, disregarding an anxious elegantly dressed negro woman waiting there. "It's going to be okay. It's not serious—I just need to have some polyps removed—he says they're quite large—that's where all this bleeding is coming from. It'll stop after the operation and I'll be fine! Let's celebrate!"

❧   ❧   ❧

Ketzel was fine, recovering quickly although Dr. Kulka insisted she stay for a few days, saying, "You could use the rest." As she's checking out he says, "I think you can go back to work in a few weeks, but until then don't overdo it." He's smiling, raising her hand to his lips.

While Ketzel's busy gathering all her things, Dr Kulka asks Miriam to step outside. He hesitates as she closes the door, then says, "Look, it's none of my business but I'm not sure what is going on with Ketzel."

Dr. Kulka took a deep breath. "She has two black and blue marks on her body, one on her back, the other on her arm. When I just began to speak about them, she said 'Oh, they're nothing,—I fell during a rehearsal.' That is not what they look like. You are her friend and I think you should pursue this—if she's with a man who's abusive, then something must be done. Is it her husband?"

Miriam can't speak for a minute, she swallows hard, then, slowly, with deep anger in her voice she says, "She's married to a man I don't like. I'm not surprised at anything he might do." To steady herself, she lights a cigarette and takes a deep pull. "She must have been careful so I wouldn't see any marks. But, of course, I'll try to talk to her and get her to admit the truth, but it won't be easy."

On the way home, in the cab, Ketzel's exhausted and quiet, pressing Miriam's hand, looking through the taxi windows as if she's seeing the streets of New York for the first time. But after she eats the chicken soup Miriam has prepared she says, "Miriam, tomorrow, I want to tell you something. I should have said something a few days ago but I was afraid to. I knew how angry you would get."

"We don't have to wait until tomorrow," Miriam says quickly. "I know what it's about—Dr. Kulka hinted at it—and—you're right—I am angry," her voice loud and harsh. "How dare a man, anyone, hit you. That son-of-a bitch—I'd like to spit in his face."

Ketzel sighs. "I knew you'd make a big deal about this when you found out and you probably spoke to Dr. Kulka too. Look, it was really nothing. Martin was upset about some other things—he'd had a hot argument with Vidali. He drank a lot and then he came home we began to argue—it's as much my fault as his—he just lost his temper …"

"That's a bunch of crap," Miriam yells. "What in hell are you trying to do, excuse this kind of behavior? There's no excuse. Who does he think you are—or he is? What kind of people are you two turning into?" She pushes aside her plate, leaning forward, her face filled with puzzlement and disbelief. "What's with you, Ketzel? Where's your self-respect?"

"Miriam—go to hell! I don't have to justify myself to you—or my marriage." Ketzel stands up, drawing herself erect, raising her head. "Let's leave it at that." At the door, she turns back to Miriam, who sitting at the table, her eyes full of pain, her voice trembling as she tries to say, lightly, "The soup was great. Thanks," but as she walks out she slams the door—hard.

Miriam sits at the table, unable to move, shaking, close to tears. For the first time, in all the years of their friendship, she's criticized Ketzel. Why did she say those things? She hadn't meant to be so sharp! But this is different—how can you let a person to hit you? Ketzel, so tenderly raised—how could she accept abuse like that?

The phone rings and she goes into the parlor to get it. Her legs are trembling and her voice unsteady as she says hello. It's Jaime, who's already spoken to Dr. Kulka and knows the surgery went well. He sounds delighted, asking what their future plans are. "I don't know what Ketzel intends to do now," Miriam answers, cold, distant. "I'll be leaving here in a couple of days."

"Miriam," Jaime says, "Please, please, listen to me. I've a few things I must speak to you about."

"If it's that you're married, I've already heard about it." She stops, adding in a flat voice, "Congratulations! I hope you'll be very happy."

"Please don't be sarcastic. What I want to tell you is more important—at least I think it is." He pauses, "I'm dropping out of the Communist Party."

She catches her breath, *My God, it's happened! Why didn't Ketzel tell me!* But, of course, it didn't matter much to her. What wonderful news. Sooner or later she knew he would see what was happening. He was too intelligent and sensitive a person not to react to the horror unfolding under Stalin. No real person could swallow it for too long. She almost says "What brought you to your senses," but she thinks she'd better not. After a moment, she tells him, "I'm so glad—happy too."

"It began," Jaime says, "When I started thinking about what happened in China, with Chiang-Kai-Chek and the thousands of workers slaughtered because of Stalin's stupid policies. Then Alana and Arthur—gone, killed. In

Spain, Dos Passos' friend, Jose Robles, mine too, disappeared. Philip Rosenblit, that's a long story.. not good to talk about it on the phone. Let's just say that he and I were involved in some financial matters with the Soviet Union and right now, I don't know where he is but I fear the worst. The ridiculous trials no intelligent person can swallow—lots of horrible stuff—I couldn't swallow it any longer." His voice slows, it sounds as if he has trouble saying the words. "I'm just sorry it took so damn long."

As he's talking she begins to feel dizzy, almost drunk. She's suddenly aware of what this could mean for the two of them. They can be together now. He's married but he can easily separate, he couldn't possibly care for that woman. She knows he loves her.

It takes her time to answer him, struggling to steady her voice. "Jaime, I couldn't speak for a moment. I've almost gave up hope for us." She giggles. "I feel like a sleeping princess who's awakened from her trance. Oh, Jaime, it's been so long." She begins to cry, tears choke her and she can't stop.

"Miriam! Hold it." He speaks harshly, as if he's in pain. Then he adds, "I don't think we can be together. It isn't in the cards for us right now." He pauses. "Hold it a minute." She could hear him lighting a cigarette. When he speaks again, his voice is pinched, flat. "I have to tell you something. Things have changed. Understand—things happen. My wife is pregnant."

"Oh, no!," the words spring from her involuntarily. She stops crying, trying to realize what he has just told her. She feels dizzy, how crazy, how stupid things are. She's hardly able to hold onto the receiver.

"She told me about it after I asked for a divorce." His voice is dry. "It was never planned—not with her. It just happened, I'm not sure how but—I'm not going to blame her."

"What about us—what about us?," she half-shouts. Then, realizing that she's veering towards hysterics, she says, "Jaime, there's nothing for us to talk about now. I can't talk! I'm going to hang up." She hears him saying, "Miriam—listen ..." but she puts down the receiver.

Ketzel's still sleeping at eight-thirty the next morning when Miriam goes to work so she leaves a note.

Ketzel dear,

Please forgive me for what I said last night. Your relationship with your husband is your own business. Also, congratulations! I hear you're going to have a baby brother or sister. I'll get back early. Love.

When she get to the house after work Ketzel greets her at the door with a hug and nothing more is said about the previous night's quarrel. But the next morning, after breakfast, while they're still at the kitchen table making plans for the day the doorbell rings furiously, non-stop.

"Who on earth?" Miriam's saying when she opens the door. "Nobody's lived here for six months!" Martin, his face full of fury, dashes past her into the hall, shouting, "Ketzel!"

After a moment of stunned surprise, Miriam follows him into the parlor.

"That's no way to enter a house—especially since you weren't invited." They're glaring at each other when Ketzel runs in, stops short and stares at Martin, her face contorted in anger.

"Digame, me amor, why did you run out on me?" he shouts, his face creased with anger.

"What?," Ketzel shrieks as soon as she gets her voice, so loudly the room echoes the sound. "You must be crazy if you don't know why."

Martin laughs, a short barking sound, comes near, putting his face close to hers. "You're a real bitch, you know. I must be loco! You run away in the middle of the night. Back to daddy—just like a little girl—a god-damm spoiled brat." He shakes his head, chuckles in mock amazement. "They all think I'm crazy. Siquieros, Caridad, the whole bunch—to come after you. They don't trust you."

"I didn't run out on you. That's not true," Ketzel retorts. "You knew I was sick." Then, scornfully, "Let me refresh your memory, Senor. Of course you wouldn't remember that night.—You came in at three—so drunk you could hardly stand up. When I yelled at you, you hit me—twice. Then you passed out—that's what happened. I guess that's what you do to spoiled little girls—you hit them so they'll be good."

She's unable to control her trembling lips and pushes him away, from her, goes to the window. Martin stands still, watching her as she hoists herself onto the window seat and sits there, her arms around her knees, looking out. Miriam, looking at both of them thinks, "It's a comic opera."

He and Miriam wait for Ketzel to say something but she pretends to be watching the milkman, coming up the steps, bringing up a morning's supply of cream and milk, the bottles clinking in a metal container. Martin moves towards her but she puts her arm out to stop him.

She puts her head down on her folded arm and beginning to sob.

"I went to Daddy. He came and got me and made me stay with him until I left—that's what happened."

Martin decides to stay and goes into the living room to hang up his over-coat. When he returns, his face has a forgiving look. "I'm staying. We have to straighten this thing out ..." He kneels beside her, tenderly brushing her hair, looking in her eyes. "Listen, darling, I swear to you I didn't remember anything when I woke up. I called your father, he hung up on me and I had to ask Car-idad to find out what was happening with you." Then, as he continues plead-ing, "Ketzel, please look at me," she stops crying.

Look," he sighs, "I took too much tequila. I should know better—it's not your fault that we haven't ... you've been sick. You know us Latins—you know how crazy we are." He presses his smooth head against her legs, looks up at her plaintively. Ketzel looks down at him, her teary face breaking into a smile.

Before anything else occurs, Miriam wheels around and quits the room. *They're going to make up for sure. What does he mean that those Stalinists don't trust her. Who can trust them? Ketzel ought to stay away from them, the whole rotten bunch! But she probably can't—not as long as Martin is one of them—and she'll stay with him.*

She heats some left-over coffee and sits down. Now she can allow herself to think about Jaime. Since she's heard Jaime's news it's been as if she's had an aching ball in her gut. *It's over now*, she tells herself, *it's final*. They can never be together. She knows she should be delighted he's finished with the Communist Party. Now she and Jaime can friends, maybe even comrades. *But I wanted him to be my lover.* She pushes the cup aside, puts her head on the table, closes her eyes, bone tired. Behind the parlor doors, rolled shut, she can hear whispering, laughing, like conspirators.

They stay in Ketzel's bedroom that night and Miriam goes up to the top floor to the little bedroom that has the nosy tree that wants to come in through the window. When she falls asleep Jaime's in her dream, climbing up the trunk. He reaches the window, opens it and gets in bed with her. "You can't stay here," she says, his body's icy. "I can't warm you, you're too cold," but he put his arms about her. "You left the window open, I have to shut it." She gets up to close it but when she gets back to bed, he's gone and she begins to cry.

She's glad when she wakes up

The next morning, Ketzel, radiant, bounces into the kitchen and catches her in a warm hug. "I thought I'd go in to work today," Miriam says over breakfast. "What are your plans?"

"Martin and I are going back to Mexico. We'll stay with the Arenals, rela-tives of the Siquieros', then we'll drive to Mexico City. Don't be angry with me Miriam ... and thank you, my dear friend!"

Miriam can't wait to get out of the house with Martin in it. She's managed not to have any contact with Martin during the past twelve hours, but as she's leaving from the front door, he comes down to hold it open for her. "Thank you" she says, briskly, moves past him.

"Miriam," he says, holding out an arm to detain her, what he thinks is a friendly smile on his aristocratic features. "You know that I don't have any use for Trotskyites but I am grateful. You've been a good nurse to Ketzel." She turns her head from him, feeling nauseated.

"Really?" She wants to laugh in his face.

"But I feel I have to warn you," he continues, his voice softly confidential. "It could even be dangerous. Be careful who your friends are. You can't trust some of them, believe me." Then he drops his arm and with his features twisted with scorn he adds, "I can assure you there's no future in Trotskyism or for Trotsky himself."

She wants to smash him! "Thank you for your kind consideration. You can go to hell. Go to hell, you and your gang of murderers." She spits out the words, grabs the knob and slams the door in his face.

❦   ❦   ❦

Miriam calls Sydney from work to let him know she'll be coming home tonight. When she gets to the 151st Street apartment she finds the table for dinner with a little bouquet of Lilies of the Valley.

"Welcome home," Sydney says. But her warm feelings toward him cool when he skeptically greets her news about Jaime's defection from the C. P. "Are you sure he's sincere. They don't leave the Party that easily, even when they're convinced about what's going on."

Miriam is astounded. "Jaime a double agent? No, I can't believe that. I think he's really upset about Rosenblit, he loved Philip. That was the time when he began to think about the other horrible murders and what Stalinism was all about No, you're wrong. Realizing she sounds too vehement she concludes lamely, "No, he's one person I could never suspect of anything dishonest."

She decides to change the subject; it's too hard to talk about Jaime without showing her feelings. After she describes her encounter with Martin, Sydney goes to get a copy of The Militant, comes back, waving it. "Look at this. It should interest you." In a corner there's a little note, a request by Trotsky to the person who wrote him recently, to get in touch with his representatives in New York.

"What was the 'certain matter' he wrote to the Old Man about?" Sydney laughs. "A big nothing. Someone pretending to be an old American Jew. He tells Trotsky to beware of a dangerous stool-pigeon in Paris, someone named Mark. He must have known this Mark well—he describes him very thoroughly, his looks, his background. He says that if they watch this person, they will find he's secretly meeting Soviet officials." Sydney stops, trying to remember. "There was more. He said that Trotsky's head was on the block and he'll soon be assassinated by either this Mark or a Spaniard, pretending to be a Trotskyist. I can't remember if it was Spanish or Mexican."

"How can you take this so lightly. I don't." Miriam said angrily. "You should have seen Martin's face. They're …"

"Well, the guy never really followed up on the notice in the paper. It says here that the Old Man even went so far as to set up a small group to investigate Mark's friend, Etienne; that's what Sevya had called him. The group found nothing. Look, it could even have been a G P U hoax. That's another game of theirs—discrediting loyal Trotskyists".

"How can we talk about it so casually?" Miriam jumps up and heads for the kitchen. "Maybe I'm crazy for worrying so much. Look! Let's forget it for now and have dinner."

Sydney follows her and as she's dishing up the food he puts his hands on her shoulders. "Okay, I'm sorry," he says. "You know I'm just as worried as you are. Look, turn around and give me a kiss." After she does, trying to sound offhand, he mutters, "Listen, we should discuss some other stuff."

She moves to the stove fishes a match from the Diamond box and strikes it gingerly, she hates the smell of sulphur. Turning to him, "What stuff?" she asks. Could he possibly know anything about what had happened in Mexico, she wonders?

"You know, oh, I guess you wouldn't know," he says diffidently, sitting down at the table, fishing in his pocket for his pipe and tobacco. The doctor warned him when he went to see him about his cough, about his two-pack-a-day habit and he's trying to cut down. But he hates pipe smoking and refuses to care for even the good pipes that Miriam buys him occasionally as presents. He never takes the trouble to clean the bowl or fill it properly. "The damn things always keeps going out," he'd grumble.

"Look," he suddenly blurts out, "while you were away, I saw someone. Not too many times, maybe two or three." He pauses, then makes himself go on. "She's a party member—we went up her place." He stops, busying himself with stirring the tobacco, sucking in air noisily.

"Go ahead." Miriam's keeping her words very matter-of-fact, intensely relieved. "Is that all there was to it? You just saw her a couple of times? Did you sleep with her?" As she asks him it amazes her how little she cares. She doesn't add that most of the male comrades would consider it a waste of time if they dated a woman and didn't end up sleeping with her.

"Miriam," Sydney protests, "Believe me, it was nothing. It was nothing to me, to her. Just one of those things."

"Yeah, I know. Like that song 'It was just one of those things—just one of those crazy things.' Let me finish pouring the coffee. I could burn myself."

Her thoughts race wildly. He's telling me about his little fling. Should I tell him about Mel? Although she can't really define what she feels, she's heard that men never could accept infidelity of their partners as coolly as women did with men. Unfaithfulness of their women reflected upon their maleness, virility or something.

Finally sitting down, facing each other, she asks, "Tell me, did you really like her?"

"Oh, God, no!," he answers, almost before she's finished. "I was just feeling very low at the time." Miriam knows the reason. Sydney had been acting Chairman of the New York chapter for a few months. "It was just after Joe Carter returned and took back his position. I know I'd been doing a good job but—I'm not one of the boys." He couldn't control the bitterness creeping into his voice. "So I was pushed back into the rank-and-file again."

"But you knew it would be temporary." Miriam's fingers tighten about the warm cup. She had been so happy for him when they asked him to be Chairman even though she knew it was for just a short period. Sydney's dream of being an important functionary in the movement had begun way back in College. Every once in a while, he'd break down, feel he was useless. There were times at night when she'd wake, hear him crying. She'd hold him in her arms but she couldn't console him.

"Of course, I knew it was just temporary." Sydney's face darkened. He was always able to conceal his depresson with a facade of genial, hail-fellow-well-met air and most people never suspected the pain beneath.

"Don't start to give me any of your little Mary Sunshine cheery talks. I just told you about this meaningless affair because I don't believe in being dishonest. I wouldn't want you to hear about it from someone else."

Miriam sits quietly for a moment, trying to pull her thoughts together, resolving to lighten up the subject. "I guess I'll have to forgive you, Sydney. I know you love me." Then she laughs. "I'll bet you don't know that Trotsky had an affair too. No, of course, you wouldn't. No one knows, except Frida and Van. Bunny too, cause she's the one who told me. It's a big secret. I don't think Diego Rivera knows about it. He'd have a fit, though he runs around screwing any dame who's willing."

"You've gotta be kidding? The Old Man—an affair with Kahlo?" Sydney looks stunned, then dismissive. "It's probably idle gossip. He's not the type."

"Why is it so hard to believe? After all, he's flesh and blood, and according to Van he always liked the ladies. There's been others."

"I don't understand it. It's not possible. He's always with Natalya. He's so devoted—at least that's the story."

"He is devoted but Van told Bunny that after his little fling with Frida he had the nerve to bring up an old romance of Natalya's from twenty years ago—one she had before he came along. Of course it came from a guilty conscience. Van said that Natalya got very upset and came crying to him, 'My little Leon doesn't trust me!'" Miriam picks up a cigarette. "Oh, brother. Men!"

"What about his affair with Frida? Let's hear!" Sydney gives up on his pipe, reaches for a Camel, lighting his and hers on the same match, his eyes lighting with interest. It was hard to accept and yet his idol was proving to be a little more human.

"According to Van, Frida went for him from the moment they met in Tampico. Here's this big-shot political Russian panting after her and they'd have these great conversations in English which, of course, didn't include Natalya. Frida would say 'all my love' when she'd speak to the Old Man and, I guess, he took it literally, writing her notes, slipping them into a book. A cute game."

"I can see why this could happen," Sydney, slowly, analyzing. "A romantic interlude, after almost ten years of being hounded from country to country. Still, I'd rather think of the Old Man being above that sort of thing. What about Rivera? Didn't he have any inkling?"

"No—It was pretty lucky." Miriam goes to the ice-box for some milk. "It didn't last long. There were good reasons. Though they enjoyed the affair, especially the Old Man, they both realized it couldn't much longer. Besides, Frieda got tired of him pretty soon. After all, he was twice her age and not so great in bed—at least not anymore. That's what Frida confided to a girl friend."

Sydney's quiet, mulling over the story. "Well, I guess he's only human after all."

Miriam asks, "Any more questions?"

"No," he says and smiles at Miriam gratefully. "We all make mistakes."

"Yes," Miriam answers, "We all do."

CHAPTER 20

New York City, 1940

Hilda calls Miriam on a blustery March day, to tell her about the B S & A U meeting they have to attend. Afterwards, they hurry to Russoff's on 43rd street, the nearest place, a smoke-filled dining room frequented by paunchy clothing manufacturers. They're both chilled and tired and don't talk until they've finished with hot soup.

"These meetings are a waste of time. The Union's really not serious about organizing office workers and with the war coming on, there'll be plenty of jobs," Hilda, says, finally. She sounds disgusted, picking up a breadstick and waving it. "Ta da da—patriotism's now the order of the day and strikes are out of style. In fact they'll probably be outlawed. But the Party expects us to do this work. Some sweet day we'll recruit someone."

"There'll be two parties very soon. The split's ... very soon now," Miriam, reading the menu at the same time, looks up and tells the surly, gray-haired waiter. "Sorry, I can't seem to make up my mind. Yeah, I'll have the fillet-of-sole." He snatches the large bill-of-fare from her hand but she ignores him. "Sydney's in the Cannon caucus and I don't know who I'm supporting. Why did you pick this place anyway? These waiters give me a pain."

"You'll know why, any minute now. Look over there. Sylvia's on her way here. Just back from Europe, couldn't wait to see you. I chose this place 'cause she had some business on 42nd Street this afternoon."

Sylvia's struggling through the noisy dining room, filled with crowded tables. Finally, with quiet dignity, she's able to reach their table. Wearing a boxy brown coat with a soft mink collar, a small brimmed hat to match, she's glowing, looking prettier and younger than she has for a long time.

After greetings and hugs, she sits back with a sigh. "Order first," warns Miriam, "before you start talking. Otherwise prepare for a lynching, this isn't Paris."

"What makes you think that they're so polite over there. Of course, in the better restaurants, they are. Fortunately, we eat in the better ones." Sylvia, smiling, slightly deprecating. "I'd better tell him what I want first."

"Well, you're lucky," Miriam quips. "I wouldn't know how to read a menu from left to right. Never had that opportunity." Then, before she realizes what she saying, she adds, "I'm not as lucky as you."

"What's with you, Miriam?" Hilda put down her glass of wine. Frowning, "You're in a lousy mood tonight."

Miriam folds her napkin into a small triangle and smooths it before saying, "I'm sorry. I didn't mean what I said. It sounds as if I'm jealous but that's not true. All of us feel the same way—we're really happy you've met this fabulous guy who also happens to have a lot of dough." Then, smiling, reaching over to squeeze Sylvia's hand asks, "When are we gonna meet him? We can hardly wait!"

"Jacques is coming to New York this summer. I'm sure you'll get to see him several times. But I want to tell you—both of you—something. About me and Jacques." Sylvia takes a deep breath and looks past the two of them, past the room crowded with diners, through the restaurant windows fogged with people's breath, to the dark street with chilled pedestrians rushing by.

"We really love each other and it has nothing to do with money. He seems to have plenty. It's true, of course, that that's good. I don't know a lot, except that his family has money. In fact I don't know much about him altogether." Sylvia stops, holding off as the waiter brings her soup, bread, wine. When he leaves, she continues, "He's not very open with me but I try to understand him."

"So what do you like about him?," Miriam asks. "What made you fall for him?"

"Hard to explain," with a sheepish grin, she says, "It could be because it's the first serious relationship I've ever had. I haven't had many. He seems crazy about me so I don't ask many questions." She picks up her spoon and turns to the steaming bowl before her. "You'll like him, when you meet him, I'm sure of that." She starts on her soup. "So, tell me, what been happening in the Party?"

After they fill her in and while they're having coffee and apple strudel, Sylvia turns to Hilda, "You're taking the same cottage this summer, right? With Browner, Shyke and Daisy?"

"We'll be there too," Miriam interposes. "Down on the Lake—same as before. We really didn't want to rent that dump again—but we couldn't find anything else. If only we could get Michael Quill to fix the toilet. Hey, maybe you and Jacques come up for a week-end? Between all of us we'll find room to put you up." Then, she adds, "It ought to be a great summer—all of us getting together."

But she really doesn't believe it, she feels pretty lousy about everything right now.

Afterwards, she decides to walk home, wending her way on winding paths through the Park, even though it's a long trek home. She needs to think, to be by herself. It'll be a long trek, but her five-year old shaggy mouton lamb is warm, it's a clear night, the moon's pearly-white in a dark blue sky and streets are quiet on a Monday night. She remembers a poem by Keats that begins, "The poetry of earth is ceasing never/on a lone winter evening when the frost/ has wrought a silence."

Walking rapidly, memories come crowding into her thoughts—splashing in the little basin beneath the big statue of Columbus on 59th street—ice cracking on the lake—running home soaking wet, one skate lost—freezing—one unforgettable Rumplemeyer treat, snowy whipped cream on dark chocolate—years later, Knute—together on a sun-warmed rock—feeling his heat and hardness through her cotton dress—water clapping on the rowboat—sweet good-bye kisses.

She feels as if she's a part of this City. She's territorial like Kootah, their tomcat who was always on the table. But Kootah's gone—like her childhood. It's gone, they say, when you know you're alone. Then we're always looking for someone to love us so we don't have to be that way. She had had Knute, Jaime, Mel … Now there's no one, like that song—"Me and my shadow, no one there to tell my troubles to." Before she realizes it, she's singing softly, "Besame, besame mucho" and "Amor, Amor, Amor," drowning in nostalgia—for Jaime!

But it's not true, she tells herself, she does have Sydney and her mother. They need her! But what about her needs? Looks like she's going to end up who knows how? She's still young so while there's life there's hope. So they say. Is she jealous of Sylvia? She's found love, real love. She sounds a little like she's trying to convince herself about that. Wish her luck. Wish *myself* luck.

She reaches the entrance and begins to walk along the dimly-lit road. The neglected paths are uneven and the benches chipped and worn. She ought to get out and walk on the street. A chilly wind whips through bare black boughs like the soft moan of an oboe and she begins to feel scared. It was a stupid idea to walk home—too damn far and too damn cold.

Columbus Circle is brightly lit, advertising, shining lights coming from the General Motors building. "Time to Retire—Get a Fisk" says a large sign of a sleepy little boy in dentons on his way to bed, holding a candle, carrying a tire around his shoulder. Near the Park Movie, wedged between tall buildings there's a small White Castle diner with slush streaked windows. When she pushes her way in, her hair half frozen, damp curls escaping her cap, a young boy wearing a white sailor hat is mopping the deserted counter.

"I've only got enough for a cup of coffee and a nickel for the subway," she tells him, perching at the counter. "Sorry, no tip today." She warms her hands, clasping the cup. He smiles at the small girl rubbing her pink nose.

"That's okay. For a pretty girl, anytime," he says and she feels better already.

Just in case she and Sydney decide to get out on their own, Miriam decides to go apartment hunting in Washington Heights. On Riverside Terrace she locates a large, dark one-bedroom on the ground floor, with two redeeming features; it's affordable with their two incomes and it looks out directly onto the shining arc of the George Washington Bridge, a safe neighborhood. Of course there's bound to be robberies, just not as many on 116th Street. A large number of German-Jewish families, recent refugees from Nazi Germany, have chosen to settle there. They don't feel or act like refugees, at least many of them. In fact, they have an air of superiority about them that can be slightly irritating. After looking at an apartment she feels hungry and stops in a store to buy a snack. Ahead of her is a buxom matron in a Persian Lamb coat, giving an order to be sent home. "Vunderful fruit we haf in Germany, big, tasty," she confided to an unimpressed clerk, waiting, pencil in hand, while she examines the fruit counter carefully. "Ve hav grapes from the Rhine valley, not like dees. De finest Reisling in the vorld."

Everything had been better there and they wouldn't have left if Hitler had not gone after the Jews. At least that was the impression one got after hearing them talk among themselves. One of the Jewish comrades in the Branch told Miriam how shocked he was when he overheard his mother and her lady friends talking during a tea party at his house. Surrounded by heavy mahoganny furniture, including Meissen ware and silver they'd manage to bring over, sipping from porcelain cups they reminisced about the good old days in Germany, their nostalgia mingling with the fragrant coffee topped with schlag.

They didn't mentioned the present, nor talked about Hitler or what was happening to the Jews who hadn't been able to leave when they did.

       ❧   ❧   ❧

One rainy Spring evening, Miriam comes home to find two letters waiting for her on the little table in the hall, one from Ketzel, a fat envelope, in her generous scrawl, the other from Jaime, typewritten and businesslike. Despite the admonition she'd given herself, a thrill runs through her and happy nobody's home sits by the window to read his letter.

Jaime writes.

Hacienda Zempoala,
Hidalgo, Mexico
March 1, '39

As I told you on the phone, I am quitting the C. P. For personal reasons, in fact having to do with Ketzel who's in Mexico now with Martin, I haven't announced my decision. I will, at the proper time. Right now, I've taken a leave of absence from the C. P. At first I was concerned that my love for you influenced my thinking. It did, but there were important, valid factors as well, which I've begun to examine and which led to my decision

What happened to Elena and Arthur, both of them dead now, continues to haunt my mind. Then, Jose Robles and Philip Rosenblit—their disappearances could only have meant Siberia or execution. In spite of my not wanting to, I began to read what John Dos Passos, Victor Serge, Andre Gide and my friend Pivert had to say about what they saw in Russia. I didn't want to admit, for instance, how Stalin used the pretext of Kirov's assassination (which he may have planned himself) to begin the great Purge, the horrible decimation of the Bolshevik leadership. This is old news to you. But I want to add that the cult of Stalin, the adulation he fosters. sickens me beyond description. Now that sentimental blinders have fallen from my eyes, I find him a brutal murderer and "the gravedigger of the revolution." I'm planning to take a back-seat politically for a while. I hope you believe me.

Concerning my marriage, it's more difficult to explain what happened. Our families have been friendly for many years, she and Ketzel are the same age. Believe me, I didn't propose marriage to Carolina until she told me she was pregnant.

To be honest, I'm confused right now. Carolina is very capable and efficient and assures me I'm free to travel, return to the U. S. if and when necessary. This has always been very important to me——being a free agent.

It all sounds great except that although I like and admire my wife I must tell you and it is to you and only you I say this, I don't love her. However, I owe it to her to be a good husband and father.

Cuidate, te quiero

Jaime

On another sheet there is a poem:

The Gift

Most of us know narrow love
love for a lover, child, family
The love I knew
intense
encompassing
covering the universe
like molten honey
like the good gray poet ...
Yet strong, deep
waging war against tyrants
yet tender
gentle
so rare! ...
Even tho' summer's gold
winter's frost
toll the years
the gift never lost
will be found again.

She sighs and holds the envelope to her burning cheek, closing her eyes. Kids playing stickball in the street, an ambulance alarm—she hears nothing. When Sydney's key turns in the lock she quickly puts away the papers.

She doesn't get to Ketzel's letter until lunch the next day. Huyler's is quiet, it's already half-past one, and as she munches her tuna sandwich she reads a gossipy account of all the goings on "South of the Border/down Mexico way"—a popular song Ketzel likes.

∾

Dear Miriam,

Mexico City, March 5

I'm sitting here in this little cafe—we've had to hold up the rehearsal so I'm using this time to write you. We're settled nicely in a little apartment right off the Zocolo. It's a good location, very close to the Palacio de Bellas Artes—walking distance and also right near a Sanborn's.

Anna Sokolow is a tremendous hit here. Our group was scheduled for just a few weeks, originally, and we did our usual numbers, "Slaughter of the Innocents" (the Spain thing) and "Lament for the Death of A Bull-fighter". It was so popular they extended the show date and now—guess what—the government has funded "La Casa del Artista" to teach Mexican girls, who are in the ballet corps, modern dance technique and, of course, Anna is in charge. So far, it's been sensational—warm energy comes in waves from the audience. Now Anna's trying to incorporate Mexican folk lore into our repertoire and we're working on a new number, "The Fable of the Wandering Frog," and we're busy making mice, cats and frog masks.

We see the Siqueiros gang and the Arenals, and also Caridad, Ramon's mother. Ramon's not around much. He's busy with a special assignment. Vidali, who I can't stand, is here too. When Tina looks at him, well, if looks could kill....

We all had a good chuckle last week. Rivera and Siqueiros had a debate at the Bellas Artes about the Mexican mural movement. "What role should the artists play?" was the subject. We were all excited, expecting a lively time because the day before they already had a hot quarrel and Rivera had pulled a gun. The whole thing was rescheduled but instead of being exciting, it got really dull! They ended up comparing how much each of them had sold to tourists! Can you feature it!. I heard this story from Anita Brenner, an American woman who lives here and who knows practically everyone in radical circles. She said that Mercader asked her to introduce him to Trotsky. Why should he want to meet him? Does he want to insult him in person. Frida refused. Things are different now anyway. I hear Frida's cooled off with the Trotsky group, gone back to the Stalin camp.

Martin sees David Siqueiros often, he's so attractive, those piercing blue eyes! A very gung-ho C P-er. If Trotsky has anyone to fear in Mexico, it's David and Vidali. As for me, I can't stand that Vidali. He showed me the finger on his right hand, his trigger finger, twisted swollen, like a large ugly worm. "I got that from shooting all those Trotskyites in Spain," he bragged. Sickening!. I'm starting to hate them all.

Daddy has sort of dropped out of politics for the time being. He's busy managing business affairs of the hacienda, preparing to be a father! Can't say I'm thrilled about the whole thing. I wish things had been different. Carolina's okay but having a baby sister or brother, twenty-four years younger! Oy Vey!

We're being called now, I'll have to stop. A big kiss and a hug.

Ketzel.

Miriam puts down the letter, feeling slightly sick. She pushes away her plate and sits, staring at the table. The waitress putting down a steaming cup of coffee, looks sharply at her. "Something wrong with the sandwich. You okay?

She looks up, managing a tiny grin. "It's fine, thanks. I guess I just lost my appetite."

*Pull yourself togethe*r, she tells herself. *We know the Old Man is in danger and Mexico is probably one of the most dangerous places he could be, but what choice dOES he have? At least, Siqueiros is out in the open. What about Vidali? Our comrades can watch the Old Man but how about the G P U—the unseen enemies?*

She feels cold, begins to shiver. Then, realizing she's letting herself slip into a frightened, pessimistic state she forces herself to take a sip but it's too hot. She gets up quickly and hurries into the street, filled with reassuring sunlight and busy, peaceful people.

She doesn't get to read the rest of Ketzel's letter for a few days. She knows Ketzel will write about Jaime's wife and she dreads reading it, but finally one evening when Sydney's away, she picks up the last sheet.

Miriam dear,

Mexico City
April, 2, '39

We just finished a wonderful performance in front of 3,200 fired-up people. It's just wonderful to dance here! The Bellas Artes is so beautiful, a white marble building with a great glass Tiffany curtain. We're used to little stages in scrubby theatres on the lower east side, we're kind of lost in such a big space.

Martin and I are going to visit Jaime and Carolina this week-end. She's nice, I guess. I've known her forever, she's just a few years older than I, very attractive, with a great figure. She's nuts about him, has always been, all over him every minute and he's embarrassed.

Miss you, wish you were here. We'd go to Acapulco in the morning and dodge the big waves at Ornos in the afternoon. Hope you're satisfied with this long letter. You owe me. A million hugs and kisses.

Ketzel

Miriam puts the letter away, a thousand emotions roiling within her. She gets her coat and calls to Clara, "Mom, I have to go out." Her mother, at the stove, hears her but doesn't respond. It takes a long walk for Miriam to calm down and when she returns she finds Sydney waiting impatiently, he reminds her they're supposed to be heading downtown to meet their comrades from the lake,

As they're leaving Miriam calls out, "Good night, Mom." Clara closes her door, doesn't answer.

"Is something bothering your mother?" Sydney asks.

"I have no idea" Miriam answered. "But I heard her on the phone the other day yakking with a real-estate broker. Somewhere she's got $700 dollars stashed away. It's burning a hole in her pocket. She's an addict, loves the real-estate game but the trouble is, she's not very smart about it. She'll never learn."

They're on their way to meet the same four comrades who'll be sharing a cottage this coming summer. They'd been together in '37, the year Harry Milton returned from Spain. Tall, handsome Franky and Beady, his wife, a short stubby girl with a Mona Lisa face, both Italian, are still a couple. They had made their affair legal with a small family wedding, just their two families. Franky has a steady job now, working and is beginning to do well, in spite of the Depression. He has a large, handsome, open face, an engaging personality which encourages people to buy life insurance, impressed by the wonderful death benefits he so ably describes. Beady's still troubled with a painful back, she's able to get around a little, but she's almost a complete invalid so the group decides she and Franky should have the best bedroom in the cottage.

Rhoda and Harold volunteer to take the garage again. "I'm not going to be here very much this summer," he tells them. "I'll be playing a lot of Pop concerts, got to save some dough. Never know when the Metropolitan Opera Company might fold or I'll be laid off." Harold, slim, with delicate hands, near-sighted, is a fine violist but a great worrier, Rhoda lives with and supports her old parents. Rhoda was a virgin when they met and Harold had wanted to marry her, do the right thing, but his mother wouldn't hear of it. Rhoda wasn't good enough for her son, It wasn't only that she was plain, short and chubby and poor. "You should find a girl with a civil service job—a school-teacher maybe, someone who has a pension." His mother nags him all the time; he'd tell the group about it when Rhoda wasn't around. It was easy to see where Harold got his worrisome nature, and the others know they'll split up soon; they're just postponing it until the summer's over.

After it's all settled, over the table filled with plates of left-over egg-foo young and chow mein, the bottle of cheap wine the management let them bring in, they toast the summer of '39. They laugh, joke and end up going to the movies to see the Marx Brothers in "A Night at the Opera".

There's been little discussion of the political upheaval taking place in the Party. A national convention is scheduled for August and everybody knows that the factional struggle between the Cannon/and Schactman/Abern Group is coming to a head. "It's very important we attend every session," Sydney says. He and Franky, half-heartedly, support Cannon The rest, confused and uncommitted, don't want to talk politics, not while they thinking about a summer vacation.

Aside from discussion meetings held at the City headquarters, branch meetings are held allotting "Jimmy Higgins" work. One of the most onerous of tasks, Miriam finds, is trying to sell 'The Militant' house-to-house. For her it is even more difficult than selling the paper at open-air meetings, and after one very frightening experience she refuses to do it anymore.

She and Ed, another comrade had been assigned to canvass a neighborhood in East Harlem, where white, black and hispanics made their home in ravaged, unheated slum buildings, a single toilet on each floor. Their job was going from door to door, introducing themselves: "We're Ed and Miriam. We're from the Socialist Workers Party. We'd like to talk to you a moment," or, "We have a newspaper we think would interest you." Mostly, there would be silence on the other side, sometimes a voice would yell, "We don't want any."

This time, after they'd knocked, a young woman in a wrinkled, baggy house dress, a tiny, unsteady baby, with a drooping wet diaper and a dirty nose clinging to her calf, opened the door. Frazzled light hair hung about her shoulders but a smile on her delicate, pale face welcomed them. An acrid sweet odor of garbage and urine hit their nostrils and Miriam would have turned to run that instant. But the woman pointed to two chairs. saying sweetly with a southern accent. "Kindly sit down. It's nice to hav' comp'ny"

Miriam remained standing, nauseated by the smell and dirt but Ed sat down, envisioning a newspaper sale, a contact, a possible new member of the Party. During the next few moments he forged ahead making friendly conversation as an opener while Miriam bent to the baby, praying silently, *Oh god, get us out of here soon.*

Ed hadn't finished more than a few sentences when the door burst open and a hefty, grizzled male in mud-caked overalls stood in the threshold. He stared, then bellowed, "Who in hell are you?" Without waiting for an answer, he strode to Ed, grabbed him by the collar, lifted him and pushed him towards the open door. Then he wheeled around to the woman and, almost gracefully for such a burly man, swung his arm, smashing it across her face.

"Bill, Bill, stop," she screamed, "They ain't doin' no harm," holding a flaming cheek.

Miriam had flown into the hall a moment after the man appeared. Ed arrived a second later. The giant looked at them, grunted, slammed the door shut. They didn't wait to hear what was happening. They made for the stairs, out of the building. In the street, under the lamp post Miriam, shaking, muttered, "Ed, that's enough for tonight, I'm going home. And you know what, I'll never do this again."

"I saw an apartment today that was pretty nice," Miriam tells Sydney one night as they're walking along the 155th street viaduct and the Hudson. "What do you think?" she asks?

"Does it make sense? To move now? If we're going to be up in the country most of the summer? Besides, your mother might be hurt if we leave."

Miriam turned to look at Sydney, puzzled. "What makes you say that? Did she think we were going to live with her forever?"

"People don't think—they feel. She's gotten used to us being with her."

Miriam's too surprised to answer. She puts her arm through Sydney's, thinking about what he had said, wondering if she was insensitive; *how come he notices things I don't. Even though, when it comes to me, he doesn't notice much.*

"Maybe you're right. I guess it wouldn't make sense for us to move now. There's plenty of empty apartments, even up in the Heights." That seems to be the answer Sydney wants to hear so they forget about it.

A few days later, when her mother's at the stove, adding salt to the soup, Miriam asks, "It looks good, Mom. Is there enough for Sydney and me?"

"It's almost done." Her answer is curt, as usual. "Help yourself when you want." Clara's about to go out when Miriam says, "Mom, I want to talk to you. Come sit down. You can spare a minute."

Her mother comes to the table, reluctantly, plunks her elbows on the table, shakes her head, smiles.

"All of a sudden you want to talk to me," she says. Then, harshly, "You haven't got time—you rush in—you rush out. You sleep here, I wouldn't know you're alive. I forget I had children."

Miriam's surprised, her voice defensive. "Ma, you know how busy we are. Working, school. It's not that we don't think about you. You know we're glad to be here." But in spite of herself, she feels annoyed. *What the hell does she expect,* she thinks. *She's got enough to keep herself busy.* She turns to the stove and sniffs. "It smells delicious, Mom." With a sardonic smile on her face, Clara says, "You could at least tell me when you're going to move out. How am I supposed to find out, from the letter-carrier?"

"Look, Mama. I'm sorry I didn't talk to you about moving. You can't expect us to live with you forever." Miriam, setting two bowls and spoons at the table, adds, "Anyway we're not moving, at least for a while. We'll be away almost all summer. By the way, maybe you'll come up to the country for a couple of days. It'd do you good.

"Knarrishkeit," her mother laughs, short, sarcastic.

"Hold it, Mom. I'm really sorry if I hurt your feelings. We just talked about moving, we weren't serious. That's why I didn't mention it." As Clara leaves, Miriam calls after her, "Listen, Mom, next fall, how about, we'll go to a show. There's a new one, 'Our Town', supposed to be wonderful."

Later, when Miriam sees the show, alone, she wonders how her mother would have taken this play about the preciousness of life, and family life especially. When she was a little kid she'd beg her mother to take her somewhere, especially on a Sunday when there was no one to play with, when almost all the kids would be out with their families. It was the worst day of the week for her.

But her mother was always too busy, busy all the time, no time to listen. And now Clara's the one who's lonely.

"Okay, Mom?," Miriam asks brightly. "Am I forgiven?"

Her mother smiles faintly, brushes past her, "Okay. Good night. Don't let the bedbugs bite." Her voice is flat.

"Spring's a little late this year," Miriam hums the song, recalling the Greek myth about Persephone who couldn't leave the underground because Pluto, who loved her, kept her there below, with him, like a prisoner. The winter's been long and troublesome and Miriam yearns for freedom on this brisk, sunny day.

She always loved walking up the easy hill of Broadway, a wide and graceful street. After a few blocks, she turns west, onto Fort Washington Avenue, passing Loew's Rio where she and her classmates went when they played hookey from school. When she reaches Bennett Park at 183rd Street she stops. *Now I'm standing on the highest point of Manhattan Island*, she tells herself, *like king of the mountain.*

From the steep grade between the Drive and the River, she can see the thick, glittering steel cables of the George Washington Bridge, across the water the sharp high rocky slopes of the Palisades, and further away, the docked luxury ocean liners, waiting for new passengers. Massive gray freighters spew black smoke into the sky; overhead a silver plane slants and then ducks behind clouds, and energetic tugboats puff along the Hudson. Nestled below, at the foot of mammoth pillars of the Bridge, she sees a small, red, funnel-shaped lighthouse which was made many years ago, its concrete molded very carefully. Now it looks like it's been painted onto the vast scene, like an afterthought. Yet, although it's much smaller than the great bridge or the big boats, people notice the little red lighthouse. She's always loved the little lighthouse since she was little. It's quaint, stolid, one of a kind. Kids love it, lots of their books have stories about it.

Now it's standing all alone in a fast moving, mechanical world with no purpose, left out of the present, just a reminder of the past, no longer needed. But it is still needed, she thinks, it's important, lots of things from the past are important … enduring.

But so is the future, including my future. She has to find a place for herself in the world and she has to change the world too. Oh God, there's so much to do.

She sits down on the low stone wall, fishes an apples from her pocket and raises her face to catch the rays of a weak sun pushing through a woolly sky.

She begins to think, she must be learn to be freer, happier, lose some of her childish illusions about love, become stronger, more independent, hold her ground, like the lighthouse. Maybe she could even be like a lighthouse—some day.

As for the S W P, she's getting impatient with some of the people, the Trotskyists and the high-fallutin' intellectual airs some of them put on. Not that they aren't smart, but except for a few of the personal friends she's made she doesn't feel much closeness or comradeship in the deepest sense of the word. There's a coldness, a disaffection … There seems to be too much emphasis on theory and politics—not enough about personal relationships … she isn't clear about the reasons for it but perhaps it's inevitable for members of a small radical group who are always isolated, always on the the outside of society. In the Commununist Party there's much more closeness and warmth. Is it because they have an anchor—the great beacon—the Soviet Union—a sense of belonging and strength that transfers into their personal relationships.

She knows she'll always be a revolutionist, that'll never change. But she has to make a living, be independent, not constantly worrying about money, like her mother. Forget about factory work, places like the Brooklyn Navy Yards, and she won't leave New York and go elsewhere, Detroit or California, and get into the war industry like some comrades are doing. The Party doesn't have work for her, paid work, like an organizer or office secretary. She isn't the aggressive type, like Pearl Kluger who got herself sent by the Party to Mexico for the hearings. She'll have to find work she's good at, she likes, is happy in, she'll have to go to College, get a degree, make it happen—herself.

The apple core is her hand is sticky. Unable to spot a garbage can, she finds a handkerchief in her pocket, wraps it, puts it in her purse and heads home. She'll stop agonizing herself about Spain, the defeat, the heartbreak, the horror. It's over. The war's coming and that's it! We can't stop it. But we have to stop Hitler. She won't put blinders on her eyes that other Jews allow themselves to wear—she shudders, feeling chilled.

Back on Broadway, at Woolworth's she orders a hot chocolate. Despite all her good intentions and will-power she thinks of Jaime. What did I expect?, she asks herself. Carolina's very attractive, and she isn't political! When a man's in the mood for love and there's an attractive woman around, the outcome is inevitable. Why should Jaime be any different?

She drinks the chocolate quickly, drains the cup and walks out. Halfway down the block, she realizes she hasn't paid for it.

"I'll pay for it the next time," she tell herself. "I just can't go back now." She stops for a moment at 155th Street and looks at the tremendous statue of El Cid on horseback in front of the Museum of the American Indian. At night, she remembers, the kids from High School used to come to this courtyard and neck in the dark corners. She leans against a stone pillar and begins to cry.

Thinking about him has got to come to an end. I'm screwing up my own life. When are you going to keep from being a damn fool?, she asks herself. She takes Jaime's letter from her purse, tears it in halves, then quarters. As she walks home, she tears the letter into even tinier pieces and watches them scatter and mingle with the other debris in the gutter.

Mexico

These days, in Trotsky's house, there is usually company for tea. In his 'fortress' visitors are always welcome, notwithstanding his followers' worries about security. One afternoon, Trotsky, Natalya and a professor from the States, sit in the cool, shaded dining room. "May I ask how did you lose power?" the professor inquires.

Trotsky replies, "One doesn't lose power as one does a handkerchief."

He answers the visitor with facts and events but back in his study he wonders if he has told the whole story. He wonders, has he told the whole story? How had Stalin, "the greatest mediocrity in the Bolshevik party," driven the most honored Bolshevik next to Lenin, heir to leadership of the Soviet Union, from popularity, from office, from citizenship, into exile? A bad joke that a sly, shabby, inarticulate man should have been his rival! A pockmarked man, possessing, using political sagacity and cunning, plotting and scheming, for control, for power.

He knows he's made mistakes. He'd gone duck hunting in 1923, and during the trip had fallen ill. All during the discussion of Trotskyism in the Party, the most crucial period in his life, he was sick in bed. As he wrote in My Life, *"One can foresee a revolution or a war, but it is impossible to foresee the consequences of an autumn shooting-trip for wild ducks."*

The year before, when Lenin was still alive, he'd ordered Trotsky to relieve Stalin of his post, but Trotsky had disobeyed, had decided to wait. And after Lenin's death, Trotsky would often absent himself or would let his attention drift during important meetings. He had not supported those who fought the destruction of party democracy. And he said nothing when the leadership decided to suppress Lenin's will, in particular the postscript calling for Stalin's removal as General Secretary. Trotsky had remained silent, a disgusted look on his face. A fatal error.

CHAPTER 21

Upstate New York, Summer 1939

The jalopy Sydney and Miriam buy that Spring is a lemon, ending up with more hours in the repair shop than on the road. Comrades grumble when they have to fork over ten dollars to keep the damn thing going but they have no choice, they must have a car there.

July is sunny and hot, the lack of rain causing drought conditions in the east, yet, fortunately, water is not a problem in the cottage. A pump over the kitchen sink supplies plenty, clear, cold, refreshing, but the problem is the toilet. It hasn't been fixed although Michael Quill of the Teamsters' Union, the cottage owner, had promised it would be. Therefore a bucket had to be filled from the kitchen, lugged to the bathroom, dumped so that the toilet would flush. Attempts to reach the landlord are futile; he got all his money before the beginning of the summer.

During the course of the day, people manage but it's different after breakfast. The first person to fill the bucket and get into the bathroom was the luckiest, others had to take toilet paper and depart for the woods nearby. Once someone visiting made an unfortunate decision to take an early morning walk and came running back, pale as a ghost. "I almost stumbled over a great white bear squatting behind a tree and grunting! For god's sake, get that toilet fixed."

One night there is a lively discussion about the Hitler-Stalin Pact, which has just been signed. The Trotskists knew that Stalin and Hitler might conclude such an agreement. Indeed, Trotsky had predicted it could happen and had argued that if such an agreement served the interest and security of the U S S R, there could be no principled objection to it. What excited the comrades was how the Communist Party members and its supporters would react to a pact between Stalin and Hitler, who been vilified in their press. It was startling to see Ribbentrop and Molotov in the newspapers, shaking hands. To most of the Jewish C P members it had to be absolutely horrifying! And there was certain to be a lot of demoralization. Such a pact with the devil was almost unthinkable, no matter how expedient it was.

"Wouldn't you expect C P-ers would see Stalin's zig-zag policies in a clear light for the first time? Wouldn't you hope they'd finally see where Stalinism leads and come over to the Trotskyist ranks?!" Everyone is so excited that night they talk for hours.

One Monday it begins to rain and the rain continues all week.

"Looks like the drought's over," Frankie grumbles. By Saturday, the interior of the tacky bungalow is so damp that the walls are wet. "If we could only have gone to the movies tonight," Miriam mourns. She's just finished drying the dinner dishes and is watching Frankie and Harold work at getting a fire going. "That lousy jalopy—I told Sydney it was too cheap," she complains. The handsome, useless car sits in back, waiting to be towed for the third time.

Sydney, his raincoat dripping, hears her as he's bringing in a cord of wood they just bought. They had already run out of the branches and twigs gathered in the woods. He bristles at her. "Just like your mother. You were with me when I bought the damn car, I wasn't sure about it but you love a bargain."

"Okay, people, let's not argue." Patient Beady, the peacemaker, speaks so softly others have to quiet down. She's nestled in a shabby morris chair, the only comfortable seat in the living room. The sofa so old it's springs stab the occupant at unexpected moments and places. "Why don't we all sit down and enjoy the fire when the guys have finished? How about charades?"

"Okay, let's," Miriam says. She pats the place next to her and smiles apologetically at Sydney. He's right and he doesn't need henpecking. He doesn't have a high opinion of himself in the first place.

As soon as the others gather, making some kind of a semi-circle about the fire, beginning to crackle, making the room seem a little less glum, Miriam says, "I've got a great word. Quiet, everyone," and begins the game. She thinks it's a good word but no one's able to guess it, even though she goes through a variety of contortions, even rolling on the floor. When she says it's a book, "The Immoralist" by Andre Gide, everyone groans and yells at her for a lousy choice. After that, the others pick easy ones like *"Duck Soup", "Pins and Needles"* and *"The Grapes of Wrath."*

"Hey, how about some wine," Frankie suggests when they declare enough of charades. "I brought a bottle for us—It's our second anniversary." He looks over at Beady, whose face lights with surprise. With half-filled jelly glasses everyone toasts the couple, then to the success of the Fourth International and the health of the Old Man. Miriam prevails on Harold to sing the new Oscar Brand song about the exploits of the King of Spain; everyone laughs at the refrain 'With his do-wacky-wacky-do hanging down to his knees"; Beady hopes no one can see her blush.

"Better feed the fire, guys," says Rhoda. She's found a comfortable spot on the sofa.

"Whoever's going to town better buy more wood?" Miriam offers. "This'll be gone by tonight."

"Will the car be fixed by tomorrow?" someone wants to know and someone else answers, "Yeah, but who's gonna drive?"

"Anyone but Harold!" Beady chirps and everyone laughs.

They're all remembering a night a week or so before, when they decided to go out to an all-night grocery for some beer and Harold insisted on taking the wheel. It's against their better judgment, they all know he's a poor driver; he jerks the car, goes too fast, stops too short. They get there okay but it's on the way home, it happens. The car's noisy, Beady's directing the Whippenpoof song, they're all singing "We're poor little lambs who have lost our way—baa, baa, baa," when suddenly there's a sharp curve in the pitch-black road. The car makes the turn and they are—sitting on a railroad track—stuck! The car has stalled—and now a locomotive, a giant black medieval monster is bearing down on them, its headlights blinding. Harold turns the key—the motor's dead—everyone screams—he turns the key again—they scream like mad-men—he jams down on the pedal—the motor starts—the jalopy jumps—leaps forward, hurtles them onto a dirt road—stops! But they're safe—thundering on behind them the monster plunges on.

Shaking, silent, they sit in darkness. Sydney takes the wheel. When they get home they drink every ounce of liquor they can find.

Now Sydney looks over at Harold and says, "You're a fantastic musician, and we've enjoyed your practicing in the barn all summer, playing that stuff from the Mozart Violin Concerto over and over 'til we're all nuts. But never, never drive the car for us again."

That memory sparks others … "Remember the time," Franky says, "when we had that big blowup about the hot dogs?" Oh, no, Miriam thinks, why doesn't he shut up? "Let's not," she says, looking over at Rhoda who's gazing into the leaping flames, cupping the little wine left in her glass.

"Hey, Rhoda, remember how sore you got when I came up that Friday night," Franky goes on. "I told you I'd been too late, I missed Marty" (Marty was his paisan from Italy, an apprentice in Gristede's butcher department.) He'd slip Franky three or four extra steaks for the group when he'd shop there for the week-end.) "I bet you don't remember. When I told you all I could get was hot-dogs, you blew your top. You were standing on the lawn, almost crying," and here Franky does a bad imitation of Rhoda's whining voice … "I work hard all week and I look forward to a decent meal on Friday night."

Miriam recalled only too well. Everyone was quiet when she stalked into the barn. Miriam and Beady began preparing cole slaw and mashed potatoes, Sydney and Harold went for cold beer while Franky set up the grill in the front yard.

"Come and get it everyone," he called in a half-hour and everyone sat, waiting for Rhoda to come out. As she approached, everyone shouted, "Surprise, surprise," and Franky, like a conquering hero, came from the grill carrying a platter of t-bone steaks and presenting it to Rhoda. "Here you are, Madame Queen" he said in his best Amos 'n' Andy imitation. She'd grinned and said, "I knew we had steak as soon as Franky started grilling. I can smell. I knew it all the time."

Rhoda says with a little laugh, says, "You know, Franky, I still don't think it was funny," but her voice is a little sad and subdued, not her usual, assertive tone.

The room is quiet now. The warmth, the fire's glow, the sound of branches brushing across the window, the comraderie makes them pensive. Franky, on the floor at Beady's feet, reaches up and takes her hand, Harold rests his head against Rhoda's legs, Sydney sits on the floor, in a dark corner of the room, near Miriam who's snuggled into an old easy chair.

"We should do this more often, get together like this," she says, softly. "The summer'll be over soon—too soon, for me, anyway.

A little later Harold breaks the silence. Speaking in a conversational tone but his face is serious, "Maybe I shouldn't bring this up now but I've been thinking about telling you guys about this for a long time. I like all of you very much—it has nothing to do with you." He pauses then plunges on, "I've decided to leave the Party."

For a few minutes no one says a word Then someone says, "That's a helluva note! What's your reason?"

Sydney looks stunned, then asks, "Are you afraid of losing your job?"

"No, but I always worry." Harold pauses, thinks a moment, shakes his head, and says, "I just don't believe in a revolutionary movement anymore. It's an illusion; I don't think we'll ever be able to …"

"You know, it's hard to believe you can say that," Franky bursts in. "Are you forgetting what's been going on in this country for the last seven years? Sure, we're a small group, nothing in comparison to the two big parties in this country." He stands up and looks directly at Harold, "Okay, it's been a long time since we had Debs with nearly a million votes in 1912 but look what's happened just recently. 1934, the depths of the depression, one and a half million workers in different industries go out on strike! In San Francisco. a general strike—the whole City paralyzed—half a million textile workers out by September—Minneapolis—We led those workers—it was classic—the C I O, the sit-down strikes …"

Sydney interrupts, angry. "What he's saying is that he doesn't have any faith in the working class."

"That isn't true. I think the working class is capable of great militancy and heroism." Harold's face beoomes red as he stammers on. "But I think that the capitalists in America are too smart for them. They'll never let the proletariat take over." He stands up, facing Franky and his voice becomes louder, almost shrill. "They pass laws—the Wagner Act—make labor legal, let them unionize, right. Meanwhile, they sew them up. Sure, they say, we'll giv'em a little, give 'em a little there, we'll put up some housing, we'll pass a minimum wage law—25 cents an hour! We'll start a New Deal, They pacify the people—and if it doesn't work, if the workers get obstreperous—they call out the National Guard—or the Marines. They'll show them what's what!" His face covered with sweat, and he fishes in his pocket for a handkerchief. Then, he sits down, looking around with an embarrassed, half-smile.

His outburst is so unusual everyone's quiet for a moment. Then Sydney, looking at the threadbare carpet as if he sees an answer there, says, slowly, trying not to be sharp, "Harold, you haven't told us anything new. We're not kidding ourselves. But, either you haven't read Marx or you don't understand his theories, but you should know that Capitalism, sooner or later, is doomed, Communism is the only solution."

Franky adds, his tone slightly mocking. "I think you've been hanging around with James Burnham and his faction too long, Harold. Just the other day he told Cannon he's not convinced it's so wise to devote his life to a cause that might not be victorious in his lifetime—I'm trying to quote his own words. In my opinion, he's on his way out of the Party, he didn't belong there in the first place. The Old Man was right when he called an intellectual snob."

"What does that have to do with what Harold said?" Miriam blurts out. She stands up, looking around at the surprised faces.

"I agree with him." Her voice is defiant. "I don't see how a revolution can happen in this country. Look what we did to the Indians—this government is so vicious—it always has been. They practically annihilated them. If the ruling class in America was ever really threatened, they wouldn't hesitate to blow the workers, thousands, to kingdom come."

Sydney looks at her with a sarcastic grin. "So, you're going to leave the Party too. Good news!" He scrambles to his feet, going over to Harold for a light.

Miriam, flushed, responds slowly. "No, I'm not. I don't agree with Cannon, or Trotsky for that matter. Russia is not a degenerated worker's state. It isn't a workers state any more, period. The workers in Russia have lost their power and I won't fight to defend it either, although Trotsky thinks we should. But, I'm not like Harold, I'll always belong to a revolutionary party. It has to exist because the idea has to be kept alive, because communism or socialism—whatever you want to call it—it's the only way for people who want to live on this earth—in peace—without war. At least that's what I think."

As soon as she's finished, she threads her way through the comrades sprawled on the floor and heads towards the bathroom. She knows Sydney's going to follow up on her remarks and she doesn't want to hear them.

Franky begins, "Of course, that's basic. A real revolutionary ..." and she hears no more as she shuts the door. When she emerges later, Sydney's nowhere to be seen, Beady's limping her way to her room, Rhoda has already slipped out and Franky and Harold are talking quietly, watching the dying fire. Loath to go to the bedroom where she's sure Sydney's probably waiting to continue the discussion, she takes Beady's Morris chair and curls up in it. Franky gets up to go after a few minutes, and she and Harold are alone in the room which is quite dark now, just a dim glow from flickering embers. He pulls up a chair close to her.

"I know what you're trying to say and I agree about what the prospects are in this country." His voice was low, confidential, "But I'm different. I haven't got the desire or the will to go on when I feel it's hopeless." He spreads open his long, slim hands. "I'm not one who can 'man the barricades', if it should ever come to that."

Miriam shakes her head. "I wouldn't mind 'manning the barricades' if we got to that point. What I hate is all the 'Jimmy Higgins' work. But we have to do that stuff, it's the only way we can make things better, what Trotsky calls the 'transitional demands' of the party, helping people get housing, jobs, joining unions, improving working conditions …" she trails off.

"You know what" she says, "let's stop talking about politics. Tell me about what's going on in the Met these days. Are you still taking viola lessons with Primrose". Primrose is one of the most highly regarded music teachers in the world and she knows Harold considers himself lucky to study with him. Harold loves music and loves being a professional. She always sensed he wan't cut out to be a communist, certainly not an active one. Like so many young New York college students he'd been caught up in the fervor of the radical movement that swept through the halls of city colleges. She feels a trace of sadness, she'll miss him … he's a sweet, gentle guy …

He loves talking about himself and music and goes on enthusiastically until Miriam hides a yawn. Saying, "Guess you're tired—I am too. I better get over to the barn … Rhoda gets mad if I come in late," he stops down to brush her cheek. "Thanks for understanding," he says.

Two days later, as Beady and Miriam are finishing lunch Sylvia appears at the screen door, wearing expensive tailored shorts.

"Oh, excuse me," she says, looking flustered. "I didn't mean to interrupt your meal." Miriam's amused, Sylvia is always so darn formal. No one else would say that here. It's part of her bourgeois upbringing, Miriam surmises, although Hilda, her sister, is much more easy-going and informal.

"Hello, come in, join us," Beady says cordially. She approves of good manners. "Sit over here, by the fan, otherwise you'll melt in this room. How about some iced coffee? Tell us all about Paris." Miriam watches Beady with amusement. Beady'd heard a lot about Sylvia's romance and, like everyone else, wonders what how she'd managed to attract such a handsome, wealthy, intelligent guy. From what she heard, he went for her right after they were introduced. Sylvia certainly isn't sexy or special in any way. Maybe it's a 'chemistry' between them, an inexplicable attraction, Beady decides, and smiles brightly at the newcomer. "Every cloud has a silver lining—just look at today. We had so much rain all last week, we deserve this nice weather."

"It's been terribly hot in the city and Hilda and I just came up for a weekend," Sylvia says. "I'd really love to stay and chat but I'd love to go out on the lake for a little while. And I even brought my own umbrella."

"I use one too," Beady says. "My motto is always, 'Be prepared'. Of course you can take the boat, at least for an hour." She's still smiling but disappointed, she'd love to hear more about Sylvia's prince charming.

Miriam likes to row, takes the oars and while she busies herself with the loose oarlocks Sylvia opens her umbrella. The decorative flowers around its border with sun shining through casts a warm pink glow on Sylvia's cheeks and she looks young and pretty. They talk and drift, enjoying the light breeze, the muted chatter of magpies, the gentle, clapping wavelets against the old boat.

Miriam's waiting for Sylvia to begin talking about herself and Jacques. She knows he's arriving very soon, Hilda's told her. Trailing her left hand in the cool water, looking down to the bottom, she says,

"I'd better warn you, Sylvia, if you go swimming here, it's dangerous here and you have to be careful—stay on the surface. Don't stand up anywhere, although it's shallow enough. There's lots of sharp little rocks—you could get badly cut." As if she had just thought of it, she adds, "If Jacques comes, be sure you warn him."

"I doubt if Jacques'll go swimming." Sylvia takes her handkerchief from her watchband and wipes her forehead. "Not that he's unathletic. He's a fantastic skier. And, of course, he's a sportswriter so he knows all about all kinds of sports. Sometimes he gets a little impatient with me because he does every-thing so well. Not that I'm complaining," her voice takes on a note of pride. "He's wonderful."

"Well, you have a lot to offer too," Miriam says stoutly. "There's only thing, he's not interested in politics. I'm not criticizing him—but I don't think I could be with someone who isn't radical. Although in some ways maybe it would be easier," Miriam pauses.

"I'm not giving up on that," Sylvia protests. "He did go with me to Rosmer's home when we had the 4th International meeting, only he stayed outside and wouldn't come in. I wanted him to meet Shachtman and Cannon and Etienne but he's got a quick temper. I've had to learn when to stop. I'd love to meet his parents but when I mention it up he cuts me right off." She sighs. "It doesn't look as if we'll get married, not right away."

"Are you sure you want to?" Miriam's puzzled. "Men with quick temper scare me. I don't think I'd ever marry one—that's why it probably won't last with Sydney even though he is political." She picks up the oars and begins to row back to shore.

"Jacques will change, I'm pretty sure. He really loves me. I think, it'll hap-pen in time." Her voice trails off and she looks down at her clasped hands. "I hope it will. I'm afraid to think it might end…. he'll be here in a few days." Sylvia sits up, straightening her narrow shoulders. "I can't wait for you to meet him."

Miriam watches her walk up the rickety dock, walking with precision, almost like an old person, placing each step carefully. She is going to phone Paris now and talk to him at exactly the time they agreed to. *I guess that's how her love affair will go, ending up in a planned marriage. That's not me,* Miriam thinks. *If it were my boyfriend, I'd be dashing up the hill right now, stumbling on loose pebbles.* She's anxious to meet Sylvia's lover. In her mind, although she struggles against it, she makes comparisons between Jacques and Jaime. They're similar in many respects. Jaime is also from a wealthy family, well-educated and sophisticated, well-to-do and handsome. But Jaime is political and—she remembers with a pang—he's no longer a Stalinist.

But—she stops walking on the lawn and finds a camp chair under a tree, trembling … Was Jaime telling her the truth? Is he really running the hacienda in Mexico, helping his sister? Is his marriage with Carolina a cover-up for some special U S S R work? She feels sick. No, no, it can't be possible. Jaime wouldn't be capable of it.

Still she knows that kind of deception happens. She often wondered what Ketzel's Martin was up to. Ketzel's most recent letter from Mexico reported that Martin was hanging around with the Siquerios gang. She was so busy with her dance group she hardly saw him or them, and Caridad Mercader and her Eitingon were away in the Soviet Union, meeting up with Caridan's son, Ramon. "The Stalinists are very busy here," Ketzel had written, "holding meetings, distributing newspapers against Trotsky, and they're beginning to annoy me. I know there are political differences but I can't stand the kind of villification that goes on. I haven't seen much of my father, he's very busy and also staying away from the Party and "the rogues" as I call them—Siqueiros, Vidali. Poor Tina looks terrible. It's really a shame, she used to be so beautiful, Spain's really done her in or was it Vidali?"

I ought to tell Sylvia, Miriam decides, she's lucky her boy-friend isn't interested in politics. Sometimes it changes people. No, not all of them, the Communists who become Stalinists lose their humanity, their values, become fanatics, murderers, like Tina, Siqueiros and Caridad, and probably her son, too.

He arrives the following week and Miriam can't wait to meet him. Although the others seem interested, they're not about to walk up the hill, it's not worth it they say, and for some reason she feels uneasy about going alone. One afternoon she decides to to and bribes Rhoda to come with her. "I'll make crepes for dessert tonight if you'll do it."

The road is dry and dusty but the long shadows from trees make the walk pleasant. As they climb up they can hear the low sweet strains of Harold practicing on the viola. Rhoda, her face wistful, stops for a moment, listening. Then, with a slight shrug of her shoulders, she quickens her pace to catch up with Miriam.

As they approach Sylvia's cottage they see a man sitting out in front, lounging on a beach chair, under a tree. His face is turned away from the road but as they come closer, and see him more clearly, Miriam whispers to Rhoda, taking her arm, "Just keep on walking, don't say a word."

Once they're safely past the cottage Rhoda bursts out, "I thought we were going to stop by and talk to the guy; I'm sure he's the boy-friend."

"I don't know. I couldn't talk to him." Miriam is upset, defensive. "He looked … mean—staring straight ahead as if he saw something frightening."

"I didn't take such a good look at him," Rhoda says. "Why's he dressed like that. Wouldn't you think he'd have on a pair of shorts?"

"But it isn't that," Miriam insists. "He didn't look like a man in love. His face was twisted like … I can't describe it! It was strange, like somethings out of whack. Why isn't he inside with Sylvia, helping her fix dinner..?" She's disappointed and disturbed. She'd looked forward to meeting a charming handsome guy, a dreamboat. Oh, well, she decides, maybe he's all of those things, I could be wrong, and after a couple of minutes, she decides to forget about it, it isn't her business. A popular song pops into her head and she starts singing. It's from a movie she just saw, with Fred Astaire and Ginger Rogers.. "a strange romance, my friend, this is/a strange romance with no kisses". She sings it all the way down a to their cottage.

They're walking quickly, Rhoda's anxious to get back to Harold. There aren't too many days left till the end of summer and she wants to be with him as much as possible. But she gets into a real stew when they walk in because there's broiled trout for dinner, which she detests. Miriam, thirsty, wants a beer but it's luke-warm because Franky's just brought in the ice. While she's waiting for it to chill, she puts the bottle right on the ice and begins to fix the switch on the ratty old fan, their sole means of air-conditioning in that hot-box of a cottage.

"So how's the new boy-friend up there?," Franky wants to know.

"I didn't speak to him." Miriam answers, hesitating, looking for the right words. "We went right by, he looked creepy, I don't know why I didn't want to talk to him. Maybe he's afraid of something. People in love usually look happy, he looked miserable."

"He probably looks like we all do," Harold says, with a small, wry smile. In a way he's right, Miriam acknowledges to herself. Franky and Beady are hardly talking to each other, she always has a backache which makes the others wonder if they ever have any sex, Rhoda and Harold are finished, just lasting out the summer and she and Sydney ... He's been standing in the doorway and he turns quickly and leaves, his lips tight. Their relationship frays with each day.

"No," Miriam shakes her head. "This is different. Sylvia says he's good-looking and he really is, in that Latin kind of way, dark, swarthy—but there's something about him, like a dark shadow ... I can't explain it."

"Listen," Franky yells. He'd been fiddling with the radio on the bookcase in the corner, trying to get the six o'clock news broadcast. "Listen! Hitler's invaded Poland! France and England are massing troops on their borders. It's begun," his face pale, "It's on every station—it's beginning ..."

Everything stops as they gather around the radio to listen and talk, going over and repeating everything that Trotsky had written during the past six or more years since Hitler has risen. War was inevitable but it was always looming in the future. Now it had arrived and it was real and frightening.

After a while Rhoda complains, "War or not war—I'm starving. Let's eat" They set to preparing dinner and gradually, while they work, their somber mood lifts. Once they're at the table with the trout, bowls of crisp green salad, golden corn and ripe tomatoes, the war begins to seem like a bad dream. Sydney tells about the C P woman who insists when she's told about the Stalin-Hitler Pact, "I won't believe it until I see it in The Daily Worker," and Franky does his Hitler imitation. When they finish they play records and end up choosing, odds or evens, who does the dishes. They finish a bottle of cheap wine discovered in a closet under the sink. It is only a long while later, after they've gone to bed, when it's dark and quiet, fear creeps in between the sheets.

"Sorry, but I'm leaving early," Harold announces on Labor Day. "Tomorrow the roads are gonna be jammed and today I can get a lift right to my door." A heavy storm is predicted on the radio and everyone, except Miriam is scrambling to leave. They're rushing, even though they don't have to ... they know it's the last summer they'll be together and everyone tries to make the departure an ordinary event. When Harold kisses Rhoda good-bye he barely brushes her cheek with his lips. Later, when Miriam goes into the barn to help her, she's packing furiously with no patience for chit-chat, and in an hour she's off with him. Beady and Franky depart next in a hired cab, and Miriam's left alone.

She walks down to the lake to enjoy the hush after all the noisy departures. A brisk breeze is wafting billowy clouds across the sky and falling leaves fill the air with a spicy aroma. The old beat-up rowboat is rocking gently at the pier and she can't resist getting in it.

"You're still here! I'm so glad I caught you." Sylvia, standing on the dock, smiles down at her, looking neat, ready to depart, in a crisp linen suit with shoes and purse to match.

"All dressed for the City. You look great," Miriam tells her. "Where's Jacques?"

"He left a few days ago. He doesn't care much for the country. He's a City person. I'm sorry you didn't get to meet him but he'll be in New York. For a short time, anyway. All of us will have to get together." Whenever she talks about him, Miriam notices, she sounds like a happy little girl who's just won a prize.

"Sure, that'll be great." Miriam tries to sound enthusiastic. "I know Sydney would like to meet him." That part is true. Sydney always wants company, it rouses him out of his moody silences. "We'll do that."

After Sylvia leaves, Miriam turns to look at the lake for the last time. The breeze is stronger, whipping up the water which has become dark grey and rough. She's walking back to the cottage when she notices something out of the corner of her eye, a large object swaying gently, half-hidden in the desolate marshes at the far end of the lake. It looks like a long box, about seven feet, caught between the reeds, bobbing from side to side, covered with yellow leaves at one end. A thought darts into her mind—a body in a coffin …

That's crazy she thinks. Walk to the end of the dock, she tells herself. *Look, show yourself what's really there.* All at once, a strong gust makes the wet leaves blow off and she sees it's just an abandoned rowboat, overturned, pierced by the sharp pointed rocks hidden under the innocent surface of the pond.

She's amused, though she feels a cold fear stabbing through her, and a feeling of desolation chases the good mood she began the day with. Loath to return to the cottage, she plods back slowly. She's promised to straighten up before she closes the place, and begins to collect the wine glasses in the living room from the night before. All the coffee mugs are dirty too, and she puts water up to heat so she can wash up properly.

As she works, the vision of the wrecked boat covered with leaves at one end, bobbing in the water, keeps playing in her mind. *It's just an old boat! Why am I so frightened?,*" she impatiently asks herself. All at once she knows why! It's Klement his headless, mutilated body floating in the Seine … It's Stalin's bloody hand—everywhere—Russia, France, Spain. Mexico?

She quickly dries her hands and runs out, into the sunshine, up the hill to ask Browner, a comrade who's still there, to give her a lift back to the City as soon as possible.

Mexico, Spring 1939

A easy, warm relationship between Trotsky and Rivera had begun and flourished since Trotsky's arrival in Mexico. They were on common ground as anti-Stalinists, they respected each other's intelligence, opinions and differences and enjoyed each other's company. But through the years vrious misunderstanding, both political and personal, have arisen between them. Trotsky has begun to see Rivera in a different, more critical light, as "lacking in self-control, having an inflammable imagination, an extreme capriciousness."

A parting of the ways appears inevitable and it becomes difficult to remain living in the Blue House which belongs to Frida. Trotsky and his entourage move into new quarters on Avenida Viena, a few blocks away. The house is a one-story Florentine-style building with a large garden, high wallls, lots of space, containing separate living quarters for Trotsky and Natalya.

They have been longing for their grandson, Trotsky's daughter Zina's boy, and have had a painful battle trying to convince Jeanne, who has been caring for him, to give him up. Jeanne loves the boy and has hidden him away, but Marguerite Rosmer manages to find him. Finally, in August, the Rosmers bring thirteen-year-old Seva to Mexico and there's a warm re-union. Trotsky and Natalya are overjoyed; Seva's a little bewildered by the many changes, different countries, domestic quarrels, but still he's a charming, well-behaved boy.

The signing of the Stalin-Hitler Pact and the invasion of Finland bring to a head the political differences raging among the Trotskyists. Many of them are unable to swallow Trotsky's "defend the Soviet Union" slogan. Articles in the American party's internal bulletin ask, "Has Trotsky become Stalin's apologist?" Two camps appear and a split appears inevitable. The majority, led by Cannon, adheres to Trotsky's view that the Soviet Union is still a worker's state, albeit a degenerate one. Shachtman and Burnham use strong arguments to defend their point of view which Trotsky, himself, presented in his book "The Revolution Betrayed." He pleads for objective thinking, urges patience and tolerance, and warns against Stalinists in the ranks of the minority which might take advantage of the difficult situation.

Letters fly back and forth between all the parties involved. Trotsky is distressed about the situation and though he has few regrets about Burnham's defecting the S W P, he has warm feelings for Shachtman with whom he has had a long association. He is sorry that Shachtman does not come to visit him in Mexico, perhaps a split might still be avoided, many questions could be answered. "If I could do so, I *would immediately take an aeroplane to New York City in order to discuss with you ..." he writes him.*

CHAPTER 22

New York City, Fall 1939

That fall, as often as she can make it, Miriam takes herself to the movies. There's a block-long Loew's on 175th Street and Broadway. On nights when Sydney is attending political meetings she goes alone, enjoying the fancy dream palace with its crystal chandeliers, blue sky star-studded ceiling and ornate alcoves with stately chairs. She feels almost like a famous movie queen herself when she decends the wide marble staircase, her feet sinking into deep pile of the red carpet.

It's a necessary escape for her; a respite from the frightful events, in Germany, the 'Kristellnacht', and the rumors about dreadful Nazi concentration camps in Buchenwald and Dachau where inconceivable horrors were happening. She'd try to make herself forget what was happening, relaxing into a plush seat and losing herself in the fabricated difficulties of synthetic beautiful creatures; watching beautiful Greta Garbo in *"Ninotcha,"* boyish Henry Fonda as *"Young Mister Lincoln"* and colorful spectacles like *"Gone with the Wind".* There were also great plays that the theatre project of the W P A had put on. She and Sydney had seen some of them done by the Group Theatre and the Mercury; one of them, "Julius Caesar" was done in everyday clothing, creating resemblances to Hitler and Mussolini.

But they don't go as often as she likes; their life together consisted more of political activity than anything else. She keeps busy, carrying eight credits in English in Hunter at night, writing papers and working three days a week at the National Social Credit Association office.

But sometimes she wonders what would become of her and Sydney if it weren't for politics. They're living together but isn't a marriage in the real sense of the word. At best, it's simply an amicable living arrangement and often not even very amicable. There are quarrels and, more important, minor cruelties, times when he fails her, when she wanted to tell him about her problems but doesn't.

At work she has three bosses and each one of them is troublesome in a different way. When she comes home after a trying day, she's like to talk to Sydney about it. Maybe not about the times when they pat her backside or hug her tightly so they can feel her breasts pressing against them—that would be too embarrassing. Anyway, most of the time she sits at her desk so she's out of their reach but she would like to complain about the rough ways she's spoken to, or when one of them yells at her for not being able to find a letter in the file. She knows she makes mistakes but she wants Sydney to say something consoling to her, something that will make her feel not so stupid and miserable. Inevitably, he'll cut her off with a curt "I don't want to hear about that crap."

As she's clearing the kitchen table one night, Miriam says, "I'm not going tonight. It's the fourth meeting this week."

"You don't have to," Sydney says, putting on his jacket. "I'll see you later."

That week-end he brings up the subject. "I hate going by myself," he says. "Last night, a comrade asked me if you're still a member."

"It isn't any of their damn business," Miriam flushes, defensive. "I know these meetings. I can tell you exactly what they're going to say. The Cannonites call the Burnham-Abern group adventurists and dilettantes. Jim says Burnham wants the party to be 'a perpetual talking shop' and so on far into the night."

Sydney tries to sound reasonable. "Doesn't Burnham call the Cannon group 'bureaucratic-conservative,' and accuse us of accepting everything Trotsky says?"

"You know what I can't stand—more than anything else," Miriam retorts. "Whenever they want to get a laugh they make a crack about the 'intellectuals.' Are they so working class? Ha! Except for the Party's successes in Minneapolis with the teamsters, the whole party membership is Ivory Soap, 99 and 9 tenths percent pure, pure intellectual and petit-bourgeois." She stops. Sydney's turned away, looking out of the window.

"It's probably me, I can't stand this stuff," she says. "I hate quarreling, name calling. Everyone knows there's going to be a split and I don't know where I stand. I agree with Shachtman, 'though he's a little flakey. But you're right. I should go to the meetings. I will, from now on."

"Don't do me any favors," he answer sulkily. "Drop out altogether, if that's how you feel. It's fine with me." But she knows his real frustration comes from knowing that he isn't go to play an important role in the Party, in New York, or probably anywhere else.

"How can we do this—plunge headfirst into another war?" she asks Sydney while she finishes washing up the supper dishes. "With us revolutionists leading the charge. We know the United States is going to be in it, and if the Soviet Union is still a worker's state, as Trotsky claims, although a degenerate one, then we'll have to defend it, even if it means joining the United States Army."

"I agree with the Old Man's premise ..." Sydney begins.

But Miriam, fired up, remembering how long and bitterly she grieved when the Spanish Civil War was lost, keeps going on.... "How can we forget that the allies—including our beloved country with it's embargo—made Spain the training ground for Hitler and Mussolini. Now ..." she pauses, takes a deep breath ..., "now that we've got fascism threatening to sweep over the world, now it's up to us, us, the radicals who fought to stop them, we're called upon to get in there, help clean up the filthy mess they've created. What a joke!"

Sydney shrugs, "You're right, Miriam. It is a joke. It's not the only thing that's a joke—and not even funny." He takes the latest Internal Bulletin and goes into the living room.

As she follows him, drying her hands, she changes the subject. "I meant to tell you. Sylvia called me yesterday. Her boy-friend Jacques is leaving in a couple of days and she wants to get together before he goes. So it'll have to be tonight. He'd like to go to a night club in Harlem—hear Billie Holiday or Bill BoJangles Robinson—Small's Paradise—the Cotton Club—something like that."

Sydney likes that sort of thing and they arrange to meet at Sylvia's apartment at seven. When Miriam and Sydney arrive, Sylvia opens the door. A tall, swarthy man is standing behind her. Although Miriam hasn't mentioned it to Sydney, she's really not looking forward to meeting the man whose scowling, dark face had upset her that day in the country.

To her surprise the man smiles cordially and kisses her warmly on both cheeks. His face is pleasant with large features and horn-rimmed spectacles, and when Sylvia says, "Miriam, Sydney, I'd like you to meet Frank Jacson," he answers in charming accented English, "I'm delighted. So happy to meet friends of my Sylvia."

When Miriam mumbles "Pleased to meet you" in response, she thinks *this can't be the same person. She must be mistaken. This Jacson looks like the man she saw and yet he seems so different. Forget it,* she tells herself. *First impressions. Why does he use a different name?*

Browner's there too. He's been invited along as Hilda's date. "I've always want to go to Harlem," he says. "It takes a visitor from abroad to get New Yorkers sight-seeing." While they wait for Hilda, delayed at a meeting, Jacques and Sydney make conversation while Browner goes the bathroom. Gone several minutes when he comes back, he's grumbling, "Some apartment. A million doors. I ended up in a closet."

"Kids'd love it here, a great place for a hide and seek," says Sydney.

"How about it?," Browner says, perking up, "it's stupid sitting around."

"What—a game?," Jacques asks. After they explain it he says, "I know, we have the same." He hesitates a second—"in Europe."

Sydney designates a heavy standing brass lamp as 'HOME' and finds a cotton handkerchief in his pocket to bind Browner's eyes. As soon as he's done, he yells, "Anybody round this base is IT—by the time I count to ten," and the other two dash quickly for a secret hide-out.

The two women stand in the living room smiling at their antics and Miriam uses this opportunity to ask her why Jacques' uses a different name. "It has something to do about serving in the Belgian Army," Sylvia explains. "I'm not too clear about it myself, but it's not important." Meanwhile the three men are playing with increasing gusto, yelling and shrieking and after a few minutes the game becomes rough, pushing hard, knocking each other over.

"They're acting crazy!" Miriam says. Just then, as Browner dashes towards home base, Jacques gives him a hard shove and he falls over a piano stool, striking his head on a corner of a desk.

"That's enough," Sylvia screams. "Stop! Right now! Are you hurt?" she asks, peering into his face as Browner staggers to his feet.

"No, it's okay," he answers holding his forehead, starting to swell a little. "I'll be okay—it's nothing."

"This is absolutely ridiculous," Sylvia scolds. "Grown men, acting like children," and goes to get a wet towel. When Miriam brings out a pitcher of ice water for the panting players she notes Jacques' hands trembling, *he's strung as tight as a bow*, she thinks. The phone rings, Hilda can't meet them tonight and so they take off, finally.

They're lucky to get a large taxi with folding seats, Browner in front with the driver. It's still light enough, and a milky, clouded sky furnishes enough light to take them on a sight-seeing tour through Harlem. As they ride north, along Seventh Avenue from 110th Street, the streets desolate and deserted, with stalking cats, refuse, and tabloid sheets flying in the air, Sylvia tells Jacques how beautiful this wide thoroughfare had been in the twenties.

"It's hard to imagine seeing it like this," she says, "it used to be so bright, music, vaudeville. Everything was here, a magnet for the world. Everyone went to Harlem, to 125th Street, to the Apollo Theatre."

Sydney adds, "It was—but the depression changed all that. Now it's one of the most overcrowded slums in the country. A few years ago there was a terrible race riot here, about 10,000 negroes ran berserk. They looted and destroyed the stores; fires burned for days. About 700 police put the whole thing down in their usual gentle fashion. People were lucky, only two killed."

Jacques, his arm about Sylvia's shoulder, leans forward, "May I ask a foolish question? Why didn't the negroes take the stores for themselves?"

"It's not a foolish question," Sydney answers. "How could they? They were arrested! It took a little while but everything was restored to its proper order. Everything's owned by the whites, stores, movies, restaurants. In a capitalist country those who own it, run it. 'The business of America is business.' I guess you haven't heard that."

"I have a lot to learn about America and its history. I'm lucky I have such smart guides," he gently teases as he presses Sylvia's hand.

"But you know a lot about New York," She looks up at him, brushing her cheek against his shoulder, shyly. "Just the other day, I were surprised when you knew your way around so well. Oh, stop here, driver!" she tells the driver, "turn right and go up Lenox Avenue. Now, Jacques, you'll see, here's a lively street."

People, children, dogs and odors seem to spill out from old cracked tenement building and the avenue teems with bars, pool parlors, cheap shops and 'gin mills.' It looks as if everybody in Harlem eats out on the street; sweet potatoes and sausages are piled on kerosene stoves, and people crowd on almost every corner listening to enthusiastic soap-box orators. As they ride by, they hear a Marcus Garvey disciple inviting his large crowd of listeners to leave America, become a part of the 'Back-to-Africa' movement.

When they arrive finally at Small's Paradise they find, to their dismay, it's temporarily closed and the other two nearby, the Plantation Club and Yeah Man, aren't accepting any more guests. Sylvia's upset, Jacques has to leave for South America, and they've been looking forward to this evening all week.

"Don't cry, ma cherie," Jacques says, taking her arm. "We'll settle for a good meal with no entertainment. Let's get out here and walk a little."

As they leave the taxi the driver suggests, "Why don't yo'all try the Monterey, folks say its real good suthern cookin'. Jes' go along Seventh Avenue, it's on 13lst St." As they walk they pass the Lafayette Theatre, still displaying signs about an all-negro production of Macbeth, directed by Orson Welles. "Wish we had seen it," Miriam says. "I heard it was different and exciting."

The taxi-driver was right. Although the restaurant had a fine reputation, since it was a week-day night it wasn't crowded and the service was excellent.

"The best fried chicken I've ever eaten," Browner says, who demolishes enormous portions of food. The coffee is aromatic with chicory and Sydney orders a bottle of cognac to toast Jacques' departure. Not used to more than a glass of wine, he becomes flushed and slightly tipsy, and spying Miriam's hat, a small, velvet toque with a tiny feather, on a chair next to him, he picks it up and puts it on his slightly bald head.

"Sydney, you look absolutely adorable," Miriam says. "Here, take off your glasses." Getting into the spirit of the thing, she says, "How about some lipstick?," and fishing out her little make-up case, applies mascara and rouge, dusting the finished work with a great cloud of perfumed face powder. Everyone applauds the result.

"Hey, you're really cute," says Browner shaking his head. Sydney, needing little encouragement, snatches Miriam's little black velvet jacket from the chair and throws it over his shoulders. Simpering, he flutters his eyelashes, wiggles his shoulders suggestively and when Jacques jumps up to present him with a rose from the table, leans forward to grab his hand. Looking into Jacques' eyes, he puts his arm around his neck, and croons "Oh, my man, I love him so, he'll never know."

Jacques, not to be outdone, begins "Darling, Je vous aime beaucoup/je ne sais pas qu'to do." Sydney yields, smiles. rolling his eyes, pouting, wiggling coyly. Jacques presses closer and strokes Sydney's face, beginning to nibble his earlobe, murmuring in husky, passionate tones, "Ma cherie, je t'aime, je t'adore." The others watch his performance for a few moments, spellbound, then gradually become bored with the charade.

"Okay, Jacques, we believe you," Miriam says. "You're a real actor—a Maurice Chevalier. Sydney, that's enough too. Let's give them a hand, folks. Thanks for the performance." But Jacques continues, fondling Sydney, whispering to him, his face flushed, as if he hadn't heard.

"Now I must serenade you," he whispers, and begins, "Parlez-moi d'amour," but Browner, impatient now, says, sharply, "It's not funny any more. Can it, let's get back to normal. Maybe we should get going."

"You're absolutely right," Sylvia says, pale, her voice sharp and grating. "I think it's time we left." Sydney reaches up, pulls off Miriam's hat, hands it back to her, and says, "Yeah, you're right. Give me your hanky so I can wipe this stuff off."

Jacques for a moment sits, looking down at hands clutching the table, his ruddy flush slowly ebbing, becoming dark and drained. He laughs, a little barking sound, and gets up. "Thank you for your applause. I've always wanted to be an actor." He signals for the check and ignoring everyone's protestations, pays for the entire meal, leaving a handsome tip for the two waiters. Then, bowing with a flourish, he says, "Excuse me" and heads for the men's room. When he returns, everyone's standing, ready to go.

Coming home that night, as Sydney's opening the door to their apartment, Miriam tells him, "You not only ruined a very good hanky of mine, but I didn't appreciate the scene—it got out of hand."

"I enjoyed it the first couple of minutes. It was your idea to begin with. It was Jacques, he just didn't know when to stop."

"He's strange. I don't get the story about the passport, using a different name. He had to buy one 'cause he couldn't use his own—avoiding the Belgian army draft or some weird story like that."

"Miriam," Sydney says, his mouth a hard angry line. "You're always so damn suspicious! You're always finding fault or criticizing people. You're probably sore at me because I ordered cognac …"

"That's enough," she yells as they enter the apartment. "Go to hell." She brushes past him to the bathroom, slams the door. When she emerges, he's sitting on the bed, his head down. He looks up and starts to say something but she says, "Let's forget about the whole thing." But she's still upset. She kisses him back mechanically. *We'll have to settle a lot of things pretty soon,* she tells herself.

Bunny calls Miriam one day in December just as she's leaving the office. "Where are you?," Miriam asks. "You're not calling from Mexico?"

"Van and I got here a few weeks ago. We're going to get married soon. How about that! I've got a lot to tell you. Are you free tonight?"

"Well, I could stay downtown. There's an open forum at the headquarters I should go to," Miriam says, reluctantly. "Why don't we meet at the Kiev, on Second Avenue. It'll give me time to pick up a little gift at Ohrbach's for Sydney's aunt." That way she won't have to spend much time with Bunny. But Bunny wants to shop too and in a little while they're both looking at clothes on the second floor. *She doesn't want anything but Bunny has a gorgeous figure and a new man and she has neither.* After fingering a pretty flowered blouse, she puts it back on the rack.

"Van hated to leave the Old Man," Bunny says. "Even tho' he wasn't easy to get along with. So sharp about being punctual." She holds up a dark red short dress with a low neckline. "What do you think of this?" Before Miriam can answer Bunny goes on, "Trotsky, he was always going out to look for those odd cactuses. Van had some scary times following him, keeping an eye on him. No, this one is too short." With a sigh she puts it back. "Van doesn't like daring things, he's a little conservative that way."

"I think the Old Man's really happy the Rosmers' came last August. They're going to stay awhile. Let's go down to the lingerie department. I need a new robe—a little more sexy." Taking Miriam's arm, Bunny leads the way to the down escalator. "They brought Seva, his grandson with them. He's a darling little boy, about thirteen, very sweet, polite. Poor kid, his mother Zina committed suicide. The Rosmers are really a nice old couple; well, as old as the Old Man. They're going to stay till next May. You'd never think Marguerite was French, she has such a dumpy figure. No style, absolutely no style. They look like nightgowns, her dresses."

"I've looked enough." Miriam' almost plaintive. "Why don't you go to Klein's by yourself? I have to go to a meeting."

"Oh, there's something else." Bunny pounces on a lacy black gown, holds it against her bosom and turns to her with a sly grin. "I almost forgot to tell you. Melquiades told me to ask you why you didn't answer his letter. He wants you to write to him."

"Yes, of course, I'll write," she answers, fleeing Bunny's needling. But she knows she won't. What can she say? Melquiades—beautiful, gentle but so little to connect them. Only the confused sweet sadness of the brief affair. Their youth—their devotion to the Old Man? When she thinks of Mel, she thinks of Mexico, it's lush, primitive, poverty stricken beauty. She's New York, European, alive, bustling, ugly sidewalks. She could never live there.

Sidney's waiting for Miriam at the headquarters when she arrives. Just then two comrades pull him away but when she looks over later she sees him, sitting alone, reading.

"I've been meaning to get in touch with you," Hilda says, taking a seat next to Miriam. "Been very busy, typing a lot of Party stuff." Her brown eyes are apologetic. "Sylvia asked me to give you a message before she left for Mexico, to tell you it was on the spur of the moment."

Miriam's puzzled. "Why did she go to Mexico? Did she go to see the Old Man?"

"No. But, of course, now that she's down there she will. But that isn't the reason. She got a call from Jacques—can't get used to calling him Jacson. Seems that the diamond business wasn't in South America, now it's in Mexico. Don't ask me. All I know is he called, wanted her to come down to join him. She said she'll write. She doesn't intend to stay more than a few weeks. After all, she's a working girl."

Miriam frowns. "The diamond business. So now it's Mexico. Well, she'll get a chance to see the Rosmers. Frankly," she hesitates, then decides to say it, "frankly, I'm not crazy about Jacson or Jacques of whatever he calls himself."

"Ruth and I aren't either, but he sure impressed us with the way he carved a chicken."

Miriam looks over at Sydney. He's peering at the papers, his head buried in an article. "I'll see you later," she tells Hilda. "Let's get together when Sylvia gets back." She makes her way back to Sydney, smiling. "I knew you'd save me a seat," she says, but without looking up he takes his coat off the seat next to him and goes on reading until the meeting begins.

Mexico, Spring 1940

There's a constant turnover among the guards but Trotsky welcomes each and every one of them with deep appreciation, grateful for their devotion. In January, when Sylvia Ageloff arrives from New York, eager to be of some help, Trotsky is glad to see her. He remembers with fondness her sister Ruth, who was a secretary during the Dewey hearings. Sylvia renews her friendship with the Rosmers and through her they become acquainted with Jacques Mornard, her lover, who is charming, obliging, has a car and is always happy to run an errand for them.

Trotsky knows that Stalin will never rest until he has destroyed every remaining Bolshevik, that Trotsky himself will not be permitted to live much longer. Yet he will not, cannot, stop writing, which is all he can do now. In April he writes a paper addressed to Soviet workers, peasants, soldiers and sailors, entitled "You Are Being Deceived." In it he tells them that their newspapers are telling lies, that their bureaucracy is bloodthirsty and ruthless at home but cowardly vis-a-vis the imperialist powers. He calls upon his comrades not to surrender to the world bourgeoisie, the Soviet Union's nationalized industry and collectivized economy, for on this foundation they can still build a new and happier society. He does not know if this message will ever reach its destination

The attacks on him never stop. On May 1, 20,000 Communists parade against Trotsky in Mexico City, accusing him of being a traitor, a fascist spy, asking for his expulsion from Mexico. Now, there are always at least four or five guards watching at the house. In addition, ten Mexican policemen are on duty outside and around the building, and sentries keep watch at the gate.

CHAPTER 23

New York City, Spring 1940

"Spring smells like iodine. Did you ever notice?" Miriam asks Sydney. They're in the kitchen, sitting over *The World*, Sunday Edition, and the remains of a big bacon and egg breakfast. A frisky breeze blows the faded gingham curtains, bringing in sounds of a stick-ball game in the street. They don't make bacon and eggs very often, in deference to Clara who, long ago, stopped keeping a kosher home but still won't eat pork.

Sydney nods. He finishes reading the letter he just received from his brother, Max, in California, folds it and puts it under the sugar bowl on the table. Then he lights a cigarette and after taking a deep drag, leans back. "Max wants me to come to California. He's working in Lockheed, says there'd be no trouble getting me in."

Miriam frowns. "He's in Los Angeles, right? It could be a great opportunity. Is he inviting us to come there or is it just you?"

"Of course he means both of us. There's probably work for you too now. They're opening up the whole airplane industry. Lockheed, others. Hey, here's a chance for us to become proletarians, join the working class—organize."

"Sydney." Miriam stops. She knows from experience and wants to be careful, not to say anything that ends the discussion before it begins. "Don't you think" she begins slowly, "we should decide what we want to do before we pick ourselves up and start heading for California?" hoping she sounds off-hand, non-committal.

Before he has a chance to respond, Clara, fully dressed, ready to leave in a new wool coat, comes in. "Isn't dot nice?" she says. "My two boarders home this morning. What's the matter? Your comrades didn't invite you today?"

Miriam groans. "Mama, please, cut the sarcasm. Sit and have coffee with us." She gets up and brings a chair from a corner. "Com'on, Mom."

Clara sits down and opens her coat. "All right. I have something to tell you." She takes a deep breath. "I just bought a house. In the Bronx. Very cheap. It was foreclosed, I got a steal." A slight grin softens her thin lips, she has an air of self-assurance, she's back in the real estate business, the game she still loves, even though she just took a bad beating. "I'm moving in the first of the month, an empty apartment on the ground floor. That's why I'm going over today. I'll have the super give the kitchen a schmear of paint but the rest of the apartment is not bad." She takes a sip of coffee Miriam hands her, "Good," she says, waiting for their reaction to her news.

Miriam would like to ask why she hadn't told them anything before, but knows it's futile. "What about this apartment?," she asks mildly. "What about us? Do you want us to move with you?"

Before her mother can answer, Sydney, shaking his head, gets up. "Excuse me," he says. "I'll leave it to you, Miriam," and tucking "The World" under his arm, departs for the bathroom.

"Right now, I can't give you an apartment there for yourself. It's three rooms, not big enough for all of us." Trying to sound offhand, she adds "You could stay here by yourself. You can afford the rent if you get a job."

Miriam's still trying to digest Clara's news when her mother says, "All right, I have to go," and gets up, buttoning her coat. "I made a good job, remodelling this material, it's very fine wool. An expensive garment, Ketzel gave me." She turns so Miriam can admire the smooth fit. Realizing she has been a little abrupt in breaking the news, she adds, "You could be okay here, it's a nice little apartment."

"Now we really have to talk." Miriam's in the little parlor, a few minutes later, waiting for Sydney who's sauntered back, nonchantly. "What's going to be with us, Sydney?" She tries to sound matter-of-fact.

"I don't know what in hell you're talking about." He tosses the newspaper onto the couch and throw himself into the battered easy chair they intended to throw out two years ago, his face taking on the grim look it always did when they discussed personal matters. "I don't think we have to move. Your mother's right. But listen, do you want to make a change? I thought we were getting along okay." When he sees Miriam start to talk, he says, "No. It's you. You have some idea—some romatic ideas—about relationships. No, let me finish …" He waves his hand, goes on. "You've been acting a little strange since you came back from Mexico." He pauses, then, as if he were trying to understand, says slowly, "Maybe it's me. I guess I could be more thoughtful."

She doesn't answer right away. Looking down at the cracked linoleum which seems to need a good washing, she hesitates, feeling sad and unsure of herself, about what she really wants to say.

"Maybe it's both of us," she says. "We both have to be nicer to each other … but we both have to change in other ways if we want to stay together." She turns and looks directly into his face, her eyes searching his. "I don't think I understand why I do things, what I do, what I really want. That's true for you too, as much as for me. If we don't know what we want for ourselves, how can we make the other person happy. Maybe that's why we have so much trouble in our relationship."

"Oh, for God's sake, Miriam." Sydney, his hand automatically going to his pocket for a cigarette. "Here we go again. I don't see that there's so much trouble. When I admit I have some faults, some shortcomings, like everyone else does, you start analzying, getting psychological. Sigmund Freud, here we come!" He lights up his cigarette, picks up the Militant and begins to read. "I'm okay. Leave me alone!"

Miriam sits quietly, realizing that this is the end of the discussion. It can never go any further or any deeper, probably never will. *Give it up,* she tells herself. *They'll simply have to accept each other, the way they are—or else.* The thought of splitting up sends a cold chill through her.

To begin with, she has to admit to herself that although being with Sydney is unsatisfying, disappointing, he's someone to come home to, to put her arms around him in bed, sleep with. They have a home together. Why did she bring up the question about staying together? She knows if she's alone, she'll be frightened. She'll be like a balloon, floating, cut loose, wandering up into a frightening, immense blue void. She can't do it. She can't break away, at least not now, not yet. Living alone in a furnished room or an apartment by herself—she'd be scared, she'd better admit it.

"I'm not even *Mrs.* Freud, Sydney," she says, with a little laugh. "I'm not going to try to change you. I'll start on myself. If I can."

"Great idea, honey. Give you something to do," and as he disappears into the bedroom he calls, "Where did you put my clean socks?"

The dialogue she's been thinking about, and dreading, for months is over. She feels dejected. Until the nippy air begins to chill her she sits at the table, watching the sun disappearing behind an approaching caravan of dark clouds.

Then, as she goes into the bedroom to get a sweater, passing Sydney she kisses the top of his head..

"Let's try to be happier," she tells him. "See what happens. I don't want to go to California. For the time being, why don't we stay here? By ourselves." He looks up and nods. She knows he's pleased with going on together, with or without Clara. On her way back to the kitchen to wash the breakfast dishes, sweep and feed the new kitten, she says, "Let's fix up the place a little better, they might have some better stuff at the Salvation Army."

❧   ❧   ❧

It's Miriam's idea to go. As usual Sydney's not enthusiastic but she persists. "Look, we can't miss it," she exclaims, waving the Official Guide Book of the New York World's Fair, 1939. "It's the greatest fair in history. It says here that they had to level mountains, fill in bogs, build dams ... true poets of the twentieth century, designer, architects and engineers...."

"Okay," says Sydney. "I heard you. We'll go."

The New York World's Fair in Flushing Meadow, Queens had opened to widespread publicity, everyone talking about it, saying it was a marvel. Newspaper articles and speeches celebrated the way twelve hundred and sixteen acres of spongy marshland in Flushing, Queens had been cleared away, resulting in a vast pleasure ground, "a miraculous change from dump to glory."

Everyone sings praises about the thousands of vibrant flower beds, the huge statue of George Washington, the trees, lagoons, waterfalls, the buildings of diverse materials and colors, the nightly shows, music and fireworks, and elaborate, detailed exhibits of machinery, autos and airplanes of the present and future. It's the talk of the town and anyone who could walk or ride in a wheelchair, visits it at least once.

She and Sydney finally make plans to go and they ask Sam and George to go along. They weren't inviting anyone else, but a few days before Sylvia calls Miriam.

"I'm home, since March, finally, your peripatetic friend. I'd love to see you. Are you busy this Saturday?"

"We're going to the World's Fair." Miriam responds, and without thinking asks, "Would you like to go with us?" Then she stops, *that* was dumb, Sylvia probably wouldn't enjoy doing that kind of sight-seeing. But she'd already asked her so she says, "There's room in the car."

To her surprise, Sylvia answers "Great" enthusiastically. Miriam tells her, "We'll pick you up about eleven," and hangs up, annoyed at herself. Somehow, although she's fond of Sylvia, she doesn't find her company very exciting and she's not anxious to hear about Jacques or Jacson or whatever he's calling himself now. She knows she'll get an earful.

It rains all Friday night and although it stops on Saturday the morning air is muggy and dense. Miriam and Sydney bring sweaters, umbrellas and sandwiches; they've heard the food prices are high.

"You girls look sleepy," Sam comments when they pick up Sylvia. "Like you just got out of bed." He and George joined the Trotskyists after a short membership in the Communist Party. They're in their twenties, clean-cut, horse-faced Jewish boys whose immigrant parents had knocked themselves out to get them the best education America could offer their children. George went to Yale, got a degree in drafting (he had wanted to study architecture but there wasn't enough money), and Sam had taken accounting at NYU. Although they won't admit it, they're shy with the opposite sex. They just don't know how to talk to them. Their idea of conversation is making critical and caustic remarks about girls' appearance or intelligence, even Miriam's. She hates when they do this but tells herself to ignore it, chalk it up to their immaturity. She wishes Sydney would tell them off at least once, but he goes along with it, sometimes even joining in the teasing.

"Well, we're not," Miriam says, shortly. "But thanks for the compliment. Let's head for the Queensborough Bridge and make sure we stay on Northern Boulevard till we hit the Grand Central."

"Why are we doing this?," Sydney asks. He puts away the cigarette he's just pulled out. He isn't happy because Sam, who has mild asthma, has asked him not to smoke.

Miriam sees Sydney frown and isn't surprised when, a few minutes later, he says, "This Fair is such a phony. In the guide book it says 'We seek to achieve orderly progress in a world of peace.' Ha! Who's seeking? Not our government, that's for sure. Such a pile of horse-manure." He'd have liked to use another word but in deference to Sylvia he refrains.

"We should split up once we get inside," George says. He doesn't want to get into an argument with Sydney. "Sam and I want to go to the General Motors exhibit."

"Maybe Sylvia and I'll skip that," Miriam interrupts. "I'd like to go to the U S S R pavillion, 'though I hear it's pretty crummy."

On Queens Boulevard they pass Howard Johnson's, a large oranged-topped chain restaurant. Miriam exclaims that they make the best chocolate ice-cream sodas in New York, but George argues that Krums ice-cream parlor uptown is the best in the country. All at once they're near the Trylon, a three-sided obelisk reaching into the sky, and next to it, the Perisphere, a huge globe, two dazzling white enormous structures dominating the barren flatlands of Queens for miles around.

"Sydney, you have to admit they've tried to create something original," Sam says, irritated by Sydney's remarks. "Some of the artists from the W P A, like William Zorach and Malvina Hoffman, contributed new ideas and I hear they're good ones."

"Sometimes we have to admit that even though capitalism stinks," George can't resist adding, "sometimes beautiful and artistic stuff in art and music comes along. I don't know if they succeeded here, but it looks like they tried to bring in a feeling for space and color."

"Right." Sydney's voice rises to score a point. "It looks very pretty. But where are the pictures of millions of acres ruined by dust storms, farmers with hungry families running away on old trucks and jalopies, trying to stay alive?"

"That's beginning to change, Sydney," George says patiently. "They're trying to improve things. The T V A...."

"You know damn well those are simply soporifics to keep workers and farmers quiet," Sydney retorts. "Anyway, we'll have good times soon enough—there'll be jobs and plenty for all. You know—we all know—World War II is on its way. The phony talk about peace makes me sick!"

"Okay, that's enough," Miriam says. "You're right, Sydney. It's a phony, bourgeois world but don't we all enjoy a lot of it, even so? Don't we run to movies and enjoy watching the rich drink and cavort, like William Powell and Myrna Loy. If you're so critical of everything, Sydney, why do we go to the movies so often? We're supporting Hollywood, aren't we?"

Sydney looks at her, his lips curled in contempt. "You know damn well why we go to American movies—just to pass the time—keep out of the cold. They don't make any decent ones, well, maybe a few. Sure, years ago, in the U S S R there was great stuff by Dovzhenko and Eisenstein, 'like Arsenal' and 'Potemkin' but Stalin put a stop to that. What choice do we have, except not go to the the movies at all?"

Miriam decides to retreat and laughs, "Oh, my God, don't ever say that! I could never live without seeing my two favorite dancers in all the world, Fred Astair and Ginger Rogers." George and Sam looked relieved, happy the conversation's lightening. "Right, Sylvia?" Sylvia nods, startled, she hasn't heard any of the discussion.

When they're almost at the entrance they hear music and Miriam says, "It looks like fun with all those banners and balloons," and after they park the car, the group splits up. The three men take off for the Transportation Zone while Sylvia and Miriam head to the Swedish and Finnish exhibits, supposedly among the best.

The glass and textiles from Sweden are sharp, economical, modern and they enjoy the music, a Sibelius symphony, which accompanies the "Land of the Forests" exhibit. But in the U S S R building they find the exhibit dull and uninspired, although at the entrance a vast sign proclaims "One hundred and seventy million people live in the first socialist country of the world." As they gaze at the bas relief of Stalin, Lenin opposite him on the other side, they feel like exiles, banished from a country they had once loved.

Miriam can't help commenting, "I aways think that if I lived in Russia now I'd be in Siberia or maybe even dead," and then adds, with a bitter grin, "It's so ironic to feel safe and glad I'm living in a capitalist country."

"Wht do you say we get out of here?" Miriam suggests in a little while. "How about the 'Gardens on Parade.' Supposed to be beautiful, hollyhocks, tulips. We can sit, have coffee. My feet are tired."

As they walk towards the Flushing River Sylvia begins talking about Mexico, seeing Trotsky, how good it is that his friends the Rosmers are there now. "There's also a new guard now, a young good-looking boy, Sheldon Harte," Sylvia says. "Did you ever meet him? He was a member in the Lower East Side Branch?"

"It makes me nervous to hear about all the visitors coming to meet the Old Man," Miriam says, frowning. "After the first time I visited there the guards never bothered to check me for any weapons and there were so many different people on guard duty."

"I know, but really everyone is very concerned about the Old Man's safety." Sylvia tone is very serious. "And almost all of the guards are older comrades, very capable." Sylvia pauses a moment and then says, hesitatingly, "I'm glad we have a chance to talk but I don't quite know how to begin …" But then she plunges in, "You know I love Jacques—I told you that last summer. I'd like to get married."

Miriam's surprised. "So the romance is going as strong as ever," Miriam says. "You're lucky."

"Yes and no," Sylvia says. "I really don't know much about him even though we've been together almost two years, off and on." She stops, frowning, recalling something that troubles her. "For example, when I was in Mexico a few weeks ago, Marguerite Rosmer went to his office address in Ermita Street. He'd told us that his office was room number 820 but there wasn't anyone there by his name. That night, when I asked him, he said "Oh, I should have told you 620." So we go to 620 to check and the office boy there says that it is Jacques' office. I don't know why he makes these mistakes; it's happened before, in Paris too." Sylvia's lips set in a tight line, her eyes narrow, she opens her purse for a pack of cigarettes. "For someone in business, it's not very business-like, is it? Or am I making too much about a thing like that?"

Miriam is in the midst of straightening her flying hair, her lips clamped around some bobbie pins. Sylvia always looks so neat, likes everything so orderly, is that what disturbs her about Jacques? That's he's not always so business like? Miriam puts the pins back in her hair and tries to come up with a rational explanation. "Could it be because he's in some kind of illegal business and he's afraid to give out the right address?," she offers.

"It's possible." Sylvia's face brightens, somewhat relieved at this suggestion. "After all, he is using a phony passport because of the Belgian Army. If he gets caught by the police, he could be in a lot of trouble, get a police record. That's why I told him that I didn't want him to visit Trotsky alone, only when I'm with him. It could make trouble for the Old Man."

"Maybe you're making more of this than it's worth and you're worried about the Old Man. You don't want him to have any difficulties with the police." Miriam fishes in her bag. "I'm all out, can I mooch one from you."

"Let's wait until we get to the Gardens," Sylvia suggests. When they reach there they take out their sandwiches and relax, enjoying the view, the white blossoms, shaded walls and terraced rock gardens, little kids plunking pebbles into the pools.

"I don't remember if it was you, Miriam," Sylvia resumes, even though she senses Miriam's had enough talk about Jacques. "He has quite a temper. He can change in a minute. He'll be so sweet and in a second, so angry."

Miriam recalls last summer on the lawn when she saw his tortured face, as if something was eating inside him—how he got so fired up in that night club in Harlem, understands what she's trying to describe about Jacques—the strange way he acts, his sudden changes in mood, from lightness and charm to dark and angry.

"But then, the next moment, he's kissing me, apologizing for his flare-up and so loveable, he makes me forget about the whole thing."

"I suppose that if it doesn't happen too often, you could overlook it," Miriam responds thoughtfully, "after all, if the Belgian army is after him, he's got enough to be nervous about."

Sylvia's saying, "Jacques' so thoughtful. He took all of us, including the Rosmers, on a trip to Taxco. He wrote me this week that he took Rosmer, who was sick, to the French hospital in Mexico City, brought him home and went to the drugstore for a prescription. He even apologized to me, which wasn't necessary, for going into the house without me. You saw how generous he was last fall when we went out to dinner. Just before I left, he took me, the Rosmers and one of the guards to Chateau Boheme, one of the best restaurants in Mexico City."

"Well, if you look at the whole picture, he's got a lot in his favor. Maybe he'll change, be more open, control his temper—it sometimes happens," Miriam answers in a cheerful voice but she wants this conversation over, she's had enough of hearing about Jacques.

"How about if we go to the Public Health Building? They've got an enormous man made of Plexiglass," she says. "It says here that all the different parts of his body are lit up so clearly you can see how they all function." She smiles, saying, "It's funny that we can look inside a man and see his stomach disgesting food but we can never figure out how his head works!"

Sylvia sighs. Miriam can tell she'd have liked to go on talking about Jacques, get rid of her worries about him by talking them out, but is too too polite to insist.

"Since when are you interested in science or anatomy?" She asks Miriam.

"I took a course in Hunter," Miriam tells her. "I was so amazed when we dissected a frog and took out his heart, how it just kept beating on and on—on the paper towel! There was nothing to keep its heart going! It was miraculous." *Like my own heart,* she thinks ... *a will of its own ... yearning for someone who's not there anymore.*

By the time they pile into the car for home it's dark. As they drive from the parking lot Sam, who's usually quiet says, thoughtfully, "You can't deny what we saw today is impressive. We're a great industrial power, leader of the world. A guy in my office, calls himself a radical, thinks he a theoretician. He says that the U S S R had to become a great industrial power in order to survive. It was the only way and Stalin had to resort to the awful collectivizations—the way he did—in order to bring the country into the twentieth century."

Miriam cuts in. "You mean your friend is really aware of what Stalin did, killing thousands, destroying villages, causing famines, millions of horses, cows and sheep dying ... and he says it's okay?!," her voice angry, sarcastic, "all of that horror in the name of 'progress.'"

Sam answers, patiently, "Anyway, my guy says that Marxism will awake eventually in the minds of millions—that an industrial class striving towards a modern way of life will emerge and he quotes Trotsky to back him up—even Trotsky believes that one day, maybe not in the near future, modern progress itself will erode Stalinism from the inside. 'The seeds of the future nourished by the victims' blood.'"

"Just tell your friend that even though Trotsky said that, and I'm not sure he meant exactly that, I don't." Miriam answers sharply. "All the industrialization in the world can't compensate for destruction, terrorizing—terrorizing and killing millions of people, creating famines, slaughtering cattle and horses."

George, who's been listening, amused at Miriam's vehemence, can't help interjecting. "Look, Miriam, Trotsky, himself, he wrote, in 1927 for the 15th Party Congress ... he said that the growing strength of the farmer class in the countryside must be opposed by a faster growth of the collectives ... Isn't it possible that Trotsky would have done just what Stalin did? ... push for industrialization ... the working class in the Cities against the peasant on the farms. Industrialization had to be achieved ... Russia had to do this to protect herself against the U S."

Sydney who up to now has been listening impatiently, adds, "Yeah, that's the C P line. But in fact, Stalin used the Old Man's theories more than once. How about Trotsky's devotion to the Party ... the single Party?"

"How in hell can you say that, Sydney?" Miriam's almost yelling. "You know how concerned he, and Lenin too, before he died, they both saw the danger, how the Party was degenerating but it was Stalin who changed the party—who killed off the cream of the Red Army leadership, opening the Party to the young, inexperienced, the greedy, buying them off with jobs and prizes—you know all that."

"Take it easy, kiddo," Sam says, soothingly. "Everyone knows that Trotsky believed in the single Party, like Stalin, but his idea of the Party was completely different, a truly democratic one ... not a dictatorship."

"Thank you, Sam," Miriam laughs, a dry little sound and sinks back in her seat. "Maybe it's easy for the theoreticians, like your friend, sitting in cozy libraries, to say that Siberia, famine, terrorization and death are necessary to achieve socialism but I bet they wouldn't volunteer to be killed for progress themselves. And neither would any of us." That ends the discussion, no one seems to want to continue.

After a few minutes, to break the silence, Sydney begins an imitation of H. V. Kaltenborn, a radio commentator, whose voice accompanies the display at the Perisphere. With sonorous tones he intones, "In this brave new world, brain and brawn, faith and courage, are linked together as men march on toward unity and peace."

It's so corny that everyone laughs and George says, "Not bad, Sydney."

"You're quite a comedian—you really did a good imitation of Kaltenborn," Miriam tells Sydney days later. "You probably get it from Shachtman. He loves to put on an act. He was really a clown tonight, rolling his eyes, squirming, screeching."

"Yeah, I know." Sydney can't help grinning, remembering Shachtman's antics at the meeting they just attended. "But you've got to admit, Trotsky's article—that title—From Scratch to the Danger of Gangrene—lends itself to parody."

"Well, Max laid it on with a trowel. What a mess," Miriam says disgustedly. "The high school and college students didn't listen to a word, laughing, joking and in the back, right out in the open!"

There has to be a split, every Party member, both majority and minority arrive at the inevitable. Sydney holds to a solid Cannon position. Miriam and Sydney argue, trying to convince each other but to no avail. "The Soviet Union is still a workers' state, albeit a degenerated one and therefore must be supported and militarily defended," repeats Sydney.

"I cannot believe the Soviet Union is a workers state—how can I, how can anyone?," Miriam answers. "The people have no power. To me, it's quibbling to claim that the workers control the means of production when they can't even open their mouths! It's as simple as that." Also, she distrusts Burham, although she can't explain why, maybe he's too much of a dispassionate Anglo-Saxon college teacher, a distance from the Sidney Hooks, the Jewish professors. But the political arguments between her and Sydney, although heated at times, never reach a divisive turn and their loyalty for Trotsky never wavers.

❦   ❦   ❦

Miriam hasn't heard from Ketzel for a long time, has even tried reaching her by telephone but isn't successful. Begining to be concerned, wondering if things weren't going well, she's glad to find a fat envelope in the letterbox.

It's already getting dark, the kids outside are trying to wind up their stickball game, quarreling about the score, a rancid smell of fried chicken drifting through the window. Settling herself in the easy chair, with a cold pitcher of strawberry seltzer on a rickety little red table beside her, she opens Ketzel's envelope.

April 30, 1940

Miriam dear,

Every time I write I apologize for not writing so this time I won't. We're good friends and you understand me. Life here hasn't been all that great, to put it mildly. The only really wonderful thing is Jaime's babies. I can't remember if I told you, they're twin boys. Fat, beautiful, healthy. As for Jaime I think he misses New York. Sometimes I find him looking out at the fountain in the garden with a little sad smile when I talk about going home. He always asks about you.

Which brings me to my news. I am coming back, I'm not sure exactly when. I've had a great experience here and learned a lot from Anna. But, as someone said the key word for Sokolow is "more"; she's never satisfied and you can get burnt by her fire. No question, she's brilliant but I've had it, in more ways than one.

It's time I branch out on my own or maybe work with someone like Doris Humphrey; she's warm and gentle, besides very talented. She just got a rave review by John Martin on her new work "Life of the Bee." Someone just showed me a clipping, I think it was Anita Brenner, a writer, who happens to be a very nice, bright woman, friendly with Frida Kahlo. I think you'd like to meet her.

Okay, that's one thing. The other is Martin. It's not only him but his whole gang. I used to think I liked Caridad, her son, Ramon, Tina and David but it's worn thin. Not that I don't find Caridad a fascinating woman (you can say snakes are fascinating too) but she's also irrational. She's lost her mind about this Russian general. Anyone with a grain of sense could see that this guy is just having a good time with her in Mexico—that is besides doing his work. Her son, Ramon, gives me a pain. He's erratic and boastful. He told us a long story the other night about a mountain climbing disaster and how skillful he is with an alpine axe.

Who cares?

They've become very secretive lately. There's something going on that smells rotten to me. Remember, I called them the "rogues Gallery." Okay, so they're all good-looking, smart and charming, but they're going around these days acting very mysterious. When I asked Martin yesterday why he's stashed two policemen's uniform in the bottom drawer he got mad at me, refused to tell me and we had a big fight. I won't go into any further details but I really think we won't be together much longer. What's so amusing, just the other day, he began to talk about having a family! Maybe seeing Jaime's kids inspired him. Over my dead body!

I'm writing to Dorothy Bird and Sophie Maslow about my coming back. I don't suppose you remember them, dancers, they were at my wedding. I might also bring back a young Mexican dancer who wants to study with Jose Limon. Honey, I could go on ten pages about my ideas and plans, I'm so full of them. Now that I've made up my mind about coming back, I can't wait. So I just say, hasta luego—a million hugs and kisses,

Ketzel

P.S. The other day I met Sheldon Harte at the Kit Kat Club, he said he's one of Trotsky's guards, a kid from New York. He was having a drink with Ramon at the bar. You know him by any chance? He's a sweet guy, awkward like a young colt, sexy. Sounds very attractive after consorting with a suave, sophisticated Spanish pain in the ass, my husband.
P.P.S. Martin just walked in. He just returned from a rally which the C P turned it into a angry, ugly anti-Trotsky demonstration. Needless to say, he was very happy about it. Enough said!

Miriam leans back in the rocker and closes her eyes. Mother Jones jumps into her lap, curls up, and begins to purr rhythmically and contentedly. Every time I get one of Ketzel's letters, she muses, my heart's on a see-saw. She's happy Ketzel's coming back but frightened her father might be coming too—with his wife and two lovely, fat babies? She could have been the mother of his children if she'd acted differently. Come to think of it, how come Sheldon Harte, one of the Old Man's guards, was having a drink with Ramon? I guess guys get friendly and talk to whoever's near them at a bar. It must have been just conversation … they certainly don't have much in common.

Miriam's at work when Sydney calls. When she begins to tell him that she has a free ticket to a Martha Graham dance recital and won't be home for dinner, he interrupts, his voice strange, "Listen, there's a special meeting at the headquarters at six o'clock. You'd better get there. Trotsky's been attacked."

The headquarter is overflowing, the air hazy with cigarette smoke, subdued murmurs and marked agitation. Sydney motions Miriam to a seat he's saved next to him, his hand trembling as he holds a match.

"Jim just received another phone call from Joe Hansen," he tells her. "He'll be back in a few minutes, getting more information."

As soon as Cannon enters the room, everyone quiets immediately leaning forward to hear his message. His usual ruddy face looks bleached, worn, tired, as if he hadn't slept all night. His voice is very low but audible in the absolute hush.

"Comrades, first, I want to assure you that Trotsky, Natalya and Seva are well and safe. Now, let me share with you the little information I have at this time. Last night, May 24th at 4 A.M., twenty-five men broke into Trotsky's house. The assailants, dressed as police and officials of the Mexican Army, were admitted at the door by our guard, Sheldon Harte. They'd already tied up and overpowered the five men stationed in the sentry house. Led by a 'Major,'" Cannon can't resist an amused grin, "the murderous gang ran through the house, penned up the guards in their rooms, shot more than one hundred bullets into the bed where they thought Natalya and Trotsky were sleeping, threw an incendiary bomb into Seva's room and left another burning at his door. They went through the library, the dining room, Trotsky's study, they sprayed the doors where the guards off shift would be sleeping. Before they left, they returned to the master bedroom and fired 5 or 6 shots into the bedclothes, thinking Trotsky and Natalya were under them."

A commotion breaks out. "Bastards! Murderers!" people shout angrily, waving fists in the air.

Cannon raises his hand for quiet. "The raid lasted almost twenty minutes. They ran out to two waiting automobiles they later abandoned, taking Harte with them. Later, on the premises, our guards found an electric saw, ladders, drills, an iron bar, and a defective bomb containing enough dynamite to blow up the entire house."

Again the conrades erupt in angry shouting. Looking about, Miriam is struck by how united everyone is at this moment, the back-biting, the rancor and strife in the party that existed for more than a year have suddenly vanished. *But for how long?* she wonders.

"Let's come to order now comrades," Jim says in a few moments. "I'm overjoyed—as we all are—all three are alive and in good condition. including the

Rosmers and the guards. Trotsky, Natalya and Seva saved themselves, little Seva hid under his bed, Trotsky and Natalya hid in a dark corner of their bedroom and were missed in the dark even though almost 200 shots had been fired.

Cannon concludes with a wry smile. "I know the Old Man must be amused by the failure of this elaborate attack. It was really a big joke," but his mouth tightens.

"There's a great deal to be concerned about. Of course we know that the G P U planned and perpetrated this entire action. It deserves the greatest ridicule and contempt. But many puzzling questions have to be answered; how had they known so much about the layout of the house? Why did Sheldon let them in? And why did they take him away?"

Cannon looks down at his notes. "I'm told Colonel Salazar, Chief of the Mexican Secret Police, arrived within thirty minutes after the raid. He seems to be very suspicious about who is involved and inclined to think, according to what the Old Man tells me, it's a put-up job organized by Trotskyists themselves. When he asked Trotsky whom he suspected, Trotsky—I heard this from Joe Hansen—put his arm around his shoulder and whispered 'the author of the attack is Joseph Stalin, through the medium of the G P U.' Salazar was so amazed by the Old Man's and Natalya's coolness and perfect self-control that he was sure that Trotsky was pulling his leg."

"That's crazy!" a comrade cries out. "Salazar must be a Stalinist stooge!" yells another.

"Please," Cannon says, again gesturing for quiet. "Now, this would be amusing, if it weren't so serious. Although the Old Man told him it would be wise to interrogate some of the most conspicuous local Stalinists, Salazar thinks this is some sort of ruse on the Old Man's part. This raid, even by Mexican standards, is so scandalous that Salazar finds it hard to believe the Communist Party could be behind it. He had two of Trotsky's secretaries arrested and three of the household servants."

A chorus of boos breaks out. Cannon pauses to take a sip of water, continuing to speak now more slowly, sounding very tired. "Comrades, in a few days we will have more information, especially, we hope, about Sheldon Harte. Natalya says that the atmosphere over the house is very heavy and that Trotsky believes it is only a freak of good fortune that everyone is still alive. We're resolved to do everything in our power to keep him safe and we must be more vigilant than ever in the future. The guards will bullet-proof the doors, windows and the tower, bomb proof the ceilings and floors and replace the wooden entrance doors by double-steel ones controlled by electric switches."

Shaking his head in despair, he added "We know how strongly the old man feels about all these safegards. He refuses to wear a bullet-proof vest, gave it to one of the guards, and won't permit visiting friends to be searched." His voice dropping in weariness, he concludes, "Comrades, that's all for now. As soon as we have more information, I'll let you know." Questions are asked from the floor but in a short while, Cannon declares the meeting over.

Miriam, like everyone there, goes through a variety of mixed emotions. She's shaken by the planned, ferocious attack, overjoyed they're unharmed, amused by the ridiculous, botched-up job. But she's frightened, and on the way home asks Sydney, "Do you think he'll be safe now? They'll be taking so many precautions in and around the house. Maybe the C P won't try anymore."

He shrugs. "I feel like the old man does. It's just a matter of time. They'll get him somehow—in a different way." He tries to laugh, "They sure messed up this time, what a joke." His face doesn't look like he thinks it's funny.

Two weeks later, more details unfold. At a meeting, Jim reads a letter from Natalya: "Trotsky gets up every morning and says, "You see, they did not kill us last night after all; yes, Natasha, we've had a reprieve."

She writes, "You cannot believe how busy he is, involving himself in every phase of the investigation, going to court to answer the never-ending lies, particularly in the pro-Stalinist press. When The Nation of New York published an article suggesting that Trotsky himself or members of his household staged the raid, he wrote back telling them, 'An infamous reptile breed these "radicals" are.' After he protested to Cardenas about the arrest of our secretaries they were released. Now he's trying to get the police to investigate the heads of the Communist Party, Lombardo Toledano and David Siqueiros. They suspect Sheldon Harte but we all know that Sheldon Harte is innocent. If he'd been a G P U agent, Trotsky insists, he could have stabbed me on the quiet, right in the house. No one believes our Bob is guilty, he's an honorable, sweet young man...."

After the first shock wears off, the political struggle within the Socialist Workers Party resumes, even more bitter than before. Miriam finds there's less and less to talk about now, since they've given up arguing about politics. It's more or less understood that they'll go their own ways regarding the split.

They spend little time together, busy themselves with work, political activity and school, in Miriam's case, attending school three nights a week. But tension increases and it isn't a complete surprise when Miriam comes home from work one night and finds Sydney packing a suitcase. *How ironic*, she thinks!

Lately, she'd often felt lonely and had had thoughts of leaving him but now he's leaving her!

He stops sorting socks and follows her. She's sitting at the open window, still holding her pocketbook. Avoiding her eyes, reaching for a cigarette, he says,

"Max called me today at work from L A, very enthusiastic. He told them, the management, he can get someone to work with him, in a few days time. Good pay, too." He takes a deep pull and exhales before going on. "What do you think? Should I go?"

Miriam tries to smile. "You've already decided, haven't you?"

"Yeah, but if you seriously object, I won't."

"Sydney," she has trouble keeping a quaver out of her voice, "you know I won't say or do anything to stop you. Now, I'll have think what's going to happen to me."

"How about coming with me? I'll wait a few days if you want to. We can just take off—clear out. The furniture here ain't worth a damn!" He attempts a little smile. "We'll leave it for the next lucky tenant. What do you say?"

She hears the question but knows it's not an invitation, there's no urgency in his voice. She doesn't answer. Los Angeles ... it's supposed to be beautiful, the city of angels, of sunshine, flowers and golden beaches, she might be happy there. But with him? Surroundings, natural beauty mean very little to Sydney. Although politics, radical politics, consume his entire thinking and attitude, he's happiest when he's with other men, the only time then he feels easy and free. It isn't that he doesn't like women, or sex but it's only good when he wants it, a sharp hunger that needs to be quickly satisfied. He craves the relationship, the companionship of males, and yearns for fun, simple fun, baseball, cold beer, Laurel and Hardy movies, with men mostly and he loves being near his brother. *Do I really expect too much?* Miriam wonders. She's seen other couples who pay attention to each other, who seem happy in each other's company. Is it Sydney or she at fault?

When he sees she can't answer, he says, "Look, I'll go. See how you feel in a few weeks. There's some money in our joint account. Meanwhile, if and when you decide to come, I'll look for a place for the two of us."

When they go to bed the night before he leaves, he's tender and loving. He wants to believe that they've been happy, it's been a good relationship. After they've made love, when he has turned away, curled in his usual position, ready for sleep, she snuggles close to his thin back. "Try to take care of yourself. Don't smoke so much." She wants to say more, tell him she's scared about living alone. But if she tells him she's frightened, he might change his mind and stay. She doesn't want him to leave but she can't bring herself to say it. She knows he should go. It's better for both of them. She begins to shiver and is almost crying when he reaches around, pulls her close and kisses her.

"I hope you'll miss me," she whispers. "You're my honey-chile," he answers, "of course I will."

During the night she awakes in a panic but the next morning, made bold by the bright sun glinting off the leaves of the coleus plant she tells him, "I'll stay here awhile. Try to make it alone. Maybe I'll get someone to share the apartment with me. I'll keep myself busy, jobs are opening up in the Brooklyn Navy Yard. Maybe I can get myself to work there," but she doubts it.

At the bus stop Sydney repeats what he said about joining him in a few weeks and makes her promise she'll think about it. Forcing a smile, she says, "You're joining the proletariat now. The Old Man should be pleased, one less petit-bourgeois in New York."

Mexico, May–June 1940

A short time after the Siquieros raid, Alfred and Marguerite Rosmer, guests of Trotsky's for the past eight months, return to Europe. Frank Jacson—the guards assume he is Sylvia's husband—drives them to Veracruz where they board the ship for France. The next time he comes to the Trotsky's house Natalya invites him in and he meets the Old Man for the first time. Although he's become friendly with the guards, he doesn't seem interested in politics.

Trotsky doesn't particularly like him and is displeased when he hears him talking about his "rich boss" and the stock exchange. He tells Natalya that it might be a good idea not to have him come anymore. "Who is this rich boss?," Trotsky asks her. "One should find out. It may be, after all, be some profiteer of the fascist type."

CHAPTER 24

New York City, June 1940

After a few days, and the first difficult night, coming home to an empty apartment doesn't seem as painful as she expected. Next door there's a friendly Puerto Rican family with eight kids, one of the little ones always running in for a cookie. On Saturday, she goes to a little store next to the big Woolworth's on 146th Street and Broadway and buys pretty blue curtains with rosebuds for the kitchen window, taking off the faded ones by herself. In the evenings, there's either school, meetings, or the movies. When she stays home she'll put on the radio and listen to "The Street Singer" extolling the beauty of "Marta, Capullita de Rosa" or the A & P Gypsies chanting "South of the Border/down Mexico Way."

Bunny, happy with her Van, calls her to talk about the raid. "Van always tried to get Trotsky to be more careful but he refuses" she tells Miriam. "He doesn't want to live in a prison; he had enough of that." She says it's a shame that the Rosmers, his good friends, had to leave two days after the raid but they had definite plans to go back to France and couldn't change them. "Jacques, Sylvia's boy-friend," she chatters on, "drove them to Vera Cruz to get the boat. He said he had business there anyway so it was no extra trouble. Trotsky's a little suspicious of him, but the Rosmers think he's wonderful, he even remembered to bring Seva a toy. Natalya was luke-warm about him but she may be changing her mind because he says he's starting to get interested in politics, thinking of writing an article. Everybody's a writer these days," Bunny says, "except me." Well, Miriam thought, hanging up, "If she could write, she could do a memoir about being an "It" girl—like Clara Bow—but it would have to be a left-wing "It" girl."

When Miriam comes home a few days later, little Miguel from next door brings her a telegram delivered during the day. 'Ketzel arriving Saturday.' As she reads the news, a rush of joyful anticipation sweep through her. She runs to looks for the key to the brownstone in her underwear drawer, and she's cheerful, the first time in many days.

On Friday she ducks out of work early, catches the subway to the lower East Side. She buys plump, oily white fish, Pechter's rye bread, sweet butter carved from a wooden tub, green pickled tomatoes and ruggelah. Then, instead of going to her house, she rides up to ll7th Street, catching the ice-man just in time. She runs about opening windows, pausing in each room, remembering Fanny and Jaime laughing, scolding, loving.

At last, spent, she trudges upstairs to the little attic room, plugs in the electric fan and throws herself down on the white cotton bedspread. The soft whooshing sound from the little tree in the backyard sways in the breeze, lulls her. For the moment she's happy, her friend who loves her is returning. Then her thoughts take a darker turn. Ketzel has a husband, a loving father, a successful career. She has none of those things. Her life should be meaningful, she wants to matter, to accomplish something, make a 'better world'. She smiles at herself, her foolishness. A better world! Just like that, a small ambition! Maybe she's got to recognize she doesn't have what it takes. She isn't a great leader or writer. She remembers one time, when they'd first met, Sydney told her, "You have so much anger and fire, you could be another Rosa or even a great speaker like Emma Goldman." Yeah, like he could be another Lenin!

She and Sydney are ordinary people, except they're class-conscious, radicals. They're not fighters, though they passionately hate the cruel, competitive world they live in. A vivid photograph she once saw persists in her mind; a line, one hundred men, their desperate faces, waiting for a factory job, cap in hand. All they can hope for, all they will be given, is a dollar for the day and they'll be the lucky ones. A sign on the entrance says only ten men are needed. What kind of society do we live in? Men waiting, prisoners on a line, looking like beaten dogs, begging for a job, begging so they can eat!

What gives Trotsky, and Natalya, the strength, the courage to go on, is that they know that they have mattered, they made a revolution, they were important and although exiled now, poor, living in a fortress, Trotsky's words still echo around the world.

But it was also that they truly love and support each other, despite misunderstandings and lapses. They didn't fall apart when the assassins came. They're strong. They know who they are. *But who or what am I?*

✤   ✤   ✤

Next morning there's the sound of a door thrown open, things being dropped, a lilting voice calling her name and she rushes down, still in the clothes she'd worn yesterday, to welcome her friend. Directly behind her, a head taller, there's a young man that Ketzel introduces. He nods his head, abruptly extending a long, bony hand, his eyes lowered. As she murmurs, pleased to meet you, Luis, she finds herself thinking that *this is the ugliest, thinnest, tallest man she's ever seen, a scarecrow in a seersucker jacket. His hair is lank and wispy, his eyes (when he looks up) a yellowish color, his nose wide, his chin heavy.*

"Luis is to my mind the greatest natural dancer in the United States, if not in the world," Ketzel says. "No one knows that yet, but it won't be long until he's recognized, at least if I have anything to do with it. He smiles, his face lights up and suddenly he's a different person, exotic, yet warm, gentle and shy. Miriam can see why Ketzel adopted him as a protege.

Just look at him when he moves." Ketzel says. They turn to watch him mount the stairs.

"You're right," Miriam says. "He doesn't walk, he floats."

"He is as nice and sweet as he's graceful. I'm going to help him all I can," Ketzel says, determinedly. "He deserves it."

As they sit down for breakfast, with the door to the back yard open, Miriam thinks how worn Ketzel looks. She's lost weight, she looks older even though her hair is beautiful, more red-gold than before, thanks to the Mexican sun. She probably had a hard time with the Sokolow group. Two bossy ladies working together! Good thing she's home now. But where's Martin?

As if Miriam's reading her thoughts, Ketzel says in a dry, hard tone, "I don't know where Martin is. The last time I saw him was two weeks ago. He'll probably be here any day now."

Luis, busy with the white fish and the bagels and the other strange foods which he devotes himself to without shyness and with open enjoyment. But he doesn't stop looking at Ketzel's face. It's obvious he adores her, regards her as some sort of a celestial creature, empathizes with everything she says though he doesn't understand a word of English.

Ketzel finishes her coffee and lights a cigarette. She leans back, stretches her legs, takes Miriam's hand, squeezes it.

"Gracias, amiga mia. That was so good. When I see you I know I'm home again. Now, let me tell you about those wonderful friends I've been hanging out with in Mexico." She chuckles and her eyes narrow. "Yeah, it's almost funny. Charlie Chaplin could write a funny movie about it. Come to think of it, someone already did—The Keystone Kops."

"Better begin at the beginning, Ketzel. I don't know who you're talking about"

"I'm talking about the 'Rogues Gallery' my friends from Spain—Caridad, Siquieros, Contreras, Ramon, remember?"

"You wrote me about them; Tina Modotti, how mad she got when you took that picture."

"I deserve a medal for thinking up a name for those gangsters. That's what they all are. Okay, here's what happened." Ketzel smokes in silence for a minute. "Martin was supposed to come to see my last performance at the Bellas Artes, the night of May 24th. Does that date ring a bell with you?"

"Of course." Miriam sits up rigid, staring at Ketzel. "Trotsky—the raid ..."

"Martin never showed up," Ketzel goes on. "After the performance the cast gave a little party for me, champagne, lots of kisses, good-byes, very nice but no Martin! I was furious!" She clatters her coffee cup down onto the table. "Instead of going back to the apartment, I went to an address on Cuba Street where I knew he hung out. For a few weeks I'd suspected something was going on, especially after I had found those police uniforms. When I got there, his friend let me in. It must have been about two A.M. and a party was going on, noisy, full swing. It looked like you were at a masquerade ball. But this was different, everybody was dressed up like a police or an army man. Siquerios was swaggering around, having a great time, being an Army Major with a false mustache and glasses, Antonio Pujol dressed as an Army Lieutenant and there were two gals who were bragging that they'd been given money to get somebody drunk and how good they'd done. Everybody was having a wing-ding time, cracking jokes, laughing, but I could see how dead serious they were about something. It was crazy and scary. When someone came out of the bedroom I caught a glimpse of guns, machine guns, black bombs stacked near the bed and when I saw what was going on, I began to scream at Martin—I began to scream at Martin...."

"So Martin was with them too." Miriam's eyes shine with anger. "The Siquerios bunch that raided Trotsky's house!"

"I tried to go into the bedroom but they pushed me away. They were shrieking 'Largate, largate' at me. 'Scram.' Martin grabbed my arm, really hurting me. He's begging me, "Ketzel, go home. This isn't your business. We're only going to get papers from Trotsky's house. It's a fun raid! Nobody'll get hurt."

"They're lying murderers," Miriam shrieks, "They were out to get Trotsky. If you'd tried to stop them they've have killed you too, right then and there."

Ketzel laughs sarcastically. "You know me. When I saw Contreras—our friend, Vidali, the murderer, dressed up as an army man, standing near me, that ugly monster, I saw red. I screamed 'Why aren't you wearing a swastika and a German Uniform like you did in Spain when you kidnapped Nin?'

He rushed at me, he'd have killed me then and there. Then, before I knew it, someone grabbed me from behind and shoved into a room, locked me up. I kept yelling and carrying on but of course no one came. After a few minutes it got quiet, I could hear everyone leaving, slamming doors. It was after dawn when a cleaning woman opened the door and let me out. You should have seen her face!" Ketzel pauses, her face covered with sweat, reaches for a glass of water, then pours a little into her palm, cools her forehead. Then she looked over at Luis who was watching her with concern. "I called Anna, she sent Luis to get me. I went to our apartment, got my clothes, then to the Hacienda, Luis with me all the time. Martin never showed up. I don't know where he is now—probably plotting some other Party caper." She spits out her words ..., "I'm finished."

Taking a cigarette from a pack on the table she turns and goes out into the garden. Miriam watches her. Always like a princess, a dancer, her shoulders, her back straight, her head high.

Ketzel's very busy the following days, putting her things away, calling friends, showing Luis the City, taking them both out to dinner. She insists that Miriam stay with her and allows her to go uptown only to get some clothes and Mother Jones. "I really need you here, Miriam. Someone's got to supervise when I'm running around town, picking out lights and drapes."

Miriam doesn't mind very much, she loves being at Ketzel's, there's always excitement and it feels like family. She's been working only two days a week now, but Sydney continues to send her checks for the rent.

Along with her plans to turn the house into a place for rehearsals and performances, Ketzel is working on a new ballet she's calling 'Maxmillian and Juarez.'

"I don't especially like the title, but I don't want to call it 'Maximillian and Carlotta,'" Ketzel explains. "I think she done her husband in. She really loved him but she was a young, aristocrtic girl, didn't have a clue of what Mexico was all about and just liked the idea of being an empress. Besides, Maximillian got one and one-half million a year and they gave her a salary of two hundred thousand plus the gorgeous Chapultepec Castle in Cuernavaca to live in."

"Didn't she go crazy in the end, after they shot Maximillian?," Miriam asks. "I feel sorry for her. She tried to save him."

"They have no business being there in the first place. Juarez was the real leader of Mexico, not the French nobility. They even had their fancy coach shipped from Vienna, all gilt, carving and brocade, but it broke down in Veracruz on the muddy roads and they had to take the stagecoach, after all, the poor dears!"

"If you're doing a ballet about these characters, don't you have to make the audience feel some empathy for them?," Miriam murmurs.

"Sure, I want to make them sympathetic as individuals and hateful as foreign rulers … it ain't easy." Ketzel sighs, "I just have to get good dancers. A few like Tamiris. I'm inviting her for dinner tomorrow, plus a few others who might be good." Before Miriam can say anything, she adds, "I know, I'm rushing it, but it's better for me this way, keeping busy."

This is as close as Ketzel comes to talking about her break-up with Martin. Although she acts cheerful and bossy, Miriam knows there's a throbbing hurt inside Ketzel…. the mirror of her glamorous marriage shattered into splinters.

Tamiris shows up the following evening, her shimmering red hair set off by her black shawl ambroidered with cabbage roses. She strides into the kitchen with a small bouquet of daisies and a large bottle of wine, pauses in the doorway and says, "So this is the Luis you told me about. He'd better be good."

At dinner, Ketzel launches into the Maximillian story. Before she's gotten past a few sentences, Tamiris cuts in, "I can see it. In the first act, when they arrive in Veracruz, we can have great dark vultures flying around the city, zipilotes, dancers all in black, harbingers of their fate." Her eyes glow. "I can't wait for us to get started."

Miriam, amused, watches the two interrupt each other all through the evening. *I hope Tamiris doesn't try to take over,* she thinks. You *can't do that with Ketzel.*

"Now, would you like to see Luis dance?" They troop upstairs to the almost completed studio. Ketzel puts on a tange and goes to Luis, smiling encouragingly. He leads her lightly, his touch sure and elegant. Then, Ketzel takes a few steps back and whispers, "Vete."

His head high, arms raised, Luis moves down to the far end of the room, turns, pauses, then runs, leaps, then again a short run and a leap. Miriam and Tamiris look up, their mouth open as he soars, his head close to the ceiling.

"Oh, my God, what elevation, I don't believe it," Tamiris gasps. "He's fantastic."

Ketzels grins maternally, as he continues to leap, caught up in motion and speed, rising up like a grotesque angel.

By the time Tamiris leaves that night she and Ketzel have hammered out the outline of a three-act ballet. Miriam hopes they'll include Lincoln in the scene. "Maybe in the middle act? You know, he helped Juarez," she says. "He let him buy arms in the Unite Sates. He wasn't supposed to, according to an agreement he had with France and England but that's how Juarez won. A lesson in how actions can change history." She stops, the bitter defeat in Spain still haunts her. "Roosevelt could have sold arms to the Republicans," she continues quietly. "It might have been different in Spain. We might have stopped Hitler. But if Roosevelt hadn't maintained the embargo and supported Franco he'd have lost the support of the Catholic Church, which was important to maintain power in this country. So to hell with the struggle against fascism—to him the vote was more important."

"Good idea, adding Lincoln in. We'll try to to use it," Ketzel says. Miriam know she won't, though. She doesn't want to get involved in present-day politics. History is safe, used as a backdrop for an interesting story.

After a few more days at Ketzel's house she decides to go back to her own apartment. She needs a little peace. Anyway, Ketzel's too busy to spend much time with her, even in the evenings. Jaime calls Ketzel frequently but only once when Miriam answered the phone does he stop to say more than hello, how are you? She knows why—Ketzel's told her that one of the babies has been ill and he and his wife are worried.

But once Miriam's back on 151st Street, she's lonely. At night, with the fusty air and the oily smell of the kitchen's peeling linoleum, she feels she can barely breathe. One night, finishing some iced tea, idly listening to the radio, the phone rings. It's Sylvia, who scolds her affectionately for being so hard to reach.

"I want to see you. I've got lots of news," she says. "I tried getting you at the office. Ruth's getting married this weekend and I have to get a new dress. I'd love if you'd come along, help me shop."

Before Miriam can answer, Sylvia adds, "Jacques inisists on coming with me. He says he want to make sure I get the right color. He's so fussy about clothes."

"Good news about Ruth. How about tomorrow, I get off at four-thirty." Miriam hopes Jacques won't be able to make it on such short notice. His darting, restless eyes, his sudden changes of mood make her feel ill at ease.

When she arrives at Lord & Taylor the next afternoon, she's happy to find Sylvia there alone. It's Sylvia's favorite, this elegant store with marble pillars, carpeted floors, lofty chandeliers and polite salesgirls grateful to serve the upper classes. *A far cry from Klein's on 14th Street*, Miriam thinks. But she has to admit she, too, likes elegant stores. When she worked in Rockefeller Center she'd often wander through Saks' Fifth Avenue on her lunch-hour. Sometimes she'd be lucky and find a marked-down blouse she could afford.

Sylvia looks pretty and cheerful. She's just been to the beauty parlor and her fair hair waves nicely, framing her heart-shaped face. "Jacques' going to leave for Mexico right after Ruth's wedding," she tells Miriam. "I may be joining him a little later. He's becoming more and more a part of the family." *That won't make her other sisters very happy*, Miriam thinks. *They feel the same as I do.*

Jacques arrives a few minutes later. His olive-skinned face is sweaty but as usual he's dressed beautifully, in a light gray summer suit that goes well with his dark, thick eyebrows and tortoise-shell glasses. With his approval, Sylvia settles on a cream-colored chiffon dress, gathered in soft pleats at her waist, her small face radiating happiness when Jacques compliments her.

"It really is very becoming," Miriam agrees with Jacques, but he's become distracted. It takes him a moment before he nods his head in agreement.

At Barbetta's restaurant they decide to have some wine while they wait for Hilda, who's meeting them there. But she's late and Jacques' hungry. He insists they order, and it's about thirty minutes into the meal when Hilda arrives, breathless, her myopic eyes popping with excitement.

"They got awful news at the headquarters just this afternoon," she pants as Jacques rises to pull out her chair. "I'm sorry I'm late. When I stopped in there everybody was in an uproar. It's about Sheldon Harte—they found his body a few days ago—in a lime pit!" She takes a drink, dabs her forehead with a handkerchief.

"Are they sure it's Sheldon?," Sylvia wants to know.

"His father identified the body," Hilda says. "They also had the Old Man identify him. His father didn't know a thing about it, about his son working for Trotsky. His parents live here, in Long Island. When they searched his room at home, they found a picture of Stalin in a bureau drawer. What do you think of that!?

"You mean he never told them he was going to work for Trotsky in Mexico?" Miriam's puzzled. "Why wouldn't he tell them he was going to be a guard for Trotsky. Being a guard for Trotsky was never a big secret for anyone in the party … unless he had something to hide."

"He didn't tell a lot of people, including the girl friend, one he'd met at Duke University and been seeing in New York. She knew him as a C P'er, an 'unreconstructed Stalinist,' she told someone. When he left New York, he told her he couldn't tell where he was going but he'd write. Then she gets a pair of leather goves in the mail a few wek later, but no address or message. When the Mexican police investigated they found he had lots of cash in a Wells Fargo account. From where? Not from his family and, for sure he didn't earn it as a guard for the Old Man."

"I can't believe it—I knew him and there's no way he could be a traitor," Sylvia protests, shaking her head in disbelief.

"Well, there were several things we didn't know about him, according to what they're saying at headquarters," Hilda says. "Apparently he spent money freely in Mexico City, like getting a prostitue for a night, going to places like the Imperio nightclub and the Kit Kat Club. He must have been getting money from somewhere"

"The Kit-Kat Club," Sylvia says, turning to Jacques, "Didn't you meet him there once and have a drink with him!"

"I don't remember, but I might have." He wrinkles his forehead as if trying to recall. "I'm really sorry to hear this about Sheldon. I knew him. I know all the guards, we became friendly when I'd take the Rosmers or Natalya for a ride. I once left my car there for them."

Hilda continues, a bit impatiently. "The Old Man can't accept the rumors that he was a C P agent. When Cannon called the Mexico today he got more of the story. When they opened the pit where he'd been buried there was lime and clay stuck all over him."

Now Hilda has to stop and swallow before she can go on. "His body was wet and shining and he was curled up, like a sleeping baby. After they cleaned him up and brought his body to the house to be buried, the Old Man walked over to the coffin and stood looking at him for a long time. He was crying, as if he couldn't help it."

Hilda's eyes glisten, her lips tremble. "Some of us cried too when we heard the story …" Then, trying to speak calmly, she adds, "Trotsky and Natalya are going to bury him in the courtyard. They are going to put up a plague with an inscription that says, "Dear Comrade ..."

❀   ❀   ❀

No mention is made of Martin but Miriam knows Ketzel expects him to turn up soon. On a warm evening towards the end of June she's at Ketzel's when Martin arrives. She and Ketzel and Luis have just finished dinner. The table's draped with a powder-blue cloth, a vase filled with yellow daisies, and the candles in an old menorah that belonged to Fanny are glowing. They're enjoying 'El Caminito' lilting on the phonograph when, tearing through the soft tango music, they hear a doorbell ring loudly, insistently. They know who it is. Miriam looks at Ketzel. "Shall I go—or do you want that privilege?," she asks sarcastically.

Ketzel doesn't answer for a moment then she says, "No, you go. I'll wait for him here," her voice deep, strangling with anger. "And when you bring him back here, don't leave the room, either of you." But when Martin comes into the kitchen her face has assumed a look of sweet expectancy, a wife, anxiously awaiting her husband, She flies to him, kissing him, "Querido, I've been so worried."

Martin's face is drawn, murky in the dim light, finding it hard to speak. He's full of dread, fearing Ketzel's anger but her warm greeting surprises him and he stands still, trying to register this turn of events. After a moment's hesitation, he goes to her, hugs her, whispering softly, "Darling, you really didn't have to worry. I'm fine."

They kiss standing there, the only sound in the room Miriam clattering dishes in the sink. She'd have liked to leave but Ketzel wants her to stay. Luis beside her, handing her soiled plates never takes his eyes off from the couple who are talking and embracing in the dim room.

After a moment, Martin whispers "Let's go upstairs, Ketzel. I know the others here won't mind." He looks over, throwing them a half-smile.

"No, darling, just let's stay here." Ketzel moves away from him, going to where's she been sitting, pointing to the one opposite her. Her voice is sweet with a tiny edge of sharpness. Miriam and Luis, hear in her tone, an ominous quiver, but Martin, whose stiff shoulders have slackened, begins to assume his usual jaunty stance. He throws himself into a chair opposite her and takes a deep breath.

"Join the party," Ketzel says. "We've been having such a pleasant evening. Miriam, is there some coffee left? I made it strong, the way he likes it. I knew he'd come here, for me." She looks at him tenderly, reaching for his hand across the table, adding softly, "We'll go upstairs later, mi amor."

"No, there isn't," Miriam answers and sits down in her chair, clasping her hands in front of her, looking at Martin, who's still holding Ketzel's hand. Behind her noncommittal expression, she has a vision of Trotsky and Natalya, crouching in a corner of a dark bedroom, bullets shattering all about them, holding onto each other. She wants to scream at this handsome, slick guy, "You arrogant bastard, you murderer." Is it possible Ketzel will once again take him back, despite everything?

Ketzel, playing with Martin's fingers, says, almost in a whisper, "Tell me what happened after I left, after I was locked up and you guys left." She grins as if she considers the whole incident a trivial, silly prank.

After glancing at Miriam, Martin, still a little unsure, trying to read her mood, turns back to Ketzel, looking into her eyes. "I went to find you in in the morning, it must have been just after you left, just a little later." Shamefaced, he confesses, "I guess I had too much to drink. I'm not sure what happened. I think I fell asleep when we all went out. The next morning when I got back to our apartment, you were gone. But I figured you went to Jaime's and I didn't worry. Then I found out you were here so I got a plane as soon as I could."

"What about your friends?" Ketzel laughs. "Did they get Trotsky's stuff, those papers they wanted so badly?"

Martin looks down at their intertwined fingers before he answers. "Darling, I know you're not going to believe me. Siquieros and Antonio, the others, they didn't want to hurt anyone—we just wanted to scare Trotsky, to make him give us his papers." He pauses, looks at Ketzel, who nods understandingly, then continues with more assurance. "Look, it's over. Siqueiros is gone—he's run to Chile. The police didn't understand what he was trying to do. No harm done. To anyone, to you, especially you, darling. It was just a childish caper," his voice, softens, pleading. "Let's forget about it. Please. It was not important, the whole thing. What's important is me and you." He gets up, stands behind Ketzel's chair and leans down, nuzzling her cheek, whispering, "I'm so happy to see you, Remember, querida, what we've been talking about, our making plans."

"Later, darling," Ketzel says, leaning into his caress. "What about Caridad and Ramon. Were they with you that night?"

"No, they're here now in New York, Ramon, Caridad, her Russian boy-friend," Martin laughs, beginning to feel at ease. "Caridad's such a fool. Ramon's busy, has an important meeting in New York." He takes her hand to pull her up, "Honey, I don't want to talk about them. I want to talk about us. Our future, it's important …"

"STOP!," Ketzel explodes in a scream. She can't play the game any longer. "Shut up, you bastard!" She jumps up, her face swollen, pink. and raising her right arm leans over and swings at his face with all her might! The sharp slap tears through the quiet, listening room. "You god-damn fool—you think I'm an idiot." Martin, dazed, holding his reddened cheek, sways back, raises his arm to strike back but Luis whips across the room, catches him at the door and pins his arms. Martin struggles but is no match for the skinny dancer with steel-bar arms. Unable to move, Ketzel screaming in his face, he screams back.

"What the hell do you think you're doing?," spitting his words. "Quita su perro maldito. Cabron—get your hands off me!," screaming in Luis's face.

"We'll see, my darling." She begins to laugh, standing in front of him, hands on her hips. Christ. When I think of how crazy I was about you. God's gift to women … What a joke!"

"No lo sueltes." She turns to Luis and goes back to the table to pick up her cup. After she's taken a sip, she's ready to speak, coolly, deliberately.

"Listen carefully. I'm looking at you and I want you to look at me. It's important because we'll never see each other again." She pulls her breath in sharply. "I'm not sure you're a murderer like your friends but you went along with them that night. They were going to kill everyone in that house, even the boy. You want us to have children but you would kill a child." She shakes her head. "Unbelievable. Of course," she says, sarcastically, "we know Trotsky and his wife don't matter to you. According to you they deserve to die—but the child, their grandson?"

"Do you really expect me to answer you while this cabron is holding me? Call off your dog," Martin's shrieking.

Ketzel shakes her head, reaches for the pack of cigarettes on the table, lights one, takes a deep drag. "No, I really don't expect you to answer. Don't bother. It'll be just more lies." Turning to Luis she gives orders to release him and waves him out. "Just go. Disappear … forever. Let's see you run."

Luis drops his arms but gives Martin a hard shove before he moves away. Martin flies to the door, rubbing his sore arms.

"Muchas gracias, hijoputa!," he screams at Luis, who walks back to the sink. But he has to have the last word. "I don't have anything more to say to you,

Ketzel." He is so angry, his mouth twists as he spits, "You're a beautiful woman, Ketzel, a magnificent dancer, good in bed. We could have been happy. But you're stupid! So stupid. You and your friend—you don't know the first thing about politics." He's shouting now, waving his arms. "Why the hell didn't you stay out of them. But no. Because you're stupid you take the wrong side."

He struts to Miriam, still at the table, rigid, her hands white around her coffee cup, her lips tight. Bending down he tells her, "Your Old Man is doomed. It'll be soon, my dear!"

Then, straightening up, coming close to Ketzel, asks sweetly, "Won't you give your husband—I'm still your husband you know—a good-bye kiss," but as she raises her arm again, he's out of the door.

It's quiet, almost dark, the candles, flickering, down to their last inch, shadows everywhere. In the dim light, Luis's tall figure is outlined by a faint beam from the window, Miriam still sits at the table and Ketzel remains in the center of the room, arms stiff at her side, her eyes dark pools of anger. After a moment, tossing her long ponytail over her shoulder, she says, her voice flat, "Okay, that's it, good-night, everybody," and walks out.

Miriam's quiet, after a moment reaching for a cigarette. Martin's words have churned up clay-cold, heavy fear. She sits a long time listening to the sounds from the yard, the light clicking noise crickets make when they rub their dry legs together, a light sweet odor from a honeysuckle bush drifts through the open door. Trying to shake herself loose from the crouching boogy-man that has haunted her since the raid, she walks outside and sits down on a white wrought-iron garden bench, closing her eyes. In a little while Luis comes to join her and they stand in te doorway, quietly, breathing the cool evening air.

Ketzel's in a good mood this morning. She's consigned her marriage to hell and goes about the entire day humming, "I'm glad you're dead/you rascal you."

In the afternoon, however, she loses it when she gets a call. When Miriam answers, a masculine voice asks, "Is Martin there? It's … important." Ketzel snatches the phone from her and yells, "No! He's not—good-bye," and slams the phone down. Her voice icy, she tells Miriam, "Another son-of-a-bitch, but always so nice and polite," she says with a small laugh, "you'd never dream he's one of the gang."

Miriam hesitates, reluctant to pursue the conversation but puzzled, asks, "Why does his voice sounds familiar. Is he someone I know?"

"I doubt it. How? You never went to Spain. When you were in Mexico he wasn't around. That was Ramon Mercader, Caridad's son." She turns and begins clearing papers from her desk. "Now he's having a big conference with Eitingon here in New York. It's a big secret. I wasn't supposed to know about it. Mama Caridad is here too, of course. Ha! She can't be away from her lover. God, deliver me from that pack of wolves!" She picks up and slams a glass paperweight so hard that it slides off the desk, falls to the floor, smashes into splinters.

Mexico, Summer 1940

The house is quiet, the Rosmers gone. and Trotsky is making an effort to work on his biography of Stalin. He is fond of citing this quotation from Nietzsche: "Whatever does not kill, strengthens me." Except for his usual problems with sleeping, his health is improving, he's regaining some of is former energy. But today he puts his work aside and reaches for the Testament he wrote in February. Although his life is in constant danger, he doesn't picture a violent end. He imagines he will die of something like high blood pressure. Afraid of a long illness, remembering Lenin's paralysis from strokes, he hopes his own death will happen suddenly. He and Natalya often speak about suicide ... and he writes in one of his papers, "I reserve the right to determine for myself the time of my death ..."

The approaching war is constantly on his mind. During the Great War, Lenin and the Bolsheviks urged the working class "to turn the war into a revolution." Now with Hitler sweeping over Europe, the rest of the world must rise to defeat fascism. Different approaches to the problem are needed—a positive, not a negative slogan. Having read a public opinion poll reporting that 70 percent of American workers favor conscription, Trotsky writes, "We place ourselves on the same ground as the 70 percent. You workers wish to defend ... democracy. We ... wish to go further. However, we are ready to defend democracy with you, only on condition that it should be a real defence, and not a betrayal ..."

CHAPTER 25

New York City, July 1940

There seem to be more jobs this summer than there's been for a long time, and Miriam tells Ketzel she's been offered a part-time, three-day-a-week office position for $15.00. "I can get along pretty nicely on that and take twelve credits at Hunter at the same time. I can't carry anymore than that because I'm taking chemistry and I'm going to have to work pretty hard. That stuff doesn't go down with me very well."

"Fifteen dollars a week isn't much. Do you really expect to live on that?," Ketzel sniffs. "Listen, I've been thinking of getting someone to help me here in the house, a secretary or someone," waving her hand at the stack of letters on her desk. She drops in her chair looking at Miriam. "What in hell am I going to do with all this stuff?" The muggy day is drawing to a close. They're sitting in the little office on the third floor, feeling dragged out. Then she jumps up. "I've been thinking of something and I want to talk to you about it but let's have a drink first."

While they relax in the back yard, with a pitcher of cold sangria, Miriam says, "I got $21.57 a week on the W P A two years and I got along just fine."

"Aren't you forgetting you were living with Sydney. He paid half the bills." Ketzel laughs shortly. "I don't think you can live on that, really. The best things in life aren't free, no matter what how the song goes."

"Of course, I'm not forgetting," Miriam's annoyed, "but we actually managed much less."

"Okay, let's not go into that." Ketzel realizes she's on the wrong tack. "Look, I've been thinking about this for a few weeks now. Jaime says he's going to turn over the house to me. He says he's got too much to handle in Mexico, with the ranch and the babies." She sighs. "So the house will be my baby now. How about it? I need help and you need a job. How about working for me?"

Miriam's surprised yet she'd sensed this offer was coming from certain hints Ketzel dropped during the past few weeks. She knows Ketzel's very generous, that the office work, taking care of bills and workmen, even running errands, wouldn't demand much time, and she'd have more time to do her assignments in school. Even be more active evenings in the Party. It's very tempting, a comfortable salary, and life would be easy.

But somehow she wants to reject the offer. She doesn't want to be subordinate to a friend who'd been her companion, her peer, for almost fifteen years. What if she goofed up on something important? How would she feel if Ketzel bawled her out? Which could happen. Ketzel has a short fuse and sounds off to anyone, anytime things go wrong. Miriam knows she'll get upset, maybe cry. They'd quarrel. Their long friendship could be destroyed. And what about Jaime? She'd surely see more of him if she worked in the house. He'd be calling and visiting. There's another reason to say no. She'd had enough heartache about him to last a lifetime.

"Ketzel," Miriam says slowly, "I don't know what to say."

"Don't you think you'd enjoy working for me?," Ketzel snaps.

Miriam hesitates, thinking that's what I'd better avoid, the minute things don't go her way, she gets mad. "Ketzel, we've been friends for a long time," she says slowly, knowing it's risky but the temptation to be honest is always there. "I want our friendship to last—I'm afraid something might happen if I start working for you."

"What in hell do you mean? What could happen? I don't know what you're afraid of."

"I'm not afraid of anything but you do have a quick temper and I might do something to annoy you. In the past ..." Miriam lets her voice trail away. Oh, boy! She's floating towards Niagara Falls. Better shut up. Even before she takes a job with her, they could end up in a fight.

"If I lose my temper, it's usually because of someone's stupidity." Ketzel's face is flushed, her voice rough. "Have you ever seen me lose my temper without a good reason?"

"No, no, not really," Miriam answers hastily. "Listen, Ketzel," she begins gently, "I'm glad you offered me a job. I know you want to make things easy for me and I love you, you're the kindest, most generous person I know."

Ketzel's quiet for a moment, then says slowly, "I love you too. I really don't mean to sound so impatient. Things haven't been so great lately." She stands, picking up the empty pitcher. "Okay. If and when you're ready, let me know. Only make it soon. I need help pronto."

You almost did it, Miriam tells herself. What makes you think that being honest is always a good idea?

As she leaves, she hears Luis and Ketzel, shouting, it's mostly Ketzel, poor Luis protests, sounding as if he's being attacked by a wasp. She walks to 110th Street, almost deciding to go into the Spanish movie house where they were playing a Dolores Del Rio film, but instead jumps on a double-decker bus that goes up Broadway.

She climbs the curving metal staircase, finding herself alone with thirty empty seats, in the open air. The bus continues up along Central Park where she sees the small dark green pond ruffled by a gentle breeze, hears the voices of children echoing in the dusk. The ride begins to calm her. It wasn't only the brief altercation with Ketzel that upset her—she hasn't felt easy for a long time—since the attack on Trotsky's house.

A few days later when she calls Ketzel, she hear her friend's voice, sweet and cool as a mountain stream.

"It's okay, Miriam. I understand, you were right. It wasn't a good idea. I've hired a girl, I'm lucky, she's very sweet and competent." Not like me, Miriam thinks. And she didn't wait long to get someone else.

"Look," Ketzel says, "Jaime'll be here a few days, his little boy needs a minor operation. The doctors say he'll be fine so we're not worried. Jaime says he'd like to see you. I'll let you know." Miriam's relieved and disturbed when she hangs up. Ketzel's sensible; she won't allow trivial incidents to interfere with their friendship. But seeing Jaime again? Almost a reflex, those familiar little birds fluttering about her heart.

Branch meetings go on as usual even though the heat and stuffiness in the headquarters are unbearable. The women make paper fans, everybody keeps drinking cold soda and lemonade. There are long-winded reports from various committees, including one on factory job availability throughout the country, and comrades are constantly encouraged to leave New York for jobs in industrial plants.

Sydney is doing his part in California, and Miriam feels proud. He's writes, urging her to come out to join him, though he mentions he's been to the movies with a girl from work. She supposes she really ought to make an effort to get into a factory but she knows she can't. She'd gone once to an automobile parts plant and that was enough. She liked the comraderie but the warm greasy air, the din, the reverberating echoes in ugly, metal cavernous drab buildings, the thundering noise of two-story machines, the pounding, had filled her with terror and nausea.

One night, she's standing in the back, impatient, ready to leave, the meeting droning on, Hilda, leading a pretty, blond girl, pounces on her.

"I want you to meet Katy," she says. "She's just here from the West Coast and wants to rent a room or share a place. I thought of you right away. You need someone, don't you?"

"I do, I sure do." Miriam, surprised and happy, grins at the chubby, brown-eyed girl with a boy's haircut and open plaid shirt and extends her hand.

As the three of them walk to the subway Hilda tells Miriam, "Sylvia's back in Mexico. She had to go down, Jacques called and asked her to. She hadn't heard from him for a month and almost went crazy. Boy!" Shaking her her head, she adds, "I really don't approve of that guy. I can't imagine what she sees in him."

When Miriam doesn't respond she goes on, "Listen to something funny. He's suspicious of her! Imagine! In Mexico, when she was there the last time, she woke up one night about three o'clock. He's at the table, going through her pocket-book! Says he's looking for matches. She uses a lighter and he knows that. Is it weird or what?"

Miriam nods but really isn't listening. Happy to get someone to share her expenses she's thinking about what she should charge.

"We'll split the expenses down the middle," she decides and asks Katy, who agrees.

"If it's okay with you?," Katy asks, "I'll move in on September 1st. My rent's paid up until then so I might as well stay where I am." She sounds like a pleasant person and Miriam's pleased. Now, I can manage on my salary, she tells herself, and carry a program at Hunter too. It seems too good to be true. She knows that just when she expects things to work out well they usually don't. Like in Buster Keaton movies. No wonder, he always has such a sad face. He walks along the street, happy, then accidentally steps on the end of a long plank that swings up and knocks him down. He just can't win, long face with doggy, pleading eyes always makes her want to cry.

Ketzel calls Miriam a week later. "Jaime's here, his baby's okay. They're keeping him in the hospital for a few days, just to make sure. Come for dinner. My new girl, Cara, cooks, I'm really happy with her."

"Don't think I can make tonight," Miriam tells her. "There's an important meeting," she tries to sound convincing.

"Look, Miriam," Ketzel's cajoling, impatient, "you haven't been around for a while and I know why. Forget all that about the job. Come tonight. Jaime can't stay long. He has to go back. It'll be great for all of us to be together."

Oh sure! thinks Miriam. But she'd better get it over with. When she arrives, she hears voices in Jaime's study and reluctantly climbs the stairs to his old room. The old victrola is grinding out 'The Barcarolle' and Ketzel is swaying and twirling to music that sounds likes lapping waves, her arms encircling her head. She looks like a great red-orange tulip, Miriam thinks, standing there watching her. At first she doesn't see Jaime who's sitting at his old desk that's been pushed into a corner. Then, she spies him and, in spite of all she knows, her heart skips a beat.

"Hello, Miriam," he says, waving, his voice impersonal.

"Hi. I think I'd better stay over here," she says 'I don't think I can get across right now." Attempting lightness, she says, "Can't disturb a private dance recital," and remains standing at the door.

He looks older and tired and by now, she thinks, he may have forgotten their affair. Was it just an encounter?—perhaps that's a better description. That night just hadn't meant as much to him. It was in this very room—she'd stood in the doorway, wearing only a loose blue terry bathrobe that somehow opened. She could still hear the old Spanish couplet he'd whispered after they'd made love. "Si duermo, sueno contigo/si despierto, pienso en ti." A bitter taste rises in her mouth, as if she'd bitten into the pit of a peach. It's over for him, it's been over a long time, so it's over, it has to be over for me too. The record ends and Ketzel drops into a chair.

"I'm glad to hear your baby's doing well," Miriam says, lifting up the needle of the wheezing phonograph and turning it off. Then she notices a handmade book covered with wallpaper and large pink cabbage roses that's lying on a set of 'Das Kapital.' Picking it up she asks, "What's this?"

Ketzel jumps up, grabs it from her hand. "Miriam, you have to hear this. It's my mother's diary. It's unbelievable! Remember once I told you my real name is Juana. I'm named after this Spanish nun, Sor Juana. a poet from way back—she defied the Church. Listen to this." She pulls Miriam down beside her. "June 6, 1914. I am in backyard under tree. Jaime made big breakfast. He says I must to eat everything and he will leave books for me when he go to work. I study every day. When I improve I will write poems for my husband, best man in world. I think God send Jaime to me. I love him very much. I want work but doctor say no, wait until baby come, rest, stay home. I hope we have girl. In three months, we no."

"What do you think of that?" Ketzel closes the book gently, "I knew that she had to learn English, she could hardly speak a word when she came to America! But I never knew she had to stop working so's she wouldn't lose the baby—me! You never told me, Daddy."

Jaime stands, with a faint smile, his pallor returning, he says "Ketzeleh, when you finally arrived we were so stunned by your beauty and strong lungs, I forgot about the wonderful time we had while we waited for you."

Miriam thinks You do have a short memory, don't you? But meanwhile Ketzel is saying "... really crazy about each other, weren't you? She was gorgeous and you looked like Ramon Navarro."

Jaime says seriously. "That's not why. She was beautiful but it was her inner beauty that I loved." He looks at the two girls, lingering on Miriam a second longer, "Like both of you."

On his desk is a large carton full of photographs. "Some day, we'll have to go through these," he says. "I'd like to find a special one, if possible, a favorite, one of you and your mother. Wait ... Here it is." He looks at it for a long moment before handing it to Ketzel. It's a photo of delicate woman under a tree holding a chubby, curly headed baby in a long flouncy dress.

"Oh, daddy, It's priceless. I'm so cute! I'm putting it on my dresser right now." She jumps off the trunk but Jaime is holding up another photograph, with his fingertips, as if it has a foul odor. "What about this one? Do you want it?," he asks. "Looks like a picture of Martin with Siqueiros and some others, your 'Rogues Gallery'. I think you sent it to me from Spain."

Ketzel takes it and nods, her mouth tight with disgust, "That's him and Siqueiros, Arenal, Vidali and Ramon Mercader. The whole gang. I don't want it anymore."

Miriam takes it from her. She recognizes Siqueiros, the famous artist, who looks ridiculous in a big cowby hat and a Pancho Villa mustache and from Ketzel's descriptions she can guess which one is Vidali, he's really gross. Martin, of course, she knows. And the other two ... one looks an awful lot like someone she's met. "Who is this one? she asks Ketzel.

"Ramon, Caridad's son."

"He looks so much like Sylvia's boyfriend. Does he have a brother?"

"Yes. a few. One, Pablo, got killed in Spain. He had a love affair with an anarchist girl and Mama didn't approve. They say she could have prevented him from going to that front, certain death. Supposed to be some strange circumstances about it." Ketzel stops abruptly. "I don't want to know anything about that family, ever, ever, again.To hell with all of them, especially my dear

Martin. They can roast in hell. I get sick when I talk about them." She snatches the photo from Miriam's hand, tears it in half and drops it on a pile of books to be thrown out. "Let's go get dinner."

She leads the way downstairs, Miriam following; Jaime lingers in the room. "Be down in a minute," he calls after them. In the kitchen Ketzel says, "He's probably rescuing momentos to take back to Mexico. My dad's a sentimental pussy-cat."

Is he? Is there anything in that room that reminds Jaime of her?, Miriam wonders. She has the letter he sent her (Or did she tear it up? She can't remember.) but she never gave him a present. The blue terrycloth bathrobe, where is it? Some keepsake! Maybe she should find it and mail it to him. What would his wife think if she opened the package. But she couldn't do a thing like that. He has a new family, another life in another country! It's over for him, it's been over a long time, so it's over, it has to be over for me. As Ketzel would say, 'stop sitting on that egg—it ain't gonna hatch.'

CHAPTER 26

August 4, 1940

Thick, clammy heat hangs like a dense curtain over the City. If she could only get away, breathe some cool air. Workmen's Circle Camp is supposed to be nice, but across the lake is Kinderland, a camp run by the C P where little kids run around singing songs about the Beloved Leader. She doesn't need that, for sure. And besides, money is a little tight.

She buys some peaches from a pushcart, warms up some stew and starts a new book, The Story of San Michele, about a mountain top in Italy and a weary doctor who finds peace there. It seems like a good escape from the war, greed and hunger for profit that are raging throughout the world and dreadful rumors of concentration camps that have been set up in Poland. But she soon tires of reading, slumps down on the sagging Morris chair in the living room and puts on the radio. Rudy Vallee's singing "Your Time is My Time" in a high nasal voice. It begins to annoy her and she makes herself get up and turn it off.

Just then the phone rings. It's Sydney. At least he trying to do his bit in California, she reminds herself, working in a factory and trying to do some organizing. She settles back to listen to a long, almost meaningless conversation that gets nowhere. He's lonely out in California but he'd be lonely anywhere. What's so funny is that he calls and then has hardly anything to say. He has so much sadness down deep inside him, roots of pain. But she can't help him, she couldn't when she was living with him and listening to him makes her feel even more tired. When she begins to tell him about herself, about what it's like for her, trying to live alone, he's not interested and says he has to get off the phone.

As she passes the round table in the living room she sees a letter from Sylvia, in Mexico, again. She pours a glass of cold seltzer (thanks to Mrs. Andino for taking care of the ice).

○⃛

Hotel Montejo, August 10, 1940

Dear Miriam,

I meant to call you all July but I didn't know what I was doing. After Ruth's wedding in June, I didn't hear from Jacques for a whole month. I was frantic. Finally, he called me, with apologies and begged me to come down here, so here I am, in Mexico, once again.

I've done a little secretarial work but mostly vacationing, taking it easy. Jacques and I were invited for tea, it was a very pleasant afternoon, the Old Man asked me a million questions about what's going on in the Party.

We expect to come home soon. I hope by that time you'll have a new boy-friend and we'll make it a foursome again. Maybe this time we'll catch Billie Holiday.

Love, Sylvia

Miriam leans back, amused. Fat chance, she'll have a new boy-friend. Not that she would mind. Meanwhile, she'd settle for a good dancing partner. She remembers she used to do a good Double Lindy, the bouncing rhythm always made her feel happy.

A few minutes later the phone rings. This time it's Ketzel. She has an appointment to see an orthopedist at Columbia Presbyterian Medical Center and asks Miriam to go with her the next day … please!

"I twisted my knee a month ago," she tells her. "I didn't want to tell anyone, I didn't want to worry you, but it hurts and it hasn't been getting better. This is my third visit." Ketzel's really worried, just stares grimly out of the taxi window as they drive up Amsterdam Avenue. Trying to make small talk as they pass the High Bridge Water Tower, built over a hundred years ago, Miriam says it looks like a medieval watch tower from Roman times. When Ketzel just grunts, Miriam adds "Edgar Allan Poe used to come here and walk across the aqueduct. I love the view," but Ketzel still refuses to be diverted.

The diagnosis is not favorable. Finally, after consultation with three doctors, it's a torn ligament, and she'll have to rest for at least six months. On the way home, Ketzel is morose, silent. Then, sarcastic, she says, "I have more good news. I was going to tell you before. My dear little protege, that is my former protege, Luis! Luis has found himself!"

"What do you mean?" Miriam's puzzled. "As a dancer?"

"No," Ketzel says impatiently. "He likes boys, or men, what have you. Maybe he didn't know this about himself. A few weeks ago Ken Dollar, in Sokolow's group, discovers him and it's 'love at first sight.' He's into this, head over heels! Moved out last week. I know he was lonesome and homesick but I felt I could always count on him … as a dancer, as a friend." Ketzel's voice is rising, she's almost screeching now. She's pale, swallowing hard, then without warning, bursts into deep sobs. "I'm disappointed—disgusted, is more like it. Everything seems to be going wrong."

"Ketzel, I had no idea." Miriam puts her arm around her, "I thought things were pretty good. It's been harder for you than I realized." She tries to hold her but Ketzel moves away, still crying, her thin shoulders shaking.

Finally, quiet, Ketzel says in a subdued voice, "Sorry for the outburst. Poor Miriam, I don't have to burden you."

"Cut it out. That's what I'm here for. And listen, having to rest your leg for six months isn't the worst sentence in the world."

"Miriam, you don't get it. I've been lonely and depressed and there's so much to do. The apartment, ours, Martin's and mine, in Mexico City, it's empty, sitting there with all my stuff. I was planning to go back, close up the place." She stops to take a deep breath, shakes her head. "Luis was coming back with me. He's flown the coop—out of the picture."

"Look, it'll straighten out." Miriam hugs her, determined to get her out of this hopeless mood. "You'll see." But she knows that things aren't solved that easily. She doesn't hear from Ketzel for a few days, hoping that her dark mood will lighten. Then, one afternoon, she get a call. Ketzel tells her Luis has just called to tell her how happy he is, how sorry he's caused her so *much dolor*. She manages a laugh. "I just hope the poor kid doesn't get hurt too badly. Ken Dollar is a fickle bastard and Luis will probably be crawling back one of these days. Meanwhile, though," she goes on, her voice sweet, persuasive, "I've been thinking and I've had a wonderful idea. I told you I had to go back to Mexico, stuff to be taken care of. I don't want to go by myself—honestly, I don't think I can. I've got two plane reservations, had them for a while." Ketzel hesitates, as if almost afraid to ask—unusual for Ketzel, Miriam observes. "Come with me—it'll only be for a week. We'll get to the beach after we take care of my stuff, mornings at Caleta, afternoons at Ornos, frozen Margaritas, dancing at night—at least you'll dance. What do you say? We could have a good time!"

Miriam's taken aback. *What about my job?* But it's been slow at the Social Credit office, they won't mind if she takes off a week, she's got enough money saved for the rent for a little while. College is closed. Getting out of this furnace for a week—it could be wonderful!

"Okay," she says, "It sounds great! When do we leave?" When Ketzel squeals with delight, Miriam realizes how lonely her friend is. *Well, why not? Why should she be different from ordinary people?*

Miriam's been putting off calling her mother, hasn't spoken to her in a few weeks. The last time she called Clara ended the conversation by saying sarcastically, "I was lucky to have children" with that bitter bark of a laugh Miriam always dreaded. Now the trip gives her a pretext to phone. At first, Clara says it's a lot of foolishness but after Miriam tells her about Ketzel being so upset, her failed marriage, her bad knee, her mother says, "Go, keep her company. A shonda ze hut so fiel tsouris" and Miriam recalls how fond her mother became of Ketzel, how they talked and sewed together under the lamplight in the kitchen."

Mexico City, August 17 7 AM

After they pack up and close Ketzel's apartment, she and Miriam deposit their suitcases in the Hotel Lincoln on Avenida Revillagigedo and flee to Acapulco, where they spend four heavenly days, swimming, watching sleek young bodies diving from high cliffs, sunning, eating, nightclubbing, although Miriam feels a little guilty when she leaves Ketzel sitting at the bar while she enjoys a rhumba with another tourist.

Nothing's changed on Avenida Revillagigedo where loud clatter and chatter in the halls wake everyone up at 6 o'clock in the morning. Now, feeling wonderful, sunburned, healthy, her skin salty, shining with coconut oil, she stretches, and plans the next three days. She hopes the Old Man will let her visit again, she hopes, she'll see Natalya to give her the folding umbrella she'd brought her as a gift, have lunch with Sylvia, go to the Anthropological Museum and do a little shopping. Ketzel's busy, wrapping up old business, meeting with people from Bellas Artes and making plans for the future.

When she calls the house on Avenida Viena, Joe Hansen, Trotsky's secretary, answers. Joe's a young, round-faced, sharp young man, a good writer. He remembers her from Party meetings back home. "The Old Man will be glad to see you," he says, "L. D. is very busy these days." He sees few visitors although two days ago he allowed Sylvia's husband, Jacson to visit. However, if Miriam can make it, she can come for tea today.

Avenida Viena is very close to Frida's Blue House. The Trotsky's now occupy a one-story Florentine type house, which is at the end of a street and a dried-up river bed. It's a mostly deserted area except for a few poor shacks nearby and the police guard house. The house is surrounded by twenty foot walls, heavy steel doors and bullet-proof towers which pierce the sky, and although the road is lined with tall eucalyptus and pink bougainvillea, it is also deeply shaded. The air is mild but a chill touches Miriam as she follows the dark path to the house.

Joe answers quickly when she rings the outside bell. "You're early, we'll have to wait," he says, and as they sit in the patio he plies her with questions about what's going on in New York. "Working here" he tells her "is great, and sad, too. Trotsky can be strange. At times he'll walk in the patio and talk to Bukharin or Kamenev and Zinoviev, and it sounds as if he's scolding them for their mistakes. He hates having so many guards, it's like a medieval prison for him. 'Precautions are useless,' he'll say. 'A G P U agent, passing himself off as my friend, could assassinate me in my own home …'

He looks at his watch, then leads her to the dining room. On their way they meet Melquiades and and as Miriam takes his hand, he blushes, his olive skin deepens. Mel's been working very hard since the Siquieros raid, Hanson tells her. "Mel takes the raid on the Old Man almost personally, as if Mexican honor has been defiled. It's foolish of course, Stalininsts are everywhere, here and abroad."

It's almost five o'clock and Natalya has begun to pour tea when Trotsky comes in, briskly attractive, his white bushy hair contrasting with the vivid blue blouse he's wearing. He's late, apologizes for it and gives Miriam a welcoming hug. Of course, he wants to know the latest news and after she repeats what she's told Joe she sees sadness and disappointment in his eyes, he's very unhappy about the split in the Party.

After a while the Old Man must get back to his rabbits and as Miriam walks with him, she tells him she's rereading his autobiography, "*My Life*." "It's a wonderful book" she says and he smiles and asks which part interested her.

"I loved in the beginning, when you describe the reapers on your farm, sleeping in open fields, under haystacks, with only porridge or vegetable soup for food. They'd get so desperate, they'd lie down in the shade of the barns and wave their bare cracked, bony feet in the air … and one summer when they all got night-blindness, they groped around the yard, stretching their arms in front of them—I can't forget that story."

The Old Man nods, but when she goes on to say "I really would have liked to know more about the days when you and Natalya first met," Trotsky moves away, ending the conversation. Miriam's disappointed. She'd hoped he'd tell her about those early exciting days, when they'd met and fallen deeply in love. But just as he'd never written about them, he couldn't or wouldn't ever talk about them.

Coyoacan, Mexico, Tuesday, August 20th 7:30 AM

Peace and serenity prevails in the house on Avenida Viena this morning. The high walls capped with broken glass that glitter in the headlights fail to depress the Old Man. Although it is the rainy season and dark clouds hang over Popocatepetl and Iztaccihuatl, the dazzling sunlight is like sweet white wine, the sky a canopy of gentian glue. He feels strong and confident this morning and as he throws open the steel shutters he tells Natalya, "Well, now, no Siqueiros can get us."

He's had a sound night's sleep and he tells Natalya it's a long time since he's felt so well. He's looking forward to a 'really good day's work.' and hurries to feed his rabbits, saying he'll get back to work on my 'poor book, Stalin,' which he put it aside after the May raid to give time to the police investigation. But before that he wants to write an important article for a little Trotskyist periodical. In his weekly mail, the librarian of Harvard University acknowledges the receipt of his archives, and pleased with this news he writes a few warm and jovial letters to American Trotskyists. He steps out of his study for a few moments into the bright sun and Natalya quickly brings him his white cap.

He finds he will have to postpone, once again, his article on "revolutionary defeatism." His Mexican attorney, Rigault, has advised him to reply at once to an attack in "El Popular" which is accusing him of defaming Mexican trade unions. "I will take the offensive and charge them with brazen slander" he tells Natalya at lunchtime.

He has dictated fifty short pages of Stalin's machinations, and shutting his machine he writes, "One more and final story and my scroll is at an end," a quote from Pushkin's drama Boris Gudenov.

"Tochka!"

CHAPTER 27

Mexico City, Tuesday, August 20 12:30 PM

Sylvia's waiting in the Montejo lobby and Miriam is dismayed when she spots her. Although Sylvia's smile is bright, it's forced; she's lost weight, her light sweater swings loosely about her thin shoulders. "Funny meeting here, I didn't expect to be here again," Miriam says, "We'll both be back in New York next week."

"I can't wait," Sylvia answers vehemently. Then she adds, "I don't know what's the matter with me." But Miriam can guess. Sure enough, as Sylvia just nibbles at her chicken sandwich, Miriam hears a familiar story. Jacques' health is poor, he's irritable, he's unfriendly to other guests in the hotel, they have to eat by themselves in the garden, he goes away for several hours. "But, I must tell you," Sylvia says hopefully, "he seems more interested in politics lately. He's writing an article and the Old Man said he'd look it over, give him some advice. When we were at tea, a few weeks ago, the Old Man was in a very affable mood, asking me a million questions about the Party. Imagine my surprise when Jacques said, 'I agree with what Jim Cannon says about Shachtman,' taking the Old Man's side against me. And the Old Man was pleased to hear it too."

Miriam thinks about her own recent conversation with Trotsky. Jacques obviously makes better impressions on people than she does.

"In any case, after that horrible raid I know Jacques is worried about what might happen to the Old Man in the future," Sylvia continues. "He told the guards that he thinks the G P U will use some other methods the next time but when Jake asked him what those methods might be, he didn't know, of course. How could he?"

"Of course," Miriam answers. "We all worry, we worry all the time," she says. Then, putting down her empty cup, she asks, "Tell me, do you think you might get married one of these days?"

Sylvia nods. "I hope so. He's really tender and thoughtful and he trusts me. Do you know, he's even given me money to hold for him." With a sigh, she adds, "He'll be different, less tense and moody once we're back in the States."

They walk to the Palacio de Bellas Artes, where Jacques is already waiting. When Miriam sees Jacques she's not surprised; his face is grim and set, his smile forced. Making conversation is difficult. Miriam fills the silences by enthusing about going to see the Rivera frescoes and visiting the Anthropological Museum, but when Sylvia suggests meeting for dinner later, Miriam's not very enthusiastic. Whatever's going on with this couple, they are not great company. Just then they hear someone calling Sylvia's name.

"Hey, glad I caught you." Crossing the avenue is Oscar Schuessler, one of Trotsky's guards, off duty for the day. He's accompanied by a pretty young woman and after he introduces his fiancee, Sylvia suggests they all have dinner together. Oscar and his girl are delighted. They discuss the various merits of El Bistro, Chalet Suiza and the Luau, everyone deciding on the Luau, everyone but Jacques, whom Miriam notices, says nothing. Apparently where and what he eats doesn't matter to him.

Before the group splits up, Jacques' says he's going to Wells Fargo to collect his mail. "I'll be back at the hotel at four-thirty to pick you up," he tells Sylvia. "We're going to the Trotsky's this afternoon to say good-bye. We'll see you at the Luau seven-thirty tonight," he tells the others. He's wearing a hat and he tips it as he walks away.

Coyoacan, Mexico, August 20, 5:00 PM

In the afternoon, after a brief siesta, Trotsky is again at his desk, but at five o'clock returns to the rabbit hutches on the patio—it is their feeding time.

Natalya, looking down from the balcony, is startled to see an unfamiliar figure standing next to L D but then she recognizes Jacson. Hansen, on the roof working with Cornell and Benitez connecting the alarm system, has seen him parking and instructed Cornell to press the electric switch. As he enters Jacson asks Hansen if Sylvia has arrived yet. Hansen is surprised, he has no knowledge of this, but the Old Man often forgets to tell his guards about such things.

For just a moment Natalya feels frightened but after a moment, relieved. He had been helpful with the Rosmers, bringing gifts for Seva and chocolates. Lately, he's come more often. Why? And why is he carrying a raincoat and wearing a hat today? He had boasted of going without a hat or coat, no matter what the weather.

Going down to greet him, she sees he doesn't appear well, his face dark, green-ish-gray, and he walks in a jerky manner, holding his overcoat against his body.

After she asks him if he feels well, he says, "I'm awfully thirsty. Could I have a glass of water?"

"How about some tea?"

"No, no. I dined late and I feel as if the food is up here," he answers, pointing to his throat. He seems nervous. "It's choking me," he adds.

Seeing some pages in his hand, she asks if this is the article he showed her husband and if it is typewritten. "Oh, yes, yes," he answers. They walk towards Trotsky working at the hutches, and he takes out a few sheets from his jacket to show her while still pressing the raincoat close to his body.

"Jacson is expecting Sylvia to call on us this evening," Trotsky says as the three stand together in the patio. "They're leaving tomorrow. Perhaps we should invite them for tea or dinner," but Natalya tells him that Jacson has already refused. The Old Man looks at Jacson, "Your health is poor again," he says. "You look ill ... that is not good. What do you say, shall we go over your article?"

Jacson had shown him the outline of the article he wanted to write two days ago. It was little more than "a few phrases—muddled stuff," but Trotsky made suggestions and hopes the finished article will show improvement. He fastens the hutches and removes his gloves. Brushing off his blue blouse he slowly, silently walks to his study with Jacson. As they enter and closes the door behind his visitor, the thought suddenly comes to him: "This man could kill me."

Coyoacan, August 20 5:38 PM

Holding the sheaf of papers Jacson gave him Trotsky sits down at his table, piled up with books and magazines. Besides the ediphone, within reach, is a .25 caliber automatic, reloaded and oiled, also a .25 Colt automatic, and next to it a switch that turns on the alarm system.

Jacson waits patiently while the Old Man pulls his chair close to the desk and sits. Jacson puts his raincoat on the table. Trotsky picks up the article. Hummingbirds chirp softly in the patio, the room is quiet. Trotsky, head bent over the manuscript, is reading ...

NOW!

Jacson takes the piolet from the raincoat—holds it in his fist ... closes his eyes, raises the ice-pick high—with all his might—swings it down on Trotsky's head—splitting his skull.

AHHHHH!

Trotsky shrieks—howling—blood-curdling—raging insanely—pulls himself up with madman's strength—throws himself at Jacson—bites his hand.

Hansen rushes from the guardhouse—through the window he sees the familiar blue jacket, wrestling with another man.

Jacson pushes Trotsky down. The Old Man falls—lifts himself up—stumbles from the room.

Hansen rushes into the library—Trotsky—blood streaming from his face—stumbling—yelling, "See what they have done to me"—*leans against the door. Another guard runs in and corners Jacson. Natalya comes and throws her arms about Trotsky.*

"Jacson," *Trotsky says, as if he wants to say,* "It has happened." *He falls to the floor.—rises, Natalya helps him.* "See what they have done" *she cries. Trotsky staggers to the dining room—collapses near the table.*

Hansen bends over to hear his voice. "Jacson shot me with a revolver," *his voice is low.* "I am seriously wounded ... This time it is the end."

"It's only a surface wound. You'll recover," *Hansen reassures him.* "No, he didn't shoot you. He struck you with something."

Trotsky presses Hansen's hand. Natalya puts a pillow under his bleeding head. Hansen presses ice on his wound, wipes away the blood. Trotsky kisses his wife's hand again and again.

"Natasha, I love you ... Oh. no one must be allowed to see you without being searched," *he says.* "Seva must be taken away from all this ... You know, in there. I sensed … understood what he wanted to do. He wanted to strike me … once more …," with satisfaction, he adds "… I didn't let him."

Cornell rushes into the study. Natalya asks Trotsky, "What about that one … Jacson. They will kill him."

"No," he answers slowly, "He must be made to talk."

Robins and Hansen beat Jacson savagely. They want to kill him—they must not—he must be made to talk, the Old Man orders. Jacson is screaming, "They have imprisoned my mother! Sylvia had nothing to do with this!" As the beating goes on Jacson fades and out of consciousness—whining pathetically.

Police everywhere, ambulance—the local doctor arrives, examines the broken skull "the wound not dangerous," Trotsky points to his heart, "I feel it here … This time they have succeeded."

The ambulance roars through the City, crowds have gathered everywhere, the streets are crowded, sirens blasting—through the blazing evening lights—the wounded man holds his wife's hand. Trotsky lies quietly, conscious, one side of his body, his hand and leg paralyzed. Natalya bends over him, "How do you feel?" "Better now," he answers, making her heart quicken with hope.

In the hospital the sisters shave his head and he smiles at Natalya saying "See, we have found a barber" trying to lighten Natalya's fears, reminding her how only this morning they had talked about calling a barber to give him a haircut. They begin to undress him, cutting away his clothing but he says, "I don't want you to undress me." and turns to Natalya, "I want you to do it."

His voice is serious and sad, these are the last words he will say to his wife. She bends over and touches his lips with hers. He answers her—over and over—again and again.

Mexico City, August 20 5:40 p.m.

Miriam can't take another step. She'd begun her jaunt at Chapultepec Castle, with its romantic, shaded walks named Poetas and Artistas, ending at the Rivera frescoes of sea life and sirens. Then she'd gone on to visit the great Museum with its wide marble entrance, high ceiling, magnificent lobby and endless rooms; three miles of centuries of statues, folk art, jewelry and weapons. Now, resting with a cold Agua de Mamey, she calls it a day.

She phones Ketzel who says she's tired, not interested in joining them but for god's sake, call Sylvia! "She's called twice, sounds anxious and upset. Jacques hasn't shown up and she doesn't know where he is."

"I hope there's no mix-up," Miriam sighs, hangs up, and calls Sylvia. "I'll be at your hotel in a few minutes. Don't worry, there must be some confusion."

A cab quickly takes her to the Montejo, where she finds Sylvia, distraught, almost in tears, waiting in the lobby. Her blond hair was nicely set a few hours ago but now it's dishevelled and her dress is stained wih fruit juice. "No, he isn't here yet. He was supposed to pick me up almost two hours ago! I've checked with Miss Noriega, the manager, twice already but there's no message."

"Let's have some tea in the patio and relax," Miriam says. They sit down and she tries to stay awake while Sylvia continues to fret and worry. When the clock shows after seven, Miriam says, "We'd better go to the Luau. Oscar and Betty won't know what's happened and Jacques'll probably show up there."

Oscar and his girl are there but no Jacques. They have a drink, wait a while longer. At eight o'clock, Oscar says, "I'm going to call the house. They might have heard something."

"No," Sylvia objects, stubborn. "Jacques couldn't have gone there. He never goes there without me."

The three women standing in the lobby hear Oscar cry out, then hang up the receiver. Pale, trembling, he tells them. "We must go there immediatly. Jacson has attacked Trotsky."

Oscar races to find a taxi, it's the fashionable dinner hour and it's difficult. They scramble in, everyone silent, numb, shaken. Then Sylvia bursts forth angrily, but white with fear, "You must be wrong, Oscar. You must have heard wrong."

Oscar is furious. "I know what I heard—the Old Man is wounded … he may die … Jacson hit him in the head with an ice-pick."

"I can't believe it—it's not true," she insists but Oscar turns away, his face sick. Miriam wants to say it must be true but she says nothing, she can't speak. *At last—it's happened—at last! We've been afraid for so long and now it's come—the evil men!—the assassins! That photo, is he one of Mercader's sons? It is possible. They've finally reached him—the Old Man, the great man, the good man, the man who struggled for socialism all his life.*

"It's not Jacques. It can't be Jacques." Sylvia's moaning now, unable to sit quietly, twisting, tearing her handkerchief.

"Why doesn't she shut up?," anger rises in Miriam's throat. Of course Sylvia feels guilty. She introduced Jacques to the Old Man, she let herself be fooled—love and kisses, expensive restaurants, boat rides on the Seine, the Tuilerie Gardens, oysters at Pruniers. Don't blame her too much, Miriam cautions herself. *Would I have fallen for the same tricks? Aren't we all little girls wanting to be romanced?*

They are on Insurgentes South, crowded with cars and trolleys, the driver of their taxi pounding his horn. Miriam sees the Old Man, in pain, precious life blood pouring from him. Bitter saliva flooding into her mouth, she wants to throw up. Just this afternoon, not far from this street, she walked in Chapultepec Park, taking in the sights, peaceful, happy. "Oh, he mustn't die, don't let it happen," she keeps saying to herself. Haven't he and Natalya suffered enough? Will Stalin, that evil man in the Kremlin, have another sweet dream tonight? Didn't he tell Buchharin that he has the sweetest dream—the night after he kills an enemy? Did he sleep well after Sevya died in agony, in the hospital, after eating a poisoned orange? She remembers Lermontov, a great Russian poet, prophetically wrote a few years before:

> *Wherefore a nacked blade is in his hand*
> *Bitter will be thy lot, tears flood thine eyes*
> *And he will laugh at all thy tears and sighs.*

They pass Pepe's Restaurant, the glare of its big Coco-Cola sign pouring into her eyes makes her dizzy. When she opens them, she sees they're very close now to Avenida Viena and Kahlo's Blue House. The cab speeds up to the end of the usually deserted Avenida Viena, now crowded with the curious who peer through the open steel gates of the fortress house where two police are standing guard. As they enter light streams from every room of the silent house.

Suddenly—screaming, "Where is Jacques—let me see that villain," Sylvia pushes past the cops, racing through the patio.

Miriam chases her, yelling, "What in hell do you think you're doing?"

They pull up, stop, at the door of the study, aghast at the sight before them. The empty room is a horrible mess; the dictation machine smashed on the floor, lamps, books and papers scattered everywhere—in front of Trotsky's desk—a bloodied pick-axe.

Miriam is angrily asking Sylvia, "What in hell makes you think Jacques is still here?" when two furious police descend on them, leading them, not very gently, to the dining room where General Nunez, head of Police, is waiting. After looking at the three women and their tired, distraught faces, he tells them to sit down and rest a few moments.

"Which one of you is Sylvia?" he asks. He looks at her and nods. "We must hold you for questioning. Jacson has been arrested. Trotsky is in the Green Cross Hospital, the Guards are at Police Headquarters. When you are calmed down, we are taking everyone there."

Miriam looks Sylvia's face. The full realization of what has happened begins to overcome her. She is agonized. Miriam, her arm about her, tries to calm her but, of course, it is useless. As they drive to the Police station, she keeps repeating—"It can't be. I can't believe it.." She sobs, her shoulders shaking, tears streaking her face, shrinking in a corner of the car, like a little old woman rocking back and forth. "His name is not Jacson. He's using a false passport. His name is Jacques Mornard," Her voice rises in a piercing wail—"He fooled me! He fooled everybody, the Rosmers, all of us. He's a murderer, a canaille."

Then, at headquarters, she's almost crazy, shouting over and over, "Arrest him! He is a G P U agent—he made love to me to kill Trotsky. He should be killed!"

They are taken to Colonel Salazar, a round-faced Hispanic, with kind intelligent eyes, who is well acquainted with the Trotskys. He sees before him Sylvia Ageloff, an hysterical but harmless woman, probably not guilty of any misdeeds but sorely in need of medical attention, and orders her sent upstairs to the Green Cross Hospital, located above, in the same building. When they put her in a room and summon a doctor, almost out of her mind she's still continues, crying, "'Kill him—he is a monster. I want him to die."

Miriam sits, waiting to be questioned. in a large room of the station which is in a fairly modern building. It's pretty much the same as a police detention room anywhere, dusty, stuffy, faintly tinged with the acrid odor of urine—here, in Mexico the ever-present nutty sharp smell of charcoal and roasting corn. She'd seen the inside of a police station only once before, in the House of Detention for Women, in Greenwich Village, a Victorian Gothic building with weird turrets and carved stone. That was when her mother got arrested one cold winter night, when she lost her temper in court and told the judge to kiss her ass.

Terribly thirsty, but afraid to ask for some water, and dizzy with a splitting headache, she tries to converse with a Indian couple and their baby huddled on the wooden benches. They'd come down from the hills to sell woven mats and stationed themselves in front of a large store whose owner had called the police. The small woman, tears streaming down her dusky face, creeps into a dark corner to nurse her tiny infant. They're tired, frightened and hungry, and Miriam, reaching into her purse, gives the husband all her pesos, reserving a few for a taxi.

After an hour's delay, they tell her she can go, she will be called again for questioning. As she stands outside the hospital, waiting she sways, faint, almost falling. *All three are here now, upstairs,* she thinks, *Sylvia, Jacques and Trotsky.* Two will live—an assassin and a gullible woman! One can die! A ghastly joke! Over and over to herself, she prays, *Oh whatever fates there be, let the Old Man live, let him make it, let him live.* Two interns standing nearby, smoking, talking about the famous patient, glance over at her curiously.

"It's a very deep wound..," one of them is saying. She wants to hear more but just as she makes a few steps in their direction, Ketzel's stepping out of a cab."

"Okay, Miriam, you've had it today," she says, putting her arm around her, pushing her into the taxi, "Let's go home."

❦   ❦   ❦

Mexico City, August 21, 1940

Leon Trotsky dies one day after the attack. His body is taken to a parlor in the Calle de Tacuba. The next day the funeral courtege threads through the streets of Mexico City to the Pantheon where he will lie in state for five days.

Before the procession from the funeral home begins, Natalya, tremulous, veiled in black, enters the room and stands beside the casket of her husband. Everyone leaves so she can be alone with her husband for the last time. She bends over, her small head close to his and remains still for a long time. Then, at last, she opens the door—a huge cry spontaneously arises—

Trotsky lives! Viva Trotsky!—Death to Stalin!

Trotsky's casket, covered with a red flag and flowers leads the procession. Behind walk Joe Hansen, Oscar and the other guards, members of

Trotsky's household and various dignitaries. A huge crowd, heads bare with respect, follows behind.

❦   ❦   ❦

Miriam walks far behind the procession with the people. She prefers to be alone, although there are many Trotskyists and familiar comrades in the precession. Mel is with the other guards directly behind the bier and she wants to say good-bye to him later.

She wants to be with the indians, the mestizos in soiled overalls, in huaraches or barefoot, the mothers with babies, the campesinos in white shirts and sarapes, the students. These people know Trotsky although they have not met him. They know his story, because Mexico's past is full of revolutionary martyrs. Trotsky is the brave revolutionist who fought for the dispossessed, the oppressed. They know him as a man with simple tastes who gathered cactus in the countryside and tended rabbits in his garden. They have heard he was a world-famous leader, a great orator, a fine writer, who fought for truth and humanity with his pen and they know that although he made errors in his lifetime, he never swerved in his fight for truth, for humanity, for socialism and for that, he was killed.

As she walks slowly through streets lined with dilapitated Colonial style homes, narrow ones like medieval passages, slums, then wealthy neighborhoods with apartment buildings and beautiful parks she thinks of the Old Man—his courage, a fighter to the end. For more than thirteen years, homeless, hounded by the Gestapo, shunted from country to country, his comrades murdered, his close friends defected, his family decimated. Yet he never gave up. Does she have his strong will, that defiance, that anger? To fight against all odds. It take courage, guts! Does she have it? *Am I really a revolutionist?* Is she a kidding herself, playing a role. Does she have the right stuff to keep on fighting in a capitalist country, to make sacrifices, giving up comforts, devoting herself to the movement, a movement that, for the present, seems hopeless? Is she kidding herself, playing a role? How dedicated is she to keep on going, against terrible odds?

When they reach the Pantheon, his final resting place, Albert Goldman, the lawyer at the Dewey hearings, Garcia Trevino, a well-known socialist and anti-Stalinist, and Grandizo Munis, who fought in Spain, all pay tribute. The cere-

mony ends with Trotsky's words 'Estoy seguro de la victoria de la Cuarta Internacional. Adelante.'

Along the way the people have been singing Gran Corridos—original ballads written on slips of colored paper, telling the story of vile Stalin who murdered Trotsky, the great revolutionist.

> *"Stalin and the assassin*
> *in frank cooperation*
> *carried their crime with precision*
> *to its final destination*
> *Expelled from his country*
> *he wandered through many nations*
> *always fighting bitterly*
> *to combat oppression."*

The emotional songs, sung with such spirit, pull at Miriam's heart and yet lift her mood. She tells herself you can't give in to despair. That's easy. Going on—isn't. But that's the way it must be.

Miriam waits until the crowds disperse, but she can't find Mel and decides he must be with Joe and Oscar. She and Ketzel are flying next morning, there's a lot to do. At ten o'clock she slips out, "I could use a drink," she says.

Mel's waiting there—at the statue of Juarez. He got her message. *My last night in Mexico,* Miriam thinks. *I'll miss the soft air and the magic of bougainvillea, the darkness hiding the sadness and poverty.* As she approaches Mel his eyes smile.

They sit on a stone bench and talk, only a little, both worn from the emotional day, from the day's long walk. She knows it's the last time they'll be together. From his pocket he takes a fine silver chain and fastens it around her neck, and when she whispers, "Estoy triste, llevo nada para ti," he laughs and embraces her.

When they linger at the door Mel asks, if she would think of coming back. Perhaps if she stays, they could marry? She doesn't hesitate, shaking her head in a tender, regretful motion. She feels like crying, there's so much she'd like to tell him, but it'd be hard enough even in her own language.

She wants to tell him that her life is in New York, she'd find it too hard to live anywhere else; that she couldn't make it here and she can't face living in poverty, that he should look after Natalya, see that she isn't too lonely these days, help her in any way that he can.

Most important, she wants to tell him to watch out for himself, to be careful, it's dangerous, the Stalinists are so aggressive and powerful here. But all she can say is "cuidate, cuidate, mi amor," and hold him close.

Near the corner, moving with his easy Indian grace, he turns to wave and look at her one more time. Her fingers reach up, touch the silver chain, then her lips and he smiles and waves good-bye.

CHAPTER 28

New York City, August 31, 1940

In New York, a few days later, a Memorial meeting at the Hotel Diplomat on West 43rd street takes place. Cannon, Farrell Dobbs, Edith Konikow from Boston speak to an overflowing audience and listen to the last recorded speech of Trotsky. American Party members had requested that his body be brought to the States so that they could have a funeral service in New York but permission was not granted.

Miriam sits in the rear of the hall, purposely avoiding meeting the comrades who are still sad, shocked and angry but have realistically accepted the awful deed and its consequences. A few of them have even gone swimming that afternoon and sitting next to them in the stuffy room the salty ozone of sand and sun drifts to her nostrils.

It's taken all her will-power to be there this evening, she's still dazed and numb. When she and Ketzel returned from Mexico she didn't do much, just hung around, doing a few chores, finding it hard to get back into the normal routine. She didn't realize she looked so glum until one morning Ketzel told her "It's awful kiddo. But you've got to snap out of it—call the office, go back to work."

Ketzel was right, of course. Day by day Miriam found herself somehow, slipping back into the usual routine, work, school, meetings.

One night, climbing the stairs at 116 University Place, she's still a member of the S W P, Cannon's group, she runs into Franky. His face lights up when he sees her. He's nicely dressed for his job, big, attractive with even fleshy features; he looks like what he's aiming for now, to become a successful insurance salesman. Smiling down at her somber face, he pats her cheek. "Cheer-up, honey. Why the gloom? Let's go some place and talk for a few minutes."

They go to a small coffeepot down the street, avoiding the Crusader Cafeteria where they're sure to bump into other comrades. They talk about the Old Man's horrible death and he shrugs his shoulders, spreading his large hands in a familiar gesture. "You poor kid," he says. "But that's that. You know, in a way, maybe, it's good it's over."

"How can you say that, Franky?," Miriam's sharp, flushing, "he was only sixty years old, it was too early for him to die."

Franky shakes his head. "That's my fatalistic blood talking. For us Italians it's a way of life. You know Carlo Tresca—one helluva great guy—anarchist—always speaks his mind. Comes out with the truth, every time. Everybody loves him—you must've seen him, walking around Union Square with that bandana and black hat. Colorful guy! Sooner or later, the Stalinists are gonna get him—he know it too. You don't win in politics—any kind ..." Jumping up, he says, "Look, I won't be around here much longer. I just came up to see some of the old comrades. I'm dropping out." He hesitates then asks, with a grin, "How about going with me to the race track sometime?"

When they reach corner, he hugs her. "Call me, let me buy you a steak!" As she shakes her head, the lift she'd felt when they first met this morning has begun to disappear. *"I won't be seeing much of him from now on,* she tells herself. *He's already thinking and living a different life, he's become a bourgeois.*

Remembering she has an appointment with Hilda, she makes her way over to 114 West 14th Street. The minority, the Burnham-Shachtman-Abern group, suspended in April by the National Committee and offically expelled in September, now have heaquarters there. Although sympathetic to Shachtman position, she hasn't been able to leave the majority. She thinks the same as the minority, that the Soviet Union is no longer a worker's state, but she decides to remain in the Cannon group. She's deeply distressed about the schism. *We were small enough, the entire Socialist Workers Party, with just a little more than two thousand members a few years ago, she mourns, when we had all those successes in Minneapolis and the labor movement. Now, with this split and two small groups, with the impending war, what we will be able to accomplish? She know how deeply the Old Man felt about it—and how desperately he tried to keep it from happening!*

When she enters the headquarters, Hilda comes flying over to her. Pale, her eyes deeply circled, "I've been waiting for you," she says. "I'm having a hard time. Some of the comrades are criticizing Sylvia and blaming her, even though they've been told over and over she had no inkling about Jacques."

"Hilda, listen. It's only natural, people talk." Miriam presses her hand. "Jacques fooled a lot of people, Sylvia wasn't the only one. Sure, everyone, you, me, especially Sylvia, should have been more suspicious. We were just too innocent. Wanting to believe everyone is good. Politics is a deadly game—and not for babes in the woods like us. We …"

Hilda trying not to cry, interrupts. "Let's go out into the hall. I can't talk here." As they stand close together in the tiny, dingy space near the stairs, she whispers, "My brother, Monte, just got to Mexico a couple of hours ago." Hilda's sobbing now and Miriam hugs her, feeling helpless.

When she finally stops, the rest comes gushing out. "He told me that this Colonel Salazar, the Police Chief, was trying to get more out of Monard so he had him brought into Sylvia's room at the hospital. When Jacques saw her he got crazy, yelling at the cop, 'What are you doing? Take me out of here.' Sylvia went beserk—started to yell, 'Take that murderer away. Get him out of here. Kill him.' But Salazar made him stay, still hoping he'd confess. Sylvia just kept screaming at him, 'Don't lie, traitor. Tell the truth even if you pay with your life.' Finally, they had to give up and take Jacques away."

Miriam's silent. All she can do is put her arms around Hilda. Sylvia! Poor Sylvia. Her life from now on, until the day she dies, will be blighted with the memory of the ghastly murder and her role in it although, everyone realizes, she was completely innocent.

❀   ❀   ❀

Life goes on but Miriam feels like she's going through the motions. Since returning from Mexico she'd developed some bad habits. When she'd come home she'd sit for a long time, the dark closing in on her, soiled dishes from last night's supper still piled in the sink. Faint rays from the lamp post would creep into the room, Mother Jones would be dozing in the rocker, the curtains swaying in a faint breeze and she'd curl up on the sofa and fall asleep.

She hasn't called her mother for a few weeks. She'd lost her patience with her, at least for a while and didn't want to be embarrassed again, at least not so soon. The last time she'd seen her she'd taken her to a movie. Right in the middle of "You Can't Take It with You," Clara decided she'd had enough. She stood up, faced the audience, announced, "Gonza mishuginah! Ich gey ahaim," and squeezed her way out, disturbing fifteen annoyed movie-goers.

Tonight, her mood is lighter, for the first time in several weeks. Ketzel called, her voice bright. "Listen, kiddo, got some great news. Let's meet for lunch." Her friend's face made Miriam feel cheerful and she had lots of good news. "Number one," she says, "Luis is back, humble, contrite. Number two, Jaime's coming to New York. I always feel good when my father's here," she tells Miriam. *Me too,* Miriam thinks. In spite of everything that's happened she can't help the tiny thrill that runs though her when she hears his name.

They arrange for Miriam to come for lunch when Jaime arrives. After she hangs up the phone she realizes her mood has changed, as though Ketzel's happiness has spread to her. Jaime! She'll always love him, in a dim, distant way, as if he were a wonderful character in a good she read. She racks her brains to remember other characters like Jaime, handsome, tender men. *Madame Bovary?* Her husband was a dolt, her lover, an unlikeable cad. Lady Chatterley's gamekeeper, although intelligent enough, talked too much, too much theorizing about sex. *Wuthering Heights,* Heathcliff? Handsome, but mean and crazy!

A few days later she's invited for lunch and when she runs up the brownstone steps that Luis cleared from a light dusting of snow she stops, listening to Ketzels' voice. It sounds light and happy. *She needs Jaime,* she thinks. *Maybe she should go live in Mexico, be near her father.*

When she pushes open the door, Jaime's waiting, beaming a warm welcome, and when he gives her a hug and kisses her cold face, the little jolt's still there.

"Everyone come to the table," Jaime says as he takes her and and leads her into the dining room. "I've fixed a good meal. We must talk—there's lots of family business to discuss."

Oh, really?, thinks Miriam, *Now I'm part of the family? Well, maybe I am—somehow.*

Over lunch Jaime tells Miriam about his twins, how quickly the little boy recovered from his operation, the hacienda, why he needs to be there full time to help Adelita and, of course, to be with his sons.

For Miriam it's strange and confusing to be sitting there as if Jaime's plans have no power to hurt her, as if she's Ketzel's sister, neither more or less. What about that night? Has he forgotten? She hasn't. She never will.

While they're having coffee, Jaime asks Miriam, "What do you thnk about Ketzel coming back to Mexico?"

"What will she do there? Do you mean for good? Or just until she's better?"

"I think I've found a her a job," Jaime answers, pouring himself a second cup. "She'll have to rest until her leg heals." He reaches over and pats his daughter's hand. "There's a lot going on in Mexico these days. In January they had a tremendous cultural event, people from Paris and London—the talk of the artistic world—an 'International Exhibition of Surrealism.' Breton ..."

"Forget all that crap," Ketzel cuts in. She's been quiet, listening to them. As she grinds her cigarette in her saucer, her voice grates ... "I can't stand that stuff. That goes for Kahlo too. She's a nut, her painting stinks—she hangs around with those Stalinists ..."

"You don't have to have anything to do with them," Jaime says patiently. "President Cardenas is not in love with the C P either but he's encouraging all the arts. There's sure to be some work for you ..."

"I don't have much choice, do I? I've got to rest. This damn knee will take time—if it ever really gets better." Her voice shakes slightly.

Jaime looks at her sullen face, decides to change the subject and turns to Miriam. "How is Sylvia Ageloff doing? I know she's back in New York. Have you seen her?"

Before Miriam has time to answer Ketzel jumps up from the table, wincing, forgetting her injury. At the door she says, "Excuse me. I don't want to hear about that disgusting mess and all those horrible people. Don't forget, I've had the dubious pleasure of being with Caridad, Vidali and Tina. Poor Tina! I'm sorry for her ..." She limps out, not bothering to finish her sentence.

Miriam and Jaime look at each other. Then she gets up to clear the table, saying "I want to hear about what happened, Jaime. What the police found out about our friend, Jacques—Jacson!" She does and yet, she doesn't. Nothing can be undone, the Old Man is gone. Now, there's only a sordid business of sorting out the truth, uncovering the deceptions and lies. It's opening a cesspool but still she wants to know about all of it.

Jaime's working in his study when she comes up later. Although mostly emptied of furniture, his desk is littered with letters and bills. "It'll take days to clear this stuff up," he tells her as she comes in. "The house will be closed up indefinitely and I've got to take a lot of material with me."

Jaime leans back in his swivel chair. "Julian Gorkin—have you ever heard of him? No, of course not. He was a leader of the P O U M in Spain, nearly killed by the Stalinists there. Luckily he escaped—Victor Serge was with him. He's living in Mexico now. Just a few weeks ago he was attacked, stabbed in the head. Fortunately, he didn't die. Who knows who did it! I met him and we had a long talk. Our dear friend Contreras is in Mexico too, with Tina." Jaime shakes his head. Miriam watches his slim brown fingers as he lights a match. *Why do Mexicans have such lovely hands? Why are they such beautiful people, so easy to fall in love with?*

"Julian called me just before I left. He knows Jacques Mornard, knew him in Spain, back in 1936. His real name is not Mornard, it's Ramon—Ramon Mercader. The police are checking his fingerprints in Spain now."

"I knew it" Miriam cries. "Ketzel knew him—she knew him in Spain." Miriam jumps up with surprise. "So that's who Jacques really is. No wonder his voice sounded so familiar when he called Martin on the phone. Ketzel wrote me about him—about all of them!" Remembering that Jaime hates shrill voices she goes on in a quieter tone but she's angry. "Her Martin was part of that gang, the Siquieros gang, Ramon's mother too, Caridad, her boyfriend, Eitingon, the Russian General, the whole rotten Stalinist gang! Sylvia wasn't the only one who was fooled."

Jaime nods, his mouth grim. "The afternoon Trotsky was killed, Caridad and Eitingon were waiting for Ramon a few blocks away in a limosene. The plan was that after Ramon, alone with Trotsky in the study—that after he'd killed him quietly, he'd leave him, dead or dying with the pick-axe driven in his brain, and he could make a fast get-away, walk out to the car and disappear."

"I think it was everyone's fault, what happened." Miriam sits back, trying to steady her voice and control the nausea rising in her throat, "including the Old Man."

In a moment, she goes on. "He was tired of being watched so carefully, he didn't want the guards with him all the time. He hated feeling like a prisoner. And he was fatalistic. But everyone is to blame. Everyone was careless. Sylvia should have checked his fake stories, his background, the passport story—it was full of holes. And the Rosmers should have detected his phony accent. He spoke French like a Spaniard, people noticed it." Miriam reaches for a cigarette, makes herself slow down. "It's almost funny, the way he travelled around so freely, going from Spain, to Paris, to Mexico, to New York, he even went to Sylvia's sister's wedding in June in Connecticut and everyone couldn't get over how skillfully he carved the chicken at the dinner table."

"How did Sylvia meet him?" Jaime asks.

"She was from Chicago, a gal named Ruby Weill, supposed to be a Party member, or at least a sympathizer. We all knew her, went to movies with her. None of us bothered to check. She played it cool, sweet, didn't talk too much, afraid to give herself away, I guess. She played up to Sylvia, got her to go abroad with her and one day, in Paris, they *just* happen to run into Jacques, Ruby's friend. Jacques—Jacson—whoever—he pretended to be smitten with Sylvia from the moment he met her!" Miriam takes a deep drag on her cigarette, adding, "I hope he roasts in hell, if there is such a place."

"You know the maximum sentence he can be given in Mexico is twenty years." Jaime, with a slight ironic smile adds, "The C P will keep him well supplied. That is, if they can't get him out. I understand they're trying very hard. In any case, they'll see to it he'll have lawyers, money and feminine companionship on week-ends. He still claims to be Jacques Mornard, he'll do so to his dying day so he can hide his Stalinist connection. It's a joke! The 'confession' he had on him made him out to be a disillusioned Trotskyite! He was well prepared if he were unlucky enough to be caught. He didn't expect to be. He thought he could kill Trotsky and slip out but he didn't reckon the Old Man's stamina and guts."

Miriam's had enough. Lately she's often felt discouraged. It seem useless to keep fighting—fighting the Stalinists—fighting the whole rotten capitalist system. She sighs, "Well, there's nothing more to be said," and is about to walk from the room but Jaime catches her arm, pulls her to a stop, looks up at her. As she stands near his desk, he asks,

"What about you? Tell me, are you working? Still going to school? What are your plans?"

She sits down and tries to tell him about herself but she knows he knows what she's been doing, Ketzel keeps him informed. She tells him about her classes, what she's reading, how poorly she's doing in chemistry, about her mother—he loves to hear stories about her mother.

Then he asks, "What about the Party ... are you still a member?"

Miriam hesitates, then says, slowly, "Yes, though I'm not as active as I could be right now, I haven't changed the way I think, the way I feel. You remember when I was a little kid, I cried when they killed Sacco and Vanzetti. I guess it's my second nature, fighting for justice, truth, etc., etc.—you name it." She smiles, ruefully, "Even when you keep losing the big ones. There may be some successes, like in the labor unions, but they're hard to find." Then, slowly, "I can't support this war even though I hate Hitler—it's still a capitalist war. Is there such a thing as a revolutionary pacificist? I'm not sure. But I know I'll always believe in socialism—that it's the only way this earth can be free of injustice and wars." She laughs lightly, looking down at her hands, clasped in her lap a bit sheepishly. "I can't imagine my life not being involved, not being active. That's me—'nuff said." She walks towards the window where sunlight pours in; she's done too much talking ...

"But ... what about *you?*" he asks. She looks up at him. Now, she understands! He wants her to say something about herself, about him, about the two of them. He wants to know if she still cares! He's standing close now, looking at her, intently, his eyes glowing with the familiar, sweet ardor she's never forgotten and she sees he's not forgotten either.

Silence ripples in the room, as when a small stone is dropped in a still pond. Her throat is tight, she can scarcely breathe. From the short space that separates them, they look at each other and she feels as if she's drowning in the amber depths of his gaze.

"Jaime ... I ...," her words come from nowhere, she scarcely whispers.

"No, don't say anything. I shouldn't have asked."

She knows she must break the spell. She walks away from him, to the door and closes it softly behind her.

❀   ❀   ❀

Ketzel calls Miriam the following week, excited. "Listen to this! I've got a great idea for a new project, I've already called a friend in Cuernavaca about it and he's interested. You know, the famous legend of Quetzalcoatl, the white-bearded god who sailed away but was expected to return to destroy Montezuma, ruler of the Aztecs. Then Cortez arrives from Spain in the ships the Indians called 'water houses' and Montezuma's afraid he's the god returned. Luckily for Cortez, Marina, a smart, beautiful Indian becomes his mistress and helps him capture Montezuma. It'll be a great part for me when I'm better, but in the meantime I can choreograph it for another dancer. I can't wait! Can't you see Luis as Quetzalcoatl?"

She'll be going back to Mexico with Jaime and he wants to get back to Mexico quickly. Adelita and his wife have been calling every day. But the fourteenth day of January is her birthday and Ketzel's determined to have a party before she goes.

She wants to invite everyone they know, making it a real celebration, "It may be my last in New York," Ketzel says. There's plenty of seltzer and wine in the house but she calls Ratner's for gefulte fish and cheese blinzes, Moscowitz & Lupowitz for corned beef, pastrami and pickles, and Delmonico's for a birthday cake. The party is supposed to run from two o'clock in the afternoon until nine at night, people coming and going. *But it's not like in T. S. Eliot's poem—they're not talking about Michaelangelo*, thinks Miriam. They're talking about themselves, their careers, here and there some snippets about the coming war and the rumors of Hitler's persecution of the Jews, but it's mostly about themselves.

Ketzel, stunning in an Nahue costume, an Indian Princess, kisses everybody, saying good-by to the dancers she worked with; Sophie Maslow, Jose Limon, Doris Humphrey, Tamiris and also to Langston Hughes, Countee Cullen and all the others who have shown up to wish her well. Miriam sees John Dos Passos, whose mild, round face is troubled. He's huddled in a corner, telling Jaime about Ernest Hemingway, how coldly he acted about Jose Robles' disappearance in Spain. At eight o'clock, with a fanfare from Andre Segovia's guitar, a cake, blazing with twenty six pink candles, is wheeled out.

It has been a 'wing-ding' party, half of the invited leave more than a little tipsy, and by twelve it's over. Exhausted, Miriam, Luis and Jaime stagger into bed, exhausted, knowing that they have to be up at seven and leave for the airport in less than two hours.

At eight o'clock a taxi waits in the street and Luis and Miriam begin loading in the luggage. As Miriam climbs upstairs, Jaime, who's been busy in his study asks Miriam if he can speak to her for a minute.

"Is it important, Jaime?," she asks. She'd rather not be alone with him again. She follows him into his study, making nervous small talk. "Ketzel is taking so much stuff, it's incredible."

He moves awkwardly towards his desk. Miriam thinks this is the first time she's ever seen him so uneasy.

Taking a set of keys from his desk, he says, as he hands them to her. "I want you to have these."

"Why? She recognizes them. "I already have a set. Ketzel gave me one in case of an emergency," she says, puzzled.

"I know that. But you should have another one." He pushes back the lock of hair that falls over his forehead—that familiar gesture. Hesitatingly, he says, "I'd like you to come and live here. Make this your home."

"What? I'm not sure I understand," Miriam, hesitates. "You're asking me to move in? To stay? Do you mean for a year? Until you come back?"

"No. I mean this house to be entirely yours. It should belong to someone who loves it—like you—you always have." Jaime embarrassed, adds quickly. "We may come here now and again, for a visit, if you invite us. But Mexico's my home now and Ketzel's also. This will be *your* house."

"I don't understand, Jaime." She's puzzled, almost a little frightened. "Why?"

"A practical reason." His voice strains to sound matter-of-fact, businesslike. "A house shouldn't remain empty. Besides, it's right—I hope it will be good for you."

Miriam, unable to speak, confusion churns within her. Then she begins to realize what he has said, what he means, what is happening. He is giving her a gift, an amazing gift, with his love. A wave of joy sweeps over her, engulfs her and she wants to embrace him.

"I don't know what to say," she exclaims, going towards him ... "Such a wonderful gift!"

"No, please!" Jaime turns away, looks down at papers on his desk. "You don't need to say anything," he says softly. "We both know ... let's leave it at that." He doesn't want her to continue.

She stands looks at him. She can't talk and she knows he doesn't want her to. So she turns and leaves, the keys warm in her hand, happiness threading through her veins, her head spinning.

Ketzel's calling her, and Miriam runs down to the taxi where she's sitting, waiting. Miriam pokes her head through the window, then her hand, showing Ketzel the keys.

"Do you know about this?"

"Yes," Ketzel answers. "I know about it. It's fine with me. I know a lot and I love you too."

A few days later Miriam returns to the house on 117th Street. They had to leave in a hurry and it's been left untidy, especially the kitchen. There's so much to do but most of all she wants to be there, to try to realize what's happened, what Jaime meant about the house, if it's really hers now. She wanders up to his study, sits at his desk, closes her eyes.

To have this house, this house she's always loved, that made her feel welcome every time she climbed the brownstone staircase, opened the heavy glass panelled door ... the light streaming through the curving bay windows, the long parlor with the stately marble fireplace, the honey colored parquet floors, the flowering garden with the nosy tree, the quiet street with its faded aristocratic air. What a miraculous gift! But the house is only a small part of it. It was Jaime, Ketzel and even Fanny—Fanny who threw her out. They had all loved her.

They're gone now. Their voices echo through the empty rooms and she will always hear them.

Now she's here. She'll be lonely, maybe even afraid. She doesn't want to be alone. She needs people. There should be others. Could there be? It's a large house, there's lots of room, room for more than two, perhaps three or four. We could all live here—like a commune?

Here! A commune! An exciting idea! Comrades always share rooms and apartments. Here's a whole house … all for ourselves! She sits down, new, exciting thought crowd into her head. She sits, transfixed with ideas and happiness. I'd get a group of comrades together, we'd share everything, we'd have meetings, we'd discuss procedure, be democratic! We'd cook together, clean, listen to music … dance … and drink—just a little.! Oh, if only we can do it! Why not! She'll call Hilda, Rhoda, a few others. Maybe even Harold, or a few other guys!

Right now, though, there's work to do, the kitchen to clean, rooms to straighten. Begin! Right now! Ready to leave, to tackle the house, she notices a book on the desk in front of her. It's open, so she's sure to see it! On it there's a note:

For Miriam,

When I read this I thought of you. Although it does not have your name on it, it was written for you. Be happy in your new home.

Te quiero, Jaime

A faint pencil line in the margin marks this passage:

"Natasha has come up to the window from the courtyard and opened it wider so that the air may enter more freely into my room. I can see the bright green strip of grass beneath the wall, and the clear blue sky above the wall and sunlight everywhere. Life is beautiful. Let the future generations cleanse it of all evil, oppression and violence, and enjoy it to the full."

Leon Trotsky

Photo Gallery

The Great Depression: Familiar scene
on city street corner

Sacco and Vanzetti

The Scottsboro Boys

Eastman, Cannon, and Big Bill Haywood,
president of IWW 1905

Leon Trotsky, head of the
Red Army 1918

Max Shachtman and James P. Cannon
leaders of the Communist League of
America, New York City

Joseph Stalin, General Secretary,
Soviet Union 1922–1953

May Day Demonstrations in New York (above)
and Mexico City (below) circa early 1930's.
Bottom photo: Diego Rivera (white shirt) and Frida Kahlo, in front.

Harry Milton George Orwell Eileen O'Shaughnessy Blair

The Spanish Civil War, 1937

Zborowski, Soviet spy,
"friend" of Sevya in Paris

Leon Sedov (Sevya), Paris

Frida Kalo

Tina Modotti a San Francisco, 1920 circa.

Tina Modotti

The Three Mercaders

Ramon Mercader in Spain

Frank Jacson in New York and Paris

Jacques Mornard with Sylvia (far right) in Paris

Trotsky, Natalya, and Sevya in
Garden in Coyoacan, 1939

Trotsky Coyoacan, 1939

The Author, Trotsky, Natalya and "Bunny"
Coyoacan, 1939

The scene of Trotsky's assasination

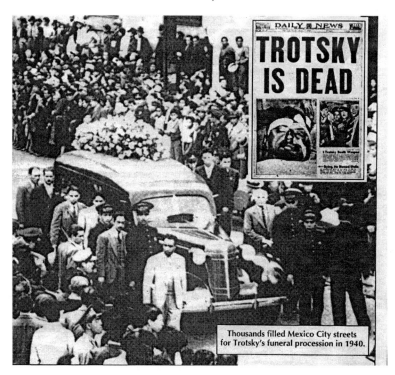

Trotsky's Funeral Mexico City, 1940

(Left) Trotsky's grandson, Esteban "Sieva" Volkov; (right) Trotsky's biographer, Pierre Broué, during speaking tour on East Coast.

NYC meetings hear about Trotsky and Soviet democracy

2001, New York City

Circa 1970, Sylvia Ageloff   Circa 1990, Seva Volkov and wife

Notes

Historical Persons

(*An asterisk denotes persons I met or knew personally)

*Ageloff, Sylvia,

Born 1913, Brooklyn, New York. Obtained a social work degree. A member of A. J. Muste's American Workers Party, joined the Trotskyists in 1934 with her two sisters. Introduced to Ramon Mercader by Ruby Weill in 1938 in Paris. After her innocence in Trotsky's murder was established, returned to private life. Married, practiced as a therapist, avoided publicity and did not resume political activity from then on. Died in 1995.

*Benitez, Melquaides

A guard in the Trotsky household, devoted to Trotsky. Disappeared after assassination.

Dos Passos, John

Noted author and critic of American society. The trilogy *U.S.A.* considered an American masterpiece. Wrote passionately about the Sacco-Vanzetti case in a "Camera Eye" episode. Went to Spain to find his friend Robles, who had become disillusioned with Soviet actions and then disappeared. Dos Passos' subsequent criticism of Russia resulted in a broken friendship with Ernest Hemingway, who supported the Soviet regime.

Eitingon, Leonid

Russian who served in Spain during the Civil War as a high-ranking officer in the NKVD, the Soviet secret police. Known as Tom, Kotov, Comrade Pablo. Organized six schools for "saboteurs." Merciless in hunting down and killing members of P O U M, C N T. and F A I and other opponents of Soviet policy in Spain. Lover of Cardidad Mercader. Shot in Moscow in 1953, along with Beria, on orders from Stalin

Gorkin, Julian,

Member of the Executive committee of the P O U M. After the Spanish Civil War lived in Mexico. Collaborated with A. Salazar in *"Murder In Mexico."*

Goldman, Emma

Russian-born anarchist, fiercely independent, deported several times from the U.S. Prominent critic of the Communist Party. Fiery orator, believed in democracy, women's rights, birth control, free love. Lived life to its fullest.

*Hansen, Joseph

Head of guards in Trotsky's house. Writer and editor of *International Socialist Review.*

Harte, Sheldon

A graduate of Duke University, where he was reportedly an "unreconstructed Stalinist." Moved to New York and joined the Trotskyists, volunteered to serve as a guard for Trotsky in Mexico. He met with Ramon Mercader at the Kit Kat Club in Mexico City. Taken away by Siqueiros after the May 1940 raid, he stayed in a cabin an hour's distance away, went to the local pub in the afternoons. Salazar reports this in his book, written with J. Gorkin, "Murder in Mexico." He was found murdered in a lime pit in June. Trotsky refused to believe he was a G P U agent, and a plaque commemorating Sheldon is in the garden of the Trotsky Museum in Cuernavaca.

Ibarrui, Dolores

Fiery Spanish Communist Party leader known as La Pasionaria. Famous for speeches and broadcasts and the slogans "No pasaran" and "Better to die on your feet than live on your knees." Changed her revolutionary aims to follow Stalin's policy of maintaining a bourgeois democratic government in Spain.

Kahlo, Frida

Attractive, dynamic, daughter of a Mexican mother and Hungarian Jewish father. Severely injured when young and a lifelong invalid, she became well known as an artist. Married Diego Rivera. A warm supporter of Trotsky when he arrived in Mexico, she loaned him her Blue House. At first his supporter, friend, and briefly his lover, she later rejoined the Communist Party and renounced her support of Trotskyism.

Lewis, Ruby Weill

Chicago member of C P, enlisted by Louis Budenz *(Men Without Faces)* to work as a spy for the Party. As a Trotskyist member in New York City induced Sylvia to go to Paris where she introduced her to Mercader and disappeared immediately afterwards.

Mercader, Caridad

Born in Cuba in 1892. Raised five children, including Ramon Mercader. Estranged from husband. Ardent Communist who boasted of killing 20 Trotskyists herself in Spain. Lover of Eitingon, who betrayed her. After Trotsky's assassination she received honors from the Soviet Union, including the Order of Lenin, for her role. Abandoned by her lover who returned to his wife and family, she ended up in Paris disillusioned, fearful of being assassinated herself, regretting her actions.

*Mercader, Jaime Ramon Mercader de Rio Hernandez

Born in Barcelona, 1914, second child of Caridad. Went to France in 1925. Learned hotel business as apprentice, served as assistant to chef at Ritz Hotel. Joined the Communist Party as a teen-ager. Fought in Spain with Eitingon, Siqueiros, and his mother, Caridad Mercader. In Moscow assigned to assassination of Trotsky. Even after the murder, continued to insist he was a Belgian and disillusioned Trotskyist and that his name was Jacques Monard. His real identity was discovered from fingerprints in Spain a year later. Spent twenty comfortable years in Mexican jail. Plots to free him, including the Soviet Union's "Gnome Project," were unsuccessful. He was awarded the Order of the

Hero by the Soviet Union for the assassination. Lived abroad when released, married and raised a family.

*Milton, Harry

Trotskyist, member of Socialist Workers Party. Volunteered in Spain in 1936. Served on Aragon front, 29th Division. Imprisoned with George Orwell and Kopp, escaped and returned to the United States. Remained a Trotskyist until his death in California in the 1980s.

Modotti, Tina

Assunta Adelaide Luigia Modotti, born in Italy 1896. Became Edward Weston's lover and studied photography with him in Mexico. Joined the Communist Party in the 1920s and recruited Frida Kahlo. Passionate lover and then wife of Julio Mella, a Cuban revolutionist. After Mella became sympathetic to Trotskyism he was shot and killed in 1929 while he and Modotti were walking in the street. Vidali was rumored to be the assassin. Modotti married Vidali, also known as Contreras, and went to Spain with him in 1935. She enlisted in the Fifth Regiment under the name Maria. Left Spain in 1939. Embittered with Vidali and the Stalinists, she died mysteriously in a taxi in Mexico City in 1941.

Nin, Andres

Popular, beloved leader of P O U M. Jailed and tortured by the Communist Party in Spain. Kidnapped from prison in a faked Nazi raid. His body never found. Vidali is believed to have led the raid.

Orwell, George

English writer, journalist, sympathetic to Communism but not affliliated with any party. In Spain he fought at the Aragon Front with the P O U M, was wounded, jailed, escaped with his life. Known for *Homage to Catalonia*, a straightforward, honest account of his experiences in the Spanish Civil War, and also for *1984*.

Rivera, Diego

Outstanding Mexican artist, muralist, revolutionist, supporter of Trotsky. Painted murals for Rockefeller Center in the U.S. Charismatic, a womanizer, with a stormy marriage to Frida Kahlo. Like his wife, returned to the Communist Party in later years.

Rosmer, Afred and Marguerite

French supporters of Trotsky, although they had some political differences in 1935. They were good friends of Trotsky and Natalya and stayed with them in Mexico for eight months. Became friendly with Ramon Mercader, whose willingness to do errands for them enabled him to enter the house freely. They left in May, just before the Siquieros raid on the house.

*Schwartz, Delmore

Born New York 1914. Poet, writer, essayist, an editor of *The Partisan Review*, critical of communists, close to Dwight MacDonald. Died in seedy Hotel Dixie in his fifties, suffering from drinking, depression and psychotic episodes.

Siquerios, David Alfaro

Prominent Mexican artist and muralist, an ardent member of the Communist Party. In 1936 did murals for Federal Art Project in New York. Fought in Spain, formed the Union of Revolutionary Artists in Barcelona. Known as the "little colonel," he commanded the 82nd Brigade at Teruel. Married to Angelica Arenal, who cooperated in the attack on attack on Trotsky in May 1940. After attack he fled to Chile with Pablo Neruda's help, then returned to work in his native country, his fame unaffected by the fumbled attack. In 1959–60 went to Cuba for Fidel Castro's first anniversary in power. In 1966 was awarded the Lenin Prize for Strengthening Peace between People.

Sacco and Vanzetti,

Two Italian immigrants, anti-clerical anarchists, living in Boston. In 1919–1921, during the "Red Scare" period of intense political repression, were entrapped by police because they owned guns. Convicted of crimes they had no connection with. They were electrocuted in 1927. The blatant frame-up drew worldwide protests.

The Scottsboro Boys

In 1931 in Alabama nine African-American youths were arrested and accused of raping two white women. Eight were sentenced to be executed. Granted a new trial by the Supreme Court, they were eventually freed, although many served time in prison. They were a cause celebre and vigorously defended by the Communist Party and the N.A.A.C.P.

Tresca, Carlos

Much-admired Italian anarchist, anti-Communist, supporter of C N T in Spain. Raised money to supply anarchists with guns and hardware. On his six-tieth birthday received telegram from Trotsky. With many enemies, political and otherwise, he often said he expected to be assassinated (*All the Right Ene-mies* by Dorothy Gallagher). In 1943 he was fatally shot on 15th Street in New York City.

*Van Heijenoort, Jean

Secretary to Trotsky for seven years, beginning in 1932. Left Trotsky for the United States in 1939 with "Bunny," an young American S W P member whom he married. Taught at Brandeis University, published works in mathematics. Years later, after he'd divorced Bunny, he was fatally shot by his third wife.

Vidali, Vittorio

Aso known as Commandante Carlos Contreras. Led the Fifth Regiment in Spain. A brilliant speaker, husky, bull-necked. Sent by the Soviet Union to restrain the leftward militant trend in 1931. During the Civil War he was known for his executions in the ranks of the
F A I and C N T. His right hand was deformed because of the incessaant use of his gun in executions. In 1938 he led the 11th Brigade in the Battle of Ebro. Was married to Tina Modotti. A month after Modotti mysteriously died in a taxi in Mexico City, in 1941, he married again.

Zborowsky, Mark

Known as "Etienne." Born in Russia, 1907. Well-educated, studied medicine. Published *Russian Bulletin* in France. Assigned by N K V D to spy on Lyova Trotsky, he became Lyova's trusted friend, lived next door to him, reporting immediately on his activities to Soviet officials (Isaac Deutscher in The *Prophet Outcast*). He fingered Ignace Reiss and Rudolph Klement for the N K V D, and in Spain contacted the Special Task Force which was responsible for Erwin Wolf's death. Went with Lyova to a Russian Hospital in Paris where Lyova mys-teriously died. Convinced Trotsky not to pursue investigation of Lyova's death. In the United States became an anthropologist, worked with Margaret Mead who defended him. In the GL 1940s he worked for the American Jewish Com-mittee and the K G B, becoming a member of Jack Soble's spy ring in the U.S.

In 1955 he was arrested as a Stalinist agent and sentenced to five years in prison. He died in 1990.

❦   ❦   ❦

Political Parties and Organizations Mentioned in Book

A F L American Federation of Labor. National organization of trade unions in the U.S.

A L B Abraham Lincoln Brigade—The XV Brigade and III Battalion of the International Brigade, created in February 1937.

B S and A U Bookkeepers, Stenographers and Accountants Union. Affliliated with A F L.

C L A Communist League of America, founded in 1928 by expelled Communist Party members. In 1934 it merged with the Americans Workers Party of the United States, led by A.J. Muste, to form the Workers Party.

C N T
Spain Confederacion National del Trabajo—National Confederation of Labor: a confederation of Anarcho-Syndicalist trade unions.

F A I
Spain Federacion Anarquista Iberica—Iberian Anarchist Federation: The federation of anarchist groups, very active in the Republican militias.

P C E
Spain Partido Comunista de Espana Communist Party of Spain. Led by Jose Diaz in the Civil war, a minor party during the early years of the Republic but came to dominate the Popular Front.

P O U M
Spain Partido Obrero de Unification Marxista—Worker's Party of Marxist Unification. An anti-Stalinist revolutionary Communist party of former Trotskyists formed in 1935 by Andres Nin.

P S O E
Spain Partido Socialista Obrero Espanol—Spanish Socialist Workers' Party: Formed in 1879 allied with Accion Republicana in municipal elections in 1931. The PSOE left the coalition in 1933. At the time of the Civil War the PSOE was split between the right and left wing.

P S U C
Spain Partit Socialista Unificat de Catalunya—United Socialist Party of Catalonia. An alliance of various socialist parties in Catalonia, formed in the summer of 1936, controlled by the PCE.

S W P   Socialist Workers Party was established in January 1938.
                   Members of the Workers' Party and expelled Trotskyists from the
                   Socialist Party.

U G T   Union General de Trabajadores—General Union of Workers.
Spain   Socialist trade union. The UGT was formally linked to the PSOE.

U R   Union Republicana—Republican Union. Formed in 1934 by mem-
Spain   bers of the PRR who had resigned in objection to coalition with the
                   CDEA, its' main support from skilled workers and progressive busi-
                   nessmen.

W P A   Works Progress Administration of the United States. It was the
                   largest "new deal" temporary agency, employing millions. Set up in
                   1935, it created jobs in almost every field of work, and included
                   work for people in many aspects of the arts until about 1940.
                   Closed down gradually before beginning of World War II.

978-0-595-49069-◗
0-595-49069-7

Printed in the United States
202949BV00003B/1-75/P

9 780595 490691